UNLEASHED

UNLEASHED

A Novel By
F. Mark Granato

All rights reserved

Names, characters and incidents depicted in this book are products of the author's imagination or are used fictitiously. Any resemblance to actual events, organizations, or persons, living or dead, is entirely coincidental and beyond the intent of the author or the publisher.
No part of this book may be reproduced or transmitted in any form or by any means, electronic or mechanical, including photocopying, recording, or by any information storage and retrieval system, without permission in writing from the author.

F. Mark Granato
fmgranato@aol.com
www.facebook.com at Author F. Mark Granato

Copyright © 2015 by F. Mark Granato
Published in the United States of America 2015

UNLEASHED

A Novel by

F. Mark Granato

Also by F. Mark Granato

Titanic: The Final Voyage

*Beneath His Wings:
The Plot to Murder Lindbergh*

Of Winds and Rage

Finding David

The Barn Find

*Out of Reach:
The Day Hartford Hospital Burned*

For my wife,
my life and love for 50 years
whose personal vision of happiness
has always been founded
on following her heart and inner voice
with stubborn patience.

"The way to make money is to buy when blood
is running in the streets."

John D. Rockefeller
*July 8, 1839 – May 23, 1937
The richest man in the world and
Chairman of The Standard Oil Trust,
once described as "The most cruel, impudent, pitiless,
and grasping monopoly that ever fastened upon a country."*

Humpty Dumpty

Humpty Dumpty sat on a wall,
Humpty Dumpty had a great fall;
All the king's horses and all the king's men
Couldn't put Humpty together again.
Mother Goose

A Letter to The Millennials
~~~ ༖ ~~~

We were the "Boomers," a generation led to believe that it was our birthright to change the world.

We were JFK's disciples, those who would leverage the sacrifices of Americans who fought both the Great Depression and a World War to build the foundation for a truly noble America.

We were the Camelot generation, enlightened by education, endowed with fortune or the opportunity to make one, endeared as the offspring of the most courageous and generous nation on earth. We would end war. We would unite nations. We would wipe out disease. We would eradicate hunger. We would suffocate religious persecution and racial bigotry, gender inequality and sexual oppression. We would take a man to the moon.

By God, we stepped on the moon but the rest of our dream died as we were betrayed and sold out by our government, by the military, by presidents, by banks, universities, corporations and Wall Street. America became the playground of self-entitled Boomers who became narcissistic politicians, stock market manipulators and worst of all, the corporate kings who ruled with an iron fist. These larger than life CEO's fed off the work of the rest of us: the bamboozled Boomers who stumbled from one disappointment and lie to another. How? Because they could. We were chained to the end of their leash.

By the 1980's we were afraid to challenge the status quo or conventional wisdom. The economic wine of America became greed, but only a few were allowed to drink from the chalice. As our nation fell into moral, economic and spiritual decay, only Wall Street and the titans of corporate America grew rich, powerful and secure. Boomers weren't allowed to have ideas or own values. Our voices were stifled by fear of retribution. This is one story of that corporate America and its inevitable, ugly end.

Turn the clock forward. The year is 2000. A new generation comes forward: The Millennials, the "ME" generation. The generation that is causing the good old boys in corporate America to rethink the playbook because the old plays don't work anymore as the new players won't play by somebody else's rules.

This is the generation that refuses to be caged in a cubicle, wants to wander in about ten and work all night. The generation that won't work for companies it doesn't respect, even if that means not working. The generation that would rather be broke than work without passion.

This is the generation that doesn't care about perks but wants the opportunity to produce, to innovate, to change. The generation that says "no" to the culture of a suit and tie because a t-shirt and cutoffs is the wardrobe of creativity. This is the generation that won't hesitate to quit an environment that sees color, nationality, religion, gender or sexual preference.

The Boomers blew it. We swallowed corporate dogma out of fear. Now it's a new generations' turn at the wheel. Don't waste it. Don't just buy someone else's thinking. Don't swallow you inner voice. Follow your passion. Stay true to yourself... and learn from the story of *Unleashed*.   *F. Mark Granato*

UNLEASHED

Prologue
~~~ ∽ ~~~

21 December 1988

At precisely 18:04 hours, Pan Am World Airway's Flight 103, a mammoth Boeing 747-121 christened on delivery as the *Clipper Maid of The Seas,* pushed back from its boarding gate at London's Heathrow Airport. As the busiest airport in all of Europe, Heathrow bustled with activity and flight delays were a common occurrence. Given the go ahead by airport controllers to taxi to runway 27R in preparation for a flight to New York's JFK only slightly behind their scheduled departure, the Pan Am crew wasted no time in taxiing into position for take off. After a brief hold, the 350-ton aircraft with its wingspan of nearly 200 feet began to roll down the 10,000 foot long runway pushed forward by four Pratt & Whitney JT9D jet engines, each generating 46,500 pounds of thrust. Seemingly without effort, the nose of the largest passenger commercial aircraft in service gracefully rose into the air as it reached a speed of approximately 150 miles per hour. Such was the smoothness of the liftoff that it barely rated a notice by the 259 passengers and crew strapped into the aircraft as it climbed into the dark English sky. The mood aboard was celebratory and complimentary champagne soon began to flow once the aircraft leveled off at its cruising altitude. The majority of passengers were American ex-patriots visiting the US for the holidays and family reunions. Also among then were 35 Syracuse University students returning home after completing a semester of study in London.

It was now 18:25 hours.

At the upper deck controls of Pan Am's *Clipper Maid of the Seas* were Captain James Bruce MacQuarrie, First Officer Ray Wagner and Engineer Jerry Don Avritt. Combined, the three men had logged more than 30,000 hours flying commercial aircraft. The crew bantered about the relatively uncomplicated departure and the clear night ahead as they awaited instructions from air traffic control to transmit its oceanic route clearance. But at 19:02 hours, just as ATC was radioing the order to proceed out over the Atlantic, all that was right about Pan Am 103 went terribly wrong and in an instant the veteran flight crew was rendered helpless to stop the chain of events that erupted in the next horrific seconds.

Just 38 minutes into the flight, as the jumbo jet reached an altitude of 31,000 feet while crossing over the Solway Firth, a large sea bay separating England and Scotland near the Isle of Man, a bomb fashioned out of the plastic explosive Semtex, which had been carefully hidden in a Toshiba cassette recorder packed in an inconspicuous Samsonite suitcase in the lower forward cargo hold, exploded.

Instantly, all radio communication between the aircraft and Shanwick Oceanic Area Control in Prestwick, Ayshire, Scotland was severed. As air traffic controllers futilely sought to establish contact with the flight crew, they watched in astonishment as the single radar echo they had been observing on their tracking screens separated into five distinct blips.

The air traffic controllers were unaware of the detonation aboard the aircraft that had blown a hole less than the circumference of a basketball directly below the "P" in the Pam Am script on its fuselage. Unknowingly, they were witnessing the mid-air disintegration of Pan Am 103 caused by the sudden ensuing depressurization of its hull. The five radar echoes were huge sections of the aircraft liberated from what had been the secure, carefree cocoon of a jumbo jet piercing the nighttime air on a normally uneventful transatlantic flight.

It would be a long while before the air traffic controllers understood the magnitude of what they had witnessed on their glowing screens. But six miles below, villagers in Lockerbie, a small town of slightly more than 4,000 residents in Dumfries and Galloway in the south-western area of Scotland looked up at the sky as the flaming explosion lit up the darkness. It would be another minute or so before the muffled reverberation of the blast descended upon them. The villagers had no idea of what they had seen. Some thought they had witnessed a small nuclear detonation.

Above them, Pan Am 103 was coming apart. Instantly, large sections of the forward fuselage ripped off, exposing portions of the interior cabin. Then the nose of the *Clipper Maid of The Seas* was sheared from the fuselage, its flight crew still strapped into their seats. The massive cone-like structure, including the upper deck cockpit peeled back from the fuselage like the lid of an opened tin can and stayed connected for no more than a few seconds. Then it tore off completely and pitched downwards to the right, impacting the number three Pratt & Whitney engine that it ripped from the pylon holding it to the wing.

In the main fuselage, now completely vented to the thin, freezing cold air and in total darkness, most passengers lost consciousness while the middle section of the passenger compartment and the two wings connected above it began a steep downward pitch. The tail section snapped off, dumping passengers into the black void like so much refuse. Within seconds, the fuselage went into a near vertical dive, shedding anything not strapped down or stowed away. First Class passengers in the front rows of seats were sucked out and ejected into the night, some swept directly into the gaping inlets of the three still operating turbofans that remained at full throttle.

As the fuselage fell closer to the ground where the air was richer and warmer, some passengers regained consciousness, cruelly left to face the impending and inescapable impact with the invisible ground below. Fully cognizant, their thoughts rushed between family, loved ones and prayer and confusion, panic and terror.

UNLEASHED

The tons of wreckage raced toward the ground and the unsuspecting village of Lockerbie. With it came a rain of carnage, millions of bit and pieces, and an undeniable truth.

At half the speed of sound, the remains of the *Clipper Maid of the Seas* dropped upon Lockerbie only 36 seconds after the explosion. Residents remember hearing an eerie rush and a growing howl as if steam was escaping from a kettle at boil. Then there were explosions all over the village and in surrounding fields, followed by an unearthly quiet, then more explosions.

Town folk who had been indoors, perhaps preparing the evening's meal or wrapping Christmas packages, rushed from their homes to find the town alight in flames and just in time to hear the ghastly thud of bodies falling from the sky onto cobble stone streets, into their gardens and atop the roofs of their simple brick houses.

A housewife heard rather than felt the squishy noise of what she at first thought was a pumpkin being smashed on her front walk. She ran to the front door, intent on catching the young hoodlums who she was sure had spoiled her steps. She flung open the door and her eyes widened at the horror lying not ten feet away. It was the body of a young man lying face down, his head shattered, blood pouring from his skull, his body twisted into an impossible position. He was dressed in a business suit and she could see that his jacket was unbuttoned and his tie had been loosened as if he had been relaxing after a hard days work. His shoes were missing.

It suddenly came to her that he had fallen from the sky and she did not understand.

The woman began to run to him, then quickly realized the hopelessness of the situation and turned to retrieve a blanket from the front hall closet. She returned and gently covered the young man from head to toe with the blanket and said a short prayer over his body, blessing herself as she finished. Only then did she happen to glance down the street. Dozens more corpses lay scattered on the road and in the front yards of her neighbors.

The young man at her feet lay at the bottom of the steps of her home for three days before the coroner came to take him away. She sat for many an hour with him just to keep the young lad company. It bothered her that he had been abandoned for so long for she was certain that he had a wife, children or parents at home, grieving for information about him. She did not have the courage to reach into his pockets and try to find some identification.

For as long as she lived, the woman would remember the outline of the boy's smashed skull on the sidewalk and the bloodstain that would not wash out no matter how hard she scrubbed. She often inquired of the Lockerbie authorities the young man's name, but could find only that he was an American businessman from a small town in New England.

Amongst the macabre shower of human bodies, some victims were completely intact and appeared only to be sleeping in grotesquely unnatural positions. The force of the detonation or the rush of frigid winds tearing at their clothes as they fell stripped others nearly naked. Still others were burned or mutilated beyond recognition.

The lifeless cadavers who only seconds before had been chatting, reading, dozing or sipping from their champagne, fell at the villager's feet, at their doorsteps and all over the nearby golf course. The nightmarish sight burrowed deeply into the minds of those who watched, their lives and visions of humanity changed forever. The accompanying and equally horrifying shower of suitcases, pocket change, packages, body parts, clothing, children's toys, pocketbooks, coats and jackets, airplane parts, tufts of insulation and everything else torn from the aircraft or its victims seemed to fall forever. Indeed, the rain of destruction was obscenely enormous and widespread.

In Lockerbie's row house neighborhood of Sherwood Crescent, a huge fireball leapt heavenward when the gigantic aircraft's main fuselage and wings sliced into the ground. The three engines still attached, fed by nearly 200,000 pounds of aviation fuel in the wet wings, continued to churn at full throttle right up until impact. The section, weighing hundreds of tons, dug a massive crater into the ground that became a crematory for the passengers remaining inside and eleven occupants of the three houses struck. A stream of burning fuel ignited a nearby gas station causing another massive explosion and fireball. Not far away, another section of fuselage, nearly 60 feet long and containing as many passengers, landed between two rows of houses but somehow missed them. A large section of the nose landed in a sheep pasture three miles east. MacQuarrie, Wagner and Avritt were still strapped into their seats, having flown the cockpit of the dying aircraft into the ground like a crew going down with its sinking ship.

In little more than half a minute, Lockerbie lay in burning ruins, eleven of its residents were dead and hundreds more injured. The bodies or partial remains of some 259 passengers and crew from Pan Am Flight 103 were strewn across the village. And the world was left to wonder.

Why?

*****

More than 3,000 miles away, as the aftermath of Pan Am Flight 103 began to unfold and word of the crash slowly spread from Lockerbie, a reluctant revelry was playing out in Hartford, Connecticut at one of many corporate Christmas parties planned in the city that Wednesday afternoon in the final hours before business would close for a few days of holiday cheer.

This particular party at the headquarters of General Industries Corporation, commonly known as "The General," was not unlike most annual corporate office holiday gatherings in that it didn't really begin until most of the guests were well into their third cocktail. Before that, the atmosphere was a sort of awkward mating ritual of corporate wannabe's, cautiously paying homage to their direct supervisors who themselves were nervously on the lookout for their own bosses. The air was tight with tension. But as time passed and the liquor flowed and tongues began to loosen, the game escalated into wholesale sycophantic behavior that sometimes advanced up the chain of command without regard to rank or consequence.

These were the musings that occupied Kevin Keller's mind as he watched the corporate headquarters Christmas party evolve from social gathering to political convention on the afternoon of Wednesday, December 21, 1988. He laughed to himself with growing cynicism as he studied the festive theater unfold around him into particular social groupings.

An especially entertaining troupe was the cubicle dwellers — those employees who wouldn't ordinarily raise their expendable heads above the shoulder high office walls they worked within each day. But eventually, with a bit of liquid fortification providing misguided courage, they were the first to begin espousing opinions of how the company should be run, or worse, who should run it. The objects of these dangerous conversations were senior executives in ridiculously expensive pinstriped suits that had survived this game and lived to ridicule it. That was one of the reasons they occupied the large, mahogany clad offices on the top floor of the corporate headquarters from where they issued the directives and policies that ruled those in the cages below.

These "Pinstripers," as they were sarcastically known, would appear to be listening attentively to the clueless victims who were under the impression that their conversation was the chance of a lifetime, unaware that they were digging their own graves. It usually wasn't until the next morning that the inescapable truth set in, not unlike lemmings that had leapt into a river only to discover half way across that the other side was hopelessly out of reach.

However, there were those few, Keller concluded over time, who despite their cubicle status had obviously analyzed the process beforehand. They had successfully identified the keys to taking real advantage of the opportunity for exposure to people who normally would have no interest in knowing their names or qualities, unless, of course, the relationship might further their own overindulged and overcompensated careers. Every year, at least one or two of those who dwelt in the purgatory below the 26th floor did actually *gain* ground as a result of a well thought out, strategically oriented conversation with a Pinstriper who didn't see the usurper as a threat, but possibly as an asset to be taken advantage of.

Then, of course, there were the Harvard, Stanford, Wharton, Sloan, Darden, Columbia, Tuck, etc., business school crowd who mostly either conversed together or stayed close to the proximity of a wall and kept to themselves.

Keller had concluded that this group, possessing extraordinary skills to connive, had been trained to recognize that the key to survival and advancement to the corporate equivalent of nirvana was patience, practiced aloofness and backstabbing. Brains and competency had little or nothing to do with getting ahead. It was all about being in the right place at the right time when the elders began their inevitable ritual of warring against each other every few years. That was when their opportunity would come. Until then, the members of this pubescent Pinstriper sect would simply sit back, avoid social or professional contact with anyone resembling a non-B school personality (meaning, they had one) and bide their time. Eventually, as the required business school course on corporate arrogance had dictated, the time would come when they would be summoned to the CEO's office and anointed and promoted on the spot. This was the result of their aloofness having drawn the proper admiration and their carefully strategized backstabbing and disloyalty plan having worked out precisely as conceived and resulting in the demise of their predecessor.

Then there were Keller's favorites, people he actually related to. These were the few who simply came, had a drink, wished everyone who would consider shaking their hands a happy holiday and then returned to work in their cubicles. There they would remain, day after day, month after month, year after year doing whatever they were told to do, with no chance at advancement or a taste of the Pinstriper world, but safe from the corporate cannibalism that surrounded them. Despite the fact that they were completely disrespected, these were the only happy people in the building because they had no real end game other than to do their jobs and collect their honestly earned weeks' wages. Most held no more than a high school or associates degree and came from decidedly blue-collar roots.

Huddled together in another corner of the anteroom where the party was being held was a group of secretaries, practically the only representatives of the female population employed at the corporate headquarters. This was the same spot where the women, those few brave enough to step into an absurdly inequitable and hostile environment, gathered each year. Either coincidentally or as a pointed message — the meaning of which was lost on people who didn't care — their meeting spot was directly beneath a huge skylight that dispersed the winter's afternoon light throughout the Chairman's suite of offices. It was the ultimate "glass ceiling," a subject much ballyhooed in the Boardroom that had many apparent male executive champions but not a single success. At "The General," it was as if God himself had coined the phrase, "It's a man's world."

The 38-year old executive assistant to the chairman and chief executive officer enjoyed studying the game and decided that he most admired those who came and went and failed to play the game. Almost as a hidden sign of his respect, the six-foot, ruggedly good-looking junior executive absentmindedly touched a finger to the mustache that adorned his upper lip.

Facial hair was very popular amongst the cubicle dwellers, although not nearly as carefully trimmed as Keller's', but consequently was hugely frowned upon in the hallowed halls of the 26th floor. The mustaches, long sideburns and beards were repugnant to senior executives, who saw the unshaven as a symptom of non-conformity that was dangerously visible in the social foundation of General Industries factories, where worker's unions thrived. It always amazed Keller that men could become enemies —akin to Rebels and Yankees — simply because they abstained from using a razor or considered it an art form.

For the junior executive, his own mustache was an innocuous and subtle way of staying grounded with the humble, almost nondescript young man he had been ten years earlier when he joined the company.

UNLEASHED

Over the years, it had been suggested to him quite frequently that he should think about shaving it. Keller had always laughed off the comment, but inside he seethed. Today he unconsciously maintained it as a badge of honor and a reminder of where he had come from every time he looked in a mirror. Now, despite his aggressive, and at times even ruthless efforts to climb the ladder, a part of him did not want to forget those beginnings.

Often, on endless flights accompanying the chairman to business meetings that took them to all corners of the globe in one of the fleet of ultra luxurious corporate jets owned by the corporation, he would stare out a window at the world, amazingly uncomplicated above the pillow-like clouds at 30,000 feet, and ponder his success. In those long hours of solitude he spent strapped into a seat of a Gulfstream III, Keller would puzzle over the personal triumphs that had opened the door for his entry into the upper echelon.

In numerous ways, he knew that he had contradicted the rules for acceptance at "The General." But his innate hunger to break away from the world in which he was bred, where failure was not only acceptable but expected, stoked the makings of a fire in his belly that only needed a spark to ignite. General Industries had supplied the match.

Surprising even himself, he had excelled at the game of winning at GIC, despite the lack of business school credentials that would have made his unusual success that much easier. At the same time, he learned that the "dance" he was forced to perform to continue his climb — basically a swagger that gave off an aura of power and arrogance — was held in higher esteem than his competence. And that disgusted him.

Kevin Keller was well read, learning far more from the books he devoured in his private moments even as a child than he ever did in a classroom. Early on in his career at "The General," he had discovered H. G. Wells' *The Time Machine*, and was immediately struck by the similarities between the class structure in the great writer's "Wellsian" society and GIC's. And it was with this appreciation that the seeds of doubt, the anxiety of being trapped, began to sprout.

On one hand there were the *Eloi*, the superficially elitist species whom Wells' protagonist, *The Time Traveller*, had discovered in the year A.D. 802,701. Keller had concluded that the *Eloi* closely resembled the executives who occupied General's luxurious offices in that their practiced behavior made them appear to be highly intelligent and productive. Nothing could be farther from the truth.

On the other hand were Wells' *Morlocks*, representing the oppressed working class whose real lives of drudgery and hard labor actually enabled the *Eloi* to subsist. For Keller, the *Morlocks* were the General factory workers and cubicle dwellers of which the Pinstripers were secretly terrified. For it was the dreaded *Morlocks*, if only they were intelligent enough to know it, who were powerful enough to deprive them of their stock options, bonuses, company cars, country club memberships and other perquisites of those who had perfected the art of being useless while appearing essential.

As he watched those employees, the simple *Morlocks* who came to offer sincere good wishes and expected nothing in return, he silently admired them for their self-possessed sense of purpose and satisfaction with simple sustenance. Now, not a day passed that his allegiance was not torn. It wasn't admiration for either of the species that conflicted him, but rather the sense that he was fast losing control of who and what he chose to be. To confess to being an *Eloi*, a man who had squandered his ability and innate values in trade for the gluttony of wealth and comfort, terrified him. To admit to being willing to settle for the life of a *Morlock* left him saddened by his knowledge of the riches and opportunities of which he would deprive his family.

The question might have forced many a man to make a choice or take a stand, thus deciding his own destiny. But Kevin Keller had learned that he could avoid the choice as well as the truth by throwing his full energy into his job and by developing his own two-pronged strategy for survival.

The first was to garner the trust of the man for whom he worked directly, the Chairman and CEO of the corporation. He did this through his impeccable work ethic and demonstrable, unquestionable loyalty. These virtues significantly helped to hide his perceived deficiencies, such as the lack of a business school degree.

The Chairman had hand-picked Keller for the job as his assistant after several years of watching him maneuver through the same corporate swamps he had with instinctive skills rather than training or Ivy League education. But what impressed him most was the young executive's dedication to the job, and most importantly, loyalty to the success of the man he reported to. The choice put Keller at the right hand of the corporation's master at a young age, with an enviable career visible before him.

Another key quality for which Keller was recognized was actually the second prong of his success strategy. It was his rigid philosophy of "Do your job" that he used as his moral compass. It had served him well in the inevitable political wars waged in the upper atmosphere of the corporate world. "Do your job" was the truth that guided him, no matter the situation or consequences. Thus far, it had not failed him. Understandably, it was not a philosophy that gained Keller admiration from all other Pinstripers.

But now, still studying this unappreciated group who had come to the party truly full of good cheer, he wondered if anything other than good fortune really separated him from being one of them. Was his strategy only a self-serving device for him to rationalize his success?

It was a question that nagged at him occasionally and one he pushed back harder each time it bubbled to the surface. Keller had long ago convinced himself that it was better to avoid facing an *insecurity* unless it might have an effect on one's own *security*. It was a bit more sophisticated than the adage, "Let sleeping dogs lie," but nonetheless as accurate.

But insecurity was what had pushed him up the ladder so far, so fast. He was an anomaly in the corporate world, neither possessing the social or educational pedigrees of many who had achieved far less.

Keller had been born and raised in the south end of Hartford to parents of Irish descent, which in itself was a wall to be climbed in the rarified, elitist atmosphere in which he worked. He was often reminded of his unexceptional heritage by those who could brag of a family tree with early American roots, but wisely chose to let the slurs go in one ear and out the other.

However, growing up on the streets of Hartford had actually taught him a few lessons that occasionally gave him a leg up on those who bragged of descending from Pilgrim Rock.

One was to know how to use your wits as well as your fists. He had learned that one could rob a bigger man of his strength without ever raising his hands, simply by disarming him with just his sharper mind and tongue. But if the situation dictated fighting as the only option, then you had better go into the foray completely committed. It was far nobler to suffer a fat lip than back down from a bully's blow, because once the Cretan had a taste of your blood, your future was in his hands. Having translated this philosophy from pugilistic into intellectual terms, Kevin Keller rarely lost an argument in the corporate suite, but when he did, he was not above using the power he derived from his proximity to the Chairman to crush his opponent when the opportunity arose.

He also learned that when a man had nothing to fight for, his taste for battle was greatly diminished. The tiny bedroom he shared as a boy with three older brothers in a small two-family flat had taught him to guard his paltry assets and sleep with one eye open. Today, his own young family gave him a bottomless well of motivation and he vowed never to drop his guard in protecting their needs.

And that was Kevin Keller's formula for success despite his lack of the conventional corporate criteria. He had climbed the ladder steadily, never swerving from his "Do your job" philosophy, but always being the first to raise his hand when the mission was distasteful or even risky, and by remembering his boyhood lessons.

The party was in full swing by now. Keller casually glimpsed at his watch every few moments for the time when he would give the Chairman a "nod" accompanied by an innocuous brushing of an imaginary piece of lint from the sleeve of his suit. It was their private sign language meaning, "You've done your job of back slapping the help, Boss, let's call it a night." A few more minutes should suffice, he thought. Personally, the end of the evening couldn't come soon enough. He might even get home in time to read a bedtime story to his three children.

As he nursed a cranberry and club at a distance just far enough from the Chairman to remain within eye contact, he abruptly felt a tug on the sleeve of his suit. He turned and faced the corporate vice president of public relations, a man he disdained for his poor work ethic and weak competency. Stan Willow survived by sucking up with unabashed fervor and relished being the butt end of every joke in the executive dining room. For some reason he believed that so long as the Pinstripers laughed at him his job was safe. Keller personally found him buffoonish and a poor public face for the company. Since the Chairman had absolutely no use for Willow either, Keller was the PR guy's only conduit to the CEO.

"Kevin, need to talk," Willow said. Keller noticed immediately that he was unusually pale and obviously distressed.

"Shit… now, Stan? I'm just about to give the boss the high sign," Keller responded.

"Yah, sorry. He's gonna want to know this."

"What is it…?

"CNN and the networks are running stories that a Pan Am four seven went down over Scotland someplace, over 250 on board," Willow said, breathlessly. "It's one of the older 100 series birds with our fuel controls. Frigging Dan Rather is reporting that it collided with a small aircraft and CNN says they've got eyewitness reports that at least two of the engines were on fire. I've got to respond."

Keller had been through this before and had his ass chewed on any number of occasions by his boss over the penchant of the media to always jump to the conclusion that an aircraft accident was the result of mechanical failure, particularly the engines rather than what it usually was, which was a cockpit mistake, short for pilot error. But the media's illogical conclusions had to be taken seriously by any company involved in the manufacture of an aircraft that suffered an accident because of the huge financial ramifications for all involved. It was an important issue to "The General" because one of its subsidiaries produced the fuel controls for the Pratt & Whitney engines. The product was a key driver of GIC's growth, profits and share price.

"Hell," Keller responded. "Is anyone reporting the last indicated altitude?" he asked.

"Yah," Willow said. "Supposedly they lost contact with ATC when the bird hit 31,000 feet."

Keller bit his tongue at the stupidity of the suggestion by even the dumbest reporter that a mid air collision with a small aircraft was possible.

"So CBS says a 747 collided with a Cessna at 31,000 feet? What idiots. You know what the boss is going to say. If I were you I'd tell him you're going to inform Rather that's a ludicrous assumption but to call Boeing or Pan Am for comment. As to engine failure, Christ, when isn't there an eyewitness who claims the engines were on fire? No matter, that's a Pratt & Whitney question, not one for us to handle. But I'd still give Rather the standard, response: 'This is an on-going investigation and we'll provide complete cooperation.' But you don't want to hear that from me, Stan, right? You want to hear it directly from the Man. So let's go talk to the Chairman."

It was a perfect set up and Keller would have bet his mortgage on Willow's gutless response.

Stan Willow hesitated, thinking about the tongue-lashing he was about to get. "Nah, you brief him. I'll handle the media as you suggested."

"Good idea," Keller responded, doing little to hide his sarcasm. "Just do your job. And keep me in the loop, will ya? This is going to be a long night. "

"Yah, thanks a bunch." Willow walked away quickly, pouting.

Keller looked over at the Chairman. They had a kind of telepathy between them as well. He shook his head. Time to go, we need to talk.

The CEO excused himself from the crowd of employees hanging on his every word, and waved a goodnight to all in the room as he headed for his office, Keller several steps behind.

The two entered the 2,300 square foot office, actually a large suite that would challenge the luxury and opulence of the working quarters of any head of state in the world. Keller always marveled that his boss' office was only 300 square feet smaller than his entire house, which was somehow big enough for his family of five. Actually, the place gave him the creeps.

Keller also had never quite gotten over the sensation of sinking into the lavish sea of beige carpeting as he walked across it. It shouldn't be surprising he thought, given the price of the pure wool, 55 ounce carpet. On more than one occasion he had noticed the startled look upon the face of a visitor to the office when he first tread into the room. It was if he had stepped in quicksand. Depending on the visitor's business, it wasn't unusual for the metaphor to be accurate.

Another mystery was the time, effort and patience that had gone into selecting just the right shade of beige. The designer, hired at enormous expense, had worked with the chairman's wife to select it, and she had actually assessed it against her husband's complexion for compatibility. After an intensive, four-month effort that had actually occupied hours of the CEO's time, they had finally decided on a shade known as Ecru, from the French word meaning "raw." Ecru, the designer explained, was more of a yellowish-grey shade of what would commonly be identified as beige, and was consequently slightly "warmer" in tone. The only thought Keller had on the selection, which of course he kept to himself, was that anything that could warm up the chairman's office was indeed welcomed. For all the money that had been lavished on its décor, the chief executive's office had all the welcoming qualities of an iceberg in the North Atlantic. It took him some years more in the rarified air of the corporate executive's world to understand that taste had nothing to do with it. The ambience was meant to be cold, if not a tad uncomfortable. It helped to counteract anyone doing business there from feeling comfortable. Having the "edge" or upper hand was always the preeminent objective.

 The Chairman sat down at his desk, an exquisitely ornate, solid mahogany replica of the "Resolute" desk that had occupied the office of every sitting US President since Rutherford B. Hayes. The original had been a gift of Queen Victoria to President Hayes and had been constructed from the timbers of the famous British Man of War ship, *H.M.S. Resolute*. The chairman's desk was a recreation but was also constructed of timbers from the *Resolute* and had cost more than his assistant's annual salary. It was a museum quality replica with a few extra options. It housed a hidden but highly complex recording system, a panic alarm linked directly to a security console just down the hall manned by several armed guards, and a door closure system, all accessible by three carefully hidden buttons beneath the desk. As the chairman sat, he reached down and hit one of the buttons. The heavy paneled door they had just come through quickly but silently swung closed and locked.

 "Ok, what?" he said to Keller, irritated already, knowing whatever it was wouldn't be good. Just one day, the Chairman thought to himself, give me just one day without a frigging problem.

"Willow just informed me that the news is full of a Pan Am jumbo with 9D's going down over Scotland," Keller responded without sugar coating the information. "A lot of people on board. Same old, same old. Mid air collision, eyewitness engine failures, etc. Willow is handling it."

"Oh, well that gives me confidence," the Chairman said sarcastically. They were silent for a moment, both assessing the consequences.

"Hard," Keller said, turning to look out over the brightly lit city skyline of Hartford through the darkly tinted floor to ceiling glass windows of the office. The effect at night was spectacular. At the push of another button near the door, motorized black out shades could render the entire environment impenetrable to the outside world. With corporate espionage becoming more and more of a problem, the shades were used at least several times a day during meetings of one sort or another. Keller also had the chairman's suite swept for electronic eavesdropping equipment at least once a month, sometimes more often.

"So many people, some kids I assume, coming home for the holidays." Keller said, shaking his head, his thoughts turning to his own family. "Whatever happened, there's going to be a lot of sad people left behind. Shit."

The Chairman looked long and hard at his assistant before he spoke.

"Christ, Kevin. You going soft on me now?"

Keller was shocked back to reality by the tone of his boss's voice.

"Whatever happened, it better god damned well not have had anything to do with the fuel controls. Jesus Christ." He walked over and poured himself two fingers of an expensive double malt from the superbly appointed bar behind him, downing it in a single swallow. He didn't offer one to Keller.

The Chairman sighed, his shoulders hunched over in frustration. "We can expect the stock to take a hit tomorrow at the bell," he said bitterly.

Keller looked at him, knowing what was going though the CEO's mind, and he suddenly felt the urge to wretch.

"I'm going to lose a fortune. So will you, dammit."

The younger man felt bile rising in his throat and a need to get home to his family.

"Jesus Christ, just when the frigging stock starts to take off. Are we ever going to catch a break?"

Keller said nothing.

"Well?"

The young assistant tried to evade the conversation.

"I'll check the passenger manifest. It was probably a London to JFK flight. We might have had people aboard."

There was no response.

"Right," Keller said, dropping it. "I'll call your driver around, sir. If anything develops tonight, I'll give you a call."

"The hell with that, Kevin. Kill the story, you understand? Tell Willow his ass is on the line. We lose a nickel tomorrow in the market and somebody's going to swing." He slammed his glass down on the granite bar top to emphasize the point.

"Yes sir," Keller responded quietly. This was not a chat he wanted to have.

"Good night, sir," he said calmly, doing his best to hide his feelings from this man whose respect he craved and had worked so hard to earn. The question, "Why?" suddenly came to him, and he had no answer.

Keller managed to get home in time to read to his three children that night, the two little boys and his darling infant girl for whom he worked so hard to be their hero. But he was robotic, his mind a million miles away. He silently tucked them into their beds and gave each a good night kiss, the innocent touch of their soft lips on his cheek almost a shock to the numbness he felt inside. He didn't notice how quiet they were for being such young children. If he had he might have understood that they were sad when they were with him.

His wife Katie said little as she watched the news coverage from Lockerbie, knowing it was the last thing he wanted to talk about. She finally went to bed, wordlessly leaving him in the world she knew from experience was impenetrable. The phone rang incessantly until about 2 a.m. with new reports from company people that added little to the mystery of what had happened over the Scottish village. He stayed glued to the television, listening to the same information broadcast on CNN over and over again. Dinner was a double vodka. And several more.

It was nearly dawn before he went to bed, still troubled. It wasn't the news that was gnawing at him, which had gone from speculation to certainty that a bomb was to blame. Neither was it the certainty that General stock and all other traded companies associated with the aircraft or the flight would take a hit in the morning when the stock market opened. Nor was it the confirmation he got around three in the morning that at least one General employee was listed on the passenger manifest and was presumed dead. Keller had already approved Willow's pro forma statement of regret for the media and he would draft a personal letter of condolence for the Chairman's signature as soon as he got into the office. He also would arrange for flowers to be sent to the widow and possibly talk the CEO into telephoning his regrets if he sensed he was in the proper mood. Sincerity was hard to fake.

No, what he could not stop mulling over was the last few minutes of conversation he'd had with his boss at the end of the day. It had underscored a weakness in the young man that he had long fought to hide. "Do your job" wasn't cutting it. The wall his philosophy usually provided to keep him at a distance from the discomfort he sometimes felt in the narcissistic, soulless world in which he worked just wasn't high enough to keep out the boogeyman tonight.

Eloi or *Morlock*? Perhaps the time was approaching when he would have to make a choice. Knocking back his last swallow of vodka, he wondered how one went about hiding a conscience.

In the fitful hour he slept before waking to face another day, he dreamt of life as an intruder in an alien world.

One

December 1997

The intruder's face and hands were numbed by the cold despite the full thermal face mask and Beretta winter shooting gloves he wore, but he was also conscious of the sweat trickling down his chest beneath the thick folds of his black parka. Nerves. He carefully unscrewed the cap from a small field flask and drank no more than an ounce of the alcohol inside to calm him.

The hidden figure had not anticipated a long wait, but already had been kneeling for more than an hour in the brush, intently watching the comings and goings around the brightly lit office building several hundred yards away. His legs were beginning to cramp. He wondered how quickly he would be able to rise should he be discovered. His mind began to race with disaster scenarios. Calm, he reminded himself. Be calm. There's no hurry. The wait for this moment had been long. He could bear the discomfort.

The shadowed stranger crouched lower as a car drove slowly into the parking lot, headlights flickering and dancing over the underbrush he hid beneath as it passed. He recognized the driver but shook off memories of him. He could not risk the distraction by letting his mind wander. Nothing was going to stop him but his own will. The moment had arrived when he would finally have the opportunity to exact the retribution he deserved with the same lack of compassion, icy arrogance and blunt expediency with which they had destroyed him. There was nothing left for him but this moment. He was almost disappointed with how easy it was going to be.

The black woolen mask chafed at his neck as he carefully reached down and unzipped the heavy canvas bag at his insulated boots. He opened it, one careful inch at a time, each gentle pull timed with the traffic moving in and out of the motel parking lot behind his wooded hideout. Reaching into the bag, he grabbed the composite, thumbhole sniper style stock of the Czech-made CZ 750 M1 semi-automatic rifle, and eased it into the darkness. Its ten clip magazine was loaded with just four rounds of .308 caliber Winchester ammunition, a lethal, long jacketed, hollow point projectile, generally intended to cause the bullet to expand upon entering a soft target so as to extract devastating, excavating wounds. Earlier versions of the rifle and its lethal load had provided assassins since the Second World War with the capacity to blow a man's head off at 300 yards. He needed just half of that distance. The combination was as cold-blooded and merciless as his targets.

He laughed inwardly as he held the weapon. His life-long disgust with the gun industry and the "sport" of hunting had disappeared quite quickly once he had begun to formulate a plan. How ironic, he thought, that a man who had once marched through the streets of Washington in protest of the Vietnam War would now be obsessed with murder.

The mechanics for killing had been amazingly easy to acquire. He had simply walked into a gun shop in Libby, a small town in northwest Montana next to the Kootenai River and Highway 2, and asked to see a lightweight rifle for long-range target practice. The shopkeeper excitedly produced the CZ 750, lapsing into a lengthy dissertation on its significant accuracy and penetration power at up to 800 yards, with low muzzle blast and recoil. As he listened to the shopkeeper's excitement, more options were laid on the table. An NCS03R day/night vision scope with infrared illuminator brought the plan he was nurturing into reality. The deal sealer was a flash suppressor, silencer and red dot finder.

And it was all perfectly legal. All he needed was a driver's license. His forged, counterfeit copy worked without a question.

Tonight, the magazine of his rifle was light. Four rounds. Two for each of his intended targets. One bullet per target was quite enough, but two would be far more satisfying, enabling the pure joy of killing men you despised, men who deserved killing, not once, but twice. He was almost elated knowing his targets would appear momentarily as a pair, as they always did. Tweedle Dee and Tweedle Dum.

As he prepared for the kill and knelt to retrieve the night vision scope, the shooter closed his eyes for a moment, breathed deeply, and willed his concentration back into focus. He knew that the act he was about to commit would not erase the pain that had squeezed his heart with every breath for so long. But it would be a hell of a good start.

He attached the scope and red dot finder and screwed the silencer and flash suppressor onto the rifle, then raised the gun to his eye and adjusted the diopter. He felt his heart begin to race, causing him to lower the gun and take a deep breathe. Then another. Calm, he told himself.

Before him, there was activity at the lobby entrance to the three-story building where he had spent several years of his life, at least 12 out of every 24 hours a day, weekends and countless interrupted vacations. But it was just a FedEx truck making its third pickup and delivery of international mail of the day. He watched as the driver pulled away from the building.

He shifted his eyes to the corner executive suite on the third floor, the black, moonless night exaggerating the brightness of its illumination. From his vantage point in the wooded blind in which he waited, it took on the appearance of a sort of theatrical stage. Any movement inside would be artificially sharpened for the murderous voyeur. For the moment, the stage was empty. He waited. They would come.

Gazing into the office, he was struck by another flashback but again fought to push it down. He thought about taking another drink but shook that off too. The biting cold helped him to refocus and he raised his rifle, using the scope with its green glow to scan the space where his targets would soon appear. Slowly inspecting the floor to ceiling seamless tempered glass sections covering over 60 running feet, the room took on a yellowish illumination from the exterior, but hid no detail of activity. Seconds later, a tall, blond woman entered the frame and he centered the cross hairs of his riflescope on the center of her bleached head. He almost laughed out loud at the thought of wasting a bullet on something so empty. She dropped some papers on a desk and walked back out of the office.

A campus security car drove slowly past his carefully camouflaged hiding place. Right on schedule. He crouched an inch lower and dropped the muzzle of his rifle nearly to the ground. The timing of the security car "drive by" was his signal. It was 7 p.m.

An instant later, two men, his targets, entered the third floor office. One had a notepad in hand and was talking excitedly on a cell phone. The other followed closely behind, gesturing angrily. The gunman smiled. The hens had come home to roost, he thought, but little did they know that the fox was as good as inside. He quickly scanned the office for collateral damage one last time. No secretaries, no security guards, no maintenance people. The two intended targets stood closely by the doorway.

"Party time," he whispered to himself, wishing he had a few more minutes to savor the exquisite satisfaction of knowing what was coming next.

With his right thumb, he flicked on the red dot finder of his weapon. Instantly, a tiny red glow about the size of a dime appeared on the face of the target closest to the door. The shooter pulled back gently on the hair trigger, immediately feeling the soft recoil punch to his shoulder that he had become accustomed to. A heartbeat later, the projectile that exploded from his rifle barrel sliced through the laminated glass window and the head of his first target exploded. A rain of brilliant red mist fogged his line of sight. The jacketed, hollow point bullet shattered the target's skull, entering just below his right eye socket, tumbling across the crest of his pronounced nose, ripping through his left eye and purging his cranial cavity of the gelatinous matter of his brain. The left side of his skull exploded outwards, spraying the wall behind him with bone, facial tissue and brain.

Without hesitation, he pulled the trigger again before the body could drop, adding a second shot directly into the man's jaw. What had been a living, breathing human being was now a headless corpse that shuddered upright momentarily before dropping heavily to the floor.

"That's one for the fox," he whispered again, almost unable to contain his satisfaction. The blond suddenly appeared at the door. No matter.

She stood, not comprehending, trying to absorb the carnage spreading across the floor and staining her expensive, six inch Chanel heels. Shocked, she looked to her right at the gaping hole that had blown through the wall behind her, brain matter littering the grass-cloth covering. Before she could even open her mouth to scream, the shooter shifted his sights to the second target that stood motionless in shock, his mouth agape in horror. The red dot finder moved a fraction of an inch to the right, and the shooter pulled lightly on the trigger again, twice, in rapid succession. The blond flinched as blood splattered her face and the delicate lines of her blouse, spraying the wad of pink "urgent" paper telephone messages she held in wet crimson. The second headless corpse also dropped to the carpet. The blond fell to her knees in disbelief, unable to even cry out.

"That's two for the fox, none for the hens," the gunman whispered even as he reached to pick up the four spent shells lying by his boots. He moved quickly, barely allowing himself the thought of celebrating a kill well planned and executed. With the sure handedness that came with practice, he carefully disassembled the rifle and tossed the components into his duffel bag. Then he crawled slowly from the cover of the bush, carefully looking for any unintended witnesses. Finding none, he stood, his legs gradually uncramping and stripped off his facemask.

Casually emerging from the brush, he walked across the street towards a motel with its brightly lit neon signs and floodlit parking lot, pausing almost arrogantly to light a cigarette. He pulled open the collar of his coat as he walked, enjoying his cigarette, appearing to anyone who might have seen him to be a guest of the motel. The assassin looked up to check the parking lot video cameras he had shot out earlier in the day, and as expected, they showed no signs of repair. Unobserved, he walked confidently to his non-descript rental car, dumped his bag in the trunk and got behind the wheel. Careful not to appear rushed, he started the car and took his time letting it warm up, then turned on the heater and lights and drove slowly to the exit.

Inside the brightly lit building across the way, no signs of the massacre had yet appeared. He was gone before they knew he had come.

Two
~~~ ᛞ ~~~

January 1990

Kevin Keller put a hand over his mouth trying unsuccessfully to stifle a gaping yawn as the speaker on the stage before him droned on and on about the effect of production "work and rework" on the bottom line in General factories. It was a classic business metric for measuring the cost of correcting defective products or parts.

He wondered silently if God had invented PowerPoint as some kind of alternative to waterboarding in the world of corporate torture. It occurred to him that the art of discussing, debating and decision-making had been displaced in business by "charts" — colorful computer-calculated columns of numbers and plot points, bars, trend lines and graphs.

Thousands of charts. Charts filled with data that had been manipulated a zillion different ways until they projected the conclusion the presenter desperately desired or had been instructed to reach. Charts had become the sacred cow of the corporate boardroom. When, he wondered, when had charts become unassailable, unchallengeable? The new golden rule was if it fit on a chart, then it must be fact.

The room was hot and in a quick scan Keller saw more than one person who was obviously sharing his struggle to stay focused, if not awake. God damned Palm Springs, Keller thought. They drag us out into a frigging resort in paradise then lock us all in a conference room for a week. Yup. Corporate logic.

"Massage the data," the manufacturing expert on the stage kept repeating, only reinforcing Keller's skepticism. "Massage the data. You will eventually see that the truth is inescapable. We are pissing away millions in earnings because of poor production practices. There is a fortune to be found in removing the rework from the work!" he emphasized, proud of his adolescent play on words.

Keller thought he was going to gag at the display of exuberance. The only thing that the young executive found inescapable was that this man's entire life was controlled and absorbed by charts. He would have bet his bonus that the idiot played with charts on his computer on weekends, completely oblivious to the world around him.

He wondered silently if any one of the hundreds of executives around him had ever given thought to the premise that the "Sword of Damocles" which hung over the head of every factory worker on the line in the General corporate kingdom — analogous to the relentless threat of a "pink slip" come every pay day — had anything to do with the quality of the product coming out of its factories. It was only common sense, at least to him, that a man perpetually fearing for his job and livelihood might be distracted enough not to perform at his best. Somehow, the issue of morale seemed to be pushed aside in these discussions, largely dismissed by annual employee surveys that predictably showed a high level of employee satisfaction after they had been "massaged" to fit a chart. His head spun with the contradiction of the whole concept.

Predictably, the speaker wrapped up his presentation with the conclusion that no US factory run by General could compete with its overseas assets that performed the same work. He urged for the continuation of moving jobs and factories off shore where products across the wide spectrum of General's predominantly aerospace, military electronics and commercial building products portfolio could be produced cheaper, faster and evidently with higher quality. Keller's ears perked up only once, at the presenters somewhat off the cuff remark about redoubling efforts to move parts and products, particularly "reworked" parts and products into markets "that have become newly accessible." He frowned. What did that mean?

Finally, the presenter found the off button, thanked his audience for their rapt attention and left the stage to what amounted to mediocre applause. Keller swore even that was supplemented by a recording. Overall, he had found the speaker's message ugly, almost unpatriotic. But to raise one's hand and suggest such a thing was to risk having it cut off.

The boardroom decision to follow such a strategy had been made and cast in the equivalent of titanium by the new chairman and chief executive officer who had replaced his former boss some months before when he had finally tired of going through the motions of working. As he had explained to his young assistant, why bother? He had made enough money through obscene bonuses and the proceeds of stock options to equal the GNP of some countries. With very little effort.

There was little wrangling amongst the members of General's Board of Directors about the selection of a new CEO, each knowing they would be retained if they elected the man personally selected by the departing Chairman as his successor. A seat on the Board was worth an easy $175,000 per year, grossed up of course to cover the required income taxes, and included at least one weeklong meeting in a tropical paradise and several in European capitals. Consequently, there was little vetting of the anointed candidate. Keller was despondent when he learned that he had guessed correctly who that man might be. For he knew that the keys to General Industries Corporation had just been handed to Satan himself.

His name was Phillip Granville, a Philadelphia born and bred blue blood who had all the pedigrees. Degrees from Harvard and the University of Virginia's Darden School of Business. A consultant at Booz Allen Hamilton.

He was tall, handsome, coy, cunning, charming and possessed a win-at-all costs competitive drive that was as intense as a migraine. His eyes were a deep blue, his hair intentionally left a tad too long to emphasize the adventuresome spirit he worked hard to project.

He also was a man without a soul.

He was ruthless, brutal, cruel, conniving, deceitful and friendless. A look of disdain perpetually crossed his face. His trophy wife lived in misery despite their enormous wealth and existed only for photo-ops. His four children detested the sight of him. Those who worked for him did so in a state of perpetual fear and uncertainty. They loathed him. Candidates who interviewed for jobs with him reported his first question as, "What were your SAT scores?"

All the qualities that a corporate Board hungry for increased profits and personal gain through cost cutting and restructuring could ever hope for.

Phillip Granville was their man, hands down. But he was even more.

He was a philanderer whose taste for extra-marital adventures ran the gamut from streetwalker to royalty. He popped uppers in the morning to give him excessive energy jolts and downers at night to keep him well rested, all made readily available by the corporation's physician who was handsomely rewarded for doing practically nothing else.

He routinely skirted the law — both domestic and international — in his business dealings, and was hardly above breaking it. In every capacity of his life that was subject to scrutiny, he surrounded himself with caretakers and protectors who hid his excesses and indiscretions with a prowess the Nixon White House would have applauded.

Kevin Keller knew the man too well. He had watched the glow of his star brighten as the executive vice president of human resources during the three years he had worked for Granville's predecessor, and concluded that someday he would be the chosen one. When it finally happened, Keller struggled not to shudder at the grasp of the new CEO's handshake and avoided looking into his eyes. That night, he came home to Katie and hugged her silently for a long time before pouring himself the first of several drinks and sharing his fears with her.

Following the transfer of power in the CEO's office, Keller himself had been unceremoniously transferred from the corporate headquarters to one of General's commercial operations, Beckham Corporation, which focused on commercial building systems and products, including heating ventilating and air conditioning and security equipment. He assumed responsibility for all of the division's product quality initiatives as a vice president reporting directly to Badr Laabi, Beckhams's president and CEO.

Keller wasn't all that dissatisfied with the move, given that he could have been thrown out with the rest of his former boss' office furnishings without a second thought. But he was well aware that what had saved him was his inside knowledge of the politics, backstabbing and questionable business transactions that were as predictable in the General culture as was the sun rising and setting each day. He knew too much, and people above him knew how much he knew. Keller figured they had concluded that it was better just to bury the young executive's knowledge in some comfortable but reclusive holding assignment somewhere far removed from the seat of power and external investigators who nearly always had General in their sights for some transgression. And from that perspective, Kevin Keller was not unhappy to be occupying a job that may not have had all the glamour of working as the top man's right hand, but took him out of the line of fire.

But what he knew about this new chairman, both from the perspective of his professional acumen and values, was knowledge that made Kevin Keller a threat to Phillip Granville himself. What he knew of the man's personal predilections made him even more so. He tried not to think about it and to stick with his creed: Do your job. The question that nagged at him was would he get the chance before becoming one of Granville's targets?

Keller knew that the whole morning's discussion, every presentation, was no more than a setup, just one more element of the brainwashing he and over 750 of his executive counterparts from around the globe were being subjected to at this annual senior management conference in Palm Springs. The big shoe would drop after lunch when most of them were overcome with boredom and the need for a nap or half drunk again from the wine that never stopped flowing. There was always just enough booze around to lull anyone with half a brain into a dull stupor and a sense of resignation.

It was going to be a really big shoe, he could sense, an objective that would send them all back to their businesses or factories reeling with a "BHAG" — a cute acronym some fat-assed, ridiculously over-paid consultant had dreamed up, short for big, hairy, audacious goal — with no clue how to achieve it. He knew from experience. In the year since he had moved from the corporate headquarters to his new assignment, he'd been challenged twice already with some half-wit's latest BHAG. He and the entire operations management were exhausted from the wasted time and effort.

However, it was inevitable that there would be a new productivity program associated with the goal that had been sold to Phillip Granville as the Holy Grail of productivity programs. Of course the new program, which would be so laden with bullshit, touch-feely meetings, useless data collection and paperwork, would ultimately prevent the productivity gains from being reached because it would occupy every waking hour of every employee. They never had time to get to really fixing the problems.

But that was ok, because the real objective was to close all the US factories anyway and to move as many operations as possible to overseas locations. Union agreements? Hardly a problem. Promises that were made to local governments where General manufactured to retain jobs in lieu of tax incentives? The pledges were broken before the ink was dry on the agreement. Patriotism? Keller had to stop himself from laughing out loud. It was all about earnings per share and how much money was going into the pockets of senior executives. How much was going into the bank accounts of shareholders and employees was just another exercise in "massaging" a chart to an acceptable number that Wall Street, the media and unions would swallow.

If you had a taste for bullshit, Keller thought to himself, this was the place to be. His stomach roiled. More and more often in his daydreams he was having these cynical conversations with himself and he knew it wasn't good. Because when this torture ended, he was going to be one of the people who would have to implement the new BHAG and the inevitable productivity program with a fervor that was worthy of an Academy Award.

Each time they went through this exercise, he had to become an actor assuming a new role. It seemed as if each script was becoming harder and harder to follow, each role requiring him to put on a new mask and assume a posture that reeked of his unwavering support. It was no different than an actor faced with the impossible task of becoming a character whose personality was a direct clash with his own.

The analogy that kept popping into his mind was of hero and villain.

On Monday, fresh from a strategic meeting with Phillip Granville that had been purposely cloaked in secrecy to add to the angst of low level employees, he would stand before his managers and pretend that he was a hero who had learned the answers to what ailed General and would save their jobs. Enthusiasm would abound because he was so good at selling bullshit. By the following Tuesday, the details of the new productivity program would have been officially announced in painful detail, making it clear that half of the people in the room would actually lose their jobs. And Keller would be expected to profess his continued undying support for the program, instantly transforming him into a villain in the eyes of people whose trust he had won just a week earlier.

He would work hard to regain their trust yet again, but just as that was beginning to happen, Phillip Granville's team would add some new wrinkle, some new caveat that would double the number of heads to hit the chopping block. Once more, Kevin Keller would have to stand before his staff and support the agenda, again making him the villain. And this insane roulette wheel of management spun around and around continuously until it stopped on the magic number of headcount reduction that Granville had in mind all along, the number that would make he and his cohorts richer still by inflating the corporation's share price through short-term cost cutting.

Kevin Keller would sit in his corner office after one of these meetings, staring out the windows in silence after having prostituted himself once more before people he genuinely cared for. All he could think about was the answer to one question.

Eloi or *Morlock*?

Three
~~~ ღ ~~~

June 1991

At eight o'clock in the evening on an early summer day in June, Kevin Keller was pretending to enjoy an after dinner brandy and illicit Cuban cigar on the veranda of the Water's Edge Inn in Westbrook, Connecticut following dinner and an all day management meeting with Beckham's senior staff. He was staring at the nose of a man standing in front of him whose lips were moving but Keller wasn't hearing a word. His thoughts were 50 miles away where he should have been at home tucking his three children, ten year-old Sam, eight year-old Ben and six year-old Julia into their beds after reading them a story about *Camelot* and *The Knights of the Round Table*, their new favorite. Allowing the fantasy to continue even as the man kept moving his lips, he thought how nice it would be to then join his wife on the back patio, listening to the symphony of cicadas, crickets and katydids tuning up as the sun set and talk about their day. They might be holding hands as they looked out over the pool or Katie might be describing her new design for an extension to the perennial garden that had become her passion.

That's where he should have been. Demonstrating his love and need for his family. Instead, here he was, looking out over the sun setting over Long Island Sound in a ridiculously romantic and senseless setting, half drunk, enveloped in the stench of cigar smoke and listening to the endless droning of a fellow executive who was as interesting as the rest of the hollow talk he had listened to all day. A part of him desperately wanted to reach into his suit jacket pocket and remove his company identification badge while blowing on the lit end of his cigar until the ember was red-hot. Then he imagined touching the fiery ember to the ID and watching it burst into flame. He would drop it to the ground and watch it turn into a puddle of amorphous plastic. Shapeless. Meaningless. Exactly what his career was becoming.

The temptation was overwhelming. But before he could fantasize any further, Keller was abruptly distracted by an obnoxiously loud neighboring conversation. What he heard was the booming voice of Badr Laabi, Beckham's president and chief executive officer berating Paul Stanton, his senior vice president for human resources. Laabi's harsh tone made it clear he was very displeased with whatever the hapless Stanton had just informed him. Stuart Brown, General

Industries' chief financial officer and the number two man in Phillip Granville's kingdom, looked on. He was a guest at Badr's meeting and looked on at his tirade against Stanton with amusement. Brown rarely said anything in social settings, and was sparse with his words even in business meetings. But he was a powerful player in GIC because he had Granville's ear and knew everything about its businesses. Including some of the things that were well hidden.

Keller flicked the inch long ash off his cigar and brought his mind back to the present, shaking his head to Sebastian Oliviero, president of Beckhams's operations that encompassed Europe, Africa and the Middle East. He was the Spaniard who had been talking non-stop to him for at least the last ten minutes.

"Yes, Sebastian, I agree," Keller said, not having the faintest idea what he had agreed to but wanting to show his colleague some show of life while he listened to the far more interesting conversation nearby.

Laabi was gesturing wildly at Stanton and stabbing at his chest as he spoke loudly enough to cause many of the two-dozen people gathered on the veranda to look in his direction.

"You heard exactly what Phillip's instructions were, Paul. Or were you not listening?" Laabi demanded.

"Yes, I heard him, it's just that…"

"Bullshit. I quote: 'Markets that have recently become accessible'," the senior executive said, stabbing Stanton in the chest again with a pointed forefinger. The American hung his head, embarrassed.

"There are laws, Badr…"

"Again I tell you, bullshit," Laabi responded, his carefully honed French accent accentuating the word so that it came out "bullsheet."

"Just get it fucking done, or I will find someone who can," he instructed Stanton, then threw the remaining contents of his wine glass over the veranda railing with disgust. "My God, where was this swill vented, Texas?" he insulted Stanton, who had made all the arrangements for the meeting. The president stormed away, pulling his cell phone from his pocket as he returned to his hotel room. The party was over.

Keller hadn't the slightest hint of what Laabi was screaming about, but his explosions were legendary. What else should he expect from a man who boasted that he had been "trained in the image and likeness of Phillip Granville." Indeed he had, Keller thought to himself. Aside from being incredibly uncouth, crude and brutally condescending, Laabi had no patience for even the slightest challenge to a directive he had given.

Badr Laabi was a French wannabe who carefully hid his Moroccan birthplace for fear that his humble, North African roots would limit his influence with Granville, who along with his other endearing traits was a discrete racist who made no bones about his preference for being surrounded by people of "highly civilized culture and only the finest education." Consequently, Badr shared Granville's most obvious trait. He was a bully.

Keller made his way over to Stanton and Brown, curious. He was oblivious to leaving Oliviero in mid-sentence.

"Americans," the Spaniard said in disgust.

"What the hell was that all about, Paul," he asked the obviously shaken Stanton.

"Nothing," he snapped. "Bastard just doesn't get it."

"Doesn't get what?"

The HR executive looked at Keller. He had a strange, pleading look, as if he wanted to get something off his chest. Then he caught himself, futility and resignation appearing on his face instead.

"Leave it, Kevin."

"C'mon, we've been friends for a long time, Paul, we can talk."

Stanton was in no mood for camaraderie. He just spit it out.

"He's worried the Abdelbaset al-Megrahi verdict is going to get in the way of his plans, alright? Like I can fix it."

Keller pulled back, perplexed.

"The what...?

"The Libyan that was convicted last January of blowing up Pan Am 103 over Lockerbie back in '88. "Don't you listen to the news, Keller?"

"But what the hell does that..."

"He's worried the Libyan's are going to be pissed off at us. There's millions at stake," Stanton explained.

"Libya? What are you talking about? We can't do business in Libya..."

"Oh, Jesus. Just leave it alone, ok? Good night, Kevin. We never had this conversation." He turned and walked after Laabi, leaving Keller completely confused.

The normally silent Stuart Brown shook his head in agreement.

"Advice you should heed, Kevin," the balding, bespectacled CFO said. "Yes, good advice, young man."

Then he too walked away from Keller, who suddenly found himself alone on the veranda.

"I guess the party's over," he thought, without a clue as to how precisely correct he was.

Four
~~~ ஒ ~~~

April 1992

"I don't know why he scheduled the meeting for the 22nd, Katie. For the last time, I don't make the frigging rules."

He was packing, again. On a Sunday afternoon. Again. A limo to take him to JFK would be arriving shortly. Again. He would be away for at least a week. Again. And their 15th wedding anniversary would fall right in the middle of his absence.

Worst of all, the meeting was in Paris. Katie's favorite place in the world.

Kevin Keller had just returned from a weeklong trip to Australia, most of it spent in the air. He'd been home exactly 40 hours when he began packing another suitcase. He lived in a perpetual state of jet lag and he wondered at times if his mind would ever catch up to his body clock. He was exhausted, spent, miserable and angry. And his wife, the most understanding and patient person he had ever known, who was practically singlehandedly raising their three children was obviously very angry. The combination had them circling like an aggressive mongoose and a wary cobra, but their weapons were limited to razor-sharp tongues.

"When does this end, Kev? I mean working for the chairman was one thing. That was like a sabbatical from our marriage, and I signed on. But I thought things would slow down after three years of that crap. This is worse than ever," she said in a voice a lot louder than he would have liked. He hated to have his kids hear them fight. It reminded him of lying in bed at night as a boy listening to his own parents screaming at each other. He couldn't remember a day growing up when he felt a sense of inner peace, a minute when his stomach wasn't aching with anxiety. It abruptly came to him that it wasn't unlike like how he felt now.

"You're never home," Katie continued to harangue him. "And if you are, you're on the phone day and night, the fax machine never stops... Jesus... is there ever going to be time for you and me? For us? As a family?"

He didn't dare say it because she'd probably throw something at him, but Keller thought his wife was particularly beautiful when she was angry with him. The corners of her mouth tended to point down just a tad, accentuating her lips and her blues eyes sparkled when she was upset. She had pulled her long, naturally chestnut brown hair back tight into a ponytail and was wearing just a hint of makeup. Her cutoff jeans and sleeveless tee was a far cry from the fashion plate she was during the week, but her casual dress was typical of the way she wanted to be with her husband on the weekends. She truly believed work ended at the front door of their home on Friday night and should not interfere with their lives or relationship for the next 48 hours.

God, he thought, she was beautiful. And so right.

The problem was, the opportunities to see her looking beautifully agitated seemed to be growing at an alarming pace. And as to casual, well, he had just put on one of his many pinstriped business suits and it was only one o'clock on a Sunday afternoon. The inequity between his working hours and the time spent with Katie and the children was growing exponentially. In fact, there were weeks on end when there was no time for family except for the telephone calls he'd manage to sneak in from some hotel room or mind-numbing conference somewhere in the world. His job was definitely getting in the way of his relationship with Katie and certainly with the kids. None of them even waited up for him anymore when he was working out of the home office and it was unusual for him to be able to get more than a couple of one word responses when he called from the road.

Well done, he thought. You've become a stranger to your own family.

"Katie, I'm sorry. I'll make it up to you, I promise. I'll take some time off next month and we'll get away for a weekend or something," he pleaded. She turned her back on him and walked out of their bedroom. Bad sign. But unexpectedly, she marched back in a couple of minutes later and sat down heavily on the bed.

"This is bullshit," she said in no uncertain terms, but now a little less angry, more pouting.

"I don't make the rules, honey," he repeated. "I hate this too. But it's part of the job. If I bail on Laabi, I'm toast. It's either his way or the highway. He couldn't give a damn about our anniversary, believe me. He's Phillip Granville all over again. A clone. All he has is his work. He expects the same from me, from all of us."

She looked up at him, the fire still in her eyes, but now they were wet.

"I'm tired of being alone, Kev." He didn't respond but hung his head in resignation. Talk about a rock and a hard place.

"Me too," he finally said. It just came out. And it was a mistake.

"Don't give me that bullshit!" she yelled. "You get treated like royalty on these trips, the whole bunch of you. Every night out for dinner, drinking, god only knows what else…" She didn't finish.

Anger flashed in his eyes.

"Look, I spend my whole god damned life in either an airplane or a conference room to bring home a big paycheck, Katie. And yah, you're right, I'm out every night. It goes with the territory. Do we drink? Yes. Out of boredom more than anything. Beyond that? You know me better. I'm not Laabi. I have eyes for only one woman in the entire world and I'm looking at her right now."

She was silent, brooding. It didn't matter what else she said and she knew it. He was leaving again.

Period. She knew he was right, but at the moment, it didn't matter. All Katie Keller knew was how much she hated General Industries Corporation and the two selfish pricks that had made her husband a virtual slave.

Sure, everything they had, the house, the cars, money to spend without thinking twice, it all came from his job. She worked too, as a physical therapist with the elderly and adored her job. But it didn't bring home anything like what it should have. Nothing near what Kevin made. The only difference was she had a life beyond work. The children, her friends, the club. Kevin had nothing. And it was beginning to show.

The non-stop business travel was bad enough. But even when he was home, they'd be lucky to see him before eight o'clock and he'd be drawn to a phone call within minutes of walking in the door. She went to bed alone nearly every night.

At 39, she was lonely, bored, frustrated and very tired. Somehow the dreams she and Kevin had shared as teens and their urgent need just to be together had vanished. "Things" had replaced their passion for each other. Expensive things that many envied, but which now held little value for either of them.

All she wanted was her husband.

She wasn't sure what he wanted at all. And that hurt the most.

It seemed that right before her eyes, her husband was becoming one of the very people he said he despised. Where were the surprise bouquets of flowers, the unexpected dinners by candlelight, the long rides along the shore roads with the top down on a Sunday afternoon?

Where?

How had the romance between them been replaced by assholes like Phillip Granville and Badr Laabi and dozens more like them?

"Don't go Kev, please," she suddenly blurted out, a tear trickling down her face. He turned and faced her, shaking his head.

"I love you," he said, his bag packed, ready to leave again with his stomach in knots knowing all was not well between them.

He was genuinely torn. Plan A was to quit the frenetic lifestyle that wasn't a life, to walk away from the existence that was robbing them of so much including their love for each other, and lose everything they had. Or, Plan B. Swallow hard and fall back into the role as a soldier in Granville's army of soulless, pinstriped robots. Take one for the team. Do your job. Happiness wasn't an option.

Just a few years ago, he was so driven for success, so determined to prove his doubters wrong, that Plan A wasn't even something he could consider. Lately, it pulled at him as he sat for endless hours in an airplane seat, staring, unseeing at the world that was passing him by just short of the speed of sound.

"My car is here. "I'll call you when I can. Say goodbye to the children for me," he said softly, then walked out of their bedroom, down the stairs and out the door without another word.

The driver took his bag and held the door open for him. Kevin Keller took a moment to stare the unsuspecting man in the face before climbing into the back seat.

Something made him look up at their bedroom window. Katie was staring down at him. His shoulders sagged in defeat. He blew her a kiss but she turned away, closing the drapes.

The time to choose was coming.

Quickly.

Five

The presenter had nearly completed his summary of Beckham's first quarter financial performance when a single sentence — a few seemingly innocuous words — changed Kevin Keller's life forever.

The Frenchman making the presentation was Jean-Pierre Chandon, chief financial officer for Beckham's businesses in Europe, Africa and the Middle East. He was a well-respected member of the subsidiary's management team, who, thankfully for the Americans in the room spoke very fluent English.

The meeting was being held on the eighth floor of Beckham's European headquarters at La Defense in Courbevoie. It was an architecturally stunning, heavily glazed office building looking out over the massive esplanade, "le Parvis" that led to the monumental la Grande Arche at the end of the Avenue de la Grande

Armée in the westernmost corner of the Axe Historique.

The view was breathtaking and a complete contradiction to the location of Keller's personal office in Farmington, which looked out over a rural, wooded area occupied by squirrels and deer, a naturalists delight. Here, thousands of office workers and tourists mingled together on the paved esplanade, either walking to one of the hundreds of office buildings in the major Paris business district or just taking in the magnificent structures that surrounded them on all sides. They seemed to sprout up as a permanent, manmade garden of steel and tinted glass. La Defense was, to some admirers of design, the Louvre of architecture.

But the world inside Beckham's impressive headquarters was hardly as inviting. The conference room was warm and stuffy and the twelve members of the European management team participating all chain-smoked. The air was thick with a pungent grey cloud from the filter-less, dark tobacco Gauloise cigarettes sporting the winged helmet of the ancient French Gauls that most of them preferred. There was a certain romance to the harsh brand, once the favorite of Jean-Paul Sartre and Pablo Picasso. But for the Americans, most of who had already quit the habit in part for health concerns but mostly because it was rapidly becoming socially unacceptable, the conference room was becoming a torture chamber. Badr Laabi was the only smoker in the US contingent, but even he was looking slightly pale.

The combination of the noxious, stale air, jet lag and too much to drink on the night flight over the

Atlantic had them all feeling slightly ill and barely able to stay focused. Several cups of thick, strong espresso did little to help. In fact the shots of concentrated caffeine only added to their overall general discomfort.

Keller had grown used to these grueling sessions, which usually began within an hour of landing on foreign soil without even the chance to shower, shave or change clothes. Time was money, and the clock began ticking the moment the American contingent's flight was wheels down at Charles de Gaulle Aeroport that morning. He couldn't count the occasions someone had remarked to him how lucky he was to "get to see the world" and enjoy travelling. At one time, he would attempt to explain the physical and personal toll such a life took. Now he merely smiled and moved the conversation along. You had to experience the "joy" to appreciate it. There also was no explaining the pit in his stomach that came with leaving home like he had last afternoon, with everyone unhappy. It made the time away so much more stressful.

Like so much in his life, all was not what it seemed.

Keller would have paid someone to open a window, but that's not how it was done. When the Europeans came to the US for meetings with Beckham staff, they suffered their own kind of torment. They weren't allowed to smoke at all and in typical American fashion the air conditioning was intentionally set low, the theory being that chilled air kept everyone alert. Their poor colleagues from warmer climates froze in discomfort.

"So, you will see that our first quarter performance has positioned us well to begin the year, and we are confident that the second quarter will be equally as successful," the tall, almost gaunt Chandon said. And then he uttered a sentence that startled Kevin Keller's somewhat addled brain into instant, total awareness.

"And with our renewed and intense efforts in Libya, Iran, Iraq, Liberia and Somalia, we are well on target to make plan for the second quarter and perhaps even exceed it."

Around the table came the sound of knuckles wrapping on the long, mahogany conference table, a demonstration of congratulations to the management team for the company's Middle East and African successes.

Lesser quality furniture might not have stood up to the aggressive "knuckling" that was a long held tradition in Europe. The table was inlaid with exquisite Zebrano hardwood detailing. It had been hand made in Cameroon by indigenous workers skilled at working with the rough, course wood with its wavy grain that was actually a threatened species. That hardly mattered to Sebastian Oliviero, president of Beckham's European division. What was important was the statement the table made. It reeked of wealth and excess, as did nearly all the accouterments of the European headquarters. The fact that the rare hardwood was nearing extinction made no difference to him. He considered the worldwide protests against its harvesting with much the same laissez-faire attitude he had about nearly everything to do with any type of authority, business policy or government regulation.

Libya, Iran, Iraq, Liberia and Somalia? The words rang in Keller's ears, jarring him from his complacency. He couldn't help himself.

"Excuse me, pardon moi," he said to Chandon.

"Oui, Kevin," Chandon politely responded to the interruption.

"Would you repeat that, please? I am unsure of what you mean."

"Repeat what, my friend?"

Keller suddenly realized that all heads in the room were turning to look at him, including Stuart Brown, UIC's chief financial officer who typically attended Beckham's financial reviews as Phillip Granville's representative.

"Libya... Iran, Iraq... the others? Renewed efforts? What do you mean, Jean-Pierre?" he asked.

"Why..." Chandon hesitated, unsure of the question.

"What do I mean? Sales of course. We have launched intensive efforts to produce export intercompany sales to former customers in these countries through local operations. And we are aggressively seeking to expand our market share." He paused. "Is there something out of order?"

There was silence in the room. Keller was struggling to process what Chandon had said.

"But, Jean-Pierre... how can this be?"

Oliviero turned to address Keller directly, somewhat irritated by the American's interruption and tone of voice.

"What is the problem, Kevin? You object in some way?" the European president demanded.

"Libya, Iran, Iraq, Liberia and Somalia?" Keller answered immediately, his voice rising in confusion. "Surely, you jest. These are all nations that have been subjected to US embargo restrictions for one form of human rights violation or another. We can't sell to these countries under any circumstances."

Oliviero's eyes narrowed as he bored holes through Keller's skull with his icy stare. Chandon shook his head, puzzled.

"I'm not clear on what you are saying, Kevin. We are in France, not the United States. There is nothing to prevent the French company from selling our products to our General companies in these — what did you call them? Embargoed nations?" He dismissed Keller with a contemptuous wave of his hand. "This is an American problem, not a French."

"Sebastian, perhaps you have forgotten why it is that our factories were ordered not to ship product to these countries some years ago? It is the same issue, nothing has changed. "

Badr Laabi abruptly spoke up.

"You are wrong about that, Kevin," he said, making no attempt to hide his contempt for the American on his staff.

"How am I wrong, Badr? Did I miss the State Department memo lifting the US restrictions on trade with these nations? Has the embargo on Libya and the others been lifted? Have we already forgotten that the Libyan Abdelbaset al-Megrahi has been convicted of the Pan Am bombing over Lockerbie and that one of our own employees died in the terrorist act? Need I remind you of the Iraqi invasion of Kuwait and 'Desert Storm'? Or of the continued efforts by the Iranians to develop nuclear weapons? Need I go on? Should we debate the terrorist activities in Liberia or the ongoing genocide in Somalia?" Keller shot back. He was angry.

Laabi leaned back in his chair, absorbing the impertinence of his subordinate. He was angrier, but more adept at hiding it.

"I have no idea of the status of the so called 'embargoes' against these nations," the Moroccan said, calmly.

"They have not been rescinded, I assure you, Badr," Keller replied, holding his ground.

"It makes no difference," Laabi responded without hesitation.

"What? How can you possibly dismiss..."

"First, because we never halted sales after these pathetic directives from your State Department and second, I have orders from my boss," Laabi finally snapped loudly. "Perhaps you were sleeping during our meeting in Palm Springs a few months ago, my friend? Could Phillip Granville have been any clearer? He is my boss, Kevin, not your president or the State Department."

His response caused Keller to sit upright in his chair. He shook his head, not sure of what he had just heard.

"Beckham is a unit of General Industries Corporation, Badr," he responded, not about to back down. "As such, it is incorporated in the state of Delaware as is GIC and is subject to the laws, policies and government regulations of the United States. There is nothing to debate here. These export intercompany sales from France to any of our companies operating in countries subject to US embargos are illegal in the eyes of the United States government. And that means they are illegal here as well."

Laabi was silent, rage building on his face. No one else in the room dared enter the conversation, including Beckham's chief legal counsel, Raymond Desmond. Keller looked over at the lawyer expecting him to back up his assertions. The American looked down at the table, silent. He turned to Brown, who also would not return his gaze.

Oh, shit, Keller thought, suddenly realizing the situation he was in.

Finally Laabi spoke, confident there would be no further challengers.

"Perhaps we should continue this conversation in private, Kevin. There is no need to delay the meeting further with debate over an argument that has already been settled."

Keller knew he could not back down although every nerve in his being was screaming to shut his mouth.

"Badr, from what you have just told me, I, as an American and an officer of this corporation have committed a felony. I am guilty of treason. And I have serious concerns that we have probably also violated the Foreign Corrupt Practices Acts multiple times in this scheme. Frankly, I am stunned."

"Foreign Corrupt Practices Act?" Laabi stuttered in rage. "What are you talking about?"

"It's known by the US government as 'FCPA' and primarily involves bribes and other illegal payments. These sales could not have taken place without criminal facilitating payments, I am sure of it.

"Furthermore, by proceeding down this path, we are continuing to violate US law. That makes us all party to illegal activities and subject to criminal prosecution. Finally, do you understand the consequences of your actions? You have already placed at risk every export license under which the divisions of General Industries operate."

"Enough, Kevin..."

"And you could trigger a Justice Department investigation that will essentially shut down all international sales of the corporation, void all contracts with the US military and prohibit our ability to bid on new business!" he continued, despite Laabi's interruption. "These sales could bankrupt the entire corporation. My God... it's possible that the Justice Department would break up the company."

The Beckham president slammed his fist down on the table.

"Enough of these hysterics, I said," he screamed. "Do you hear me? Have I made myself clear?"

Keller did not respond but neither would he look away from Laabi. He'd come this far. He couldn't do any more damage.

Laabi ignored Keller's objections and turned his attention back to Chandon and Oliviero.

"Sebastian, this discussion is over. You are to continue with your efforts in the territories as instructed. And if there is any interference — from any member of my staff — you are to let me know immediately."

Again, he stared directly at Kevin Keller for long moments, waiting for a reply. A vein on the side of his neck bulged in anger. He was like a pit viper, coiled to strike if the challenger so much as opened his mouth again. Keller knew it was pointless to pursue the argument publicly any further.

"So," Laabi said in a voice dripping with satisfaction, like a bully who had taken control of the schoolyard by terrifying anyone who would stand up to him, "have I made my self entirely clear?"

He leaned back in his chair and took his time lighting a fresh Gauloise, taking a deep drag and blowing it in Keller's direction before speaking again.

"If there are no other objections, let us continue," he growled in his deep voice. The meeting went on.

Kevin Keller sat silently in his seat, looking in the direction of the morning's presenters but they were invisible to him. Later, he would not remember a word that was said after his confrontation with Laabi. He felt as if every eye in the room was upon him, as if he was a lone juror resented by his colleagues for holding out for justice.

Inside, his stomach was in knots. He had to keep fighting the urge to step out of the meeting and call Katie, to share with her what had happened and to hear her say he had done the right thing. But the man in him would not allow him to move from his seat, knowing full well he would be admitting to defeat.

It was a while in coming, but suddenly it struck him that he had more than likely destroyed his career by standing up to Laabi. At first, it was only a thought. But as the moments went on and it lingered, the consequences of his actions grew to monstrous proportions in his mind. Finally, there was no doubt in his mind that he would be fired, if not by the end of the day, certainly immediately upon return to the US.

Oblivious to all around him, he began to wonder how he would explain what had happened to Katie.

"The world has ended, my love," he imagined himself saying.

Sadly, it did not enter his mind that their replies would be far more sane, far more in touch with the reality that he should be living, instead of the life he was: "We are your world. Come back to us."

Instead, when the meeting finally ended in the early afternoon, he felt the touch of Paul Stanton on his shoulder. Keller was unaware that the discussions had ended nearly ten minutes before and that he was sitting in the conference room alone.

Stanton's bloodshot eyes told Keller what he needed to know before he even heard his words.

"Badr thinks you should catch a flight home first thing tomorrow morning, Kevin," the vice president of Human Resources said. "There is no need for you to participate in the rest of the scheduled agenda. We will talk more when we return on Friday from Paris."

Keller looked at him, a man he had worked with for more than a decade and knew well. There was no friendship, no compassion in his eyes. There was nothing but two black holes looking down on him as he mouthed the words Laabi had instructed him to.

Keller nodded without comment.

"I suggest you do not mention this morning's debate to anyone, Kevin, it will only make matters worse. Do you understand?"

"He's wrong, Paul, you know he's wrong."

Stanton did not reply, nor did he turn away.

"You heard what I said, Kevin. It's in your best interests."

Keller closed his eyes. He needed time to think, to understand the consequences of his next move.

"No," he finally said in a soft voice. "I will not be quiet. There is far too much at stake."

Stanton shook his head.

"That's just dumb, Kevin," he said. "You're not thinking this through. The consequences. For you."

He hesitated.

"And for others."

"Others? They have been taking orders. I doubt that the penalties would be severe."

Stanton looked into his eyes for long seconds. He shook his head again. "You really don't get it. You don't understand what's at risk."

He paused.

"Or perhaps I should say… who is at risk."

It was the way in which Stanton said it that jarred Keller, sending a shiver up his spine.

"What do you mean by that? Who is at risk?"

Stanton stood up and walked away.

"This conversation is over, Kevin. Think long and hard before you do or say anything."

"Is that a threat?" Keller said, jumping up from his chair?"

Stanton shook his head again, but this time there was almost a look of pity in his eyes.

"There is more at stake than you are considering. Much more. Listen to me again. Think long and hard. Get on an airplane, go home and keep your mouth shut."

The human resources head walked out of the room, quietly closing the door behind him.

Keller realized that his hands were shaking. He needed a drink.

Stanton's words turned over and over in his head.

"Who" was at risk?

Six

Kevin Keller chased the setting sun back across the Atlantic the following morning, after a long, sleepless night.

Strapped into his Air France business class seat, he barely moved a muscle during the long transatlantic flight, playing the confrontation with Laabi over and over in his mind. He kept coming back to a question that he struggled to answer, for to do so would take courage he couldn't seem to summon. In truth, he knew the answer, but could not face it as it endlessly stirred his confusion.

Had he taken on Laabi intentionally, knowing the consequences? Was what he had done the equivalent of professional suicide?

Laabi was a consummate bully, an ugly, mean freak who enjoyed confrontation and the power to verbally crush a man, especially when he had an audience. He reveled in the reputation that he had been cloned in the "image and likeness" of Phillip Granville, a man of the same detestable qualities, the only distinction between them being that the chairman, more experienced in the arts of cruelty and narcissism was meaner and more powerful.

But on painful reflection, Keller wasn't entirely sure if it was Laabi — or himself — who had been the actual antagonist.

Of this much he was certain. He hated the person he had become, the life he led, the thought of facing even one more day as Kevin Keller. He was filled with self-loathing, a man who had sold out his own happiness, and unwittingly, that of the only people in the world who meant anything to him.

He didn't sleep on the eight-hour flight home either, his brain so shocked by what had happened in the last 24 hours that his body could not slow the flow of adrenalin on which he was functioning. He ate nothing, he drank heavily. He wondered if this was what it was like to be the walking dead.

The closer he came to New York, the more his mind turned to what he would tell Kate later that night. The dread built up in him hour by hour, until finally he buried his head in a blanket and cried in silence from the sheer agony and confusion of defeat.

That was it, wasn't it?

He was going to have to tell her that he had been beaten, that he had screwed up, that he was, after all, exactly what those in his past had predicted he would be.

A failure.

He tried desperately to script in his mind exactly what he would say to her. But words would not come to him, other than the only truth.

Kevin Keller.

Morlock.

That night, after a long, silent ride from JFK to their home in Canton, he walked to the front door carrying his suitcase and stopped. He couldn't bring himself to put his key in the door and open it. He could not face them.

He stepped off the cobblestone walk and stood in front of the picture window, peering inside at the only people he truly loved and knowing they were the only ones who cared for him.

Kate, looking as beautiful and radiant as she always did despite working a full day and coming home to care for their three children, was just finishing the dinner dishes. Predictably, Sam, Ben and Julie were playing a video game, a few minutes of utter joy they enjoyed each night before being herded off to do their homework.

The thought struck Keller that it was a scene a modern day Norman Rockwell might have painted. He wondered if Rockwell had ever painted a beaten husband and father, a failure rather than the patriarchal figures for which he was so admired.

As he stood there, watching, it began to rain, a cold early spring downpour that startled him because it was the first thing he had felt, the first thing that had touched his senses since his words with Laabi.

Inexplicably, he dropped his suitcase and fell to his knees, the rain soaking him, adding to his utter dejection and abject defeat. Tears streamed from his eyes. Kevin Keller had never felt so conquered.

It was the sudden deluge that caused Kate to casually peek out the picture window. Her eyes widened and she sucked in her breath, moving closer to the glass. Several seconds passed before she realized her eyes were not deceiving her. Her husband was on his knees on their front lawn. In disbelief, she flung open the front door, startling the children and rushed to Kevin, falling to her own knees beside him. Sam, Ben and little Julia followed her.

"Kevin, darling, what...?" She said, holding his face in her hands. "What's wrong?" She didn't know where to begin.

"Are you alright? Are you hurt? Why are you home?" she pleaded with him in rapid fire, so jolted by his appearance that she didn't know what to be concerned about first.

He reached out to her, shaking now from the cold rain that had soaked him through, but was unable to look into her eyes. Kate wrapped her arms around her husband, holding on for dear life.

"Daddy, daddy, what's wrong?" Sam kept repeating, frightened more by his father's unexplained emotional breakdown than any nightmare he had ever imagined. This was his hero, his Dad, a man who was invincible in his eyes. On his knees, crying. The boy fell on to Kevin's back and enveloped his neck, holding him as tightly as his small arms would allow. Ben lunged onto the pile too, trying to squeeze his body into any small space that would allow him to touch his father. Julia cried too, because everyone was sad.

UNLEASHED

In the darkness of that night, only a few feet from the door to the house with a roof that kept the Keller's warm and dry, a family that had already begun the slow process of disintegration because of the dysfunction of one, came together to console the man they all loved. They didn't know why he was so inconsolable, nor would they ever be able to comprehend what Kevin Keller had lost before finding his way home. But for the few minutes they held each other in the torrent, they were a family, and they were together, and they were safe.

None of them could have guessed that their time together was as fleeting as the icy cold rainstorm.

Seven

He arrived at his office promptly at 7:30 a.m. the next morning as he did whenever he wasn't travelling, prompting perplexed stares from his secretary and staff who had not expected his return until Friday. Ignoring them, Kevin Keller atypically told his secretary to hold his calls and that he did not wish to be disturbed, then vanished into his private corner office, closing the door behind him. He tossed his briefcase onto the calfskin leather couch across from his desk and sat heavily into his chair. The dark screen of his computer begged to be turned on. He ignored that as well. Instead, he turned his chair toward the corner windows, those that gave him the widest vista of the heavily treed woodlands surrounding the corporate headquarters of Beckham Corporation, and looked at the landscape.

It was something he did often, usually sneeking a quick glimpse before turning back to whatever emergency was at the top of the list at that moment. He had always found the scene so incongruously peaceful to the world inside the steel and glass building from which he worked.

In his growingly repressed frame of mind, Keller imagined the world he saw outside his windows as freedom beckoning him to just lean out and breath deeply of its sweet fragrance. It was so at odds with the stench of tyrannical management and the anxiety, corruption and backstabbing that reeked inside the tomb. The lovely scent he dreamt had been calling to him for quite some time, just a trace at first, but lately in a powerfully seductive aroma. He had fought off the allure, much like a lonely, desperate sailor who resisted the siren call of sea nymphs who would lure his ship onto rocky shoals. But now, after hours spent in confession with his beloved Kate through the long night and into the early hours of the morning, he knew he could no longer resist the deep unhappiness that had run his life aground.

Still, at dawn's light, he returned to this office, the only place that had ever given him a semblance of belonging. But his reason for being here now was entirely different.

Once, he had been certain that he fit here, that he was unique among men and had earned the right to work alongside the *Eloi,* despite his reticence to completely embrace their elitist philosophies. But he was confident that he could hide among them until the day that his stature had grown to the point where he had the power to reach out to the *Morlocks,* for whom his empathy increased daily. His legacy would be to raise the stature of the workers, to free them of their drudgery in a new order of shared equality. And in the end, he would be the hero, not only in his professional life, but as a man, a husband and father, as well.

He'd been an idiot.

So idealistically naïve. So blindly arrogant, even pathetic.

Ironically, it was Kate — the very person that he long had blamed as the reason he had taken this ignorant, testosterone fueled career path — who showed him just how big a fool he had become. He had been so wrong, so off course about what she desired and expected of him.

He shook his head now in wonder as he recalled their conversation.

In the kind of intensely pressing, just short of crushing way that only a truly loving woman who deeply understood her partner could, Kate had finally opened his eyes to the fact that Kevin Keller had abandoned the man he was meant to be. He had exchanged his whole being to become someone else — all, as she reminded him of the words he used constantly to defend himself — in the hope of securing her eternal love by providing for her every want and need.

It was not only misguided, she had concluded. It was all a lie. A lie that he had planted so deeply inside his ego that he no longer saw it as such. It had become his reality, his mantra and he wore it with swollen pride. And in the process, Kevin Keller had become a man that she still loved, very much.

But didn't like.

He felt his eyes moisten at the memory of the look on her face as she said those words.

Fool, he silently screamed to himself. He unwittingly caught sight of his reflection in his blank computer screen, and for a moment wondered who the man was looking back at him.

Not surprisingly, Kate had taken control of the situation last night, helping him inside and in to a warm shower, calming the boys and tucking them into their beds with the reassurance that their father would be fit and fine in the morning after a good night's sleep.

"Your daddy just needs some rest, boys, okay? Sweet dreams, my darlings, nothing to worry." The tone of her voice was as comforting and calming as it always was, no matter what was on her mind.

As usual, Kevin had underestimated her.

Long ago, as a young man, he was attracted to Kate by her beauty: an exquisite face that deserved the cover of Vogue, her toned and athletic body, her soft brown hair, blue eyes you could swim in and lips that could take a man's breath away. But ultimately he had fallen in love with her intelligence and wit, but most of all her heart and her courage. As he talked with Kate last night, he was ashamed to silently admit that he had forgotten why he loved her so much.

After the children had fallen asleep, Kate and Kevin shared sips from a snifter of brandy as they talked in front of a warming fire in the living room, sitting side by side in the oversized leather chair they had picked out together just so they could sit like this. She next to him tucked into the crook of his arm, her legs over his, he holding her close, his hand around her delicate shoulder. Somehow, they had never seemed to find the time — or the mood — to use the chair for its intended purpose. But tonight, it was just the right place of refuge to share secrets that had been building between them for years. Secrets that had crept into their marriage as Kevin's life had spiraled more and more into the miserable existence he now suffered, his life verily controlled by people he detested.

"Why, Kevin?" she had asked him, not out of surprise, but confusion. "Why have you allowed these assholes to take away your life? Aren't we enough for you?"

He didn't respond immediately. This wasn't the boardroom where every point had a counterpoint and hours of debate usually ended not with a thought, but an edict. This was real. No one had ever held his attention more than his wife did at this moment. Because he knew she was right.

"You know that they control you, Kev. I see it. Not just in the way you jump when one of them calls, but in other ways..." she continued, adamantly refusing to stop the pursuit of the reason for her husband's unhappiness.

She had no choice. Kevin was at the center of her world and he was oblivious to it. At stake was not only the foundation of her own personal happiness, but even more importantly, so was maintaining the intimacy and contentment of the family who meant more to Kate than anyone could conceive.

It was not only the heart of a wife and mother that beat in her chest. No. Within her veins beat the pulse of a woman desperate to provide a sanctuary for her family that enveloped them in love and caring. She didn't crave material things, but increasingly her husband seemed incapable of demonstrating his commitment to them through any other means than by showering them with "stuff." With each passing day, as she had watched Kevin slip further and further away from his emotional attachment to them, she realized that he had lost the plot of the story they had begun to write the day they exchanged their vows. But she refused to give up on him. He was central to the happy ending she was determined they would find together.

It had never been the promise of material riches that had drawn her to Kevin. She had watched the wives of so many of his colleagues completely obsess over the wealth and rewards that were rained upon them. Kate had silently wondered if any of them knew at what price their lives of leisure and excess were bought. It seemed to her that their husbands — including her own — were selling their souls for unearned riches that didn't appear to bring them even a smattering of happiness. In fact, she grew numb to the countless stories Kevin shared with her of alcoholism, broken marriages and affairs and children with emotional problems that were rampant amongst the people he worked with. She found it all so appalling but kept her true feelings hidden, hoping that her husband would someday find the courage to discover the truth on his own. She deeply regretted her silence now, but still puzzled over his fate. Why? Because she found it so hard to accept that as a man, he had lost himself.

From the earliest days of their relationship, what had most impressed her about Kevin was the promise she saw in his inner self. His spirit and drive belied his upbringing; her husband wasn't even aware of how badly he had been abused by violent, alcoholic parents. Yet what he wanted for her was happiness — that was obvious from their first awkward date. From the very start of their relationship, all he talked about was his promise that he would not let history repeat itself. He was determined to break out of the cycle of his upbringing; not only the poverty, but also by providing the love, kindness and caring that he knew should define a family. He had no experience to lean on, but he understood innately what Kate dreamed of and he was determined to make it real. Until... until...she searched desperately for the words, but couldn't finish the thought. She really didn't know what had caused her husband to lose sight of everything they wanted together and to create a whole new set of priorities on his own. He had completely lost his identity.

And now, they were on a precipice from which they could easily fall. But she refused to watch her husband and their young family shatter into a million pieces. It was time to make choices.

He held her closer and kissed her hand when he finally answered.

"I've let you down, Kate, let you all down..."

"Why would you say that, Kevin?" she asked him in astonishment. "Don't you understand that this is not about things? We have everything. What we want is you. And you have gone missing."

He stared at her for a long moment, then sighed.

"No, I've let you down in that I couldn't just play the game, Kate, shut my mouth, collect the rewards and go home," he said quietly, almost in a whisper. "I thought I was a hero to have values, to argue that we should do things the right way... to treat people right..."

He shook his head again while staring into the fire and drained the last of the brandy.

"And now I've probably lost it all. Short of crawling into Laabi's office and begging on my hands and knees for another chance, I'm done. Plus I'd have to be willing to continue to be an accomplice to a felony." He buried his face in his hands. "A felon... can you imagine? Committing treason for a lousy buck?"

He lapsed back into silence. Kate held his arm tighter.

"I'm done. But I'm not going to go as quietly as they expect me to. I'll take this as far as Granville and the Board if I have to," he continued. "Otherwise I'm as guilty as that son of a bitch and all his cronies in Paris."

Kate looked into his eyes. Her worry was hard to hide.

Her concern did not escape him.

"What?" he asked. "Don't worry, Kate, one way or another, I'm out of there. Nothing is worth losing you or my family." He squeezed her hand to reassure her. "Nothing."

"That's not what worries me, Kevin."

"Then what?"

"If they're capable of all you claim, why do you think *they'll* go quietly? Are you sure you want to take these guys on?"

"It wouldn't be the first time that I've put myself out there. The difference is I already know the outcome for me. But I'll stop them from this treason."

They were silent again for a while, both pondering what was to come.

Kevin stared into the fire for long moments, squinting, his fists clenched.

"Do you remember that night, Kate? The night of the Christmas party?"

She squinted her eyes, puzzled. "No, I… what Christmas party, when?"

"December 21, 1988. Not only the night of our corporate Christmas party, but also… Pan Am 103. Lockerbie, Scotland. 259 passengers and crew, 11 more innocents on the ground, all murdered. By a Libyan terrorist named Abdelbaset al-Megrahi who placed a bomb onboard. The Libyan government helped him do it. That desert thug, Gaddafi."

Kate closed her eyes, remembering the night vividly.

"Yes, I remember. "But what does that have…"

"Libya was already on the State Department's list of embargoed nations because of its support for terrorism. It was illegal for any US company to do business with any entity, any person or organization of that country. Libya was off limits, period. It was illegal for us to do business with them in any way shape or form, whether it was a jet engine or a sheet metal screw for an air conditioner. And we knew that. Yet we sold to them through backdoor channels. Knowingly."

"But you didn't do anything, Kevin, you weren't involved…" Kate implored him.

"You don't get it, Kate. You don't know why I'm struggling with this so much."

"I understand that it's illegal but…"

"Don't you see, we owed it to them to respect that law. We owed it to all of them. This isn't just about flag waving."

"Now I don't understand…"

"There were 189 Americans on that flight, Kate. 35 of them were kids from Syracuse University coming home from a semester abroad in London… and one…" he couldn't finish, and looked longingly into his empty brandy snifter.

"One what?" Kate asked, the horror playing in Kevin's mind becoming clear to her.

"One of them was a General Industries employee," he said, his face hardening. "I knew him. A young guy who lived not far from here in West Hartford. We all went to his funeral…Granville, Laabi…all of us."

He began to cry at the memory. "We owed it to every American… hell, every person on that plane not to do business with a country that supported terrorism. But what's worse is that we continued to do it and now we're pushing like hell to grow market share in all these shithole countries that are still harboring terrorists or enabling it. Just to build market share and profits that we can bury in the earnings of another General business unit."

He sucked in a long breath and let it out slowly.

"Laabi is thumbing his nose at the US, at the State Department…even the family of the guy we lost that night.

"I can't just stand by and watch that happen, or even worse, participate in it. Blood money, Kate. That's what it is."

They both finally fell asleep sometime after midnight, emotionally exhausted and still cuddled together in the chair. Kate awoke the next morning to find her husband had already left for the office.

Keller spent the entire day in his corner office staring out the window, reflecting on the long talk with Kate and his future. He never turned on his computer, checked for e-mails or asked his secretary for his calls. For all intents, he had taken the day off, a rarity in his career.

If he had checked, he would have found a half dozen e-mails from Paul Stanton and at least as many telephone calls, all referring to the subject of having a meeting with Laabi on Friday morning, two days away. The buzzards were already circling the carrion. But Keller knew that, instinctively.

And although he might have appeared to be taking advantage of a little time not filled with meetings or trapped in an airplane, Kevin Keller was actually using his time very productively.

For when Friday morning came, he had no intentions of being the main course for the animals he worked for.

Whatever happened, he thought as he walked out to his car that afternoon, there would be a battle. And there would be blood.

He had no idea how deadly right his prediction would prove.

Or that the thought of blood would not be a metaphor.

Eight

After a half dozen telephone calls to colleagues in the finance department went unanswered the next morning, the truth finally hit Keller. It was jarring. The truth had come to him during the long sleepless night. They were freezing him out.

Angrily, he stormed out of his office for the first time in two days, walking past members of his staff as if they were invisible, and took the escalator to the third floor. He went directly to the office of the assistant controller, an old friend, and found his door closed and locked.

He knocked, once, then again, louder. Nothing.

"Jack, Jack Lunge, are you in there?" he said, louder than he intended. Hearing the disturbance, Lunge's secretary came hurrying from the coffee room. Her eyes went wide when she saw Keller.

"Marie, is he in there, for Christ's sake? I've been trying to reach someone in this department all morning," Keller hollered.

The girl was flustered by his tone. "Um, yes... I mean... he told me he wasn't to be bothered, Mr. Keller. You can't disturb him." She was terrified.

"What? What the fuck is going on..."

Suddenly the door swung open. Lunge said nothing, just waved Keller in. "Hold my calls, Marie, please," the balding, middle-aged accountant said quietly.

"I'm so sorry, I tried..." she said, her hands trembling.

He shook his head. "It's okay, not your fault, just don't let anyone else in." Lunge closed the door.

"What can I do for you, Kevin?" he asked while making his way back to his desk. "What the hell are you so worked up over?"

"Don't bullshit me, Jack. I called you and at least five other bean counters hours ago. No one is answering my calls." He was beyond angry and shouting.

"Why not, Jack?" Keller demanded.

Lunge hesitated.

"How the hell would I know, Kevin. Maybe everyone is busy?"

"Don't give me that crap. With Laabi's direct reports in Paris all week this place would normally be a playground."

"That's not fair, Kevin," Lunge replied, his head down, not wanting to make eye contact.

"Okay. Then why wouldn't you open the door for me?"

"Shit. Because... oh, Jesus. Just because. Okay? Kevin will you just drop this, just let it go?" Lunge pleaded.

Keller was startled at the response.

"Let what go? I haven't asked you anything."

"Yah... but we all know what you're looking for."

Lunge picked up his head and shrugged.

"So you know what happened in Paris?" Keller said.

"Yah."

His instincts were correct, he was being frozen out.

"And it's all true?"

"Kevin, I can't... I mean, I don't know what you're talking about. Now would let me get back to work — and take my advice?"

"If you've participated in it, or even if you know about it, you're complicit ... you know that, right, Jack?"

Lunge exploded out of his chair and yanked open the door to his office.

"Kevin, get out of my office. Don't make me..."

"Don't make you what?"

"I've been instructed to call security if I have to. I don't want to do that, Kev. For the love of God, let this go. For all of us."

Keller sighed. What was happening here was obvious. He pulled himself out of the chair and stood up, staring right into Lunge's face.

"It's not that easy, Jack."

Lunge was silent, staring at the floor.

"Wasn't Steve a friend of yours too?"

Lunge was shocked at the name.

"Oh, shit, Kevin. That was a long time ago." He suddenly looked ill, then turned away.

"Get out, Kevin, please."

Keller waited a moment, hoping his old friend would say more. Lunge would not look at him. He left.

As he walked back to his office, he couldn't help but notice the absolute silence on the floor and that the door to every office was closed. It was usually teeming with people and conversations, near bedlam on some days as numbers from around the world were continually crunched to fill the treasure chests of Beckham Corporation, and in turn, its parent General Industries.

Gazing across the empty office, Keller had an eerie vision of Phillip Granville standing at his tall, imposing bookkeeper's desk that was filled with stacks of gold coins, and like Ebenezer Scrooge frowning as he notated his counting's into large ledgers. From time to time, Granville would take stacks of the cash and place it in a vault behind him. Occasionally, he would look around to be certain he was not being observed, and stealthily slide a few of the golden coins into his own vest pocket.

"I need a drink," Keller whispered aloud, only then realizing that his owns hands were trembling.

He quickly returned to the security of his own office and placed a few more calls, some overseas. In every case, no one was available to speak to him.

He reached for his private Rolodex, thumbing through it rapidly then abruptly stopped at a business card with simple black letters and a name. It read the "Federal Bureau of Investigation" and an agent's name.

It was a man who had deposed him many years before when he was working at GIC headquarters and the company was being investigated for fraudulent billings on US government military contracts. Keller had spent days with the agent and actually came to respect him even though the agent had made it clear his objective was to find the truth, even if that meant shutting down GIC permanently and putting everyone involved in the scheme — including Kevin Keller — behind bars for a very long time. The fact is, the agent's philosophy was not all that different than his own: Do your job.

Keller held the card in his hand and reached for the telephone. He hesitated, deciding to think about the consequences of making the call. They were huge. It struck him that this earlier experience with being investigated by the government was probably the instigator of his alarmed reaction to what he had discovered in Paris. If found guilty, the penalties for everyone involved could be extremely harsh, involving huge fines and prison time.

On the other hand, a telephone call to the FBI would be a first step in a "qui tam" or "whistleblower" suit that could put a stop to the illegal activities of his company and even potentially reward him for having initiated the suit. There could be millions involved.

But he had to face facts. He had no physical proof and those who had it were holding him at bay. The screaming match in Paris with Laabi hardly would constitute hard evidence of wrongdoing. That would take months of forensic audits by the government during which time Beckham's ability to do business on a global basis would be significantly hampered.

And what about the risk to his... suddenly, a chill went up Keller's spine as his last conversation with Paul Stanton in Paris came to mind. He replayed it in his head, over and over.

"Kevin, you're not thinking this through. The consequences. For you," Stanton had said.

"And for others."

"Others? They have been taking orders. I doubt that the penalties would be severe."

Stanton looked into his eyes for long seconds. He shook his head again. "You really don't get it. You don't understand what's at risk."

He paused.

"Or perhaps I should say... who is at risk."

"What do you mean by that. Who is at risk?"

Stanton stood up and walked away.

"This conversation is over, Kevin. Think long and hard before you do or say anything."

"Is that a threat?" Keller said, jumping up from his chair."

Stanton shook his head again, but this time there was almost a look of pity in his eyes.

"There is more at stake than you are considering. Much more. Listen to me again. Think long and hard. Get on an airplane, go home and keep your mouth shut."

Keller asked himself the same question again and again. Who was Stanton referring to? Who was at risk?

But the more he thought about it, the more convinced he was of the answer. He knew — but was terrified to face the truth.

So this is how they would keep him quiet.

He put the telephone down and placed the business card back in the Rolodex. There would be no further calls until he heard what Laabi had to say in the morning.

Keller got up from his desk and walked over to the windows facing the wooded area outside the building. He stared for several long minutes before he felt it. The sense of freedom the scene once gave him was abruptly gone. Now, life on the outside of Beckham seemed to have danger written all over it. Something was telling him that being on the inside was the smart move.

That was exactly what they were telling him, wasn't it...

Coming to the realization that he might truly have forced himself into the life of a *Morlock* was one thing. But to be out there alone, without the shelter and security of Beckham...with no way to defend himself, his family...

His family. Keller grabbed his briefcase and ran from the office all the way to his BMW sedan in the parking lot.

He had to see Kate and the kids.

Now.

* * * *

She was waiting for him as he pulled in the driveway, even though he was hours early. Keller could tell by the look on her face that his wife was rattled. It took a lot to make that happen. But she beat him to the punch.

"Are you alright, Kev?" she asked as he got out of the car, her voice somewhat shaky. "You're home so early." She looked into his eyes trying to find the truth.

"Of course," he said reaching for her. He kissed her on the cheek as the kids came around from the backyard to greet him.

"Dad, you wanna shoot hoops?" Sam asked hopefully. Julia ran to him and jumped up into his arms. She planted a wet kiss on his cheek.

"I'll get the ball," Ben said, running off to the garage, excited. It wasn't often that he saw his father during daylight hours.

"Just let me talk with your Mom for a few minutes, guys, and then we'll play, okay?" Keller replied, a sudden wave of guilt dampening the joy he should have felt at the desire to be with them. He couldn't remember the last time he had played with his children or taken Kate out for a surprise dinner. He had everything a man could want, but was completely blind to his real wealth.

"Come inside, Kev, please?" Kate asked, taking his hand.

He kissed Julia and put her down then followed his wife into the kitchen. She poured him a drink while he hurried upstairs to change out of his suit. He was in the middle of changing his pants when she appeared at the doorway to their bedroom, his drink in hand. A look of alarm was all over her beautiful face.

"Kate, what the hell is it?" he asked. "What's happened?"

She handed him his drink and sat down on the bed.

"I'm not sure, maybe I'm imagining it."

"Imagining what?" he asked.

"I didn't have any clients today so I was home," Kate explained. "And there was this black van parked across the street all morning. I didn't think anything of it until I noticed that there was someone sitting behind the wheel. The truck was there for hours."

"Well… was it some workmen, one of the utility companies… one of the neighbors having something done?" he asked.

"I couldn't see any activity from inside. So, right after lunch I opened the front door and stepped outside. Immediately, the van started up and drove away, quickly. I swear the driver turned his head so I couldn't see his face."

Keller tried to hide his worry.

"Kate, you sure you're not just letting your nerves get to you? I know things have been stressful around here these last few days. Perhaps it was just coincidence that the van drove away when you came out."

"At first, I tried to convince myself of that. But then an hour later it was back. It drove slowly by the house, as if checking to see if anyone was home. I hid inside. It happened twice more over the next few hours. "

Keller knew his wife was not prone to seeing the boogeyman and when she was genuinely upset. She was upset and he was catching up to her fast.

"Did you happen to catch the guy's plate numbers?" he asked her. "I can call the police and report a suspicious vehicle in the neighborhood. The registration number would be helpful."

"Funny thing. There were no license plates, Kev, I checked each time, front and back. And I tell you, it was as if whoever was driving was trying to see if anyone was at home or if the house was empty. I had the distinct impression they were checking us out."

He took a sip from his drink, thinking. Why would anyone... suddenly he felt a chill as one reason came to mind. But he wasn't about to share it with Kate. Or his own experience at the office.

"Listen, I'm sure it's nothing, Kate but just to be sure I'm going to call the police and file a report, ask them to keep an eye on the house. Okay? You said it was a black van? Year, make, model?

"Sorry, Kevin, I don't know. It looked newish. Other than that, I don't know enough about vans to tell them apart."

"Get a look at the driver? Did you see his face or hair at all? Was he wearing a uniform of any kind?"

"I don't know, I couldn't tell. He was wearing a black baseball hat, but went by so fast that I couldn't catch any other details."

"Okay," he said to his wife, calmly. "It doesn't matter. But just to be on the safe side, I'm going to call." He went upstairs again and disappeared into his study. Kate could hear him talking. The conversation was brief and ended with Kevin laughing.

"What did they say? Why did you laugh?" she asked when he came back down, clearly still shaken.

"Oh, the cop I spoke to was giving me a hard time on all the details I wasn't able to provide. He was just ribbing me, honey. Promised they'd have a patrol car watch the neighborhood and said to tell you not to hesitate to call if you see the van again."

"That's it?"

"There really wasn't much more he could say. He found it a bit odd that you didn't see any registration tags... relax, Kate, nothing to worry about." He reached for her and she wrapped her arms around him. They were quiet for a moment, enjoying the security of a hug.

"I've got to meet with Laabi tomorrow morning," he finally said. She shook her head while still holding him. "I suspect I'll be home early again."

He stepped back from her. "Very early."

Keller searched his wife's eyes for a sign of concern or disappointment. What he saw was relief.

"Kevin, you have no idea how happy I'll be to see you get away from those people and that ugly world. You deserve a life. And we need you."

He pulled her close again and kissed her, a long, soft kiss that told her a lot. Her husband was back.

"We'll be alright, Kev, if you stay strong. I guarantee you'll find another job. You have an incredible resume. And you're a good man."

"Well, one out of two ain't bad," he said, smiling.

"What do you mean?"

"I mean being a good man is not exactly a quality much admired or in demand in my world."

Now it was her turn to look into his eyes.

"If that's the case, Kevin, then it's time you set your sights on a new world. Don't ever stop being a good man. Promise me?"

"Even if it means we have to give up..."

She interrupted him. Her eyes blazed up with irritation.

"Give up what, Kevin? Can you tell me the last time we've had a night out together, when we danced or held hands? Can you remember the last time we did something as a family? Spent time together without you having a cell phone glued to your ear? Give it up. It's not as great as you think it is."

He hung his head, chastised.

"Don't do that. I know how we got here. I love you for wanting to give us the best, but it's not what we want."

He nodded.

"It's not what I want either, Kate." He kissed her again.

"Now forget about that disgusting French wannabe you work for and go outside and enjoy your children," she said, pushing him towards the door.

"You don't have to tell me twice," he smiled.

But as he made his way outside to play with Sam and Ben, it hit him.

The question of whether he was an *Eloi* or a *Morlock* was about to be answered. What troubled him was that he really would have no voice in the decision. He was past that. The minute he had raised his voice in defiance, it was over. It was like stepping off a cliff, falling from the mountains of the privileged where the air was sweet and clean, to the bedrock far below where the sun didn't shine and it was hard to breath.

He knew that taking on Laabi and Phillip Granville would not only cost him his job, but he would be blackballed in the corporate world. The only world he knew. The thought of becoming a whistleblower… he pushed it into the back of his mind. It would still be there tomorrow when he knew more.

Sam threw a basketball at him and it him in the chest before he saw it coming.

"Ooof," he said, grinning at his laughing children. "That hurt, you turkey."

Years later, the memory of that moment and their innocent laughter would haunt him.

The pain had just begun.

Nine

"So, it would seem we have a rogue, my friend," Phillip Granville concluded for the head of GIC's Beckham unit, Badr Laabi. "Isn't it interesting that he is the only one to object? Fear of retribution has closed the mouths of a thousand plus. Wealth makes them all behave like lemmings." Stuart Brown, expressionless, shook his head in agreement.

The three senior executives were sharing an exquisite Francois Voyer cognac and ironically, an embargoed Cuban Habano cigar smuggled in from Vuelta Abajo, comfortably sitting in Granville's lavish office.

The flabby, wrinkled Laabi was hardly an example of the type of executive that typically appealed to him. He always seemed in need of a shave and could be brutally heavy-handed, the UIC chairman thought. But despite his unhealthy and disheveled appearance, Badr Laabi was a workaholic, like himself, who ruled his businesses with an iron fist and a tongue that could rip a grown man's confidence to shreds in seconds. That he was cruel, almost to the point of being sadistic made the executive that much more useful to Granville. For having Laabi around meant that he never had to get his own hands soiled when there was dirty work to be done. And there was always dirty work to be done in Phillip Granville's world.

Both men were keenly aware that they were universally despised by all within the GIC companies, yet each wore the hatred as a sort of badge of honor. It had not escaped either that those who would desire to rise within the conglomerate's ranks would understand that Phillip Granville and Badr Laabi were their role models, men to be emulated. It was a simple yet pitiless creed they shared in developing business leaders: Do as I do, the way I do it, no questions asked, and you will be rewarded.

On this Thursday night, Laabi was particularly sloppy having just arrived on a late flight returning from Paris. Within minutes after the wheels of his company Gulfstream III executive jet had touched down at the corporations private airfield, he was back in the air aboard a helicopter for the short flight across the river to the General skyscraper in the heart of downtown Hartford. The sun was setting as the pilot expertly placed the sleek helo on the building's rooftop landing pad. The telephone in the helicopter rang immediately. It was Phillip Granville's secretary telling him to come at once to the chairman's office.

Kevin Keller was very much on Phillip Granville's mind.

"Yes, Phillip, out of nowhere it seems, Keller has found religion," Laabi confessed to his superior. "Apparently he was not aware of some of our financial transactions involving businesses in 'embargoed' countries. He was highly offended and judgmental, the little son of a bitch, " he reported, emphasizing his last words with unbridled sarcasm.

Granville was silent.

"I ordered him to return to Farmington. He has been here several days, attempting to get information from the financial people. They have not responded to him, as instructed. They wouldn't dare," he grinned, enjoying the power. "We have also taken steps to watch him... and his family."

Phillip Granville raised an eyebrow at the mention of the word "family," but did not comment.

"Like most Americans, he is a patriot," Granville replied. "I don't mind a little flag waving, but I refuse to let politics get in the way of commerce. There are those in the Secretary of State's office who are aware of our, shall we say 'transgressions'... but as you know, they are quite well rewarded for their cooperation."

"It is nonsense, Monsieur Granville," Laabi responded savagely. "Les Etats-Unis has no right to prevent Beckham entities in other countries from doing business with whomever they please. The French have no quarrel with the Libyans — or the Cubans for that matter and those other countries the State Department has placed on this devil's list. I personally dare your government..."

Granville cut him off sternly.

"Badr... let us not be stupid," he chastised his subordinate. No matter how much he liked the ugly Moroccan, he could not tolerate such naiveté. Laabi's shoulders sagged.

Stuart Brown atypically interjected a thought.

"Do not underestimate the State Department, or the Justice Department," he said. "The consequences of our actions could be very severe if they were known."

"But how..."

"You are being naïve, my friend," Granville said with authority. "We do not own the State Department. We have friends, or let us say, 'facilitators' inside. But I have no doubt that they will turn on us in a second if things became uncomfortable."

"I am confused, Phillip. What is it that you would have me do? It is my intention to fire Keller tomorrow morning. I should not proceed with this plan?" the Moroccan asked.

Granville stood up, taking Laabi's glass with him to refresh their drinks. He poured liberally, allowing his subordinate a moment to think through the situation.

"Here," Granville said, handing the freshened cognac to Laabi. "This is quite spectacular, wouldn't you agree? An excellent way to end a long flight."

"Qui. But of Keller..."

Granville calmly sat back down and stretched his lanky frame, placing his custom made shoes atop a glass coffee table worth the price of a new Ferrari.

"First, be mindful that simply firing Mr. Keller will not prevent him from coming to me with whatever evidence he may think he has, if any. Nor will it stop him from going outside of our nest... perhaps to the

Justice Department. His obsession with patriotism could very well lead him to the status of 'whistleblower'."

A puzzled look came over the Beckham president's face. "What is this 'whistleblower'?"

Granville laughed out loud. The US government had no idea how foolish the rest of the world viewed it.

"A whistleblower is someone who has filed a 'qui tam' suit, alleging fraud against the government under the False Claims Act. If successful, the "whistleblower," as this person becomes known, stands to reap between 15 and 25 percent of any award or settlement the company agrees to. It can also lead to criminal prosecution of individuals. Given those two facts, I'm sure you would agree that the stakes are high for all involved."

"Vous plaisantez!" Laabi shouted, nearly spilling his cognac.

"No, I'm not kidding, Badr. And Mr. Keller is quite correct in further noting that GIC could be stripped of its international export licenses. If convicted, my friend, we could be bankrupt in a single day and have the specter of years of legal battles to contend with to defend ourselves from going to prison."

Badr Laabi's complexion suddenly turned a shade similar to the smoke given off by the Habano he had been enjoying.

"Mon dieu," the Moroccan whispered, slumping into his chair.

"My God is right. Keller is not to be taken lightly, Badr."

"Qui. So I see."

The three men were silent for quite awhile, each lost in thought. Laabi was first to break the silence.

"So, the plan… it is not enough?"

"Perhaps as a first step," Granville replied without hesitation.

"A first step…? Pardon, Monsieur Granville. I do not understand," Laabi said, puzzled by the cryptic response.

Granville sighed. He hated to be specific.

"A problem of this nature is not unlike a cancer that will grow — unless it is cut out." He paused. "Eliminated, down to the final cell of its existence."

Laabi leaned closer to his supervisor but said nothing. He stared intensely into Phillip Granville's eyes for several long minutes, then brought the crystal tulip glass to his lips and drained it. The alcohol did little to put color back in his cheeks. He placed the glass on the coffee table and stood.

"I must still visit my office before this day is done, Phillip. Good evening."

"Good night, Badr. My best wishes to your lovely wife and children." Stuart Brown nodded. They watched as Laabi turned and walked away.

Suddenly, Granville called after him.

"You know, it is true that many men see their family as their higher power and their only real reason for living."

Badr continued to walk as Granville spoke. At the door he stopped and looked back at Granville and Brown, nodding his head.

"Qui. We shall see, my collègues.

"We shall see."

Ten

The morning sun was breaking through the sheer drapes on the bedroom windows when Kevin Keller put on his suit jacket and leaned down to kiss his sleeping wife goodbye. He was leaving to face Laabi.

But Kate had only been pretending to sleep while she watched him get dressed. They had spent the night making quiet, gentle love and cuddling, both aware that their lives were about to change forever. Holding each other gave them a kind of security against the uncertainties they were determined to deal with together. For some reason, she felt much more confident last night. Now, she was afraid, but could not say why.

"I'll always love you, Kev, you know that, right?" she said when he kissed her, stroking his freshly shaven face. "No matter what happens, we have each other, the kids…"

"Shh," Kevin Keller responded, putting a finger to her lips.

"A slight setback, that's all, babe," he said, "Today, we start fresh. Just gotta go state my case to these guys and let them know this isn't going to happen as easily as they think."

Kate flinched at the words. She understood the conflict her husband was fighting inside, but a part of her wished he would just let it go. Type up a letter of resignation, pack a box and walk out the door. But that wasn't Kevin. Instead of telling him to turn his back on them, she reached for his hand and squeezed it, then pushed herself up from the bed and kissed him gently on the lips.

He grabbed his briefcase and stood at the door for a moment taking in her beauty. He wondered how in the world he had ever let anything else become more important than her happiness.

Keller smiled, reassuringly.

"Call you after I face the firing squad," he promised with false bravado, then left.

She heard him as he walked down the hall stopping to peek into each of the children's rooms. She imagined him blowing kisses at them as he always did.

Kate listened as he started his car in the garage and pulled out, then suddenly was overcome by a wave of panic. She jumped out of bed and ran to the window waving at him frantically as he drove away. She watched until his BMW disappeared from sight. Inexplicably, tears came to her eyes and she sagged to the floor on her knees. A chill rose up her spine and she shivered uncontrollably.

"No, no, no..." she sobbed, fighting off the sudden terror that she would never see her husband again.

Less than 30 minutes later, Keller pulled into the parking lot of Beckham headquarters in Farmington. He swung his car into a spot reserved for him and looked around. He was the first one to arrive. In an hour, the parking lot would be full. And with Laabi and his senior executives back in town, the energy and anxiety levels inside the building would shoot up like a thermometer under a blowtorch.

He slowly walked the 20 yards to the front door, realizing that it might be the last time he ever entered the building. He nodded to the two security guards at the front desk, took the escalator to his office and threw his briefcase on the couch. Then he sat at his desk and waited for the phone to ring. From his seat, he was able to see every one of the executive team arrive and walk into the building. It was only 15 minutes before Laabi pulled in.

Surprisingly, it was Paul Stanton who first emerged from the car, stepping out of the passenger seat of Laabi's newest toy, a jet black Mercedes S600. It was worth the equivalent of the salaries of a half dozen factory employees, a fact that the Beckham CEO delighted in pointing out whenever the opportunity arose. Stanton looked over at Keller's car and said something as Laabi emerged from behind the wheel. Then they both laughed.

As prepared for this confrontation as he was, the sight of Laabi and Stanton together still unnerved him.

"We'll see who has the last laugh," Keller said out loud. He glanced at his watch to see how long it would be before the phone rang summoning him to Laabi's office. He guessed no more than 10 minutes, considering that the CEO had obviously already met with Stanton to get their plan in synch. Less than eight minutes had passed when it rang.

Keller looked at the phone for a moment, the thought coming to him that he should just let it ring and have Laabi come searching for him. But that would only turn the ugly man into a raging bull.

"Keller," he said into the phone without hesitation and as indifferently as possible.

"It is Badr. Come to my office at once," Laabi said curtly and hung up. Keller stared at the handset for a moment, marveling at how crude his boss was. He had a thought to call him back and say, "Fuck you," but fought off the urge to sink to his level.

It's show time, Keller thought. Out of habit, he grabbed a legal pad off his desk and checked to make sure he had a pen in his suit jacket. He stopped momentarily to stare out of the corner windows of his office at the heavily treed woodlands he found so peaceful. Just for a second, he thought he picked up that faint scent again, the sweet fragrance that he equated to freedom.

"Get a hold of yourself, Keller," he whispered aloud, somewhat alarmed at the thought. Now was not the time to brood. He sucked in a deep breath and left the safety of his office.

He took the escalator upstairs to Laabi's suite of offices and entered without knocking. The CEO's secretary, Lorraine, a tall, buxom blond, prone to wearing absurdly inappropriate short skirts and five-inch heels was just coming out of his office. Every time Keller saw her he could not get over the thought that if he passed her on the street he would mistake her for a hooker. The fact that she had the IQ of an overripe watermelon didn't help. She was a constant problem in communicating with her boss, a fact that "endeared" her to members of the senior staff who were constantly scrambling to clean up her scheduling mistakes and forgotten messages. But Laabi loved her. That much was obvious from the designer labels that draped her eye-popping figure. The man paid well for blind loyalty, especially if it was nice to look at.

The secretary nervously perked up as Keller walked toward her, and she anxiously smoothed out imagined wrinkles in her skirt to avoid making eye contact with him. No doubt Laabi had already said something to her about the reason for their meeting.

"Good morning, Kevin," she sang at him. He even found her voice annoying.

"Mr. Laabi will see you immediately."

"I'm sure he will, Lorraine. Thank you."

She tilted her head to one side and gave him an awkward smile as he passed by her, then quickly pulled the door to Laabi's office shut. The sound of the latch catching startled Keller. He suddenly felt like a moth helplessly trapped in a spider's web.

His hands trembled but he took the initiative.

"Good morning, Badr, welcome back," Keller said politely.

The Beckham CEO, bent over his reading desk, ignored him, feigning interest in a spread out copy of the morning's Wall Street Journal. A minute passed, then two. Finally, he spoke.

"I see we have learned some manners in the last week, yes Kevin?"

Keller bristled.

"I don't know what you mean, Badr. You called me here, I came. Is there something on your mind, or have you forgotten?" He had no intention of being bullied any longer when the outcome was already apparent.

Laabi's head snapped back at the impertinence of his subordinate.

"Still the wise guy, I see. Alright, have it your way." He walked to his desk, pressed a button on his telephone and instructed Lorraine to have Paul Stanton join them.

The door opened immediately and Stanton entered the room.

Keller couldn't help but laugh. "Jesus, Paul, have some class, will ya? You guys could have worked on your timing a bit."

Laabi turned red.

"Take care of this, Paul, I have tired of Mr. Keller's disrespect."

Keller lost it.

"Disrespect? How in God's name have I shown you disrespect, Badr? By challenging a decision you made? A decision to break the law? Certainly, you jest..."

A look came over Laabi's face that might have frightened someone not prepared for it. But Keller had seen it before and had more than enough time to anticipate it. If he was about to officially join the ranks of the *Morlocks*, he was prepared to take these two pathetic *Eloi*'s with him.

Stanton tried to take control of the situation.

"Kevin, you've been insubordinate. Let's not make this any worse than it has…"

"Insubordinate? You sycophant motherfucker," Keller shouted at the hapless human resources executive. "You just shut your god damned mouth, you fucking two-faced whore."

"I will not be spoken…"

"The hell you won't, Stanton. When I'm done with you, the only words you're going to remember are a judge telling you how many years you're going to be someone's boy toy in a federal prison."

"Why you son of a bitch…" Laabi screamed and launched himself at Keller, intent upon throttling him. The younger man simply stepped aside and the overweight Moroccan lost his balance and fell heavily to the floor. He jumped up, his face crimson with anger. A vein in his neck was bulging.

"You're through, Keller, do you understand me, you are through!" Laabi screamed shaking a finger at Keller.

"Tell me something I don't already know, asshole." He turned to Stanton. "Don't bother cutting me any kind of severance, Paul. I don't want your blood money. Besides, all I need is enough gas in my car to get me to the FBI's office in Hartford. I'm sure they'll be quite happy to buy me lunch when I tell them my story."

Laabi's shrill laugh turned Keller's attention back to him.

"So that's your game, is it my patriotic American friend?" he paused, breathing hard but calming himself. He needed to be smart.

"You are a fool, Keller."

"I hardly think I am the fool, Laabi. You've left yourself — and virtually the entire management team of this company — wide open to criminal prosecution.

"But you know what's worse? You betrayed that young man who died at the hands of the Libyans over Lockerbie. He was one of us. I'm going to make sure his story is told, Laabi. You're going down, asshole, and I'm taking you there."

A wicked grin came to the CEO's face. Stanton stood beside him, his arms folded. He shook his head in resignation.

"Jesus, Kevin... I warned you."

"Warned me of what, Stanton?"

"You're playing with fire," he said, knowing what was going to happen next.

Laabi was still grinning.

"Save your breath, Paul. He has already lit the match."

"What are talking about, you arrogant bag of shit?"

The CEO sniggered. Not unexpectedly, it was an ugly, ridiculing well-practiced laugh that was intended to humiliate an underling.

"Did your wife not receive the message I left for her yesterday, Kevin?" Laabi said quietly, his emotions now in check. "Or is she the type that enjoys being watched? I would have thought she would be nervous for the children…"

Keller stared at the grinning European, not sure what he was saying. Then it hit him.

"The black van..."

"Ah, so she did share with you her concerns. I am delighted."

Keller crossed the room in three steps and smashed his cocked right fist into Laabi's pudgy face before the man could move. The Moroccan fell against his desk, blood pouring from his nose. Stanton grabbed him before he could throw another punch.

Laabi lifted himself off the desk, reaching for a handkerchief to put to his nose.

"You have no idea what you have begun, Keller," he growled. "You are a dead man..."

Keller laughed in his face.

"Come for me, you prick. And tell Granville to come with you. I'll be waiting."

"And your family?" Laabi sneered.

Keller stopped as he continued.

"Will they be waiting? Will they know why...?"

"What? What about my family? Are you threatening my family?" he screamed, taking stepping towards Laabi. "Are you, you son of a bitch?"

Stanton grabbed Keller by the shoulder and turned to his boss.

"Shut up, Badr. Think of what you're saying man..."

"He knows exactly what I'm saying," Badr Laabi spit back as he looked directly into Keller's face, blood still trickling from his nose.

For a split second, Kevin Keller thought he was looking into the eyes of the devil, and for the first time truly understood that the man was capable of anything.

He dropped the legal pad he was still unconsciously clutching in his left hand, shook himself loose from Stanton's grasp and slowly backpedaled away from the two men. Then he turned and ran to the door before either of them could stop him. He kept running, not even bothering to stop by his office and retrieve his car keys and briefcase. He took the escalator two steps at a time and raced by the security desk, ignoring the two guards who called to him to stop.

He sprinted across the parking lot to his car and reached under the driver's side front fender where he kept a spare ignition key in a magnetic holder and opened the door, his hands shaking so badly he had trouble fitting the key into the lock. Jumping behind the steering wheel, he jammed the transmission into gear and roared out of the parking lot, neglecting his seatbelt and blowing through a red light at the intersection of Route 6 without so much as a glance for oncoming traffic. He had the powerful BMW six-cylinder moving at over 90 miles per hour before he even dared look into his rear view mirror. There was no one chasing him. Yet.

It didn't matter. He wouldn't have stopped even for the police. He had to get home to Kate and the kids before… He forced himself not to complete the thought.

Several miles up the road he downshifted hard into second gear, the sports sedan whining in protest of the abuse. He swung the nose of the BMW on to New Britain Avenue, fishtailing across both lanes as he floored the car again. Swerving left then right he picked his way through slower traffic, fighting to keep control of the speeding car. His mind was racing as he replayed Laabi's words: "Will they be waiting, Kevin? Will they know why?"

Panicked, he thought momentarily about calling Kate from his car phone, then resisted the urge. It would only frighten her. He drove faster. The only answer was to get to them. "Calm down!" he screamed to himself.

He hung a hard right on to Route 177 and then came upon Route 4 with the gas pedal pegged to the floorboard. The busy road was going to be filled with traffic, he knew, but it was the most direct route to his home in Canton, just ahead. He simultaneously downshifted and yanked the steering wheel hard to the left, causing the BMW to slide through the intersection, its brakes locked up and tires screeching as they desperately worked to grab a hold of the slick blacktop. Cars on both sides of the road scattered, swerving to avoid the mad man who had suddenly appeared out of nowhere. A black and white Farmington police car parked at a convenience store across the street from the intersection saw Keller's erratic driving and gave chase.

"Just what I fucking, need," Keller screamed as his rear view mirror suddenly filled with flashing lights, but put his foot down harder on the gas pedal. The BMW howled. He wasn't about to stop for anyone until he pulled into his driveway.

The BMW nudged up over 110 miles per hour as Keller shifted through the gears into fourth and swung in and out of traffic. He was less than five minutes from home when it happened.

Just as he was about to cross the bridge on Collinsville Road over the Farmington River, a driver in front of him panicked when he glanced in his rear view mirror and saw the speeding car coming at him with a police car close behind. The cruiser's red and blue flashing lights and screaming siren terrified the innocent driver. Insanely, the panicked driver slammed on his brakes and pulled his car abruptly into the right lane, directly into the BMW's path. Keller couldn't stop in time.

Instead, he instinctively mashed the gear lever into second and swung the steering wheel to the left trying to swerve around the slowing car ahead of him. But his path was blocked by a flatbed truck carrying several tons of road construction equipment. The lightweight German car bounced off the truck, which pushed the nose of Keller's car hard to the right, nearly perpendicular to the traffic behind him. Before he could stab at his brakes, he was into the retaining wall of the concrete bridge at over 90 miles per hour. The impact was so intense that for miles in each direction, people thought there had been some kind of explosion nearby. 911 emergency calls would flood the police dispatcher in Canton and several nearby towns for the next 15 minutes.

The collision instantly blew the front drivers side air bag, which absorbed the forward momentum of Keller's body caused by the crushing head on crash. But the enormous speed and energy carried into the impact caused the car's still spinning right front tire to grab the lip of the concrete wall and catapult the powerful sports sedan high into the air off the bridge, corkscrewing out over the river. Keller could do nothing as the car quickly lost upward impetus and nosed over towards the river, 50 feet below.

His body slammed forward again into the now deflated steering wheel air bag when the car hit the rock strewn riverbed only 15 feet or so off the surface of the shallow, but turbulent river. Keller was jarred into reality as his head smashed into the roof of the car and he felt ribs on his right side crack. Dazed from the blow to the head and unable to breath from the injuries to his chest and rib cage, he began to lose consciousness. But somehow, as the world began to turn black around him, he heard Laabi's voice again.

"Will they know why, Kevin?"

His head cleared for a few seconds as he suddenly felt the shock of icy water climbing up his pants legs. The car was quickly filling with water. He thought again of Kate and the children. He had to get out. Ignoring the fierce pain of his crushed side and blood trickling into his eyes from a deep gash in his head, he forced himself to kick open the driver's side door and push out. The heavy current running through the river yanked him free of the car and he began fighting toward the surface. But the powerful undertow prevented him from swimming upwards and instead dragged him across the murky river bottom. Ten feet from the ruined car he blacked out.

As the rushing waters dragged his body down stream, the last image to cross Kevin Keller's eyes was the sneering face of Badr Laabi, again asking him the question that would haunt him into eternity.

"Will they know why, Kevin?"

Eleven

December 1997

The bouncing headlights of the battered pickup truck flickered as the driver picked his way cautiously over the deeply potholed dirt and gravel road. The jumping lights cast eerie shadows over the scrub brush and withered pines lining the single lane road that was little more than a path to a derelict cottage set reclusively on the Old Saybrook shoreline at the northern edge of Long Island Sound.

The truant property owner had long ago lost incentive to make the parcel more visible or attractive from the main road, realizing that his transient, often odd tenants were usually a lot more interested in isolation than landscaping. Set back about 100 yards from Saltus Drive off Main Street, the cottage more resembled a tumbledown cabin than a vacation rental.

But 500 feet of beachfront, directly overlooking North Cove and adjacent to the solitude of Riverside Cemetery made the shack attractive to romantics in search of rustic, seaside ambience, or more typically, people with a reason to disappear for a while. The driver had signed a one-year lease, under an alias, for just that reason.

The truck pulled slowly up to the front door and ground to a stop, its brakes squealing and springs creaking. The man behind the wheel killed the motor, set the brake and sat for a few minutes, finishing his cigarette and scanning the perimeter for any unusual signs. He unscrewed the cap of a pint of Popov, hidden in a brown paper bag under his seat, and took a long, thirsty pull, wincing as it hit his stomach. Sated for the moment, he pushed the bottle into the pocket of his faded, black jeans.

It had been an exhilarating night, bringing the satisfaction that comes with settling a score. His adrenalin was still surging as he spent a moment recalling the rush he had felt watching his targets fall, fractions of a second apart, in a shocking transition of power. But now he was nearing exhaustion and he sighed with the recognition of the tasks that had to be completed before daybreak. He was fairly drunk, having spent the last four hours nursing tall glasses of vodka over crushed ice, sitting alone, avoiding conversation, drawing only enough attention to be seen and vaguely remembered.

It was a fairly busy night at the ramshackle *Silo Bar & Grille* off Route 6, only a few minutes away from where he'd pulled off his successful ambush. There was just enough activity to help him blend in but not be invisible. It was exactly what he had hoped for. The barstool on which he positioned himself was within eyesight of a large, antique neon "Pabst Blue Ribbon" clock that hung high on a wall above the entrance to the men's room. It gave him precisely the vantage point he wanted.

He smiled, recalling his discovery one recent night after settling in at the bar where he had once been a regular. But that was a long time ago. With his new look and a Red Sox cap pulled low over his eyes, there was no one in the place who would have remembered him. But that clock. That clock had been a find that had enabled him to literally turn back time. It was key to his escape strategy.

While relieving himself one night at the dirty, leaking urinal, he had looked up to see two thin wires above his head, exiting the wall and running directly into the light switch at the entrance to the dimly lit room. He quickly surmised that someone had tapped into the electrical box behind the switch and spliced off the power line to supply electrical juice to the Pabst clock on the other side of the wall. The connection was dangerously stupid, enough to shut the place down if an inspector saw it, but an idea had suddenly come to mind when he saw the jury-rigged wiring. It was the last piece of the puzzle he had been slowly putting together for months.

Last night, a half-hour before closing time, he had slipped into the rest room, locked the door and clipped one of the exposed wires, effectively killing power to the clock. He went back to his stool at the bar, occasionally checking the clock to see if he was right. It had stopped. About 20 minutes later, he pushed back from his tall vodka and visited the men's room again. Inside, he pulled out his pocket knife and in all of about four minutes, stripped the two ends of the wire he had cut, and twisted them together to reconnect the power. He re-emerged from the bathroom, sat back down and allowed himself a quick glance over his shoulder at the clock, which now read 20 minutes slow. No one had noticed, not even the bartender who knew him as "Mike," a recent regular.

Sure enough, when he walked into the bar tonight, after carefully hiding his rental car in the dark shadows of the small parking lot in the back, the clock was still 20 minutes off. No one had given it a second look. He sat down at his favorite stool in silence and the bartender set him up with his usual tall vodka over crushed ice without being asked. The stranger thanked him with a mumble and put a $20 bill on the counter, a sign he would be around for the evening. When the bartender came back to wipe the counter, he made a point of asking him for the time. Without looking up he nodded at the Pabst antique.

"Never wear a watch, Mike. Just gets covered in crap," he said. He looked up at the old wall clock. "That old thing is usually on the money," he added.

Casually pushing the baseball cap higher on his forehead to give the bartender a better look at his face, the stranger smiled. "Guess they don't make 'em like that anymore," he replied.

He took a long sip from his drink, satisfied that according to the clock and the bartender who had served him, he was sipping his first vodka of the night exactly nine minutes before the killings had occurred just a few miles away.

There was a college basketball game playing on the television hanging over the bar that he pretended to watch. A half-hour passed and things were still quiet. Then, a local news anchor appeared on the screen and described a "massacre" at the company headquarters of Beckham Corporation in the well-to-do community of Farmington. Two were known dead, the newsman reported and there were others possibly wounded. Video images showed numerous police cars and ambulances at the scene and a crowd of office workers gathered outside despite the cold.

"Names of the victims have not yet been released," the newsman said, "but a source who declined to be identified has confirmed that they were executives of the company. We'll provide details as they become available." A murmur spread though the bar. The stranger sat stone-faced as the game came back on and went back to his drink.

Just sit still, he told himself. Stick with the plan.

About 45 minutes later, two men entered the bar and every head in the place turned to size them up, then turned away. They were obviously plainclothes detectives just stopping by for a quick scan, looking for anyone who might be the least bit suspicious. The stranger eyeballed them just as quickly and went back to his business. He was street smart enough to know that if he hadn't checked them out like everyone else in the bar, it might have raised their antennae. He had no intention of giving them any reason to find him interesting.

The two detectives sat down at the bar several stools away and called the bartender over. He took his time sauntering over, then shrugged his shoulders and shook his head a few times to questions that were out of earshot. The cops pointed to a few people in the bar, including the stranger. Mike looked over at the clock and talked for a minute or two, then nodded in the stranger's direction. He pointed at the clock again and shook his head. Getting nothing out of him, the two cops turned and studied everyone in the room for a few minutes, then got up and left. The news came back on the television to announce that the two victims of the Beckham "massacre" had now been identified as Badr Laabi, 50, president of the General Industries division and Paul Stanton, a vice president, age as yet unknown. Someone laughed loudly in the back of the room, oblivious to the news. No one else seemed to care except the bartender who was just looking for an excuse to talk to someone.

"That's something, hey Mike?" he asked the stranger without taking his eyes off the television.

"Yah. Sounds like they were big shots," he replied.

"Not anymore. Don't think I've ever seen them in here before," the bartender replied. "Guess we don't rate enough Michelin stars," he laughed.

"What'd the cops want," he asked Mike. "Saw 'em looking in my direction."

"Wanted to know when you came in tonight," he laughed. "I told him I knew exactly when because you and I had been talking about that old clock. Ten minutes to seven, you came in, I told them. They were looking for somebody that came in sometime after seven."

The stranger smiled and pushed his glass forward on the counter. "One more for the road, bud," he said.

A half hour later he left, careful to not be seen getting into the 1976 Ford F150 pickup truck that he had parked in the lot earlier in the day. He had already wiped down the rental car in the back lot for fingerprints and with his closely cropped hair there wasn't much chance of a stray lock giving an investigator a DNA sample. The truck started right up and he pulled slowly on to Route 6, conscious that he'd had more than enough to drink to warrant a traffic stop. He wound his way toward Farmington center, got on the highway to take him to Route 72 into Middletown and then onto Route 9 that would bring him to Saybrook. In 45 minutes, he'd be snug as a bug in his hideaway, far away from all the excitement in Farmington, he'd thought.

Now, sitting in the truck outside the rented cottage, he took another pull from the bottle of Popov and looked around carefully before getting out. Satisfied that all was as it should be and that he was alone, he stepped out and walked to the back door. The screen door swung open with an irritating screech that he had learned to ignore. He stepped inside, flipping on the switch to the single light in the kitchen and he entered the bathroom to splash some water on his face.

Catching a glimpse of himself in the mirror he was startled by his reflection. Once, some considered him handsome, and women teased him for having soft brown "bedroom" eyes. Now, he badly needed a shave, the shadow on his face doing little to hide his sunken eyes and the deep black circles under them. He had always been trim, keeping himself in good shape. But now he was thin, gaunt and gray and looked years older than he was. Pain and solitude had aged him.

He had a fleeting thought that what he looked like didn't matter anymore. The die was cast, his future decided months ago when he put his plan into motion. What he'd done on this night was just the first nail in his coffin. But there were others to be hammered in.

Wasting no more time reflecting on what was to be, he grabbed a flashlight and a set of keys from the pantry, relocked the door and went to the back of the pickup. Reaching into the truck bed of the old Ford, he lifted out a long, black zippered bag and carried it around to the back of the house, using the flashlight to find the narrow path, and continued on to the shoreline to a small dock jutting into the cove.

Tied up at the weathered single pier was an early 70's Bayliner cuddy cabin that had seen better days. He had picked it up at auction for only $1,200, intending to use it no more than a few times on short runs that wouldn't bring him very far from shore. Nonetheless, always comfortable around engines, he did a quick top end rebuild of the 165 horsepower Chevy stern drive, tuned it, polished the prop and replaced the gimbal bearing just to be on the safe side. The stranger had cut power to the running lights; he had no intention of being seen from shore or another boat, despite the odds against it. The only thing he added to the boat was a depth finder that he had paid cash for at a yard sale in Niantic several months before. It scanned the ocean bottom depth from zero to 2,000 feet. He wouldn't need more than a fraction of its capability.

He stepped into the boat and hoisted the heavy canvas bag into the cabin. With a turn of the key, the motor turned over and he let it idle and warm up for a few minutes. Casting off the single rope line, he stopped to cover the canvas bag with a tarp, then returned to the wheel and slipped the transmission into reverse, backing the boat slowly away from the dock. Despite his life-long love of the ocean and the seashore, he had very little experience with boats, so he moved cautiously, taking his time, thinking through every step. He turned the boat into the cove and headed out into the Sound, at a leisurely pace, careful to minimize the phosphorescent trail of his wake. He did not want to be seen.

He checked his watch, a cheap Timex he'd bought a few months back in a Walmart. It read 1 a.m. Perfect, he thought, right on schedule. He aimed the boat due north, further into the Sound and closer to the shipping lanes he had studied on the chart maps he had copied at the Essex Public Library. About 30 minutes later, he checked his watch again, and fired up the depth meter. The sounding indicated 20 fathoms, about 120 feet of water beneath the hull. He stopped the boat, letting it idle, and uncovered the black bag.

Unzipping it, he removed the components of the black rifle he had used so successfully a few hours earlier. Unceremoniously, he leaned over the bow railing and dropped the rifle stock over the side, watching as it quickly disappeared from sight, only the momentary phosphorus splash giving away its trip the bottom. Then he turned the boat north again, traveling at full throttle for about ten minutes, and after checking the depth finder reading once again repeated the process, dropping the night vision scope over the side. Twice more he replicated his actions, first in a southerly direction and then due west tossing the rest of the rifle parts overboard. When he was done, the components of the lethal weapon were scattered over the bottom of Long Island Sound in its deepest waters, over an area covering more than 10 square miles. He kept no records of the various positions. The rifle was gone, forever.

His work done, the lone figure drained the rest of the bottle in his pocket, then set course for his dock. Upon reaching shore, he staggered up the path to his cabin, barely able to fall into the pile of dirty, gray sheets that passed for his bed. His head was spinning, both from the vodka and exhaustion. He pulled himself up and sat on the edge of the bed, his head in his hands.

Then overcome with the nights work and a lifetime of regret, he began to weep and rage.

He wept for his sins and for those who had sinned against him. He wept for his lost childhood and his failure as a husband and father, hating himself. He raged, knowing that the premeditated acts of horrific violence he had committed tonight had satisfied only a sliver of his immense pain. His voice was guttural as he admitted to his failed life, and to the bright promise he had given away.

Finally, he cried for his wife and children, in great heaving sobs, his heart broken again, still shattered from the loss he could never overcome. He had loved them with his entire being, had lived for them, and had dreamt endlessly of all that he would give them. In the end, they were gone, lost to him forever. His pain was immeasurable, like an open wound crudely stitched directly to his soul.

He staggered up from the bed, went into the kitchen and took a quart bottle of vodka from a cabinet. With the small of his back against a plywood counter for support, he uncapped the bottle and drank from it deeply, draining nearly a quarter of its contents. Then he stumbled back to the bed and fell into it, the vodka coursing through his veins directly to his brain.

In the last moment of his consciousness, he wondered, again, why all was as it was.

Twelve

"Do we have anything here?" the detective asked his partner as he took in the room full of forensics investigators poring over two headless corpses and every square inch of the crime scene at Beckham headquarters in Farmington. The plainclothes cop wearing a rumpled, lightweight raincoat despite the cold had long ago gotten used to the blood and gore that came with the job, but this was a frigging execution if he ever saw one.

Two suits with their heads literally blown off. A trophy secretary in a near catatonic state with blood staining her oddly expensive shoes. Four whistle sharp bullet holes that had pierced the room's shatterproof window glass in a circumference less than that of a nine-inch dinner plate. He couldn't help but admire the marksmanship.

Two men were busily digging spent slugs out of a wall in the next room. The four bullets had pierced the glass, the targets and the wall behind them before embedding themselves in another wall 20 feet away. There'd be no know way to identify the caliber until the results of lab testing came through, but the detective only had to look at the remains of the two mutilated skulls to know they'd been hit with high velocity, hollow point rounds. The kind used to make sure a target didn't survive one hit, let alone two.

About the only thing evident was whoever had pulled this off was a pro or a very well trained amateur. It was going to take them hours still just to find the shooters nest. The angle at which the rounds had hit their targets would give them some clue, and another whole team of uniforms was scouring the wooded area in front of the Beckham building for evidence. He bet they wouldn't find anything more than some matted weeds, if even that. The fire department had sent its rescue truck to the scene to provide floodlights for the searchers.

Detective Dennis Leery shrugged his shoulders at his boss and partner of three years, Detective Sergeant Michael DeStephano. The two had proven to be a good team, known by the rank and file in the Farmington Police Department as "MOP" — actually a term of respect for the rate at which the 'Mick" Leery and the "Wop" DeStephano successfully closed cases. Of course, no one in the department would dare use the acronym to their faces. But the partners were well aware of it and did nothing to squelch its use behind their backs. It wasn't a bad thing to be recognized as good at something as ugly as solving the worst of the department's cases. And the respect was useful — not only in getting things done inside but in being recognized on the street as a couple of gold shields not to be messed with.

Leery was comfortable working with his partner. DeStephano was as good as they got and you never had to worry about him having your back. But he couldn't say he knew much about him personally. Any time he had probed about a wife or kids his boss brushed it off quickly and changed the subject. What he did know was that he wasn't married, in fact seemed to spend every spare moment of his free time helping out his widowed sister-in-law with her three kids. Leery had a feeling that most of his boss' paycheck went in that direction as well. But he had never opened up about the situation. It was okay. Cops were funny like that. You either knew everything about them or very little. Some guys liked to separate the badge from the home fire.

"I dunno, Sarge," Leery said, at five foot, ten inches, a full six inches shorter than his senior partner. He watched the forensics team at work, occasionally yelling to someone to bag an item. "We're not going to find anything in here or outside either, partner. This was well thought out. Somebody took their time and knew how this place works."

"Yah," DeStephano responded. "Guy who worked here once told me he wasn't the happiest of campers while employed by Beckham. Mentioned to me that it was a real 'Goose-Steppers' parade.'"

"Huh?" Leery looked up, puzzled.

"It's how they used to describe the way German troops marched in parades during the war. The press ridiculed it as a symbol of blind obedience. Get in line and do what you're told, no questions asked. And we know how happy that story turned out to be."

"Who is he? Why don't we just talk to him?" Leery asked.

DeStephano hesitated for a moment and looked out at the uniforms scouring the wooded area with handheld flashlights. The awkwardly moving, darting and crossing lights cast eerie shadows in the woods. The property was dense with foliage, he thought. It was an easy hiding place, especially for someone who knew how to hide.

"He's dead." He didn't say anything more. Leery didn't press it.

"Do we have a time?" DeStephano asked.

"Just an approximate," Leery answered, moving on. "We only have video of the anteroom, where the secretary's desk was located. Nothing in here," he said pointing to the inside office where the slayings had occurred. "This is the president's office. The tape shows no activity for at least an hour before the two deceased walked into this office at 7:02 p.m., on the button. The secretary goes in one minute later. Then nothing until a guy comes in to the outer waiting room about 20 minutes later. Told me he had an appointment at 7:30 with the head knocker."

"Who was?"

"The shorter, fat guy in the pinstripe suit was the president of this operation, guy by the name of Badr Laabi. We think the taller one is Paul Stanton, he was VP of Human Resources. He's got no ID on him but his secretary came running in here a while ago, screaming his name."

"Doesn't seem like El Presidente was a real popular guy based on the number of people stopping buy to say hello," DeStephano observed. "Human resources? Goes without saying he didn't have many friends."

"Dunno," Leery responded. "We haven't had a chance to interview anyone yet at any level. Suppose we ought to start with the people who reported to Laabi and Stanton."

"Where's the guy who had the appointment?"

Leery motioned to a heavy-set man in a dark grey suit wearing horn rim glasses. He was balding, looked to be about 40 or so.

"Guy's pretty shook up. He sat out here for at least five minutes before checking to see if anyone was in the office. He called security when he saw all the blood."

"He didn't go in and check on the bodies?"

"Apparently not. Would have had blood all over his shoes. There's no tracks. He's still shaking like a leaf."

"Yah. Well, maybe he'll get a bigger bonus."

Leery smiled at his boss, quizzically. It wasn't like him to be so sarcastic. Odd. He let it slide.

"Yah," he said, forcing a laugh. "I'll start with him. I'll do it myself. What do you think?" he added, nodding at the man sitting on a small couch, wringing his hands. "Engineer?"

Now it was DeStephano's turn to laugh. "No way. Accountant. Look at the glasses."

"I think you be right, boss. Sure does look anxious, huh?"

"Probably just shock. Like him or not, it must have given the poor bastard quite a start to see these two characters minus their heads."

"Yah, I suppose." He reached for a notebook in his jacket pocket and turned to walk toward the waiting man, then suddenly stopped.

"Say, who was that guy you knew who used to work here? Maybe I can track down some of his old buddies. When did he die?"

The look on DeStephano's face changed to deadly serious. He thought for moment before responding.

"A long fucking time ago, Dennis."

Leery waited for more. That's all there was.

"Let's get going. We got a lot of people to talk to," the Sergeant said, changing the subject. "Make sure somebody speaks to the security guards at the reception desk. I wanna know who came and went from this building today. And get me the name of the number two guy from human resources and whoever is in charge of payroll. I'll talk to them myself.

"Let's see if anyone's been given the old heave-ho around here lately, maybe got an axe to grind."

He stopped for a moment and rubbed his chin, thinking. "Anyone call this Laabi's boss to let him know?"

"That would be that guy... uh... what's his name..."

"Phillip Granville at "The General", General Industries Corporation. Headquarters is downtown, in Hartford."

"Oh, yah, Phillip Granville. Friend of the working man," Leery said sarcastically. "I'll call him myself."

"No," DeStephano snapped, "I'll do it. I want to arrange an appointment with the big cheese while I'm at it."

"For tomorrow?"

"No. Tonight." He caught his partner's look of surprise.

"Don't worry," he said to Leery," from what I hear, Phillip Granville doesn't have much to go home to. And I'll be very surprised if someone from this operation hasn't placed a call downtown by now."

"Ok, I'm on the rest of it, partner, let me know when we leave to see Granville," Leery responded as his boss turned back to the crime scene.

"Nah, I'll do him myself."

Leery didn't respond but eyed his boss for a moment, tossing around a nagging thought that the senior man was holding back on him.

"Guy dies. So what's the big secret?" his partner mumbled.

Thirteen
~~~ ☙ ~~~

Detective Sergeant Michael DeStephano had heard the stories of Phillip Granville's palatial office, but he'd written them off as just hearsay and evidence of the universal dislike of the guy by people at every step of the food chain. "They weren't exaggerating," he thought, casually letting his eyes roam around the office high on the 26th floor of the General Industries Corporation headquarters in downtown Hartford.

"Dislike" was an underestimation, he decided. "Disdain," perhaps. He was more comfortable with that and it was aligned with his own feelings for him. He simply despised the guy, wouldn't piss on him if he was on fire.

It was nearly nine o'clock but Granville, chairman and CEO of the $40 billion international conglomerate was still more than an hour or two from his usual departure time. The guy was a legendary workaholic. DeStephano laughed, knowing that Granville was proud that people thought of him as such. Ignorant bastard. He was too stupid to know he had nothing else but work.

He laughed to himself again as his eyes took in the priceless works of art dripping off the mahogany panels in a room bigger than his entire house, remembering the quote Granville's last wife (number three?) had given to a reporter on the court house steps after their divorce.

"Phillip Granville is living proof that there is a form of life lower than pond scum," she said with a tone that would melt glass. For a man richer than Midas, more powerful perhaps than even the President of the United States, Granville was a man who couldn't even send a Christmas card without conjuring up ill feelings.

Tired of being kept waiting, DeStephano figured he might attract some attention if he "accidently" broke something of Granville's prized collection of primitive African sculptures while examining it. He wouldn't give a shit, the detective knew. Granville had dozens of such artifacts all over the office. It was his way of impressing people who visited him with how worldly and well travelled he was. Just as the detective was about to drop a small, probably irreplaceable terracotta sculpture smashing to the white Italian marble floor that lined most of the office, he was interrupted.

"Be ever so careful with that, would you Detective DeStephano? It's actually rather priceless, you know," the articulate voice of Phillip Granville filled the room. He was standing in the private doorway that led to a suite of rooms — actually a private bedroom, bath and full kitchen — attached to his office. "Nigerian, 5th century, from the Nok culture. Oh, what the Nigerians wouldn't pay to have that back in their country," he gloated, testing and getting the expected reaction from the detective.

DeStephano waived an arm around the office. "Bet you could say that nearly everything here had another home at one time, hey Phillip? A wonder how it all got through customs and ended up here. Why, I'll bet a single call to INTERPOL..."

Granville chuckled in contempt, carefully masking his irritation at having been called by his first name, a crime more than one subordinate had paid dearly for.

"Now, now, Detective, I'm sure that my art collection is hardly the reason for your visit at this late hour. However, if it is, I would be happy to have one of my people produce full documentation of every piece on display to satisfy your quizzical mind. Tell me, do you always assume one is guilty before even being asked?" Granville said, his voice drenched with sarcasm.

For just a second, DeStephano regretted not bringing his partner, Dennis Leery with him to question the General Corporation chairman. He would have liked a witness when he gouged out his eyes with his two thumbs.

Granville didn't wait for a response but quickly strode the length of the room and extended his hand to the detective. DeStephano hesitated before shaking it. Even the touch of the man's hand repelled him. It was soft, squishy. The son of a bitch had never done a days work in his life.

"So why have you taken time off from catching bad guys to visit with me tonight, Detective?"

"That's detective sergeant, thank you," he replied.

"Oh, forgive me, I hadn't realized. It's been some years since we've spoken last, hasn't it? I didn't realize that congratulations were in order... we should have a drink, celebrate your success."

"I'm working..."

"Ah yes, we should get to that."

Granville walked behind his desk, big enough to serve as a conference table that could seat six. DeStephano bet it had cost as much as his first house. Or maybe the one he owned now.

He swept his arm magnanimously to the chairs surrounding him.

"No. I'll stand, thank you. And let's say we stop the game, Phillip."

"Game? Whatever..."

"I suppose you're going to tell me that you're unaware of the murders at Beckham HQ earlier this evening?" DeStephano said as a matter of fact.

The color drained from Phillip Granville's handsome face. At six foot three, he was a rather imposing figure, especially with his movie star looks, hundred dollar haircut and dark probing eyes. DeStephano had learned in his ugly line of work that such attributes gave a man a false sense of security because he just assumed his opponent was intimidated. But with that one question, the detective, hardly a match for Granville's looks, finishing school or tax bracket, seized the high ground.

"What? What murders?" the CEO responded, genuinely shocked. DeStephano was surprised, there was no hiding it.

"So I guess it is true," the detective laughed. "Your own people are too afraid of you to give you bad news. You know, Adolph Hitler had that same problem. Probably cost him the war."

"Who?" Granville demanded, almost stammering in his speech.

The detective reached inside his wrinkled raincoat pocket and pulled out a notepad. He flipped a couple of pages, taking his time. There wasn't a thing he wouldn't do to get under the CEO's skin.

"Ah, here it is. My eyes aren't as good as they used to be, takes me some time to find scribbled notes these days… "

"Who, god dammit…"

"Well, I see I have your attention, Phillip."

Granville glared at him.

"These aren't confirmed, of course. Hard to tell who they were. Both victims were decapitated. Heads blown right off their shoulders. Looks like two shots apiece from long range. Damn good shooting…"

Granville reached up and grabbed the edge of his desk to control his anger. "Who?"

"We think the first one was Badr Laabi. He was the head knocker at Beckham, right? According to the passport in his suit pocket, he was Moroccan."

"Laabi? Badr Laabi? This is impossible."

"Ooh, I don't think so, Phillip. But unless you're familiar with what the insides of his brains look like, you'd have a hard time recognizing his face now. It's pretty much gone. We're going to have to wait on fingerprints and the autopsy for an official identification." DeStephano had never had so much fun.

"Who was the other?" Granville was grey now.

"Again, not sure. He got it the same way. But a secretary who claimed to work for him said he was Paul Stanton, the HR clown for Laabi... would that make sense?"

"Yes, they worked very closely together," he responded and then became silent.

"Yah, too bad... assume they had families?"

"Of course..."

"Awful shock. What will make it worse is that it will be at least 24 hours before we can confirm the names. Their families will be in limbo until then," DeStephano said.

"My God, this is horrific," Granville muttered to himself."

"Really? I don't recall you saying that some years ago when my family suffered a loss and you were the so called 'human resources' chief. If I recall, you were a prick about it. And believe me, I do recall, and I do know what a prick is."

Granville said nothing, but glared back at the detective. His rage was nearly to the boiling point.

"Will there be anything more, detective?"

"Oh, yes, Phillip, there will be more, lots more. But that's all I have right now, other than the obvious question."

"Which is?"

"Do you know of anyone who would want these two guys dead? In a very spectacular, surgical kind of way?"

The CEO didn't even consider the question.

"Of course not."

"Well, I don't know much about 5th century Nigerian Nok terracotta, pal, but I can tell you a thing or two about guys with vengeful agendas. And what we got here is one pissed off fella who's got a way with things that go bang in the night."

He casually turned and began to walk away, leaving Phillip Granville to absorb that tidbit. Then he suddenly stopped and turned back to the CEO.

"Ya know you might want to give my question some thought, just to make sure you haven't maybe pissed off the same guy at one time or another. Things like this… they seem to spread before they're over. Vengeance is very contagious."

"I'll give it some thought," Granville replied smugly. "But I tend to pick my friends carefully."

DeStephano nearly doubled over with laughter. He slapped his knee to emphasize his amusement.

"You dumb fuck," the detective said.

"You're so arrogant that you wouldn't understand that it's not your friends you have to worry about. It's your enemies."

"I have no enemies."

"You have no friends, either, but you're way too full of shit to know that. Tell you what, it's been a long night, Phillip. Let's not argue, we'll just split the difference. Let's just agree that anyone who knows you hates your guts."

DeStephano turned and walked away, then stopped one more time.

"Seriously, you should give it some thought. I got a hunch you're on the same list as your two buddies were.

"And by the way," he paused to look around the office, "you're right, it's been some years since we've seen each other. I guess congratulations are in order for you as well, you've come a long way, Phillip. I'd guess that climbing the corporate ladder to get here is like finding an escape from the slums."

The detective slowly turned and took in his surroundings, smiling. "Wow," he said.

"It's gonna be a helluva fall."

Granville could no longer contain himself.

"Oh, Detective Sergeant, give my best to your family. I've always wondered. Were they able to keep the house? Were they forced to apply for food stamps?"

DeStephano looked long and hard at the man behind the desk. With a single look, the SOB could stop a man's career dead in its tracks.

The detective merely grinned, long ago hardened beyond anything a punk like Granville could say trying to get under his skin.

"I'll be sure to tell them, Phillip, I know they think of you all the time," he said, so facetiously that he could swear he saw Granville's hand shake.

"And don't forget. Think about my question."

He turned and walked away, pausing just as he got to the door and chuckled just loud enough for Granville to hear.

"Funniest thing…I've just got this hunch…"

Fourteen

The gunman awoke from his brief, fitful sleep the next morning, alone in the shack on the beach. On the horizon, the sun was beginning to crest. He was cold. The vodka usually helped him get a few hours sleep, but no more.

He stumbled into the bathroom and splashed water on his face, trying to forget the nightmares that had kept him company while he slept. He turned on a small transistor radio that hung from the doorknob. It was already tuned to an all news station. Not surprising, the murders in nearby Farmington were the lead story.

As the stranger struggled through the haze of a pounding hangover to make a pot of strong coffee, he listened to a female reporter at the scene summarize what police knew, or at least what they had released to the press.

"While the Farmington Police will neither confirm or deny this," the newswoman said, "my sources here tell me that the two men who were brutally killed last night in a gruesome execution were two senior officers of Beckham. They are Badr Laabi, the company's president who is known to be working in the US on a Moroccan passport, and Paul Stanton, vice president of human resources, of Farmington. These same sources say at this time they have no suspects or motive for the chilling murders that happened here early last evening.

"Both men appear to have been shot by at least one sniper from a location hidden in a wooded area some distance from the building. I can tell you that the area police are now searching is hundreds of yards from the location where the bodies were found in a third floor office last night, suggesting that the gunman or men were highly trained assassins. We'll bring you further details as they develop and will be live at the press conference that is scheduled at days end with Farmington Police Detective Sergeant Michael DeStephano who is heading up this investigation." The report ended abruptly with a promotion for supporting the Salvation Army in shopping centers through the holidays.

Good, the stranger thought. They got nothing. He held his hot coffee in both hands to warm himself then stepped outside onto the small deck that looked out over the ocean and breathed deeply of the cold, salty air. It was refreshing. He chugged down the strong black liquid to clear his head, suddenly aware that he had to get going. There was much to be done today. But just for a moment, he paused to reflect on what he had accomplished the night before.

He felt no remorse, yet no overwhelming sense of victory. He was so full of desire for vengeance that he wasn't sure he would ever be fulfilled. However, his plan had gone off to the letter and there wasn't a stitch of evidence left behind that would point guilt towards him.

Him? A painful smile came to his face. There no longer was a "him." He was now a man without a name, an identity, not even an address. He no longer existed. And later, when his work was completed, that would be a critical measurement of his success — for those he loved, those he would leave behind forever.

Not more than 30 minutes later, he left the cottage, being sure to lock the doors. He'd run an electric razor over his entire head and face, leaving little to resemble the man he once was and limiting the chances of him being identified. He threw an overnight bag into the front seat of the Ford pickup and stopped to pull on a worn, vintage leather jacket before getting inside. Then he placed a pair of dark mirrored aviator glasses over his eyes. Together with his scruffy blue jeans, Irish knit sweater and walking boots he was practically indistinguishable from the average tourist. That was the plan.

There'd been a heavy frost the night before that was still visibly shining on the scrub brush lining the rough dirt road that led back out to the main road. But the strong sun was now working hard to sweat out the chill and he figured it was going to be a mild day for mid December. Perfect flying weather.

Carefully, he drove through Saybrook, merging on to Route 9 and then picked up Interstate 95 to bring him to New Haven. Traffic was sparse and he was in no rush so he kept the old pickup at the speed limit until he pulled into the parking lot of the Parisian-inspired architectural gem, Union Station.

A rush of memories hit him as he slowly maneuvered the pickup through the lot in search of a dark spot in which to park. Years before, he'd spent countless hours in this building, waiting for a Metro-North train to take him into Manhattan on business. The stranger had always admired its neoclassical architectural style taught at the École des Beaux-Arts in Paris that had been copied when it was designed in 1920. He had never complained about a late train because it gave him more time to study the exquisite building. As well, he had always preferred the train over the helicopter that was typically available to him for travel to New York City. For what he gained in convenience, he paid a price in having to be shoulder to shoulder with people who made his guts churn. On the train, he could put up his collar, sit low in his seat, read the newspaper and be completely inconspicuous. And that, too, was very much in the plan today.

For a moment, he wavered. The memory had been painful, about times when his mind was filled with things other than hate and vengeance. He couldn't allow himself the luxury of feeling again.

He went inside, bought a ticket and was soon comfortably seated aboard a train for the two-hour ride into Grand Central Station. From there, he would board an express bus to JFK airport where he intended to purchase a one-way ticket for an international flight to Spain. His trail was deliberately complex and always moving, and even while he read the newspaper he had purchased in the lobby just before boarding, he had one eye measuring those surrounding him at all times. He had no intentions of being caught because he had been stupid. He'd made that mistake once, and it had cost him dearly.

The stranger took off his coat in the heated coach, rolled it into a pillow for his head and fell asleep as the train sped to New York. Almost at once, he began to dream, reliving the last tumultuous years and the agony of his loss.

The nightmare ended when he was jerked awake as the train stopped at Grand Central Station. Stretching as he stood up, he shook his head vigorously to clear his head. The bad dream had actually been a good thing for him, he thought. It refocused him on his mission.

He chuckled at the thought of the enjoyment he would get from his first visit to Europe in many years.

But some, he knew, would find it unforgettable.

F. MARK GRANATO

Fifteen

April 1992

The cold.

It was not fear for his Kate or their children, Badr Laabi's sneering face or even his painful injuries that woke Kevin Keller. It was simply the cold of the spring night air.

He regained consciousness lying on a muddy bank of the river, his body still half submerged. Somehow, the turbulent waters had plucked him from the bottom of the Farmington River and thrown him ashore before he drowned. He had no idea how long he had been out or where he was. But he was alive. And freezing to death in his soaking wet clothes.

He pulled his bruised and broken body out of the water and managed to raise himself up to a standing position by pulling on a low hanging tree branch. His broken ribs brought stabbing pain with every movement and he was woozy. His head hurt. For long moments he stood, more draped over the branch than standing, trying to get his bearings. What had happened? Where was he?

Then gradually, as neurotransmitters began reactivating in his bruised brain, the wild series of events that had brought him to the brink of death came back to him in terrifying clarity.

They were going to kill his family.

Laabi, Stanton, probably Granville, too. They were all in on it. They were going to murder him and his family for what he had discovered. It was the only way to keep him quiet, to protect them from rotting in jail.

From the depths of his soul, a scream of anguish escaped his mouth as he recognized the hopelessness of the situation he was in — and the consequences for his family.

He had to get control, he thought, he must get to them.

No, wait.

He thought again.

The police, I must get to the police.

They will protect us. My family.

He began picking his way along the riverbank, repeatedly falling back into the water as he slipped on the muddy bank that ran irregularly along the water's edge. In the pitch-black night, it was slow going.

He walked for what seemed like hours. Then suddenly, he saw lights ahead and heard muffled conversation. He wondered if they were searching for him. He moved closer, cautiously.

Finally in frustration, he thought to yell out for help. He pressed his right arm against his ribs to immobilize them. He needed to yell. He took a deep breath, preparing to holler, then... he stopped. He shook his head with a new thought.

What if they thought he was dead?

What if they couldn't find his body?

What would it mean to the safety of Kate and the children?

Would Laabi and Granville leave them alone? Would they be satisfied that Kevin Keller's misfortune had taken care of their problem?

He sagged to the ground, unsure of what to do. He needed to think this through before he took another step.

Then his imagination hammered him with another horror.

Were Kate and the children all right? Had anyone gotten to them... the black van?

Instantly he knew that his priority was to get home, to see with his own eyes what the situation was. It wasn't far. That had to be Route 4 ahead, probably the bridge that had nearly killed him. He was only a few miles from home. He turned and pushed into the thick underbrush lining the riverbank and began making his way through the trees back toward the main road. He was in agony. But the fear that was choking him was far worse than the pain. He had to know.

After an hour of fighting his way through the undergrowth, he made his way back to Collinsville Road, roughly a half mile from where he had gone over the bridge. He watched from the security of the heavy brush cover as police and fire department personnel were still guiding traffic around the right lane on the damaged bridge and splaying searchlights back and forth across the river looking for him. He thought there was a boat in the water. That meant they had divers who would find the car empty.

Keller emerged from the brush standing tall and walked as normally as possible considering his broken ribs, then casually crossed Collinsville Road, passing between stopped traffic. He walked another 50 feet to River Road and a few minutes more so as not to attract any attention. As soon as he was out of sight of the main road, he ducked back into the woods. A hundred yards ahead was his house. In another few minutes he was at the edge of his back yard, and stooped low in the tree line that he had planted with Kate when they built the house. It gave them privacy and deadened some of the road noise.

Slowly, on his hands and knees, he crawled closer to the house coming up along the side yard so he could see his driveway and the street in front. He was shocked to see dozens of cars there, including at least three police cruisers in the driveway. He inched closer still and recognized some of the other cars as those belonging to friends.

As well as Paul Stanton's silver Cadillac.

A flash of rage stormed through his mind. It took every bit of his willpower not to stand up, march into his living room and strangle Stanton with his bare hands.

He closed his eyes and mapped out the rest of his plan, stealing a car, finding Laabi tonight and killing him, too.

Somehow, he managed to control his anger and stayed where he was, forcing himself to watch what was happening in his own home. He was rewarded very soon.

Stanton emerged from the house, accompanied by a uniformed police officer. They were talking. Keller scurried closer through the brush bordering his side yard to listen.

It's just terrible, Officer, just terrible..." Stanton was saying to the cop who just shook his head. "It's so sad to see his wife and children going through such agony."

"Yah, Mr. Stanton, it's always such a shock when these things happen. Really rough on kids," the policeman replied.

"But as I told you, we should have seen this coming. Kevin has been acting so strange as of late. Just crazy. Leveling all kinds of accusations against management. He's been scaring people lately. We should have known something was wrong."

The rage was building in Keller's throat as he listened to Stanton's blatant lies. So this was the plan. He wondered what Kate had said, but imagined the police had just discounted it as the words of a wife and mother in horrible pain.

"How long will they continue the search, Officer?" Stanton asked.

"Well, probably at least through tomorrow," he replied. "Mr. Keller hit that retaining wall pretty hard. No telling what kind of condition he was in when the car went into the water. I'm assuming that he was dead before the current pulled him out. It runs pretty fast through these parts so he could be miles down stream by now. It's heavily wooded along those riverbanks and there are a lot of underwater pockets that could hide his body. I hate to say this, but we might never find him."

"Oh my God," Stanton said, making sure the cop noted how upset he was. "Well, thank you for all your efforts, Officer." He handed him his business card. "Please call me if there's any change." They shook hands and Stanton walked to his car. Before he even started it, he was on his car phone, probably talking to Laabi. He spoke only for a couple of minutes then pulled out of the driveway and down the street. Keller watched until he was out of sight.

As he waited, he saw that people began leaving the house, probably their close friends who had done all they could to shore up Kate and the kids at an unthinkable time. When the police left some time later, he surmised that they had finished with their initial interviews with her but would probably be back in the morning.

Finally, only Kate's brother and his wife, her only living family, were left inside and it appeared they were staying for the night. He was grateful for their kindness. But guilt was tearing him up. His wife and children should never have had to suffer like this. And he alone had put them at risk.

As he sat pondering his next move, the cold air numbed his physical injuries but his grief continued to build. Because it became clear to him that there was only one course of action he could take to ensure that Kate and his children would be safe.

He had to be dead.

That conclusion came to him with a stunning finality that both broke his heart and filled him with a fury he had never felt before. But he was sure there was no recourse. Even if he were able to prove that it was Laabi, Stanton and probably Granville who had masterminded the treason General Industries was guilty of, the danger to his wife and children would never go away.

Keller was certain that the ingenious plan to exploit the US embargoes ran deep within GIC. Granville had cultivated a culture within the corporation that thrived on corruption. There were billions of dollars at stake. Consequently, so long as anyone involved escaped discovery, Keller's family would be at risk. They would come at Kate and his children to get at him. In the end, they would all be murdered.

Reality was inescapable. He could not live with that. Better that he die so that they might live.

Just for a moment, in a reckless display of anger, he stood up in full view of the house in which his family was now secure. He clenched his fists.

"There will be a price, you bastards. There will be a price," he whispered into the night.

"I promise Kate, you and our children will always be safe."

He paused, closing his eyes to conjure up a lasting image of his wife and children even as he uttered a final vow.

"There will be blood.

Sixteen

Kevin Keller watched in hiding for two days as mourners visited his wife and children at their home in Canton. He was only yards away from the people that meant more to him than life itself, but was powerless to confront them, his accident and disappearance still a mystery.

From time to time, a Canton or Farmington police cruiser would pull into the driveway and uniformed officers would remove their hats and enter the house. He guessed the visits were to provide updates on the search for the body they would never find.

Around noon on the second day, still hiding in the thick brush and woods surrounding his house, he was startled to see Kate and the three children emerge from the house and sit together around the patio table where they once celebrated summer barbecues.

He wasn't close enough to see what state they were in, but he could hear them crying as Kate did her best to hold them together. Keller's heart broke at the scene. All he had to do to alleviate their grief and misery was emerge from the brush with a cock and bull story of having been lost in the river and suffering from temporary amnesia from the accident.

A voice in his head continually tempted him. "That's all you have to do, Kevin." The voice would go away when he would ask, "Then what? How do I protect them?"

He pondered the question over and over until he thought he would go mad. There was no answer. He had no idea how deep the conspiracy went within General Industries and how many people were aware of it. But he was certain that so long as anyone at GIC knew he was aware of their crimes, he and his family were as good as dead. He could not arrive at any other conclusion. He knew that Phillip Granville, Badr Laabi and countless others were capable of anything — any depravity — to retain the flow of illegal riches into their pockets. The illusion of his death must be permanent. It was the only way to save the four people he watched, holding each other for comfort, missing him, wanting him.

It could never be again.

That night, Keller stole away from his back yard under cover of a moonless sky, and went in search of food. He hadn't eaten in nearly three days and he was dangerously cold and dehydrated. He had about $300 cash in his wallet and useless credit cards that would give him away the second he used one. His driver's license was equally worthless.

When he got to Route 6, he quickly crossed the road with the collar turned up on his suit jacket and his hands in his pants pockets. His hair was tousled and he hadn't shaved or bathed since the morning of the accident. For all intents, he looked like a homeless person or a derelict on an extended bender. He intended to keep up the façade.

Food would have to wait. First he had something to do.

He stumbled into the woods on the other side of the road and went to the bank of the Farmington River. Keller pulled out his wallet, removed the cash and was about to throw the leather case into the rapids, then stopped. He had forgotten about the family pictures he always carried with him, the small snapshots that had accompanied him on business trips all over the world. On countless nights in as many countries, when sleep in yet another strange hotel room bed would not come, he would reach for his wallet and take out the small, plastic encased set of pictures and stare at his family, remembering their good times together, how much he loved and missed them. Often he would kiss each of their faces on the small Kodak images, hoping they would feel his lips wherever they were and know that Kevin Keller the husband and father missed them unbearably. It was not unusual for him, even as a grown man, to cry himself to sleep and waken in the morning still clutching the pictures.

Now he had to let them go. Kate knew the pictures were in his wallet. They must be with his other credentials when the leather case was found, as it inevitably would be sooner or later.

He sat at the river's edge and pulled out the pictures one last time, studying each of them by the dim light of the streetlights some distance away and the neon signs of a nearby convenience store. He pored over the images of his beautiful Kate and their exquisite children, permanently burning their smiles and the magnificence of their innocence into that small area of his brain that could never forget. His heart was pumping, painfully so as if it would truly break into a million pieces. He felt so much pain inside that he had forgotten all about the gash to his head and the broken ribs that would have stopped a normal man days before.

Finally, he knew the time had come. Gently, he pressed his lips against each of their faces, then placed the pictures back into their protective plastic and into his wallet. He looked at the lump of soggy leather in his hand, all which remained of Kevin Keller. He brought it to his nose to add the smell of the leather to his memories, then without another hesitation, flung it as far out into the river as he could. The raging waters swallowed all presence of it instantaneously.

He squeezed his hands into fists and punched them into his face, wanting to hurt himself so that he could remember the pain of this moment. A pain so deep that it would give him the strength to live in the world of anonymity for which he was destined.

And the courage to make them all pay.

Seventeen

May 1992

Nearly a month after his disappearance, Kevin Keller had successfully made his way out of Connecticut, cautiously following Route 44 to the northwest corner of the state where he crossed the border into the small town of Millerton, New York. He was nearly invisible, sleeping in the underbrush a hundred yards from the road at night, taking advantage of the heavily forested terrain. By day, he played cat and mouse with passing traffic, desperate to remain unnoticed. He had no idea if local police had been alerted to his disappearance and were looking for him or if he had just been written off in the accident. He bathed in icy cold streams and washed out his clothes in the winter runoff from the foothills, a part of him refusing to become totally reclusive. But still, with his hair and beard grown out, he struck an odd pose dressed in a rumpled business suit and white dress shirt. He had a few hundred dollars in cash, but was fearful of going into an establishment of any kind for fear of being recognized, so at night he would rummage through the garbage pails and trash bins of restaurants and fast food places for sustenance. He kept this up for weeks and had not yet experienced a run-in with police, but he knew his time was running out. He was bound to attract someone's attention eventually and that could end his run for freedom — and the protection he was providing for his family by disappearing. So long as Laabi and Granville believed him dead, Kate and the kids were safe.

He needed a plan.

Just outside of Millerton, he came upon a road sign for Rhinebeck, 10 miles west, a small New York state village he and Kate had driven to many times when they were dating. With the top down in Kevin's decrepit old Triumph TR4 two-seater, a picnic basket of sandwiches and cold beer in the back cubby, they had endlessly explored the village's pre Revolutionary War development and growth into one of New England's earliest centers of commerce. They were also frequent visitors to Hyde Park, the former estate of President Franklin D. Roosevelt. The area reeked of history, for which they each shared an insatiable appetite.

He stared at the simple sign and felt his eyes fill with tears. Life would never be so simple or beautiful again. Unconsciously, he turned down Route 199 and began walking toward Rhinebeck, certain that the plan he needed would come to him in this place where he could remember being with his Kate.

Several hours later as the sun was setting, Keller walked into the Rhinebeck Village historic district, having attracted no undue attention. As he strolled through the early European-American settlement, the landscape came flooding back to him along with his memories of holding Kate's hand as they passed by the mansions of its earliest settlers and even the Beekman Inn, claimed to be the oldest continuously operated such establishment in the country. He and Kate had stayed there several times. He closed his eyes and squeezed away tears.

The Inn was where he had proposed to her. Where they had made love for the first time. Where they had laughed and talked endlessly over glasses of a locally produced Reisling and set in motion their plans for happiness together, forever. His knees buckled, and he stopped and leaned against a tree, staring at the magnificent old Inn, letting the memories sink in for just a few moments. If he allowed himself anymore, he knew he might never move again. He wondered if Kate and the children ever thought of him. He hoped not.

That was when the plan began to come to him.

A half block up the street he stopped at a convenience store and asked if there was a bus station in town. The young man behind the register grunted without looking up at him and pointed over his shoulder. "Greyhound, about a mile north."

He left without another question or even buying something to eat, despite being famished. The few times he'd caught his reflection in a window, he noted that his new life had taken its toll. He was already gaunt looking, having probably lost over 20 pounds in just the few weeks since he'd gone missing. The dark circles under his eyes, straggly hair and scruffy beard added to his overall ill appearance. What he didn't notice was that the light in his eyes was gone, replaced by the dull emptiness of a man living with a dark and painful secret.

Keller turned left onto East Market Street and began walking towards what he hoped was a Greyhound terminal. Conveniently, a Salvation Army store was just up the road. With where he planned to go, a change of clothes would make sense and the suit he'd been living in for weeks was hopelessly soiled. He went in and bought blue jeans, a baseball-style cap with no markings, a couple of plain t-shirts, underwear and socks, a lightweight military surplus work jacket and a pair of second hand boots with rugged rubber soles. He also found a well-worn canvas backpack that appeared to have spent most if its life on a college campus. He already had sunglasses; they were in his suit jacket pocket when he crashed and somehow hadn't broken. He paid for the merchandise and left as quickly as possible. The only thing he couldn't buy was identification of some kind. Getting a license or credit card was out of the question. Eventually, he was going to have to do something about that. He needed a name and at least the story of a former life.

With his supplies stuffed into the backpack, he walked quickly towards the bus station and was relieved to find it was indeed a Greyhound depot. He could go anywhere from here, no questions asked.

He didn't know why it came to him, but the destination he thought of was the most remote place he knew of in North America.

"One ticket to Butte, Montana, please," he asked the clerk inside the station.

"One way sir?" the older man behind the barred window asked, looking up only to see Keller's nod. His fingers sped across a computer keyboard, following the path of the customer's destination and where he'd have to make transfers.

"Now that's not a place I get many calls for," he said, making conversation. "Got family out that way?"

"No. Just seeing some of the country."

"Hmm, I see," the clerk replied, knowing there was no more conversation to be had.

"It will take you two days, 14 hours and 35 minutes and the first bus leaves at 8:10 a.m. in the morning," he said. "At least four transfers, but I'll take care of all that."

Thank you," Keller said, relaxing with the man's easy going banter. He was keenly sensitive to raising attention and was on high alert for signs that there was anyone searching for him. It was reassuring to know that with his long hair, full beard, baseball cap and sunglasses, he bore little resemblance to Kevin Keller.

He was unaware that he had already begun shedding many of Kevin Keller's traits, and not just his appearance. Inside, his mind was slowly undergoing a metamorphosis that was slowly twisting his thoughts into a simmering rage, kept from coming to a boil only by the overwhelming weight of sadness and loneliness he was carrying. Kevin Keller was already no more. The question was: Who and what was he to become?

He spent the night hidden in deep brush in the village park, sipping from a cheap bottle of vodka he'd bought for his dinner and catching 20 minutes of sleep every now and then. He had been sleeping like this for weeks now. Every time he would doze off, images of Kate and the kids would shock him awake. The alcohol kept him warm and somewhat numb but he was much too afraid of being discovered to rest anyway. He prayed that the farther away he got from New England the more at ease he would become. But Keller was smart enough to know that he would spend the rest of his life looking over his shoulder even if was successful in dropping off the face of the earth. Deep within him though was the dream of finding a way back to the surface, back to Kate and the kids with nothing to fear. Every time the thought crept into his consciousness, he pushed it back down, hard. The situation was hopeless, and he knew it.

The next morning he waited until just before final boarding to get on the bus, his dark glasses on, hat pulled down low and collar up, and took a seat in the back alone next to a window. Outside, a Rhinebeck police patrol car drove slowly by the row of parked busses and he nearly panicked. Had he given himself away? Were they looking for him? He took off his jacket and slunk down low in his seat, turned away from the window and buried his face in a copy of the Greyhound magazine he found in the seat pocket in front of him.

The driver of his bus stepped outside and approached the patrol car. Keller's stomach clenched.

Harmlessly, the two drivers shared a laugh as friends would do. He heard the cop holler, "Safe trip," as the bus driver returned to his seat, prompting a wave. Then the driver donned a pair of sunglasses, adjusted his review mirror, buckled his seatbelt and greeted his passengers with a cheery "Good morning" over the PA system. He slowly pulled the long silver motor carriage with it's passenger load of about 45 people out onto main street and headed north.

    Keller remained slumped low in his seat until the bus crossed the village line and blended into traffic. In a few more minutes, the bus was approaching the Kingston-Rhinecliff Bridge across the great Hudson River and he pulled himself upright in his seat to take in the spectacular view. He and Kate had crossed this bridge many times together and were always spellbound by the view. Its mile and a half continuous under-deck truss design allowed unimpeded views of the dense spring foliage now in full bloom along both riverbanks as far as the eye could see. It was also a trifle challenging to anyone with a fear of heights. At 150 feet off the ground, the heavy metal guardrails that protected vehicles seemed flimsy at best. Kate had always white-knuckled it across, but smiled the length of the ride in their tiny sports car glorying in the beauty she could almost reach out and touch, the wind in her hair, the sun on her face.

    Kate, Kate... Keller's mind would not let her go. He closed his eyes hoping to sleep. But images of his wife and children danced in the shimmering blackness beneath his eyelids and there would be no escape from his torture. The only time he truly slept now was when he passed out from exhaustion.

He stared out the window, trying to block out the memories. Instead, he saw a reflection of two men, their eyes intensely watching him, a smirk on their lips.

Keller turned around quickly, scanning the seats beside and behind him for the source. They were empty. Then he heard a voice. He turned back to the window. One of the faces was Phillip Granville's, the other, Laabi. Granville smiled at Keller's attention, baring his teeth. They were stained with blood.

"Keep going, patriot. Run, and never look back," he growled in the reflection. "Or they will drown, too, Kevin. In their own blood."

Instinctively, Keller drew his fist back and punched at the image, his hand bouncing off the window. Granville and Laabi began to laugh.

No one saw. But surely, he thought, everyone on the bus must have heard the hideous laughter that filled the air. Keller put his hands over his ears trying to shut out the noise. It was impossible. He grabbed his coat, leaned forward until his head hit the seatback in front of him. Wrapping the coat around him, he locked his arms over his head to shut out the noise. Finally, there was silence. Beneath the canvas jacket, he trembled in fear and remained hidden in his seat for nearly an hour.

When at last he found the courage to sit up and look into the window, the faces were gone. The trembling had stopped. And he was no longer afraid.

Keller put his back against the soft seat and let his aching neck relax. He willed his mind to go revisit what he had just experienced and quickly understood that the impetus for the hallucination he had suffered was not Granville or Laabi, but actually within himself.

It wasn't his loneliness or suffering at the loss of his family. It wasn't concern for his own safety. Nor was it his hatred for the men who had taken everything from him.

It was fear.

Fear of what they might do to those he loved. And fear that he would not be able to stop them.

His instincts had been correct when he stopped at the crossroads outside Millerton at the sign that read "Rhinebeck." He thought the plan he needed might come to him there. And it had.

But he couldn't run forever.

F. MARK GRANATO

Eighteen
~~~ ❧ ~~~

He slept the sleep of the dead for the next two days, rousing only when awakened by a Greyhound driver alerting him to the next transfer as he made his way across the country. His body and mind were completely exhausted from the abuse he had suffered for weeks and had finally given out. But even as he slept, his mind would not surrender, dragging him back, so far back...

Granville was already in his office, on the phone, speaking in French but in a tone that suggested he was very unhappy with the hapless person on the other end of the line. He didn't have the courtesy to stop the tirade even after his secretary escorted the young widow, her brother-in-law and the chairman's assistant into his office to wait.
Phillip Granville was the executive vice president of human resources for General Industries, Inc. and the hands

on favorite to succeed the current chairman in the near future. Kevin Keller was attending the meeting at the order of his boss so he wouldn't have to face the woman himself. It was not the first time he had been used as an envoy so that other senior officers of the corporation could avoid difficult conversations. It wouldn't be the last.

But Keller knew this one wasn't going to be just difficult. It would be heartbreaking. The woman, in her early 30's, wrung her hands incessantly. Looking at her, he assumed that she had once been very beautiful, but the horrors of the last few weeks had probably robbed her of that natural glow forever. Her eyes were dark and lifeless and the black circles under them couldn't be hidden by any amount of makeup. He thought she was suffering terribly, probably on the verge of a complete breakdown. Keller knew from some experience that what was coming was only going to make it worse for her.

He took a deep breath while Granville continued to act out his tirade. Watching him perform, he couldn't help but think to himself what an obscene title the man held. "Human Resources." Phillip Granville saw people only as irritants, so much refuse that must be dealt with in order for him to achieve his objective. And there was no limit to the ardor he would employ in destroying anyone who got in his way. He was consumed by power and devoured those unfortunate enough to challenge him, even if unintended. Despite being protected by the mantle of working for the current chairman, Keller felt no sense of protection from this man's wrath. He knew instinctively that his own boss would toss him into the trash at the slightest complaint from his HR executive, the man he had enthusiastically picked to succeed him upon his upcoming retirement. The decision only needed approval from the full General Board of Directors.

Kevin Keller had wondered over the selection from the moment he had understood the inevitably of Granville's ascension. He was so perplexed by it that he finally confronted his boss and straight out asked him, "Why?"

"Kevin, you surprise me," the CEO had replied, chuckling. "I thought you had a better grasp of the game. Certainly, personalities have nothing to do with it. I personally think the guy was spawned by an African Puff Adder," he laughed, comparing the future chief executive officer to a snake whose savage, ripping bite and insanely powerful venom usually brought death to a victim within seconds.

"Phillip Granville is a despicable human being, " he concluded.

Keller remembered being stunned by the response. So he repeated himself.

"Why, then?"

"Because it's all about the money, Kevin, and when you've made enough of that, then it's all about the power."

Keller thought he was going to be sick.

"This guy is so ruthless he's going to drive the stock price through the ceiling," the chairman continued. "He'll be a darling of Wall Street. The more ruthless, the more viciously driven he is, the more they'll love him. The problem is, I'm not mean enough to do the job. He is, and he's going to make me rich because I own a helluva lot of stock in this company. Do you know what my stock options are worth alone? Ha! It makes me laugh out loud every time I think how much money I'm about to make for doing nothing but choosing the most hideous person I can to lead this corporation. You'll be rich too, ya know. How many thousands of options are you holding right now? Just think about it. Your family is going to be rich.

"Now won't that be nice?"

There was only one response Keller could think of.
"But at what price?"

The memory faded as Granville finally slammed down the phone, his victim having been properly dispatched, and turned his attention to his visitors. He looked to the woman first and gave her his seemingly undivided attention, turning on his seductive charm in the blink of an eye. Keller half expected the long, slithering tongue of a Chameleon to dart out of his mouth. The guy was amazing.

"Mrs...." He stood and reached across his desk to shake her hand.

"Lucy," she interrupted him. "Please call me Lucy."

"Lucy..." he nodded, then turned to the man accompanying her. "And you are?"

"Her brother-in-law. Call me Mike," he smiled.

Simpleton, Phillip Granville thought to himself, but forced a look of friendly amusement.

"Of course. Now what is it that I can help you with?" he asked them. Keller flinched. Granville had been completely briefed. The woman was equally surprised. How cruel.

"My husband..." she began.

"Oh, yes, forgive me. That awful thing in Lockerbie. You have my condolences. Ed was a valued..."

"Stephen," she corrected him.

"Ah, yes, silly of me... Stephen was such a valued employee. His death was a terrible shock... to all of us, I mean," Granville responded. Keller's stomach churned at the insincerity Granville was laying on the widow.

"But... if I am not mistaken, his death is part of the FBI and the international community's investigation... I mean INTERPOL believes it was an act of terrorism, am I not correct?"

"Yes," Lucy responded, her voice shaking. She glanced over at Keller, waiting for him to intercede. He didn't say anything.

"So," Granville continued, "I am uncertain as to why you are here."

The look on the brother-in-law's face had quickly changed, Keller noted. There was an edge to him he hadn't noticed before. The kind that said he didn't suffer assholes gladly.

"Excuse me, Mr. Granville," he interrupted quickly. "In case there's any confusion here – it would appear you don't know what the issue is..." he too glanced over at Keller. "We've come to talk about my brother's pension and health insurance for his family."

Granville didn't skip a beat. "We? I'm afraid I can only discuss such matters with your brother's wife, Mike. We have laws..."

"Which I'm sure you adhere to rigidly," Mike replied with sarcasm.

"In fact we do, Michael," Granville answered quickly, forgetting the informality agreed to. He turned to Lucy. "Now what exactly can I help you with, Lucy?"

"Well..." she hesitated, suddenly very unsure of herself. "It's about his vesting."

"Yes? I assume he was an employee for more than five years? Stephen's pension and benefits would have automatically vested after his fifth year anniversary with the company. Is that not the case? I admit that I have not reviewed his file," Granville replied. "Simply no time."

Keller went wide-eyed. The two of them had reviewed the man's file in detail the day before.

"Well, that's just it," Lucy continued, her hands shaking. Her brother-in-law reached over and placed his hand on hers for comfort. She grabbed it.

"Stephen began work at General nearly four years and ten months before he died. He would have vested in his pension, small as it would have been, in just 62 days. But more importantly, his survivors would have lifetime medical and dental coverage and a life insurance policy worth five times his salary also would have vested." She paused.

"Those benefits are so important to us…"

Granville raised a hand to stop her in mid sentence.

"Lucy…I'm not sure what you're asking me to…"

To Kevin Keller, it appeared that Mike was about to come out of his chair. And for the first time he noticed that the man had very big hands and there was a decided bulge under the armpit of his cheap, untailored suit. He wondered if it was a gun.

"You're not sure of what…?" Mike responded, menacingly.

"Mike, please," Lucy implored him, reaching over and grabbing his hand, hoping to calm him. It didn't work.

"What the fuck is this, Granville? The lady — wife of your former loyal employee — is asking you to waive the 60 days he was short on vesting. He left three kids behind as well as Lucy. That money and those benefits couldn't be more important. Is that clear, or are you still confused?"

Granville smiled as if to diffuse the situation. Actually it was a sign of gratification that he knew he had the upper hand. The wife was a mouse and the brother-in-law was a hot head. Nothing he couldn't handle.

"Ah, Mike. I am sympathetic. But I'm afraid my hands are tied. There are the laws, you understand."

"The insurance company assured us that you had the authority to waive the 60 days, considering he was murdered while traveling on business for your company," Mike shot back, not about to take Granville's bullshit.

"That's simply not true, Mike."

"What's true is that you are pure bullshit, Granville." He stood up, towering over the arrogant executive.

"You understand that they will lose their house and will have no income or insurance based on your unwillingness to help them, Mr. Granville?" he said pointedly and with rising anger in his voice.

Granville sighed, feigning concern. "My hands are tied." Keller himself would have wiped the smirk off Granville's face if he'd had the nerve. He didn't.

"Let me be completely clear, Mike," he began. "General Industries had nothing to do with the death of Lucy's husband or the difficult financial circumstances in which he has left his family. All of these issues will be addressed by the United States Government in the months ahead, I am sure. In the meantime, you cannot expect this company to bend the rules any time an employee — or former employee, as in this case — encounters difficulties with his personal life. We are a corporation, and consequently answer to shareholders who would not approve of such largesse. We exist only at their willingness to invest in UIC because they expect a profit on their investment. Giving away unearned pensions, health care coverage and the proceeds of insurance policies is hardly good business."

He paused.

"Now... am I perfectly clear?"

Mike reached across the desk and grabbed Granville by his tie, pulling him forward. The look on his face would have stopped a train in its tracks.

"Perfectly," he growled. Both of them knew that with one good yank by the bigger man, there was a good chance Phillip Granville's neck would snap. Keller knew it too, and unconsciously hesitated before stepping in.

"Mike, Mike, let go Mike," Keller said, finally jumping up to grab the big man's arm. "You don't want to do this. Don't make me call security. Please…"

"Mike, let him go, this is hopeless, don't make it worse," Lucy yelled to her brother-in-law.

Mike slowly loosened his grip and Granville pulled back, adjusting his tie out of habit.

"I believe we are quite finished here. Kevin, please show our guests out," he said, slightly flustered.

"We are hardly finished, asshole. I'll get the money for a lawyer somehow and I know a few reporters. They'll love this story."

"As you see fit. But lawyers are expensive and I warn you, precedent is against you. And reporters? I'm afraid that falls into the same weak threat category. I'm sure Mr. Keller would be glad to give you a tour of the third floor of this building, which happens to be where our public and investor relations people work. There are more than 100 employees working the job. So, good luck with that," Granville said with an icy arrogance that made the hair on the back of Kevin Keller's hair stand on end.

"We'll see, Granville. But in the meantime, don't ever cross the street without looking both ways." He looked at Lucy while Granville theatrically flinched at the ugly threat.

"I'm sorry, Lucy. But it seems everything your husband told you about this heartless bastard was right on the money. Let's go." He grabbed her by the hand and pushed by Keller.

"Thanks for nothing, Kevin. We came to you because word was you had a conscience. Well, you're no better than the trash you work for. Hope you never need help, you two-faced bastard."

Keller followed them out the door.

"Mike, Lucy, please, I had no idea..."

"Bullshit, Keller. Tell your chicken shit boss he hasn't heard the end of this," Mike yelled over his shoulder as he pulled his sister-in-law away.

The young executive needed to explain that he was just a pawn in the process. He chased after them.

"Mike," he said, putting a hand on his shoulder.

The angry man turned around and savagely brushed Keller's hand away.

"You're no better than any of them," he spit, pushing Kevin away with both hands. Keller went sprawling.

The shoving wouldn't stop no matter how hard he tried to brush away the man's hands. Finally, he swung wildly at his attacker who backed out of the way just in time.

"Sir, sir... I am sorry to wake you but we're at the final rest stop before Butte. Don't you need to use the rest room? You've been sleeping for more than 12 hours."

"What?" Keller replied, groggily. He slowly was emerging from a thick fog and for a moment could not remember where he was. "Get off me!" he said to the driver, struggling to sit up.

"Sir, do you require medical assistance? Are you alright?" the driver asked following company procedure that dictated he first cover his ass before throwing the unruly passenger off the bus. He was at the end of his patience with this one, having been behind the wheel for the last six hours knowing he had an unconscious passenger in the back. He didn't know if the guy was drugged out or even dead. Actually, he didn't care one way or another so long as he could get him off the bus without breaking any company rules.

He reached down and put his hand on the passenger's shoulder again and shook him, repeating himself.

"Sir, do you require medical assistance?" he said.

This time Keller threw a punch that bounced lightly off the driver's shoulder. But it was enough to get him tossed.

"Ok," the driver said, out of patience. "Apparently you're well enough to want to fight. Get up, get your things and get off my bus, now, or I'll call the police."

Keller heard the man's voice but his words were slow to register. The dream that had been torturing him was quickly fading and he slowly was getting his bearings again. He finally realized he had to get away or there would be police. The last thing he needed. But where in hell was he?

"Did you hear me? Get off!" the driver said menacingly.

He didn't argue and dragged himself to his feet, his joints stiff from sleeping so long in cramped quarters.

"No problem, I'm going. Sorry, I was just dreaming," he said to the driver.

"Yah, probably about where your next bag of dope is coming from," the man said harshly. "I don't appreciate passengers trying to take my head off. Just get off or I will call the cops."

Keller stumbled down the narrow aisle of the bus, lugging his canvas backpack, the driver close behind. He hesitated at the front stairs, scanning the station he was about to step into. There were no police waiting for him. Nothing seemed unusual.

He turned to the bus driver.

"Where are we?"

"Bozeman. Another couple of hours and you would have been in Butte. Good luck. Now get off," he responded tersely.

Keller descended the stairs and blended quickly into the crowd of passengers milling around the station. He knew nothing about Bozeman. For that matter, he knew nothing about Butte. All he knew was that he had to get out of the station. There were far too many people here and he had no idea if anyone was looking for him. He found a rest room and hid in a stall for a few minutes, clearing his head and trying to decide what to do next.

Keller decided he had to get back on the road with a minimum of attention. Maybe he could find someone outside the station heading west. He just needed to keep moving. An image of Kate flashed through his mind. He pushed it down, hard.

He splashed his face with some water from the sink, then put his sunglasses back on, pulled his hat down low over his brow and got into his work jacket, even though the temperature was hovering near 60 degrees. Then he grabbed his backpack and ventured back out into the station. Spying an exit sign, he walked straight for it and out into the main parking lot. There were dozens of vehicles, mostly pickup trucks, some empty, some with a waiting driver. He didn't have a clue about how to steal a car and quickly dismissed the idea as stupid. To the best of his knowledge he hadn't broken any laws yet and wasn't about to start leaving a trail.

He scanned the parking lot until he saw an older man, his longish gray hair sneaking out of a well-worn cowboy hat at the wheel of a ten-year-old Ford pickup. The driver had stopped near the curb a few feet away to pick up a younger man who threw a bag into the back of the truck.

He hesitated for a moment, then rapped on the right rear fender as the driver began pulling away, stopping him. He went to the passenger side window and smiled. The young man inside, who appeared to be the driver's son, smiled back and rolled down the window.

"Hi, I'm sorry to bother you but I was wondering if you..."

The passenger cracked a grin.

"We're heading towards Cardwell, about halfway to Butte if you're looking for a ride, friend," he offered without hesitation.

Keller almost didn't know how to respond at the immediate friendly response.

"That... why that would be just fine, if you don't mind, sir. I'm trying to get to Butte. Half way is better than no way," he smiled.

"Well, hop in the back, it's about an hour's drive."

Keller climbed up over the rear fender and sat down against the back of the cab, pulling his jacket collar up to hide his face from onlookers in the parking lot. The truck pulled away.

Almost immediately, the pickup left the crowded Bozeman business area and merged onto Interstate 90. He'd never been a geography buff but wished now that he knew more about this part of the country. As they drove, he marveled at the beauty of the seemingly endless mountain ranges and the rolling hills covered in bluebunch wheatgrass that the highway cut through. Several times he spotted herds of cattle and horses in the open ranges. There was a strange smell in the air that he couldn't identify right away. Then it struck him that it was the clean, crispness of it that he didn't recognize coming from the Northeast and especially after having spent the better part of the last two days on a diesel-powered bus.

About the only thing he remembered about Montana from his school days was its nickname, "Big Sky Country." Now he understood. Not a single tall building interrupted the natural mountain skylines. He sucked in great breaths of the sweet air and for a moment, lost his troubles in the back of that truck, the wind and sun on his face infusing him with a taste of hope he had almost forgotten.

Too soon, the pickup pulled to the side of I-90 just before an exit ramp marked, "Cardwell."

The man in the passenger seat got out and told Keller that was as far west as they were going.

"You're welcome to come into Cardwell with us, friend, but if you're still needing to get to Butte, this is about the best spot to hitch a ride. Shouldn't take you long, lot of truckers come through here."

Keller thanked him but feigned some urgency of getting to Butte. He still felt the need to keep moving. He grabbed his backpack, jumped out of the bed of the pickup and waved as the two men pulled away. He was still surprised at how kind they'd been to him.

Ten minutes later, an oncoming, unmarked 18-wheeler slowed after seeing Keller with his thumb out and down shifted to a stop 20 yards beyond him. The driver leaned over and opened the passenger door even before Keller reached him.

"Where you headin' for, son?" the driver hollered over the roar of the big diesel engine in front of him as Keller came alongside. He was grinning through a long, unkempt handlebar moustache and wearing mirrored sunglasses and a soiled John Deere cap. His deerskin work gloves were soiled black from the countless hours he'd spent at the wheel of the huge truck. From the looks of the fast food wrappers and empty coffee cups that littered the floor of the passenger side, it appeared to Keller the driver kept his rest stops to a minimum. The big man reached across with his hand extended.

"Name's Dave, Dave Havok. I'm rolling toward Hamilton. You?"

"I'm, uh… Pete," Keller responded, thinking fast to give himself some identity. "That near Butte?" he asked as he hopped into the passenger seat.

The driver laughed. "You ain't from around here, huh? Yah, maybe a couple of hours. About four, five more on I-90 gets you to Washington. Downtown Spokane, at least. Butte's about an hour from here," he said as he put the truck through its gears again. "Something special waiting for you there?"

Keller stared at the driver for a moment. Something special. With a stab of pain he remembered there was no one anywhere waiting for him.

"Not really… truth is, I'm just looking for work," Keller lied.

"That so," Dave replied slowly. He didn't seemed convinced.

"Not running, now, are we son? You can tell me if you need, none of my business. Everybody makes mistakes..."

"Me? Running? Uh, no, absolutely not. Just nothing back home for me. Just picked up and left."

"Where's home?"

"Hartford," Keller replied, a little too quickly.

"Connecticut?"

"Uh, no,... uh, Vermont."

"My mistake. You know there's something like 20 towns in this country named Hartford?" Dave said, trying to make conversation.

"That so..." Keller replied.

"You don't sound like you're from Vermont... Pete."

He was tiring of the conversation. The grilling was annoying.

"Well now, Dave, what should I sound like?"

He turned toward the big, gentle truck driver with the easy-going smile on his face and they both laughed spontaneously.

"Actually I was born in Madison, on the Connecticut shore. My family moved to Vermont when I was five." Lying was beginning to come to him easily.

"That right," Dave said without further comment.

For the next hour, they rode in silence, Dave expertly steering his highway chariot while Keller feigned taking in the scenery. Actually, now rested, his head clear and in no immediate danger, the ache in his heart began anew.

Suddenly, Dave started in again.

"Listen, Pete… if that's really your name…"

Keller rolled his eyes. It didn't escape the driver.

"Now, now, just trying to be helpful, that's all," he said.

"Appreciate that Dave, it's just that…" He paused, not knowing how to finish the sentence.

The truck slowed as they approached a steep upgrade and the driver expertly worked a downshift to build up a head of steam to make the climb. They had slowed to about 50 miles per hour by the time the truck crested the hill, but the sight in front of them brought out another big grin on Dave's face.

"Yessiree… nothing like two miles of downhill grade to give a man a chance to relax and save a few dollars on the go-go juice," he laughed, shifting the big rig into tenth gear, the equivalent of allowing the monster truck to freewheel.

He turned back to Keller.

"Like I was saying, just trying to help."

"Yah."

"A man can get lost in country like this, ya know. I don't mean like lost in the woods, living off the land, that kind of thing. I mean just blending into the backdrop."

Keller didn't respond.

"More than one man who calls Montana home never dreamt of being here. It was fate that dragged his tired or hurting ass out here. Sometimes to hide out from something that's chasing him. Sometimes to regroup. Sometimes to gain a different perspective on how life ought to be."

Keller turned to him. This guy knew things.

"What do you mean by 'regroup' and 'how life ought to be?'"

"Well, sorry to tell you young fella, but one look at your face says two things: you ain't from here and you wish you weren't here. Something's got you running. In fact, you've spent so much time running away you don't even know where you're running too. Worse, even if you get to where you think you're trying to get, you won't know when you're there."

"What?" Keller said, both mystified by the strangers take on him and stunned by his accuracy.

Dave summed up his analysis.

"You are, as they say, a lost soul, son."

They rode in silence for the next few miles, the only sound in the truck being the constant whirring of the truck's huge wheels on the endless highway blacktop and the roar of the giant diesel pulling the rig.

It was Keller who finally broke the silence, his head spinning. For a moment he considered that he might still be dreaming. But the racket in the cab was real.

"You know all this about me... how? I met you 15 minutes ago. Who the hell are you..."

"Someone who ain't from here either. Someone who got chased here and has made a life being invisible," David answered even before Keller had finished his question.

More silence as he mulled over this strange conversation. A reflection of Kate and the kids stared back at him in the windshield. He shuddered.

"So… say I am a lost soul."

The grin came back to Dave's face. For the first time, Keller noticed how lined his face was. They weren't only signs of age. Some of those lines came from worry. And maybe fear.

"That's a damn good place to start, son. The second thing to figure out is why? If it's obvious, like say you robbed a bank or shot a man over a woman then you pretty much have your answer. But if you're lost because someone or something is pushing you to hide, well then…"

"Then what…?"

"Well then, we're back to what I said a while back. It's time to regroup, think about what it's going to take so that you don't have to spend the rest of your life hiding." He suddenly swept his right hand across the vista in his windshield. "Although, there aren't many better places to stay lost in. Guess it all depends on another factor."

"Such as?"

"Whether or not you left something behind that means a lot to you. Enough to take the next step."

Keller was completely absorbed by what this stranger was telling him, but about to explode in anticipation.

"For Christ's sake, Dave, will you stop talking in riddles?"

The carefree grin on the driver's face disappeared in an instant. Keller thought he had offended his new friend.

"There's no riddle here, Pete. I'm about as serious as I can be. Not playing with you, boy." His tone was deadly serious.

Keller's eyes were glued to the man.

"If you decide you've been pushed here and have something worth living and fighting for back home, if you've got some unfinished business, then the next step is to learn the things that can change your perspective on life."

Keller turned his face toward the open road, fighting back tears that were about to completely give him away.

"We're different out here, son. We don't like Commies but we don't like suits, neither. We respect a man for his values and his courage, not for how much he makes or what he owns. That's the prison a lot of us ran away from."

Keller turned back.

"Some took to life and the way it is here and stayed. Like me. Some others learned how life ought to be and went back because they needed to. But with a different set of tools to work with."

"Tools?"

"Yah, tools. Easy to remember. Three words, and they all begin with the letter 'P'. Priorities. Patience. And penance."

They rode some more miles together in the quiet roar of life on the road, Keller intensely trying to interpret the unexpected lecture.

"How does one go about enrolling in Dave's school?" Keller finally asked.

"It's a hard process," Dave said, the grin poking out from under his unruly moustache again.

"Oh? Money, favors, promises? What?"

"Nothing quite so sinister. Just a question."

"A question?"

Dave laughed out loud.

"Jesus, you sure as hell ain't from around here, son. You got no manners. I'll bet your mama already taught you the words."

Keller spread his hands apart, palms up, pleading for the answer.

"You simply have to say: May I?"

Keller shook his head, laughing in disbelief at the conversation. It struck him that it was the first time he had laughed in weeks.

"May I, Dave?" he asked.

The driver reached over and slapped the young man on the thigh.

"Hell boy, what took you so long to ask?"

They laughed at that.

"Who are you?" Keller asked the driver pointedly.

The grin faded quickly from Dave's face.

"Someone who had a lot, lost more and gave up his life for the wrong reasons. A man with a lot of regrets who has learned to live with a big ache in here." He pounded his chest over his heart with a fist.

"All I got left are memories, man. Cuz I didn't take care of unfinished business. I let it take my life away."

He paused and squinted his eyes as if he was seeing something way off in the distance.

"But I'm also a guy who's been searching for a pupil for a long time. Someone to teach what I've learned in this gateway to heaven." He waved his hand at the brilliant blue sky and the endless mountain range. "Maybe just for the joy of seeing him make his world right again."

He went quiet. Then:

"Even after I've shown him how much it's going to hurt."

Nineteen

The long ride to Hamilton, Montana in the roaring eighteen-wheeler with Dave Havok was a turning point for Kevin Keller. It was on that long, lonely stretch of road that he stopped running — and began learning.

Havok pulled the giant rig off the highway at the outskirts of Hamilton without explanation and wheeled it expertly through a 10-mile stretch of snaking two-lane blacktop. His passenger had made up his mind miles back to stop asking questions and at least for the moment, go along for the ride. The driver had already proven to him that he had an acute sense of people and particularly in sniffing out those who were in pain. Kevin Keller was so lost in a world of trouble and anguish that he was just stumbling, running towards nowhere and nothing. What did he have to lose?

Still silent, Dave began gradually downshifting his rig until it came to a near crawl, than swung the nose of the tractor far into the oncoming lane before sharply pulling right into a barely noticeable entrance cleared in the heavy brush lining the road. Slowly he drove the truck along a dirt path just wide enough for the truck's tires. The dirt road appeared to have been cut by a bulldozer some years before and wound its way circuitously up a mountainside. After ten minutes or so of climbing the grade by zigzagging across the slope, Keller couldn't resist.

"Where the hell are we going, Dave? I thought you were headed for Hamilton?" he said, perplexed at his newfound friend's detour.

"Hold your horses there, Pete," he laughed, emphasizing the fake name Keller had given him.

"I thought you said you were interested in going back to school?"

"Well... I am. But is this where you hold classes?" he asked sarcastically.

"Listen. The first thing you need to do out here is blend in. To do that, you need a job. To get a job you need a name. An identity. Understand? 'Pete' isn't going to cut it. We're going to see a friend of mine about that problem."

"A friend?"

"One of *my* teachers," Havok said. "Trust me, son."

Keller looked long and hard at the truck driver. "I'm not sure why, but I do, Dave."

Havok laughed aloud again.

"Good first lesson, my student."

Abruptly, the truck reached the crest of the carved road and pulled up in front of a log cabin that was neatly hidden in a grove of thick, tall pines. The driver pulled his rig around to the back, sounded his air horn twice, then killed the motor. The immediate silence was almost shocking to Keller's ears after two hours of the diesel engine roaring and huge truck tires pounding the pavement. Havok opened the door and stepped down from the rig without a word. Keller opened his own door and hesitated. The smell of pine hung heavy in the air, which was as clear and crisp as anything he'd ever felt in his lungs.

"Well, hell boy, I told you my friend lives here, not the boogeyman. C'mon."

Before he could get out of the truck, the door to the cabin opened and a burly man in a red plaid flannel shirt stepped out onto the worn, cedar porch that stretched the length of the house. His long grey hair was pulled back into a ponytail and he had a beard that probably hadn't been trimmed before Keller was born. He was as broad in the belly as he was in the chest, and likely tipped the scales at better than 300 pounds. The suspenders he wore only emphasized the enormity of his gut.

"Well, I'll be a son of a bitch. Look what the cat dragged in," the big man said, a grin that must have been eight inches wide breaking through the huge beard. "How is it, Dave?"

"It be just fine, Sam... and you, old friend?"

"Got through another winter with a couple of cords of split wood left over, a freezer still full of venison and some of them trout you and me snagged last fall... suppose you could say I'm doing just about as good as a fella could do, Dave," he replied. He pulled a Briar pipe out of his worn denim pants pocket. "Could use a bit of tobacco though."

Dave Havok chuckled. "Its always something, you old geezer. Next run through I'll bring you a few tins of Redman, ok?

"Don't be long, boy. You know I like my smoke after dinner on the porch during the summer. Just love watching that sun ease down behind the mountains."

"Yah, I know what you mean, Sam. There are times when I'm driving back east that I have to remind myself what real living is all about."

"Yes, sir, Dave," the old man sighed. "Pity the fool who's never seen life from this angle, hey?" They both laughed. Keller wasn't sure why. The country was beautiful, but it was desolate, too. A man could get awfully lonely living this far from civilization. And what he'd learned about being lonely already was enough to make him wish he really had died in the crash into the Farmington River. He stepped around from the passenger side of the truck, surprising the old man.

"Sam, meet my new friend, 'Pete'," Dave said, introducing him with that same sarcastic twang. Sam caught on immediately. "Pete, this is my friend — and muse — Sam Dawkins. He's at least 200 years old and wiser than a parliament of owls. "

"Well, now... uh, ... it's good to meet you, son, but that won't do at all," Sam said. "No sir, not at all."

"Good to meet you, Sam," Keller said, sticking out his hand. The old man's grip was like a vise.

"What won't do?" Keller asked.

"Well, let's just say 'Pete' ain't too convincing. Man's got to have a solid name to live in these parts. Especially if he wants to earn a days keep and sort of blend in, if you know what I mean."

Keller caught Dave's wink at the older man.

"Uh, yes sir, Sam, I think I'm beginning to catch on," he said. "But how is it I go about fixing that problem," he asked. "Because I do need to find work."

"And he'll be needing to do some learning, too, Sam," Havok interjected.

"Oh. I see." The merriment of the moment faded from the grizzled face of Dave's friend.

"Dave, at the risk of offending your passenger here, maybe you and I might step inside for a minute and chat before we start to think about Pete's problem."

Havok's eyes narrowed. He was puzzled.

"Why sure, Sam." He turned to Keller. "If you don't mind, Pete…"

"Of course not," Keller replied, more confused than ever as to where he was and why.

"We'll just be a minute, Pete. Why don't you mosey on down to the barn while we're gone and meet the Mule. Jest don't walk behind him, is all."

"I'll do that Sam, thank you," Keller replied. "What's his name?"

"The Mule."

"Yah. What's its name?"

"The Mule," Sam repeated, looking oddly at Keller as if there was something unusual about his response.

Keller shook his head as if he understood and turned toward the stall. For a moment he thought about sticking to his original plan. To keep on running. Maybe he should have stayed out on the highway and found his own way to Butte. His stomach churned in anxiety. No. It was time to stop running and either dig in out here where no one would ever find him or think of another plan.

He walked over to the Mule's stall and stroked the animal's head. The grey beast was old and gentle, and welcomed the attention from the stranger. There were loud voices coming from the cabin. Keller wasn't sure what the issue was, but it was clear that Sam wasn't entirely comfortable with him. He heard the old man yell.

"I'm telling you, I can see it in his eyes. He ain't got the balls for it." Dave replied in a calmer voice but Keller couldn't make out his words.

Just five minutes later, Dave and Sam emerged from the cabin looking like nothing had happened.

"C'mon over here, Pete," Dave called. "Let's go inside."

Keller sauntered over wondering what was next.

"You hungry, son?" Sam asked.

"Uh…"

The old man shook his head then grabbed the young man's shoulder.

"Christ, you can't even tell the truth about being hungry," he said, angrily. "What kind of man are you? Just what the hell are you running from, son?"

Keller was caught off guard by the sudden change in Sam's disposition.

"I just didn't want to impose…"

"Bullshit. If a man is hungry, the answer is simple. Yes. It doesn't require any humility or courage to respond. Save those qualities for more important shit, understand?"

Keller shook his head.

Dave put his hand on Sam's chest.

"Slow down," he said. "Give him a chance."

"Chance, hell. I'm too old to waste my time on a lying pansy," he said.

He turned to Keller. "Sit down…Pete," Sam said sarcastically, pushing Keller towards a rough wooden table and a mismatched set of chairs. Keller did as he was told.

"So, let's hear it," the old man demanded. "Get it out, or get out. You get one chance."

"What…"

"What my friend 'Gentle Ben' is trying to say here Pete is we need to hear your story before we go any farther.

"My story?"

"Who or what are you running from and what's your plan," Dave interrupted. "And calm down. This old dog only looks like he's going to kill you. His bark is worse than his bite."

No one laughed.

"What the fuck…" Kevin Keller said. "I didn't come here for…"

"What did you come here for, Pete? Let's start there." Sam may not have been in a killing mood but he wasn't in any mood for bullshit.

"I was headed for Butte."

"Why."

"Needed to get away."

"From where?"

"Home."

A look came over Sam's face that would have given a rattlesnake reason for pause. He abruptly stood up, grabbed his chair and threw it across the room where it splintered against the stone fireplace.

"See what I mean, Dave? I'm too old for this crap. Too old to deal with a man who can't even tell you his real name. And he has the nerve to play 20 questions with me. He's nothing but an Ivy League pampered aristocrat who got his tit in a wringer somehow and he's running. Screw him. Get him out of here. I've had more intelligent conversations with The Mule."

"Whoa there, Sam..." Dave responded. "Since when have you been so quick to judge a man? If we'd played by these rules, you would have thrown me out too."

"I should have, you ingrate. Bringing me this worthless pile of cow shit."

Sam went to the fireplace to retrieve the remnants of his chair, which had now become a stool. He carried it back to the table and slammed it down on the floor and flopped his wide backside on it.

"You get one more chance, Pete. You want our help, answer the question. Who or what are you running from?"

Keller swallowed hard, struggling with the decision of placing his trust with these two strangers. Men who seemed to have put their lives back together again after some kind of tragedy, disaster or loss. Maybe all three.

He rolled the dice.

"I found out my company was breaking the law."

"Big fucking deal," Sam replied, unimpressed.

"They threatened to kill me and my family if I turned them in. I realized they were going to kill us all no matter what I did, just because I knew. I had to run to protect my family. So long as the guys who run my company think I'm dead, my family is safe."

Keller spit out the words in a monotone, barely hearing them himself. The simple act of admitting the truth made him shudder.

"My wife, my three kids think I died in a car accident. No body. I just disappeared. About two months ago."

Sam sucked in a huge breath of air and blew it out slowly.

"Now that is a big fucking deal," he said.

"I've lost everyone I love. I can never go back or they'll kill them." Keller's eyes filled with tears before he could hold them back and he let out a primal scream. "My life... is over."

He slammed his fists on the table in rage, over and over again.

"Maybe its not, Pete..." said Dave.

"Kevin. Kevin Keller is my name. From Canton, Connecticut."

Sam's eyes narrowed. There were signs of life in this young man afterall.

"Like I said, maybe you're life is not... Kevin Keller," Dave replied.

"How? If I go back, if those bastards find out I'm alive they'll kill my whole family! Kate. My boys, my little girl. They're gone. I'll never see them again. I can't go home, I can't protect them..." The tears overwhelmed him.

Sam suddenly pulled a huge hunting knife from a sheath taped under the table and slammed it into the rough wooden surface.

"Do you want justice, Kevin? Do you want to kill those bastards who took your wife, your kids, your life away from you? Do you?" Sam screamed.

Keller closed his eyes, relishing the vision that came to him.

"Yes... God, yes... I want to stick highway flares in Phillip Granville's eyes and cut the testicles off of Badr Laabi... I want them all dead. And I want them to suffer, to scream in agony as they die slowly. And I want to watch!" He was screaming as he spoke the words.

"I don't know those fella's, but it sounds like they given you good reason to be riled up enough to want to kill them. But prove it, Kevin, prove to me that you're angry enough to kill," Sam challenged him.

"What? How..."

Sam pulled the knife out of the table and threw it into the wall. Then he walked to the fireplace and pulled a shotgun off the wall over the mantle and threw it to Keller.

"Follow me, Kevin," Sam said, walking out the door. Dave followed.

Keller wiped the tears from his cheeks, his hands still trembling from the anger coursing through his veins. His face was beet red. At that moment he could have strangled a man with his bare hands. He pushed back from the table and followed the two men out of the cabin, carrying the shotgun in his hands.

Sam and Dave were already at the barn when he stood on the porch.

"Come here, Kevin," Sam called to him.

He walked to the two men, his rage still burning inside.

"Kill the Mule, Keller, shoot this evil bastard," Sam ordered him.

"What?"

"I said shoot this evil, good for nothing animal. He is the devil that is keeping you from your wife and children. He is Satan, he is the monster who has ruined your life, who is making you run! Shoot the Mule, Kevin, now!" Sam screamed.

Kevin Keller, who once upon a time would have trapped a housefly with his hands and let it go outside, who lived only to love his wife and children… raised the shotgun to his eye, aimed it at The Mule and pulled the triggers on both barrels without a second thought.

He stood stock still after firing the gun. There was silence.

Dave walked towards the young man and carefully pulled the gun from his hands. Keller was gripping it so tightly he had to pry his fingers off the stock and triggers. The Mule brayed as Sam pulled a piece of apple out of his pocket and fed it to the beast, then led him back in to the barn, unharmed.

The gun was not loaded.

"We had to be sure, Kevin," Dave whispered into Keller's ear. "We had to know how deep your rage was…and just how crazy it's making you."

Keller looked up at Sam as he emerged from the barn, his hands still shaking from the adrenaline that was pumping through his heart. He was still raging.

"You'll make a fine student, Kevin Keller. And your life is not over."

His words hung in the air as Sam shook his head side to side.

"Not yet."

Twenty

June 1994

From the moment Kevin Keller was lost in the Farmington River on that early spring day in 1992, few traces of him had ever been discovered. Despite weeks of searching the turbulent waters, his remains had simply vanished. The case had lingered for a few more months and there were several neighborhood searches organized by volunteers that combed miles of the river, but the only evidence ever found was a leather wallet. In it was Keller's driver's license, a couple of credit cards and some ruined, water soaked family snapshots of his wife and children. It was the only proof ever found that linked his disappearance to the crash but provided no hint of what had prompted his bizarre behavior leading up to it.

For the Farmington Police it was enough to place the case in an inactive status and in January 1993 a court ruled his death in abstentia, based largely on the extreme violence of the accident, eyewitness accounts and the discovery of his wallet. Locals figured that eventually, probably when the river swelled some spring after a winter of heavy snowfalls, his body would surface miles from the accident, perhaps even in the Connecticut River or Long Island Sound. For now, his remains were likely caught in the many hollows and crevices that lined the banks of the river.

The absence of a body made his disappearance and likely death that much more painful for the Keller family. Kate yearned to hold her husband's hand, look into his eyes and brush a kiss across his lips just one last time. To Sam, Ben and Julia, their daddy had just never come home. It was impossible for them to find closure when they had not even seen his body lying in a casket.

There was no church or gravesite service marking his passing. Kate, despite her overwhelming grief, desperately held on to every memory of being with her husband and every conversation she could remember. Faithfully, she satisfied Kevin's wish that only a simple congregation of friends and family gather to pray for his passing. It was an agreement they had made together after a brief, awkward conversation they both knew was necessary and made it official in their wills.

The couple had also agreed that their remains should be cremated and turned over to the surviving spouse. But Kate didn't even have an urn holding her husbands ashes. He had simply vanished as if he never was. Within a year of his disappearance, his personal belongings disposed of with Goodwill or put away in boxes stored in the attic, the only thing remaining of Kevin Keller was the sizeable estate he had left for Kate and the children. Between stock options, the generous company bonus General paid in the year of his court ruled death, his company 401K and life insurance, he had left his family well cared for. The house was paid for and Kate did not have to worry about their financial survival. He'd left them financially unburdened.

If only he had been able to plan so well to hide the nightmares he left behind.

Kate, terribly unstable after the shock of Kevin's loss, went into a deep, lasting depression. She had arranged for counseling for their children immediately after his death, but it never occurred to her that she might need it herself. She had virtually no family to turn to for support, as both her mother and father had died early in their marriage and she was not close to her only brother. Kevin had been estranged from his abusive parents since graduating from high school. He'd left specific instructions in his will that neither of his parents were ever to have any contact with his children so long as they were minors. Any relationships they'd had with remaining family was either fractured or had long ago evaporated.

Alone, her life had come to a sudden and brutal halt, and she lived each empty day going through the motions of tending to her children. She quit her job as a physical therapist for the elderly, having lost the compassion that had driven her to success as a specialist in the field. Now, their incapacities had become merely aches and pains for which she had no patience.

She was unaware of what she had become: lonely, so terribly lonely and obsessed with memories of her husband and the brief time they had shared together. She filled her hours following his death poring over old scrapbooks, yearbooks and family photo albums, searching for the slightest mention of his name, pictures of him (even when he was in the background), and worst of all, seeking out those few photographs where he had been in the family spotlight. The more time she spent in the effort, the sadder she became. He was in so few of the images. Kevin had simply not been around much, almost constantly working.

As well, despite the fawning of dozens of corporate executives, including Phillip Granville himself who showered her with shallow and hopelessly superficial notes and letters, she could not purge her memory of the last conversations she'd had with Kevin. The wild allegations about federal crimes, treason, doing business with embargoed nations. It was nearly more than she could bear.

Finally, after more than a year of discussions with her therapist and from time to time with Granville himself, who seized every opportunity to manipulate the widow, she became convinced that Kevin had been on the verge of a complete mental breakdown in the last months of his life that had filled his head with crazy schemes and plots. Looking back, she began to remember his bouts with discontent that she now understood as "depression."

She spoke with some of his colleagues who reluctantly agreed that her husband had seemed to be struggling with emotional challenges, some which struck them as somewhat "psychotic" in nature. It took all of her strength to gather up the memories of their last weeks together, including those that had overjoyed her, and to park them in a deep recess of her mind where she could bury them. She'd had her suspicions and concerns about Kevin's "new leaf" — a plan to quit Beckham and General Industries and start anew. They had filled her with hope. But now she knew they were the ranting's of a man who wanted and needed her love while he was slowly going mad.

But ultimately, it was her Sam, a boy of 13, who dragged her out of the black hole into which she had fallen.

The spitting image of his late father, Sam dreadfully missed the man he had never fully gotten to know, but hid his pain for the sake of his two siblings. His brother and sister leaned on him for support in the absence of their father, and worse, the emotional detachment of their mother. For as much as he mourned his dad, it was the smile on his mother's face when she saw him, the sparkling love in her eyes for each of her children and the laughter with which she filled their lives that he missed even more. He did all he could to help his mother, sensitive beyond his years to her loss and despite his own confusion and sense of betrayal. But he was wise enough to know that he alone could not fill the hole in her heart.

But for the sake of Ben and Julia, if not his own, he knew he had to bring his mother back to them.

One afternoon after school on a cold winter day more than a year after Kevin's death, Sam came home to find his mother sitting at the kitchen table, staring darkly into a half empty cup of cold coffee. She didn't acknowledge his presence. Without even knowing why, it angered him.

"What the hell are you doing, mom?" he asked her, unaware of the menacing tone of his voice. She jerked up, suddenly aware of him and his anger.

"Sam?" she said, alarmed. "What is it? Why would you speak to me like that?

He dropped his book bag to the floor and banged a balled fist on the table.

"Because I'm sick and tired of coming home to find you wasted, that's why mom," he said, his anger unabated.

"Wasted? What are you talking about? I haven't been drinking. This is coff.."

"You're acting like you're completely stoned, mom. Don't you get it? Where are you? Where is your head? I'm your son, remember? You can't even say hello!"

She saw the hurt in his eyes and was stunned by it.

"Sam, I'm so..."

"So what? So sad? So depressed, so lonely, so tired?" he screamed at her. "So what?" he yelled again, louder, but his voice began to break.

Kate pushed away from the table and slowly stood up to embrace him, but her son would have none of it.

"We're all sad, don't you get it? Ben and Julia miss him. I miss him. But you don't understand, mom."

"Understand what?" she said softly, not sure how to defend herself or if she should.

"He's not coming back! Dad is dead! Forever... he's gone, mom, he's gone." He slammed his fist again on the dining room table. "He's fucking gone! And there's nothing you or I can do that will bring him back... nothing. I pray every night. It's all bullshit."

Kate hung her head, badly needing to hold her son. But he wasn't ready to let go of it.

"He might still be out there..." she said, feebly.

Sam's jaw dropped. He had no idea she had been holding on to such fantasies.

"Out there?" He took a step closer to her and grabbed her by the shoulders. He was as tall as she was, no longer a little boy. Kate looked into his eyes and saw her husband's, the same steely blue that had gotten her attention so many years before.

"Mom, there's nothing out there... a body, maybe. But dad is gone. You've got to deal with it."

She began to sob and fell into her son's arms. He held her as tightly as he could, recognizing how shattering this moment was for her. He let her cry for a moment, wondering what to say next.

"But we're still here, mom. Ben and Julie and me... we're still here for you... with you... we need you, mom. "

Kate pulled back from her son, a look of shock on her face. It was as if someone had just slapped her.

"I'm here," she whimpered.

"But you're not, you're not with us. We're all alone, mom, you've left us, too. Dad is dead, you're alive. But there isn't much difference for the three of us."

Tears ran freely down her cheeks, her heart breaking again. It may have been the first time she had felt anything but grief in over a year.

"Please, mom... let him go," Sam begged his mother. "We're all still here for you to love. You'll never be alone, I promise."

And that was how Kate Keller began to put the pieces of her future together again, spurred by the love of her children and the final shocking recognition that the love of her life wasn't coming home again.

She would always grieve for her husband, and her children would always carry a weight of sadness at the loss of their father. But life would go on for all of them. Slowly, little by little in the next months, they began to recover, to find each other again. At every opportunity, and especially at family moments when the hurt hung over every birthday and holiday celebration like a dark, damp cloud, Kate found it in herself to dig down deep and share with her children a fond memory of her husband and their father that would make them laugh.

But some 2,300 odd miles to the west, the man Kate was desperate to put behind her was living a quiet, nearly invisible life, working as a day hand at a small ranch in Hamilton, Montana on the southwestern border of Idaho. In the tiny, one window cabin where he bunked on the ranch, the only reward of long, 12 hour days of back breaking field work on which he subsisted, he awoke each day to the glorious sight of the Bitterroot Mountains. It was part of the Rocky Mountain range that ran from Alaska to Mexico.

In the few seconds after daybreak in which his red-rimmed, sleep deprived eyes watched the majestic mountain landscape emerge from the darkness, Kevin Keller's heart was free from the sadness that enveloped his existence every day of his miserable life. It was only a momentary relief from the agony that would immediately follow. At times, the loss of his family threatened to overwhelm him like the swift, bitter cold and crushing weight of an avalanche.

The world in which he lived in total anonymity, save for the innocuous identity that he had stolen so that he could find work, was far different from that which he had come.

As far as he could see, there were no ivory towers here, no steel and glass skyscrapers with offices that overlooked cities where people lived like hamsters on a wheel to make the rich richer, the powerful, more powerful.

There were no factories run by men and companies that could not tell the difference between order and concentration camps.

There were no caste states, no cubicles, no ridicule for facial hair or the color of one's suit.

No, in this breathtakingly beautiful but gloriously inconsequential sliver of the world in which he was hiding, none of that mattered. It was a world where a man could have a soul, where he could own an opinion without fear of repudiation and earn a living by simply working — doing his job — rather than through vicariously driven, evil-minded plots to steal and plunder, no matter the pain to others. He didn't have to worry about who was slithering closer or who would rob him of his just dues at the end of a hard day.

And most importantly, here he no longer had to worry about the boogeyman, that hideous creature surrounded by gluttonous thugs who had robbed him of all that was important to him, of all that he loved. His new world gave him the time to think with the clarity he needed to map out his plan of vengeance.

He watched in awe as the snowcaps of the Bitterroots came into view and took a single moment to gloat in the ecstasy of knowing that perhaps the tables had turned.

For now, he fantasized, maybe it was the boogeyman who wondered and worried if his former employee was ever coming home.

Twenty-One

December 1996

The winters were the most difficult time.

It wasn't the harshness of the snow and cold, the short days and long nights or even the quiet of the wilderness that could drive a former city boy crazy. No, it was the beauty and isolation of winter, the sparkling clear nights where thousands of stars peppered the cloudless skies, each one a memory or a face that a man desperately tried to remember, or forget.

Tom Pulling, a.k.a. Kevin Keller, felt each day of each winter in Montana as one more slice of his life slipping away, one more image becoming a little fuzzier, another memory that much harder to recall.

But four years after he had begun to run, four years after he had put 2,300 miles between him and the danger that lurked over his family, his day of resurrection was nearing.

In his quiet, nearly invisible life working as a ranch hand, he had carved out a peaceful existence that some would suggest was a life without purpose, or "meaningless."

In the many hours of solitude that filled his life in those harsh winters, he had often analyzed that word, so cruel in its very definition. For Pulling, as he was now known by his "teachers," life was really not so much about meaningless as it was about empty. For he knew that even after all his brutally painful preparation, after all the hours of intense "learning" at the hands of Dave Havok and Sam Dawkins, and eventually, even after he had successfully achieved his plan of revenge and salvation for his family, his life would remain empty. What he would have to show for his efforts was the knowledge that those he still loved in this world would be safe, forever. And that was why he took solace from the absurdity of knowing that while his life appeared meaningless to those who might judge him, it was actually brimming with purpose and profoundly important.

In the spring, it was the work and the learning that eased his mind, allowing him to refocus on his future task and releasing him from the past.

Four years had seemed like a lifetime. But working side by side and being mentored by men who had spent a good portion of their lives learning to hide, to protect and defend as well as to punish and avenge, the time had passed more quickly than he could have imagined.

His learning had begun with an understanding of who Dave and Sam were, as well as the many others he met over the ensuing months that made up the small, mountain community largely hidden from the world.

Some were men who had broken the law and were literally running from a life in prison. Others had gone AWOL from the military, despairing of the regimented, sparse life that held values they were stunned to discover they did not share. Still others sought to escape their broken hearts, struggling through each day in perpetual mourning from the loss of a loved one. Perhaps it was the death of one revered, a spouse or child. For others it was the inexplicably cruel ending of a relationship from which they could not recover. For these men, the loss amounted to an emotional amputation, such was the depth of their sorrow.

Finally, there were the "patriots" — men who knew too much, had stumbled over a secret or crossed paths with an evil they had not understood. Consequently, they had unwittingly become a threat to powers far greater than they. These men ran from organized crime, from the military and intelligence agencies, from secret sects and unions and political leaders, or from corporations that had taken to interpret the concept of shareholder value as a license to ignore the law. In the judicial system, they were known as "Whistleblowers." In the criminal or fraudulent world from which they sought to escape, they were considered vermin of the lowest order. But as such, these men were frightfully dangerous to the guilty, and every man had a price on his head.

Dave Havok had gone AWOL during the Vietnam conflict, having finally been overcome by the blood of hundreds of horribly wounded teenage boys he worked desperately to save as a Marine medic. Sam, a licensed psychiatrist once held in high regard in the medical community, had lost his wife and three children to a drunk driver who had been exonerated in court for lack of evidence. The man had never served a day of jail time for his crime. Sam Dawkins had eventually stalked and murdered him, strangling with his bare hands the unremorseful monster that had taken all the joy from his life. He had been hiding in the wilderness for nearly two decades.

And that was why Dave Havok and Sam Dawkins had given refuge to the man they now called Tom Pulling. It was a combination of relating to the young man's plight and compassion. For on that fateful morning when he had hopped aboard Havok's 18-wheeler, Pulling unwittingly had entered a secret world of survivalists — men who had endured such pain in another life that they had sought and found an alternative way of living. They shared a common bond of unspoken pain, relying on their isolated mountain lifestyle and Sam's teachings to help them cope.

Sam Dawkins nurtured their understanding of his three P's philosophy: Priorities, patience and penance. These were the keys, he argued, to finding a new life or recapturing the old, to rediscovering happiness or accepting their fate. Without total commitment to these precepts Sam contended, they would wander aimlessly for the rest of their lives.

Dawkin's coaching was repetitive almost to the point of programming. One must identify and commit to priorities, he taught, find within him the patience to reclaim them as his reason for being, and finally, be willing to suffer or mete out the penance required to guard them.

These weren't just words, the man formerly known as Kevin Keller had discovered. They were an honest to God roadmap for existence for men who had teetered on the brink of despair or self-destruction. But it did not escape him that Sam's use of the word "penance" hid his true meaning.

Pulling pressed the older man in private conversations to clarify his understanding of penance, primarily because he needed validation of his own growing "violence begets violence" philosophy.

"I don't lobby for the dignity of murder, Tom. But Matthew 26:52 offers a clue, hey? Jesus himself said, 'For all they that take the sword shall perish by the sword.'"

Pulling was silent for a time after hearing Sam's response, digesting the words.

"I don't know what's percolating in that mind of yours, young fella, but I suspect mayhem is very much on your mind."

"From sunup to sundown and in my dreams, Sam," Pulling said. "There is no way for me to get my life back. But I can fulfill it by saving those I love. My own life means nothing to me.

"I need to sleep on that some, Tom. Because thinking and doing are two very different things. If that's your chosen path, we've got to help you learn the means of walking it."

It hadn't taken long for the grizzled old Sam Dawkins to bull his way through the cloud of confusion that had saturated Kevin Keller's brain when they were introduced. Sam had given the young man a bunk in his cabin until he could "arrange" a few things and promptly disappeared. Those few days alone in Sam's log cabin were better than any five star hotel Keller had ever stayed in after weeks of being on the road, sleeping in the outdoors and foraging for survival.

He was sleeping when Sam shook him awake a few days later. Dave Havok was with him.

"Wake up, 'Pete'..." Dawkins said as he shook him lightly. Keller was up like a shot. He'd been dreaming again, of what he couldn't remember, but terrifying enough to have him soaking wet with perspiration.

"Got a gift for you."

"A gift?" Keller replied in surprise, pulling himself together.

"Yah. You might call it the start of a new life. What you do with it is up to you," Havok said. He handed him an oversized manila envelope. "Open it."

Keller wiped the sleep from his eyes and took the envelope. He unclasped it and folded back the top, emptying out the contents. Inside were a new driver's license, a social security card, its cardboard edges bent and carefully aged, a worn copy of a birth certificate officially notarized, a U.S. Passport with only a single stamp — Mexico —and a brief dossier on the life of the man named in the official looking documents. Thomas H. Pulling, 41, of Horseshoe Bend, Idaho, population 668, 20 miles south of Boise and located near the Payette River. The town had voted heavily Republican in the last four elections and most of its inhabitants held no more than a high school diploma. Ranching, logging, agriculture, hunting and fishing were the mainstays of employment for the 90 percent white community. Boise Cascade operated a sawmill and was the town's largest employer.

Tom Pulling was unmarried, his parents were both deceased and he had no living relatives. The town hall had burned down several years before, and all tax information, voter registrar data, academic records from the town's only school and personal information on every citizen had been destroyed in the blaze. It would take a seasoned FBI agent a month to find there never had been anyone by the name of Thomas Pulling living in Horseshoe Bend. Of course, that federal agent would never have found anyone who would answer questions about the man none of them knew. Simply because it was a federal government employee who was asking.

Thomas Pulling was a man with no recorded past, but who held documents that said he was born and raised in Horseshoe Bend and was a U.S. citizen.

There was another smaller, sealed envelope inside. Keller opened it to find $5,000 in $20 bills and a set of car keys. A 20-year-old Ford F150 pickup badly in need of a paint job sat outside.

Dave Havok was right. Inside those two envelopes was a new life — or the means to get back his old one.

Kevin Keller was reborn that day under the guise of Thomas Pulling—who immediately began the training that was to help him make the decision as to which path he would take next. The new identity had given him the chance to examine his perspective on living, one that allowed him to choose to abandon his former life completely and exist in anonymity, or to follow another road that would enable him to finish his business with those who would kill him — and guarantee his family's safety forever. He had a difficult choice to make. But at least he had a choice.

Sam dragged the answer out of "Tom Pulling" with relative ease.

"Welcome to Hamilton, Tom. So...in which direction are you headed?"

The young man didn't hesitate. Looking Sam directly in the eye, he uttered one word and a simple objective.

"Home. I've got unfinished business."

Sam grinned. He personally knew the satisfaction of coming to terms with an impossible situation.

"Somehow I ain't surprised. But you know we got work to do, right? Learning..."

"Right," Pulling said. "When do we start, Sam?"

And that's how it began. The lessons on "priorities, patience and penance" were the focus of much of the coming months, each night at Sam's cabin, just a few miles away from the ranch where the old man had gotten him a job as a ranch hand tending to horses.

Every night a small group, usually a cross section of a core of about 50 people who lived in various, discreetly located cabins spread out over the foothills of the Bitterroot Mountains, would gather at Sam's and talk about the state of the government, about life, about their own frustrations with everything from taxes (that none of them paid) to the increasing difficulties of buying guns and other items overseen by government statute. The intense conversations were intended not only to keep the men connected with the world, but to remind them that the path they had chosen, whatever that was, may have been the correct one. But it also motivated them to revisit their decision, and to change their course it they desired.

Dave Havok would always join them if he weren't on the road. When he did, he would report on what he had seen in the northeast, from Washington to Maine, where his road-hauling job led him.

"Washington is completely focused on the Middle East and terrorist flare ups all over the world," he told Sam and a group of his followers following a several weeks long trip north in spring 1996. "It would seem that every governmental system in the world is being challenged.

"But Clinton and his boys aren't worried about anything in particular. Congress is out to lunch as usual, completely disengaged from anything other than the pork barrel crap that gets them elected to begin with. Wall Street is making money hand over fist, employment is high, interest rates are low and if you read the newspapers, everything is hunky dory. But it's when you pull into the truck stops, talk to folks at a diner, that's when you get the real sense about what's happening in this country."

"And that would be?" Sam interrupted.

"Well... folks ain't happy. They just ain't happy about the way things are going. Those fat, happy bastards on Wall Street are making more money than God himself can imagine and they're unchecked. They have no rules accept if it's excessive, then it must be ok. The average guy is just getting buy and praying he don't see a pink slip every Friday. See, although employment is high, it's just a game. The corporations are moving all the manufacturing jobs off shore — particularly to Mexico and China — and the guys left holding the bag are finding work at Taco frigging Bell. But still, it allows the government to report low unemployment."

"Same old shit," someone in the audience chimed in."

"Yup," said Dave. "And what's worse is that the average guy is building up more and more debt trying to keep his kids in college and they're borrowing money on their houses because their equity is just going through the roof. But that bastard Greenspan has the balls to testify that, "Irrational exuberance may have unduly escalated asset values." Can you believe that? He's admitting that it's only a matter of time until the whole house of cards comes tumbling down. But those SOB's on Wall Street and in the corner offices wearing their thousand dollar suits will still get their obscene bonuses even as the poor sucker who borrowed on his house — which eventually isn't going to be worth a shit when the whole friggin' thing turns to shit—gets foreclosed on. I'm telling you, it's the corporations and Wall Street that are running this country right into the ground. There's a tidal wave coming at us and the only guys who know it are building new tennis courts and hiring illegal aliens as cabana boys at their mansions in the Hamptons."

There was a tittering of nervous laughter across the room.

"Tell us how you really feel, Dave," Sam Dawkins said, a grin on his face as he packed his old Briar pipe.

The room erupted in laughter and someone brought Dave a beer.

He wasn't smiling.

"I'm telling you," he said, deadly serious, "the next thing that's going to happen will be another war. It will kick start the economy even higher with the frigging 'guns and butter' mentality that's built this country and the fat cats are going to get even richer. But someday, we're gonna pay a helluva price, you mark my words. Whether it's another Oklahoma City nutcase right here in the good old US of A or some rag head taking another crack at the World Trade Center, some bad stuff is gonna go down. There's just to many really pissed off people in this world, too many hungry babies, an incredible disproportion of wealth all over the world... it's a bomb ready to explode."

Now there was silence in the room.

"But you know who the real culprit in this shit is? You know who's going to eventually turn the world into a shooting gallery? I swear, it's the Pinstripers..."

"The who?" a voice called out in the room.

"You tell him what I'm talking about, Tom," Havok said to Pulling. "You tell him what they're doing — and what they're capable of."

Tom Pulling grabbed his long neck and took a slow draw from the bottle. He thought for a moment.

"Everything... and anything that will make them richer," he said. "You'd think some of these third world countries that don't have a pot to piss in couldn't afford the kind of weapons they show off, ya know? But guess again. Some of the poorest countries in the world are using the tax dollars of people who can barely afford to buy bread or rice for their children to buy new weapons, spare parts, shit...anything that will cause bloodshed — from U.S. corporations."

"That's illegal," someone said. "Don't we have sanctions against that kind of stuff...?" someone asked.

"Yah, embargoes. The State Department maintains a whole list of countries that U.S. companies are forbidden to do business with, and that doesn't just include the sale of weapons. Cuba is the most typically known, but there's also the Balkans, Burma the Congo, Haiti, Iran, Iraq, Lebanon, Liberia, Libya, North Korea, Syria, Vietnam and a half dozen African countries including Zimbabwe. Shit, I could go on."

"How do you know so much about embargoed nations, Tom," a tall, bespectacled man who had recently joined the group asked from the back of the room. "State Department after you?"

Tom Pulling didn't even crack a smile.

"Don't ask. But these are countries that have been charged with human rights violations, drug running, human trafficking, harboring or abetting terrorists...any number of despicable crimes. Of course that doesn't stop U.S. corporations from routing their products through foreign subsidiaries. They don't give a shit. As long as they get paid and show grotesque profits and Wall Street is happy enough to buy their stock, those bastards would sell cancer to their mothers."

The conversations dragged on until nearly midnight each night, giving every man a chance to examine a perspective from which to see the world. Most were content to remain hidden away, either long forgotten or of low importance to those who had once pursued them. Many had accepted being "dead" and welcomed their nearly invisible lifestyles. Then there were men like Tom Pulling, who lived each day with only one quest in his mind. Not a minute of any day passed that he didn't think of what he had been forced to leave behind, the pain he had caused those he loved, and the satisfaction he would feel when his inevitable opportunity for revenge would come.

The men he lived with taught him the hard skills he would need to fulfill his fantasy. These were capabilities he could never have absorbed in his former life, nor would he have ever wanted to. But his nightly visions of Kate, Sam, Ben and Julia pushed him to excel at talents few would ever want or need.

Tom Pulling became an expert at murder and destruction.

Trained by men who had learned all there was to know about military weaponry, explosives, hand to hand combat, survival on the run and the art of deadly improvisation, Pulling had metamorphosed from Kevin Keller the "Pinstriper" whose only weapons were his glibness, a business degree and the ability to manipulate financial data on PowerPoint slides into a lethal killing machine in just a few years. He became proficient with virtually any handgun and remarkably adept with the M16 — the standard military issue automatic rifle since the Vietnam War — to the degree that he could have earned a Marine Corps marksmanship badge of "Expert."

His accuracy had become honed to the point that he was almost as precise as a top military sharpshooter, probably within reach of the most skilled Special Forces snipers. On a particularly good day at the range, he had peppered a six inch target 300 yards away within a 1.5 inch MOA — or minute of angle — with five rounds in less than 10 seconds. It was nearly as good as hitting a target three football fields away five times in the exact same place — in less time than it took to light a cigarette.

Dave, a Vietnam veteran who had trained with the M-16, achieving a "Sharpshooter" qualification, watched in awe a few days before Christmas as Pulling shot a perfect 250 points in a shootoff.

"50 rounds, five points each, every shot dead center," Havok said in amazement. "How could a corporate pansy go from banging on a keyboard to being a crack shot in just a few years," he added. "Some men can spend entire careers in the military and never learn to shoot that well. Hell, the mechanics of killing seem to come easy to you, son."

"That's just a paper target, Dave, I haven't killed any one yet. But every time I squeeze the trigger, I think about the bastard whose head I want to blow off his shoulders," Pulling replied. "They're going to pay, Dave, believe me, they're going to pay."

Havok took a deep breath of the cold mountain air and let it our slowly.

"I believe you, Tom, and I believe you are justified in whatever you're planning on doing. Not many men could live with the heartache you have. But remember, you're going to end up paying a price too, you know that, right? The first time you pull that trigger, you're fate is cast."

Pulling didn't respond immediately, busying himself with replacing the clip on the M-16.

"What price, Dave? What price haven't I already paid? Fate? Are you kidding? I've been a dead man for the last four years to the only people in the world who mean anything to me. Do you think I give a shit about being punished? My only concern is about how much punishment I can get away with before they get me."

"Seems like you've pretty much got your 'P's in order," Dave Havok said. "Priorities, patience and penance. Betcha thought I was crazy when I told you how we live here, Tom."

"That was a long time ago. I was crazy... with fear, with sadness and anger," Pulling replied. "Maybe I'm still crazy. But if I am, there's never been another man more comfortable with being nuts. I know who I am, what's important to me... and who must pay."

He abruptly dropped to one knee and unloaded an entire clip from his M-16, shredding the center of the target nearly 500 yards away. Havok raised his binoculars to his eyes to check the target and and shook his head in amazement at what he had just witnessed. Pulling stood up and turned to him, handing his friend the empty rifle.

"So call me crazy. I've a feeling some of those boys I'm going to visit back home might be using stronger language than that very soon now," Pulling said.

"C'mon. I've got to take a drive into Libby to see a man who's got some gear with a little more range. I could use the company," Pulling said.

"Libby? Hell, that's 250 miles northwest. You can go to any Walmart to buy a rifle. Why drive four and half hours?" Dave asked, puzzled.

"Because what I need Walmart wouldn't inventory, and unless you're aware of a NATO base in the area that's in the business of lending out sniper equipment and plastic explosives…"

"Sniper? Explosives? Jesus, Tom… what are you planning?"

Pulling opened the driver's door of his old pickup and answered his friend.

"A one man war, Dave."

Havok was aghast.

"They'll kill you, Tom, you know that," he pleaded with the younger man.

Pulling shrugged his shoulders. "Maybe." He paused.

"But not if I kill them first."

Twenty-Two

September 1997

"Don't know how to thank you, Sam," Tom Pulling said, shaking the old man's hand.

"You don't have to, Tom. We're brothers. Each of us lost our way and a lot more. It's been a pleasure for me to watch you unscramble your brains, son."

"Even knowing what I plan to do, you still think I'm sane?"

Sam stared into his eyes, knowing the anger that still raged inside his friend despite his irreversible decision to free his family from a danger they didn't even know existed.

"I've never shared this with you, Tom, but a long time ago when I was in medical school I had a professor I admired tremendously. His name was Dr. Victor Frankel. He was psychiatrist, a very tragic figure who suffered terribly in a Nazi concentration camp during the War. But after being liberated he wrote extensively about his experiences in a book he wrote, *Man's Search for Meaning*."

"Can't say I'm familiar with it. It wasn't on the syllabus in business school," Pulling said. "Actually, nothing relevant to living was," he laughed.

"Well, you can imagine that Professor Frankel's experiences were horrific," he continued, intent on making his point. "But after all he had been through, one of his most profound observations was the following: An abnormal response to an abnormal situation is normal behavior. "

Pulling's eyes narrowed as he considered the remarkable words.

"Given your situation and all that you and your loved ones have suffered, I'd say that Professor Frankel would agree with me that you are quite sane. Even if your intended actions would argue against it."

Pulling looked up to the mountains again, shaking his head.

"This is what I have to do, Sam."

"I know, Tom. Just remember, justice served will not heal your wounds… or save you."

Pulling shook his head.

"I'm alright with that. The reward is worth my fate."

Dave Havok revved the diesel in his 18-wheeler pulled up outside Sam's cabin. He was going to drive Tom Pulling back east, disguised as his partner in the hauling business he ran. Pulling's old Ford pickup was hidden in the huge trailer.

"Let's go, Tom, time and fuel are wasting away here," he said, half seriously.

"So long, Sam. I can't promise to write, but I suppose you'll eventually read about me."

"Suppose I will, Tom. Good luck. See ya on the flip side, buddy."

Pulling chuckled.

"I imagine we're headed for the same next stop, Sam."

The old man grabbed his belly at that and had himself a good laugh.

He looked up at the sky. There was already snow in the clouds.

"Well, wherever that is, let's hope it's warm!"

Just after darkness a week later, Pulling rolled the pickup off Havok's trailer at a rest stop on Route 95 in southern Connecticut. The false wooden bed of the pickup held the supplies Pulling had acquired over his years in the Bitterroots.

"Got everything, Tom?" Havok asked.

"More than enough to do what I need to and then some," Pulling replied.

"Remember I always got your back, son. Come through this way pretty often. Just use that number I gave you to reach me. Never hesitate."

Pulling's eyes grew tight as he tried to hold back his emotions.

"Roger that, Dave," he said, blinking hard. "But if you don't hear from me..." He finally succumbed and embraced the man who had plucked him off a Montana highway, as lost a soul who ever lived. "I'm going to make right whatever I can. The rest I've already accepted."

Havok shook his head, fully understanding the cryptic words.

"Shove off, pal, before some State cop pulls up and wants to take a gander at my manifest."

"Right." He turned and walked to the truck, then stopped and faced his friend. "Three P's," he said.

Havok smiled.

"That there are, son," the truck driver replied. "Three P's. Let them guide you."

Pulling climbed into the drivers seat of the pickup, flashed his lights at the man who had begun his resurrection and drove off. A half-hour later he pulled into a convenience store and picked up a copy of the local newspaper. He turned to the real estate ads and almost immediately found what he was looking for.

He went to the payphone outside the store and dropped a quarter in the slot. A voice answered after several rings.

"Hello?"

"Hi. Name's Tom Pulling. Saw your ad in the paper. I'd like to lease that cottage you have available in the North Cove in Old Saybrook."

Twenty-Three

New Year's Day 1998

As the gunman made his way through the darkened streets of Seville, he marveled over how little had changed since his last visit there several years before. Something about the brightly lit Flamenco bars and the drunken artisans reveling in the celebration of the New Year made him angry. This was still such a happy place. It was a contradiction to the state of his own life, caused in part by the man he intended to visit that very day before dawn.

Walking with mobs of partying Spaniards across the Puente de Isabel II, a bridge that defined the point of entrance into the ancient Triana neighborhood on the other side of the Guadalquivir River, he kept his head down and tried to blend in. He was not in a mood to celebrate.

His destination was just ahead on Calle Betis, a street that followed the river, and he stopped to gaze at the home where he had been the dinner guest of Sebastian Oliviero. It was a great honor for the American to have been invited into Oliviero's home and the evening had been exquisite. A devilish grin broke on his face as he thought of how he would soon repay his host.

He remembered being mesmerized by the Spaniard's lovely young wife, Adonia, with her flowing black hair and sensuous dark brown eyes who Sebastian had coerced into dancing the Flamenco for their guest. And they had gotten very drunk on a red tempranillo wine from the Valdepeñas region that the charming Spaniard explained he had purchased specially in honor of Keller's visit because it was American author Ernest Hemingway's favorite when he wrote for a time in Spain.

He blinked hard at the memories. He wondered how something so sweet could leave such a vile aftertaste.

Tonight, the stranger knew that Oliviero and his wife would be entertaining another old friend for the New Year's celebration, Jean-Pierre Chandon, an unmarried Frenchman visiting from Paris.

None of them would be expecting his unannounced visit, which he believed would be brief — and memorable.

But as he approached Oliviero's three-story apartment overlooking the river near the famous *Casa Anselma* flamenco bar, the stranger experienced a twinge of remorse. Adonia, his wife should not see him. He preferred to leave her out of his plan and rather, like his own wife, be left behind to mourn her husband.

Quickly, he modified his plan to accommodate this new thought, including his all important exit strategy. He reminded himself of the importance of leaving here tonight, undiscovered.

There were so many more visits to make.

He took the disposable cell phone he had purchased out of his pocket and dialed the number to Oliviero's apartment. It rang several times before Adonia answered.

The lilting voice of the slightly drunk Spanish beauty spoke into the phone.

"¿Hola? Que hay de nuevo?"

With no fear that she would recognize his voice, he answered.

"Hola, señora," he replied. "Es el Sr. Oliviero en la casa, por favor?"

"Sí, un momento, por favor."

He heard the voices of Oliviero and Chandon questioning who would be calling at nearly four o'clock in the morning.

"Sí, este es el Sr. Oliviero. Quién está llamando?"

"Feliz Año Nuevo el Sr. Oliviero, es un viejo amigo," Keller responded in the little bit of Spanish he knew. " Happy New Years, Senor Oliviero, it is an old friend," he repeated in English. "Do not be alarmed, I am here to surprise you."

"Surprise me? Who is this?" the Spaniard asked suspiciously.

"Oh, you will ruin the surprise if I tell you. Please, join me at the Chapel of El Carmin. It is just two blocks from you at the Puente de Isabel. I have a gift for you and Jean-Pierre."

"Jean-Pierre as well?" he laughed, dropping his guard. Keller heard muffled conversation between the two.

"Si, we will be right there. I hope this is worth the walk!"

"Oh, trust me, my old friend, I have been looking forward to this for some time..." The stranger could barely keep from crushing the cell phone in his grip. He hung up then carefully removed the SIM card from the device, removing its data and rendering it useless. Looking around to make sure he wasn't being observed, he walk back to the bridge, leaned over the railing and threw both pieces into the river. Then he made his way to El Carmin, a Moorish Revival chapel that stood at the entrance to the Triana Bridge, Puente de Isabel.

As he expected, the door was opened. He pushed one of the great, ornate wooden doors aside and slipped into the dark room, lit only by the reflection of the multi-colored decorative lights hung off the bridge outside. The miniscule amount of light entering through the chapel windows gave him the perfect shadows in which to hide. Tinges of red and yellow light painted the inside of the chapel in an eerie, if not appropriate vestige of the unholy trial that would soon be played out here.

Reaching behind his back, the stranger pulled out a small, 12-gauge flare gun, the type used by mariners in distress, that he had purchased at a hardware store upon arrival in Seville. One did not need a gun permit to purchase the device and he paid for it with cash. His next stop had been a plumbing supply shop where he purchased a harmless four-inch length of galvanized pipe, no questions asked, that happened to be the exact dimensions of the plastic barrel on the flare gun. The final stop on his odd shopping spree was at a sporting goods shop where he had purchased a half dozen 12-gauge shotgun shells loaded with 00 buckshot.

He had removed the plastic barrel on the flare gun and replaced it with the galvanized metal pipe at his hotel room shortly before leaving for Seville and all that was left to do now was to load the first of the shells. With that complete, his sailor's tool — an object intended to bring mercy and salvation to those in danger on the seas — became a lethal weapon capable of taking life in dramatically gruesome fashion.

Within ten minutes, the gunmen heard the loud, drunken voices of the two Europeans and stepped back into the darkness to hide himself. Oliviero opened the door and peered inside and seemed afraid to enter but was pushed inside by a laughing Chandon. The two men stood side by side, laughing, when their "surprise" stepped out into the light.

"Ah, there you are!" Oliviero laughed.

At first the two were delighted upon seeing the man with the orange colored, clown like pistol in his hand. Then they took a closer look at his face. The stranger pulled down his collar to give them a closer look. Chandon gasped first. Oliviero stepped back in fright. That was when the gunman pulled the trigger, firing directly into the center of where they were standing, hitting both, the 00 buckshot doing its job.

Oliviero screamed and fell to the floor. Chandon slumped to his knees. Each was bleeding extensively from multiple wounds on their arms and chests. The lightly choked shotgun shell had exploded in a wide, flesh tearing pattern. The gunman took his time, pocketed the spent shell casing and reloaded.

"Hello, gentlemen, do you remember me? Allow me to wish you a Happy New Year again. Do you like my surprise?"

Before either of the Europeans could scream a response or plead for his life, the gunman aimed his makeshift killing tool at Oliviero's head from no more than four feet away and pulled the trigger. The explosion of buckshot, masked by the noise of the revelry outside, hit the Spaniard full in the face and throat. His head slumped to one side, nearly torn from the neck, and he fell heavily to the ground, dead. The Frenchman screamed.

"Don't bother, no one can here you," the gunman said as he again pocketed the spent casing and reloaded again. "And so you don't think I am more favorably inclined to the Spanish than the French, allow me to give you the rest of your surprise, Jean-Pierre." He pulled the trigger again, this time decapitating his victim.

Calmly, without hesitation or emotion, he reloaded twice more and shot each of the unfortunates directly in the chest, flaying them open like wild game being field dressed.

He reached into his pocked and pulled out one last shell.

"Pity, such a waste," he said, reloaded and shot Sebastian Oliviero in the groin just for the satisfaction.

"You won't be screwing anyone else, my friend."

Moving quickly now, the gunman hid the flare gun in his belt and zipped up his coat. He reached into his jacket pocket and counted the empty shell casings. Six. Then he stepped around the bodies, careful not to step in the pools of blood or to brush against the ooze sliding down the walls and benches of the chapel and opened the door a crack. There were hundreds of people milling about outside, oblivious to the carnage inside the venerable El Carmin. He squeezed through the small opening and stepped briskly into the moving pedestrian mobs without being noticed.

After re-crossing the bridge, he turned left and one kilometer down the street found the parked SEAT Toledo sedan that he had stolen in Seville earlier in the day. He jumped in, hotwired the ignition to start it and pulled into the light traffic without incident. He drove five more kilometers away from the Triana Bridge before pulling the car over and killing the engine. Walking across the street, he stepped up to the railing protecting pedestrians from the Guadalquivir River and after checking to see that he was alone and unobserved, tossed the flare gun and the shell casings as far out into the river as he could. The splashes were undetectable.

Returning to his car, he drove another ten kilometers then pulled off the road and hid it in a commuter parking lot. He pulled out a handkerchief and wiped down all surfaces of the car that he had touched then stepped outside and did the same with the door handle. Without stopping, he turned his back to the car and began walking towards a bus stop two kilometers away. Just as he reached the waiting zone, the first bus of the morning arrived, its lighted destination placard reading "*Aeropuerto de Sevilla.*"

He boarded the bus, taking his time and avoiding eye contact with the few other passengers. Slouching down in a seat next to a window in the rear, he leaned back and closed his eyes. The sun was beginning to rise. In the distance, he thought he could make out the sound of police sirens. He ignored them. In an hour he would be at the airport.

Despite his efforts to stay awake, the adrenalin that had been streaming through his body for the last 24 hours had taken its toll. He told himself he could fight through the fatigue.

Unexpectedly, the face of a woman appeared in his eyes. She was crying and small children were holding on to her black skirt, tugging at her, their faces also lined with tears. In her hands she clutched a small red rose. He watched as she took a step forward and placed it next to a photograph placed on a small table at the foot of an altar. They were in a church.

A tall, thin man, a priest, took her hands and squeezed them. He was wearing vestments embroidered with real gold and precious stones. It shimmered in the light and cast a halo around him. She was startled to see that the priest wore custom made shoes and a very expensive gold watch. The priest spoke to her, quietly, trying to sooth her. He touched her face. She pulled away from him, repulsed.

The woman turned, leading her children back to a pew in the front row of the church. The priest returned to his altar then climbed the few steps to the top of a pulpit and began reading. The woman bowed her head and wept. The children drew closer to her, trying to console her.

Abruptly, the priest stopped talking, climbed down the steps of the pulpit and walked off the altar without another word. In the church, people began to stand up and exit their pews. The stranger noticed they were all men. He was frightened.

He saw that instead of leaving the church, the men began to walk towards the woman and her children. He screamed for her to run from them, but she could not hear him. She remained motionless in her seat, surrounded by the children, continuing to weep.

Suddenly she sensed the presence of the mob of men around her and she spread her arms to gather the children, drawing them to her. A look of terror crossed her face and she screamed, but no sound came out. The men moved forward, blocking his vision of her. He yelled to her to fight back and began running towards her, to save her…

"El Senor, Senor, por favor despierta. Hemos llegado al aeropuerto de Sevilla." He opened his eyes. A man was shaking him. He lunged up and grabbed him by the throat, trying to push him away.

"El Senor," the driver said, choking. "Lo siento, pero que estaban durmiendo. Hemos llegado al aeropuerto de Sevilla."

His heart was racing as his mind slowly cleared and he **remembered** where he was. He shook his head to the bus driver, saying several times "Lo siento, lo siento," I am sorry.

The driver smiled, feeling victorious. "El Senor, Aeropuerto de Sevilla, el Senor!" he repeated, pointing in the direction of the terminal.

"Gracias, gracias," the stranger said and managed to get out from his seat and shakily stand up.

He walked down the aisle with the driver in the lead and departed the bus. He had been sweating in his sleep and the cool fresh air immediately helped to clear his head. He hurried off in the direction of the terminal not wanting to create any more of a disturbance. The terminal was already busy with people and he walked awhile trying to blend in. Assured that he wasn't being followed or watched, he reached into his pocket for the small key to the locker he had rented when he arrived from New York yesterday. He needed a shave and a change of clothes. He looked at his watch for the first time in hours. It was 06:15 hours.

He checked the departures board for flights to JFK. Iberia flight 3951, departing 13:50 hours with a stop in Madrid. Just what he wanted.

Before purchasing his return ticket, he found the locker he had rented and retrieved his overnight bag. He paused to take advantage of the small bit of privacy afforded by the narrow metal chamber and pried up the bag's false bottom before pulling the bag out into the open. Underneath the thick cardboard were several counterfeit US passports, matching driver's licenses and credit cards. He had used one set of the fake identification to leave New York and pass through customs in Seville. He selected another for the return. The documents were the best investment he had ever made, difficult as they were to come by even in the world of secrecy and isolation he had discovered. They came with a steep price but from people he would trust with his life.

Looking over the array of false documents in the bag, he thought for a moment about the long road he had travelled to become good at disappearing into the shadows and going completely underground when it was required. But more importantly, he considered how good he had become at exacting retribution from those who had taken his life away from him.

He picked up the fraudulent passport, license and credit card that gave him the documented individuality necessary to pass through borders or for renting a car or a room, and stared at them. The stranger grimaced at the obscenity of the things. They had replaced him. He no longer had a real identity.

By forcing him into the dark and robbing him of a meaningful existence, those who had taken his life had rendered him not only nameless, but empty, as well.

There remained only one reason for his continued being and survival.

To finish the killing that would save the ones he had loved and lost.

Twenty-Four

Nearly 20 hours later, the stranger pulled his old pickup onto the single lane road off Saltus Drive in Old Saybrook and drove the final 100 yards to the decrepit cottage he'd rented. He was completely exhausted, but eager to see if there was any mention of his visit to Seville on the news. Following his usual security precautions, he sat in the truck for several minutes after killing the headlights and listened and watched. The only noise was the sound of him unscrewing the top off the pint of Popoff he had hidden under the front seat and the soft splash of the nearby surf. He put the bottle to his lips and pulled deeply as he scanned the property around the derelict cottage. All was as quiet as he had expected.

    The door of the truck squeaked as he pushed it open and he waited again for any sign of intruders. Then he walked around to the front of the cottage and down to the beach, checking the sand for footprints with a flashlight he had taken from the truck. The water was freezing cold, but nevertheless looked inviting. Not yet, he told himself. There will be peace in the waters, but not yet. There was more to be done and he had to be sure before he found his own way out.

He quietly let himself into the cottage and intentionally left the lights off. Finally convinced that he was alone, he turned on the transistor radio and listened for news of Seville. There was nothing.

He almost felt let down, but quickly told himself that no news was good news. It bought him more time. But he was smart enough to know that it was only a temporary reprieve. As certain as the morning's sunrise, the noose was already tightening around his neck. It was inevitable. But perhaps those who would hunt him were finding his trail more difficult to follow than he had anticipated.

He pulled the bottle out again and drank from it, then lay down on his bed. He forced himself to relive the past two days, desperate to find an error or a crack in his plan that might have given him away.

Even has he cleared Customs at JFK with his fake passport, he wondered how he been able to manage so much carnage without a slip up that would have the law breathing down his neck. He was intelligent enough to know that police and probably federal agencies on at least two continents might be looking for him, especially if they had discovered that the same company employed all four of the murdered victims.

Eventually, fatigue and alcohol combined to knock him out. He no longer really slept. The only time he rested was when his body gave out. But his mind never stopped working, thinking, reliving.

There was no escape from the living hell in which he found himself trapped. The moment he closed his eyes, as always, they were upon him, feasting on his torment, feeding his mind new horrors to contemplate.

He was out for no more than two hours when he awoke with a start, soaked through his clothes with sweat, unsure of where he was.

Then he remembered. All of it.

He lit a cigarette and took another pull from the bottle trying to clear his head.

The stranger pondered if those who were left knew he was coming for them. The others hadn't, but how could they? They must have been convinced that he was long gone. But by now, perhaps they were panicked, worrying that they were wrong. And that he had been watching them the whole time. No, he concluded. They would have no reason to think of him. He had been dead too long.

But worse, he imagined, was the truth that must have hit them by now. A monster with an insatiable desire for bloody vengeance was stalking them.

And it was their own greedy arrogance that had unleashed him.

Twenty-Five

Detective Sergeant Michael DeStephano and his partner, Detective Dennis Leery pored over the information coming into Farmington Police Headquarters via computer link with the Federal Bureau of Investigation and the International Criminal Police Organization, or INTERPOL.

It was late and the two men had been living off cold coffee and cigarettes most of the day. But the news that was coming in from INTERPOL's headquarters in Lyon, France about the murders of two Beckham executives in Seville, Spain less than 24 hours before had them mesmerized.

"Christ, what is this, some kind of medieval corporate takeover?" Leery said sarcastically. "Kill off all the big swords and pillage whatever's left? "

DeStephano was a bit more studied in his approach.

"Four senior executives of Beckham murdered in less than 96 hours. I'd say someone is pretty pissed off. There's not a chance in the world that this is coincidental," the senior detective replied.

"Especially given the way they were taken out. I mean, these guys were not just murdered, they were executed. A shotgun at close range. That will get your attention."

"Yah, whoever's working this plan is one angry guy," Leery replied. "Or maybe 'guys.' That's a lot of killing for one person. Whether it's one or a bunch, they're moving fast."

DeStephano laid eight by ten glossy photos of the four victims side by side on his metal desk. He had to clear away a dozen case files and a bunch of empty Styrofoam coffee cups to make room.

"What do we know about these four guys, except they each earn more money in a month than the two of us combined make in a year?" the detective asked.

"And don't forget the cars. They all get hot shit cars," Leery added.

DeStephano laughed. "And I'll bet they all pay alimony. Life at the top isn't always what it's cracked up to be, Dennis."

"Yah... but I wouldn't mind a go at it."

The two detectives studied the photos. Other than their place of employment, the victims shared little in common. Only one was American and had no criminal record. Hell, DeStephano thought, Paul Stanton was as close to a model citizen as you might find. A typical Farmington swamp Yankee, the best schools, even played some baseball. The rest were all

Europeans. Check that, he thought to himself. Laabi wanted to make you believe he was European. But last time he checked, Morocco was part of the African continent. North Africa, heavily influenced by the Europeans, but Africa nonetheless.

"An American, a Spaniard, two Frenchman," Leery said.

"Correction. One Frenchman. One African."

"Morocco...?"

"Yah."

"Sorry. Didn't cover much geography at the police academy," the junior detective countered.

"Read a newspaper."

"But..."

"Sports section doesn't count," DeStephano bantered.

"Yah, I guess. So what have we got?" Leery asked.

The lead detective paused and thought hard. A couple of minutes passed.

"Nothing. I'd say absolutely nothing. Except someone's obviously got a real hair across his ass for Beckham... or maybe General Industries."

"Or maybe Phillip Granville, your old friend," Leery added. "What better way to get at Granville then to take his goon squad apart one by one. Actually, the way this guy's going at it a better description would be piece by piece."

DeStephano looked up at his partner. "Interesting idea."

"I'm no Wall Street whiz, but I hear tell that the financial analysts — the guys that keep Granville living in the style he's accustomed to — don't much cotton to upheaval or uncertainty on the management team or in the Board Room," Leery added. "Our man could be attempting to bring Granville down off his lofty perch."

"True... but why not just take him out? Lord knows Granville's got no friends other than the guys who are making him money. And those aren't really friends... just hangers on who are getting fat and happy with him."

He thought some more.

"Nah... it's more. They're something else driving this. Something real personal, I think."

"Like the guy got fired? Pretty extreme reaction, ya think?"

"No, more than that." Det. DeStephano silently puzzled over what slight could make a man so angry with his superiors that he would murder them. In a way that was sure to attract a lot of attention.

"Well, if ain't revenge... what could piss off a guy enough to make him go serial?" Leery asked.

"Maybe it's not revenge at all. Maybe it's fear."

"Whoa...now there's a twist, boss. But guys who are afraid usually run. Hide. Go to Wyoming or build lean-to's in the woods where there's nothing but bears and snakes to worry about. This guy is front and center. He's not advertising his identity, but he sure as hell isn't hiding."

"Yah," DeStephano said shaking his head. "Usually a man goes on the offensive to win. I wonder if our guy has come out of hiding to protect."

"Protect what?" Leery asked, not sold. "I dunno. Granville's a big enough scumbag to convince me he's got someone who hates the smell of him hot on his tail. And whoever it is, they're just toying with him by knocking off his buddies one by one."

Leery took a sip from his cold coffee and lit another cigarette. He studied the pictures again and sighed.

"You might be right, Dennis," DeStephano said. "But something isn't right here. Just can't put my finger on it." He took the photos from Leery then threw them down in disgust.

"Waste of time. These aren't going to tell us anything. Unless there was something these guys shared. Some kind of secret that our guy was on to. Something they knew about the guy who sent them to the promised land."

They were quiet for a moment, each lost in thought.

"Notice how we've suddenly narrowed this down to 'one guy'?" Leery asked.

His boss raised an eyebrow.

"Call it a hunch. I've had a couple of those lately."

"So where do we go from here?" Leery asked. "I've got a hunch of my own that this isn't over. That our friend has another target — or targets — in mind. I don't have a clue how to get ahead of that. Developing a list without knowing his motive is going to be a bit difficult."

DeStephano mulled over the question. Leery was right. He had good instincts for a fairly young guy. That came with being naturally cynical.

"Let's start by interviewing the first line of people who reported to these guys. INTERPOL will help us with the Europeans. We can handle Laabi and Stanton's people."

"Ok." Leery sighed. It was going to be a long night for a lot of people.

"And while we're at it, let's wake up a judge and get a subpoena to make General Industries supply us with a list of every executive it has let go — under less than friendly circumstances — over say..." he thought about the time frame, "the last five years." He paused again. "No, make that the last ten. Guys who are this pissed off tend to hang onto their anger a long time."

"I'm on it," Leery responded without question.

"And let me have the subpoena. I'm going to drop in on Mr. Granville again tonight and it will be my pleasure to hand deliver it. And the news."

Leery looked up.

"What news?"

"I've another hunch that however many more people might be on our guy's list, Granville's name is at the top. Actually, he'll probably be the last to be targeted.

"Sort of like dropping the cherry on top of a hot fudge sundae. It's the first thing you look at, but the last thing you eat."

Twenty-Six

It was pushing 10 p.m. by the time the senior detective came calling at Phillip Granville's office in the headquarters of General Industries in downtown Hartford. He had no problem pulling his unmarked police sedan into the covered parking garage adjacent to the 26-story skyscraper, but was met by two burly, uniformed security guards when he tried to enter the building.

"Evening, gentlemen," he said pleasantly to the two retirees, both of whom he recognized as former Hartford cops. "Hope I'm not taking you away from reruns of *Starsky & Hutch* or something similarly educational," he bantered.

"Don't bust my balls," the heavier set of the two quipped to DeStephano. "It's late, there's no one here. Why don't you go back to Farmington, buy a dozen doughnuts and then take a nap behind the Post Office for the balance of your tour like the rest of your crew," he said sarcastically.

The detective laughed out loud.

"Christ, the good times are hard to forget, hey pal? Betcha that scam worked pretty well for you to be able to pull your 20 in one piece and land this little piece of heaven. Why, you could probably do this corporate gig for another 30 years and never break a sweat, some kind of record. Speaking of doughnuts, you might want to look into Weight Watchers or something..." He patted his belly and shook his head in disgust at the paunch the guard was carrying around his middle. "Livin' the life, hey Sarge?"

"Look, we don't want no trouble here, just doing our jobs, Detective," the other guard said trying to diffuse the tension. "But unless you've got official business here, my partner and I are going to have to ask you to leave or we'll call the HPD."

"Oh, geez, a voice of reason," DeStephano said mockingly. "He reached into his suit jacket and pulled out the subpoena and handed it to the guard.

"You can borrow my reading glasses if you need, old timer, or I'll save you some time. It says produce Phillip Granville pronto. That means now."

"But..."

"But nothing, butthead." He pointed to an obscenely sleek car parked in an oversized slip with orange parking cones surrounding it. It appeared to be doing Mach 1 just sitting there.

"That's the man's sweet ride parked right over there, if I'm not mistaken. An Aston Martin, right? Vanquish? Sure. Top of the line for the discriminating man. In Cobalt Blue. I dare say, properly British. I'm told he doesn't leave home without it. So, if he's upstairs, you both better lead the way unless you want me to call the HPD and have your fat asses arrested for obstruction. You dig, boys?"

The junior guard looked puzzled.

"How do you know so much about the guy's car? You got some sick interest in Mr. Granville or something?"

"Let's just say I know everything there is to know about Phillip Granville and then some, slob. Including that yes, I have an overwhelming curiosity about his sick interests."

"You mother..." the heavy one began.

"Yah," the Farmington detective said. "Mine says hello, too. Get moving asshole."

The guards exchanged glances, knowing that DeStephano had them by the short hairs. It was either take crap from Granville's chief of security or spend the night in a holding cell. This guy wasn't kidding.

"Follow us, detective sergeant,'" the obese guard said with ridicule. They led DeStephano to an elevator that took them to the 24th floor and then to another private car that took them to the 26th floor, which was reserved strictly for Phillip Granville and his direct reports.

The big guy picked up a telephone in the lobby of 26 and dialed a single digit that connected him directly to Granville's office. He sputtered through an explanation of the situation to Granville's secretary who was obviously giving him a hard time.

"I got no choice, Cindy, the son of a bitch has a subpoena... yah. I'll hold." He looked up at the ceiling, talking to himself. "Like I need this shit..." He waited a few minutes then perked up at the sound of a voice, before turning an unhealthy shade of pale.

"Uh, yes sir. We'll bring him right there."

The guard turned to DeStephano. "Ok hotshot, you got your 15 minutes. Follow me."

"No need, big fella, I know the way. Wouldn't want you to get your sweat socks damp. Thanks for the hospitality," the detective said and marched off to Granville's office leaving the two guards with their mouths agape. Surprisingly, the chairman and chief executive officer met him at the door to his private suite of offices with his hand outstretched. Despite the inexplicably warm welcome, DeStephano thought he looked a little green around the gills.

"So what do I owe the pleasure of your unannounced visit — even if court approved, Detective DeStephano? It's always such a pleasure to see you even at this late hour. And how is your lovely family? You know, I do admire you. Giving up your own life to help raise those children. Not many men would do it. Your loyalty is a trait I respect."

The mention of his family sent a stabbing pain up the detective's neck. It was the kind of physical reaction he always had when he was confronted with a slime ball he wanted to choke to death with his bare hands. Unconsciously, he moved his left arm in such a way that he brushed the 9mm Smith & Wesson semi-automatic service pistol hanging in the shoulder holster under his jacket. The invisible touch allowed him a second to fantasize squeezing off a round aimed directly between this prick's eyes.

"Thanks for asking, asshole. I'm sure your wife and kids are waiting up for you, too. You strike me as the real huggable type, Granville. And as to your admiration, the only thing you should remember is that I'm loyal to a badge which stands for putting bad guys in jail. And you, big boy are my number one priority. Now how's that for loyalty?"

The CEO's blue eyes glistened at the retort by the detective. He was a sharp one, all right. Too bad his morals were stronger than his lust for the finer things, Granville thought. He ignored the detective's threat.

"As you well know, marriage and I have had a rather rough go of it, detective. Intimate relationships are not my strong suit. It seems we make strange bedfellows." He laughed at his own lame joke.

"Ya got me there, Granville, a real knee slapper," DeStephano replied, ridiculing the man who could buy and sell him a thousand times over. "But actually, I'm not interested in your love life, or whatever you might call it. I have some serious questions that need some answers. Shall we go to your office or would you rather I begin with a couple of security guards and your private secretary as witnesses?"

"Come right in, detective. My, but we are efficient."

DeStephano laughed.

"You know, that must be your key to success, Granville. There is simply no way anyone could take you seriously. You're just a pathetic piece of shit who likes people to believe that you're j a harmless, charming biz whiz. But I know the truth, hot shot."

"And that would be...?" Granville smiled, enjoying how easily he could get a rise out of the hapless cop.

"That you are a ruthless, disgusting pig who hurts people for the fun of it. And one of these days I'm going to nail your ass, buddy and you're going to spend some time far, far away from this little pleasure palace built by your idiot shareowners and have lots of fun being your cellmate's boy toy."

Granville's smile faded quickly.

"Let's get this over with, Detective, I've got other plans for the evening. What is it that you want?" He was suddenly all business.

"For starters, this subpoena requires you to provide us the names and last known whereabouts of every executive level employee that has left General Industries Corporation under any circumstances over the last ten years. By the way, the last four on the list should be easy to come up with. Hell, the bodies in Seville haven't even cooled yet."

Granville had his back to the detective, pouring himself a drink as DeStephano finished. The CEO's hands visibly shook at his visitor's last words.

Nonetheless, he turned and faced the detective with cool calm.

"Yes, quite disturbing news from Spain. But I trust the Spanish authorities and INTERPOL have the investigation well in hand. These last few days have been quite stressful and a tragic loss for our shareholders. The financial analysts who track our stock are quite concerned. I must address that situation without delay."

"Oh, sorry, didn't know you or your shareholders were all broken up by the well planned murders of four of your corporation's top executives within a 96 hour period. How silly of me. And you in particular, Mr. Granville, seem terribly saddened. I must get in touch with my inner self and learn to be more sensitive in such situations." DeStephano's hatred of this guy was so deep he couldn't resist any opportunity to stick it to him.

"I'll take that as an apology, Detective Sergeant," Granville responded.

"None extended."

"Ah... some grudges never fade, do they... your family's pain has..."

DeStephano's head felt like it would explode.

"You so much as mention them again," he interrupted, "and I will have no recourse other than to rip your rib cage out of your chest with my bare hands for resisting arrest."

The CEO's eyes widened. For the first time, Granville was genuinely wary of the Farmington policeman. He had pushed him too far. And he was smart enough to know that it would take far more protection than the "rent-a-cops" he employed who were parked outside his door to protect him.

The CEO nodded to the detective, whose face was still the color of a nearly ripe plum.

"My apology," he said with disingenuous remorse.

"Yah. The list, Granville. I want the list. By tomorrow, noon. Understand? If you let someone go in the last ten years for so much as stealing a sugar cube from the company cappuccino maker I want to know about it and where to find the culprit. Understood?"

"Of course, Detective. But I must ask the reason for this, shall I say, request. I mean, you can't possibly think that horrible business in Seville has any connection to what happened in Farmington last week? Or that someone who was once in the employ of General Industries felt so betrayed or mistreated as to become a serial killer? My God, man…"

DeStephano shook his head.

"What exactly did you score on your SAT's, Granville? Of course they're connected. Or do you typically have four top executives of your corporation murdered on a weekly basis? This isn't coincidence, you brick head."

Granville was silent, staring into his glass, bristling at the disrespect.

"Guess it doesn't take much to run a big company after all…" the detective said, watching and enjoying the powerful man wince.

"And as to God…"

Oh, how he enjoyed this.

"If I were you, I'd start praying to the big guy. Because I've got a strong feeling that whoever is pissed off enough at you or your company, mad enough to brutally murder four men in very graphic fashion, then…"

DeStephano paused, waiting for the obvious to sink into Granville's brain.

"Then what?" the CEO asked a little too quickly, obviously unnerved.

The detective laughed quietly to himself.

"We'll then, I'd say that you and my brother actually had something in common."

Granville smiled. Finally the opening that would give him the last laugh.

"Now what could that possibly be?" he asked arrogantly.

DeStephano didn't hesistate.

"Fate."

Granville's eyes went wide.

"Fate?"

"Yup.

"God himself couldn't help either one of you."

F. MARK GRANATO

Twenty-Seven
~~~ ~~~

February 1998

Phillip Granville was a man who generally slept well and without disturbance, unbothered by the pressures of running a $30 billion multi-national enterprise that employed more than 200,000 people. One would think that the tremendous burden associated with managing the day to day operations would tend to keep him somewhat anxious if not entirely obsessed.

But Granville had long ago learned the art of surrounding himself with those who would worry for him, those who would lie awake at night fretting over mountains of issues and predicaments to which Phillip Granville himself held them accountable. Consequently, his most powerful managers lived their lives in a constant state of agitation and anxiety, a psychological hell that kept them razor sharp to signs of failure by their subordinates with zero patience for slipups. Granville held their blind loyalty by paying them obscene amounts of money that allowed them lavish lifestyles and gave them unassailable power that only he could question. They were his personal army, their allegiance sworn to him without hesitation or even the thought of ever questioning his orders or decisions. The cubicle dwellers saw them as Granville's "keepers," a group that ensured the CEO would never have to dirty his own hands with the nasty work that was required for keeping his empire in order. It was simply taken care of without him even asking.

In truth, Granville's army bore similarities to a pack of savage hyenas ready to pounce and rip out the throat of any one who would challenge their leader. Badr Laabi, Paul Stanton, Sebastian Oliviero and Jean-Pierre Chandon were all members of this pride and managed their own families of two legged corporate thugs to see that order in Phillip Granville's kingdom was never challenged.

But now they were gone. Four of Granville's most trusted assassins had been murdered, their own hideous behaviors eliminated in an instant by a judge and jury even more merciless than the CEO had ever imagined. One by one, his band of mercenaries was being stalked, hunted down and murdered.

And for the first time in his career, Phillip Granville felt the pangs of anxiety as he tried fruitlessly to sleep after Detective Sergeant Michael DeStephano's parting words.

"God himself can't help you…"

Granville leaned back in his ridiculously expensive desk chair and sipped from a snifter of brandy.

"God," he silently mused. Was that an entity he should be afraid of? Was the possibility that there was actually a day of reckoning making him anxious? He took a deep pull from his glass and chuckled to himself. After all, he didn't really believe in God. To believe would require him to admit that he at the least had an equal, and that would not do.

He waited in his throne room as those members of his pack that he had called were assembling in the conference facility. He had put out the call two days ago. Some of his army had a long way to travel on such short notice. No doubt they would be anxious too, for it was unusual to be called with no explanation, no warning. Yet they each instinctively knew why they had been called. And they were not unaware that there would be four empty seats in the room.

The lights on the top floor of General Industries Corporation were burning late again, Detective Sergeant Michael DeStephano observed from the driver's seat of his unmarked police car parked on a side street in Hartford. He was way outside his beat, doing stakeout work where he should be depending on the local cops to help him out. And they would, he knew, with just a phone call. But this was personal. Very personal. He would just lay low, cause no trouble. For all he wanted to do was observe the arrival of the other General executives he believed were on the killer's list, those no doubt having been summoned by Phillip Granville himself.

He had been tipped off by a well-placed source in the U.S. Customs Service. His partner, Detective Dennis Leery had asked that they be alerted to any unusual influx of General and Beckham executives coming into the country shortly after DeStephano's last meeting with Phillip Granville. He'd had another hunch that Granville would be pulling his troops together for a strategy session. He was right, judging by the number of limousines that had been pulling up in front of GIC headquarters since early evening, each usually carrying only one passenger. The helicopter pad atop the building had also been busy all night the detective had noted, probably ferrying in troops from JFK and Logan airports. It was unfortunate that he could not witness those arriving by helicopter.

He thought back to the conversation he'd had with his partner after the last late night meeting he'd had with Phillip Granville, trying to make sense of it all.

"I think I scared him, Dennis, if that's possible," DeStephano explained in debriefing Leery. The two were organizing evidence on an oversized blackboard mounted in his office. He stuck four photographs to the board.

"He's lost at least two of his most trusted 'Bosses', Laabi and Oliviero, and two very important 'Capos', Chandon and Stanton," the senior detective said, describing the wounds inflicted on Granville's corporation in terms the Mafia would recognize.

"Granville is his own 'Consiglieri,' he takes no counsel from anyone. I would bet there's not a man working for him that he really holds in respect."

"Right. What he holds is their 'coglioni,'" Leery said, " and I don't imagine he's afraid to squeeze."

"Yah," DeStephano smirked. "I often wonder how guys like Granville can justify intimidation... nah, make that fear as some sort of a sign of respect."

"You never see any of them quit, Mike," Leery countered. "The only way any of the top guys ever seem to leave General or Beckham is in a body bag marked natural causes."

"You got the list we asked for?"

"Yup. Granville's people delivered everything required in the subpoena right on time. No questions asked. Everything tracks. I checked with the IRS, Social Security, US Customs, INTERPOL, the FBI, the top international corporate headhunters... hell, even their proctologists," he said, trying but failing to lighten DeStephano's mood. "No one at an executive level has left GIC in more than 10 years under any other circumstances than their natural or accidental death. They don't quit and they don't get fired."

DeStephano shook his head.

"I don't understand. That company employs more than 300,000 people. You'd think there'd be some kind of natural turnover among the top one percent, at least. You mean to tell me none of them ever gets a better job offer?"

Leery shook his head.

"Looks that way boss." He shrugged his shoulders. "Maybe the General perks are just too good to give up."

"No job is that good. What about their compensation? Can we get a look at what these guys are making?" the senior detective asked.

"Not really," Leery answered. "The U.S. Securities and Exchange Commission only requires the disclosure of the top five officers of publicly traded corporations on an annual basis. It's in a financial statement called the '10-K,' which is normally filed within a couple of months after the end of the company's fiscal year." Leery feigned a yawn. "It's real light reading, the kind you want to curl up in front of a fireplace and…"

"Get to the point, Dennis," DeStephano said impatiently.

"Yah. Well the 10-K tells you just about anything you ever wanted to know about GIC, including Phillip Granville's total compensation, his travel expenses, stock options, bonus, maybe even the address of his tailor."

The senior detective finally laughed. Is that what makes a man successful he asked himself? He wondering what it felt like to wear a custom made suit. He couldn't even remember the last time he had bought one — off the rack at Filene's Basement.

"These are independently audited financial statements, and they typically go into organizational structure and list all of the company's officers. That list is 50 strong and there's nothing about their compensation or anything to suggest why these guys are so loyal. There have been numerous attempts by shareholder groups to require corporations like General to disclose the compensation of every executive, but it always gets shot down by management. Gee, wonder why. There's no doubt that money is the key to Phillip Granville's track record of holding his management team together."

"How far did you go back," DeStephano asked.

"Ten years. It took 20 off my life."

"I can imagine. But you found nothing that would give us a clue, something that would point to a pissed off former GIC or Beckham exec?"

"Nada. Not a single thing. The only people who've left the company over the last ten years did so because they keeled over and died. That's all. I even examined the death records of the eight people involved."

DeStephano raised an eyebrow.

"Yah, only eight over the last ten years."

"Amazing. Must be all that good living."

"The only death that was the least suspicious is that young guy, you remember, the one who went off the bridge in his Bimmer in Canton a few years back. Seemed to have had some kind of nervous breakdown. He went into the Farmington River after a wild ass road trip from Beckham headquarters, the motivation for which remains a mystery. His body was never recovered.

"Keller was his name, Kevin Keller. Left a wife and three little kids," Leery concluded.

"Case was closed, court declared him legally dead. There was nothing in the investigation to point a finger at Granville or even Laabi who was already running Beckham."

DeStephano cocked his head at that. "Badr Laabi was running Beckham then? You don't say."

Leery looked at his boss, knowing what he was thinking.

"Listen, Mike, the Canton Police were all over that thing. Think it happened back in 1992, April or

May, not sure. We helped them out with some interviews of Beckham employees. Only thing we came up with were some statements that indicated Keller was pretty depressed and talking some pretty crazy shit. Claimed there was a major conspiracy led by Granville and Laabi that involved the sale of goods to what the State Department had declared to be embargoed nations."

DeStephano raised his eyebrows.

"I did some research and found that if it were true, General would have been in deep yogurt with Federal violations and at risk to lose their ability to conduct any foreign business, export or import. Would have put them out of business. Keller was claiming illegal sales were ongoing to a whole bushel of countries identified as having committed some violation, mostly human rights or terrorism. You know, like Cuba and Libya, places like that. If what Keller claimed was true, General would have been in a whole world of hurt."

Leery caught DeStephano's sudden flinch.

"Something wrong boss?"

The senior detective shook his head.

"No, nothing. Anyone other than an executive of GIC or Beckham ever confirm Keller's behavior?"

"Yah. His wife, in fact. Said he was going through a very difficult time, hated his job, was raging about Granville and Laabi raking in millions in illegal sales. She said he was going to threaten to go to the Justice Department or State if they didn't stop. His wife confirmed everything."

"Hmm…"

"Aw shit... Mike, that was six years ago. They never found the guy's body. Probably washed out into the Connecticut River or even the Sound. It's a dead end," Leery pleaded.

"Pull Keller's jacket from the Canton PD," DeStephano said. "I want to go over it myself. You're probably right, but a fresh look can't hurt."

Leery sighed. "You got it."

Now sitting in the unmarked car outside the towering headquarters of General Industries, Detective Sergeant Michael DeStephano wished he had brought Kevin Keller's file to occupy him while he observed the top echelon of the corporation's management arrive for an unscheduled visit. He'd left it on his desk. He'd get to it first thing in the morning he promised himself. DeStephano was a man who made a living gambling on hunches. He had that tingling feeling in his gut that there was something waiting to be discovered in Keller's file. The detective reached for his coffee cup on the dashboard and put it to his lips. Yup. Cold. He wondered how many hours he had sat in an unmarked car drinking cold coffee while eyeballing some scumbag. Too many. But he would do it for the rest of his life to nail this one.

Inside the office building, far from the prying eyes of the police, Phillip Granville finally made his grand appearance in the huge room that served as his private conference facility on the 26th floor. The opulence of this chamber rivaled the penthouse of the world's finest hotels and served as the CEO's secure, encrypted teleconferencing center, management meeting chamber and Boardroom. With seating for 100 people in a theater-style setting, he could, from this room, speak face-to-face with any of his senior managers via digital television broadcast on a cinema-sized screen any time of the night or day, seven days per week. The satellite-based system was more capable than any such business facility in the world and rivaled US government, military and intelligence installations.

At the opposite end of the conference facility, a 60-foot long conference table that could seat as many as 50 people held first time visitors spellbound. Hand carved out of a single slab of a Tasmanian mountain ash tree that was nearly half a millennium old when felled, Granville had personally picked out the prized specimen of the *Eucalyptus regnans* species because of its pale blond color and extraordinary long, clear grain sections that were virtually free of knots. Its highly polished finish was the centerpiece of the contemporary aura that saturated the environment.

Private glass-walled salons were scattered throughout the facility in seemingly haphazard fashion, but actually were brilliantly conceived as nearly invisible, yet highly functional individual meeting places. Caviar finish stingray leather, dyed to a cognac color adorned every chair and couch in the facility and were placed on more than 5,000 square feet of Italian white Calcatta marble with bold grey veining. Strategically hung and carefully lit on white walls also covered in the marble, were an astonishing collection of impressionist, post impressionist and early modern works by artists such as Monet, Degas, Gaugin, van Gogh, Cézanne and Matisse.

Visitors, especially investors, found the overall effect breathtaking. Instead of being put off by the obvious extreme cost of the masterful design and its contents, they were strangely reassured by its innate statement of power, confidence and success, which they transferred to the whole of General Industries Corporation. But Phillip Granville's conference room really had been built with only one statement in mind: "Welcome to my palace."

The Chairman took his customary seat at the end of the table and discretely flipped one of several switches in a control panel hidden beneath it. The switch initiated locks on every access point to the room and also electronically jammed any radio transmission that might be emanating from it or trying to penetrate the environment. He studied the faces of his most loyal and valuable generals who had arrived from all over the world. Each ran an important segment of GIC's business or administrative function and also reported directly to Granville himself. The administrators were his most prized hit men, those who ensured he never had to dirty his own hands with the complex and sometimes "off book" operations of his corporation. Stuart Brown, his most valuable operative, sat to his right. The significance of Brown's position at the table was not lost on the attendees.

Each man's value to him was priceless. Yet he detested every one of them. To acknowledge their strengths or successes either publicly or privately would endear them to him, and that was unacceptable. Emotions led to failure.

His feelings were not unknown to the men gathered around the table. They were completely aware that the man with the hollow eyes sitting at the head of the table would sacrifice any one or any number of them at the slightest whim. That was the power he held over them and why none of them ever made a mistake and cleaned up failures in such a manner that they were never discovered.

He had their undivided attention as he began.

"Gentlemen. I thank you for coming on such little notice. Some of you must be near exhaustion. You can be assured that the matter on which I have convened this august group is of an urgent nature, involving each and every one of you."

There were nods of understanding around the table from each of the 48 men present.

"By now I am sure you are aware that we have lost, in just the last several weeks, four of our colleagues. Badr Laabi and Paul Stanton at Beckham h eadquarters in Farmington, and Sebastian Oliviero and Jean-Pierre Chandon in Seville, Spain have been brutally murdered. The investigating authorities here and abroad have concluded that each was essentially assassinated in carefully well planned operations that have provided not a single shred of evidence as to motive or guilt."

There was complete silence in the chamber as Granville spoke. He looked for indications of shock on the faces of his subordinates but found none. What he saw was puzzlement and anxiety.

"Our own internal investigation has uncovered no unusual activity or circumstances affecting any of these men, in fact, all were performing to my highest expectations."

He paused again, letting his words sink in.

"I grieve for these men, they were not only our colleagues, but friends," Granville said, stone faced, daring any man in the room to question his sincerity.

He knew, of course, that none of them were naïve enough to think he was sincere, but accepted that it was what he must say to them. Of far more concern to them was the issue of their own individual fates in what they all knew, without saying, was a conspiracy to murder them all off, bring down the corporation or both. None of them gave any more of a damn about the victims than Granville. What they wanted to know were the answers to the two most fundamental questions lurking unsaid in the rarified atmosphere of Phillip Granville's palace: "Who" was responsible and "What" was the motivation of the person or persons accountable?

The nerves of each of those seated at the table were frayed, but not because of the sudden, brutal executions of their colleagues. What they feared was the knowledge that each of them was loathed by all those they ruled within GIC, making the list of their enemies almost limitless in scope. They were ruthless men who made bitter enemies. The venomous hatred of their subordinates was held in check only by the richness of their rewards. Instinctively, each man began spinning through a list of possible culprits, mentally shuffling through a Rolodex of candidates. They quickly realized it was an exponential exercise.

"Given the failure of the investigating authorities to provide any inkling as to a motive of the killings or perhaps a clue as to who has attacked us, I am sure you are wondering the reason for this meeting," Granville began again, emphasizing what he knew they were thinking: They were all at risk.

There was no response, only the same unwavering attention to his words.

"It is an unequivocal fact that General Industries Corporation has been wounded by the loss of our colleagues. But perhaps of more vital concern is the damage these cowards have inflicted on our collective psyche," he continued. "Perhaps they have caused some of us to doubt our mission, which of course is to provide our investors with the greatest possible shareholder value."

He waited again. Not a man flinched.

"Or perhaps to doubt some of the decisions we have taken in order to continue the profit levels Wall Street has come to expect from us.

"Without fail, I remind you."

Several men dropped their heads, knowing where Granville was going.

"There have been those who have doubted some of our strategies," he continued. "We have found their arguments naïve, parochial, insular… and have pushed their objections aside, despite what I have always considered idle threats of retaliation. Those who might have seen a vision of success through rose-colored glasses have been rewarded well to keep their ideals locked within."

He intentionally waited before finishing the thought.

"Or have been dealt with appropriately."

An almost perceptible pall descended upon the proceedings. Several of the invited turned away from Granville's gaze. The CEO picked up on the sudden shift in temperature immediately. He moved quickly to erase any doubts as to the continuation of power at GIC.

"No doubt, our success, quarter upon quarter, year after year, fueled by our relentless and aggressive search for growth and profit have made us numerous enemies. Adversaries who are frustrated by their inability to tap into the rich markets that we have come to control through carefully cultivated, discrete relationships."

He paused, using the excuse of taking a sip from a glass of water to give them time to absorb his words.

"Let me remind those of you who may have any doubt as to the correctness of our course that there are several incontrovertible principles by which General Industries Corporation will continued to be managed."

Every head in the room swung back to gaze into Phillip Granville's dark, hollow eyes. The look on his face reflected a man of absolute conviction as unmovable in his beliefs as he was void of compassion.

"First, there is only one chief executive officer of GIC, and he is speaking to you now. There will be no debate or questions regarding my decisions, at any time or in any situation. You will follow my orders without query — or doubt.

"I remind you, this is not a democracy."

He left no time for analysis.

"Second, an attack on General Industries is an attack on all of us. We will respond accordingly. I understand that each of you must deal with the laws of the lands from which you operate and even international treaties and agreements. No matter. The law of GIC — my law — predominates all others. Deal with the irritations in your own backyards."

There were those who travelled home later that night mulling the thought that at that moment they had been looking into the eyes of Satan.

Indeed, as he spoke, Phillip Granville's grasp on reality was slipping away, his anger so deep and overwhelming that his hands shook.

"And finally, let me remind you that you are all very wealthy men. The sustainment of your privileged lives depends on your ability and willingness to follow orders and to execute them with complete confidence and enthusiasm."

He paused again, letting the words sink in.

"And do I need to remind you of the greater rewards that are within your reach?"

Granville smirked as he watched a grin bloom on the face of every man sitting at the table and how none attempted to suppress the urge. It still amazed him how quickly greed could wipe away anxiety.

"My expectations of you are unchanged. You know your financial targets. Achieve them, no excuses. There will be no change in our strategy, no course corrections in our business operations or methods. However, recognizing that we are facing new risks, you are to immediately upgrade your personal and facilities security and communicate any unusual activity in your operations to me, directly. You will receive a briefing tomorrow by a private security agency we have hired to help you evaluate and improve your defenses."

He paused again, letting it all sink in.

"Now. Are there any doubters among you?"

The room was silent. It appeared that Granville's words, as so often before, had quelled their anxiety.

"Are there any questions before we move to more urgent business? What I refer to is a case of a magnificent cognac I have been saving for just such an occasion as this. It is a very rare, 40-year old Château de Montifaud Heritage Louis Vallet that I discovered during a recent visit to France. Its exquisite aroma alone will make the unpleasantness of our business tonight disappear, I promise you — and remind you of the wealth we will share in the years to come."

Surprisingly, from the opposite end of the table, a voice, it's French accent lending an air of worldliness to the proceedings in the small New England city, interrupted with a question.

"Monsieur Granville, please excuse me for keeping you and my colleagues from this superb cognac, I am fortunate to know of it." It was Didier Michad, the French executive whom Granville had hand selected to replace the murdered Jean-Pierre Chandon as chief financial officer for Beckham's European operations."

Granville was somewhat taken aback but hid his displeasure.

"Yes, of course, Didier, what is it?"

"Monsieur Granville, it is quite clear from what you have said that the authorities have little evidence to help conclude their investigation into the murder of our colleagues. Qui?"

"This is true, Didier. Continue, please," Granville said, patiently.

"But I am puzzled..."

The CEO frowned.

"Get to the point please, my French friend..."

"You refer to the culprits in the plural sense,

qui? And you speak of a conspiracy, which by its very nature would suggest more than one is responsible for the murder of our colleagues. Yet we know not whether it is many — or one — who has attacked us. This is true, Monsieur Granville?"

For those sitting closest to Phillip Granville, the only detectable indication of his displeasure with Michad's question was the redness that appeared to slowly climb from the base of his neck until his entire face took on the hue. Then they watched as the chief executive, his eyes intently focused on the French manager, slowly regained his poise and his complexion returned to normal. But a large vein on the side of his neck pulsated at an unusually fast rate, suggesting his response would be quick — and harsh. Several of the more senior executives sitting at the table closed their eyes in anticipation of the wrath that they knew from experience was forthcoming.

But Granville's long delay in responding was intentional. Although it appeared he was mulling over a response, he was actually waiting until he could fully regain his composure. Inside, he was fighting the urge to leave his seat, walk to the Frenchman and gouge out his eyes for the sheer audacity of questioning him. But he would not allow that to happen now; Michad would be dealt with later.

Finally, he spoke.

"Didier, I ask you to look around this table, at your colleagues to your left and your right and tell me what you see."

Michad was confused by the directive but nonetheless, slowly looked to his right and to his left. He nodded.

"Quite impressive, Monsieur Granville. We are a powerful team, if I take your point," he replied.

"Precisely. The people sitting at this table are the power that fuels this corporation. They are the best in their respective businesses and disciplines. Would you not agree?"

"Oui, bien sûr!" Didier Michad responded immediately in agreement. "Without a doubt."

"Then can you imagine a single person attacking this corporation knowing the might and determination they would be up against?"

The Frenchman shrugged his shoulders nervously, finally recognizing that he had irked his boss. He answered quickly.

"Only if that person was truly insane, Monsieur Granville."

"So I take it you would agree with me that what has transpired must be the work of an entity with substantial resources and motivation, yes?"

"Qui," Michad said in a low voice, sinking a bit lower in his chair, silently chastising himself for being so stupid to question Granville."

The chief executive officer, once again firmly in control of his army allowed his soldiers to stew in silence for several moments.

Then he smiled. There was quiet laughter around the table as the ice melted.

"The cognac awaits us gentlemen," he said. "Let us drink to the fact that we are united as one as we prepare to fight a war. Our invisible enemies will not be able to hide for long. And when they become visible, we will counterattack."

He waited for a comment that he knew would

not come.

Then he rapped the knuckles of his right hand on the tabletop and repeated the action, slowly picking up the tempo. He was joined by all of his guests. Eventually, the sound became a deafening wave of commitment to their commander's words and his dedication to justice. Phillip Granville's brand of justice.

Parked far below in the city street, alone in his unmarked car, Detective Sergeant Michael DeStephano yawned, wondering what was happening on the 26th floor of General Industries' headquarters.

"What I wouldn't give..." he said aloud, imaging what he could learn if he had a wire or a mole in place. He had neither. There wasn't enough evidence to convince a judge to issue a warrant allowing for the placement of wiretapping and recording equipment in the building and it would take months, maybe years to successfully plant a source within GIC's management ranks.

He would have to listen to his instincts, bank on the hunches that had rarely failed him in his career to nail the bastard who seemed to find murder so easy. Then his thoughts wandered to the victims and their boss, a man he sorely despised for many reasons, including some that were very personal.

Abruptly, Stefano felt a chill and tried to shake off the thought that had triggered it.

It came with the sudden silent recognition that he was actually rooting for the bad guy.

Twenty-Eight

Stuart Brown did not share Phillip Granville's ability to sleep well. He was essentially paid to relieve his boss of worries, shouldering the myriad problems that would have made Granville an insomniac. Consequently, Brown was a workaholic who survived on precious few hours of rest, but, like Granville was well fortified by a steady diet of barbiturates, amphetamines and benzodiazepines supplied by the corporation's executive physician, Sid Keitel, MD. Keeping Phillip Granville cool, calm and mean and Stuart Brown stoned were the doctor's sole reasons for existence at GIC.

The combination of uppers, downers and mood stabilizers allowed Brown to sleep when he needed, work for days on end if necessary and maintain a calm demeanor whatever the situation. He was widely recognized for his remarkable intelligence and ability to present complex financial data and analysis, sometimes speaking to Wall Street analysts for hours without a single note. On the other hand, he was legend for not communicating a single word for weeks on end.

His emotional state was a complete dichotomy. He could order the layoff of thousands of workers without a sign of remorse despite complete awareness that his decision would result in their financial ruin. At the same time, he was an avid student of poet Maya Angelou, a champion of the human spirit, and mythologist Joseph Campbell's philosophy of "Follow your bliss." He rarely spoke in social environments, but when he did, he often quoted freely from both, often shedding a tear at the compassion and benevolence of their thoughts.

Within the General inner circle, it was widely accepted that Stuart was Phillip Granville's right hand, brightest counsel and most loyal attendant. Beyond that, the man was a total mystery. In truth, he was a drug addicted, ruthless, asexual, emotional time bomb that was possibly the only human being Granville truly feared.

With his thick, horn rimmed glasses and sparse, slicked back grey hair, the short, thin man nearing his 60th birthday was anything but intimidating in his appearance. But the secrets he carried in silence rattled continually in his brain. His mind was a file cabinet full of every illegal business transaction, every financial transgression, every inhumane act ever committed by GIC under Phillip Granville's leadership as well as his predecessors. Those files carried the potential to be the gravestones of Phillip Granville and his soldiers, and the chief executive knew it. Stuart Brown had the unique ability to bury them all. And that made him a very valuable — and very dangerous — accomplice.

Not surprisingly, Brown lived alone in a large chateau-inspired brownstone house on Scarborough Street in the city's elite west end, behind high walls, fences and gates. Brown lived simply with just the assistance of a housekeeper who came once a week to dust and change the sheets. His only other perquisite was a car and driver, his poor eyesight making the commute to and from the office a dangerous chore. He took his meals at General Industries headquarters in the executive dining room, never vacationed and studied stock reports and the financial data of acquisition candidates in his few leisure hours at home. He did not own a television or carry a cell phone. The only pastime that interested him was reading. Fiction, non-fiction, biographies, histories, it did not matter. He absorbed and expanded his knowledge from the printed page.

He had no reason to fear anyone or anything, always knowing that Phillip Granville's minions were there to protect him and cater to his every need.

But Stuart Brown did have an Achilles Heel.

He was terrified of spiders.

A life-long arachnophobic, the man who could move the share price of GIC with a phone call or determine the fate of a thousand employees with a simple nod was scared silly of anything with eight tiny legs. The mere sight of an arthropod, no matter it's size, would send the man into a complete state of fear and panic so intense that he risked suffering a heart attack. On several occasions in his earlier years he had been rushed to the hospital in pulmonary and cardiac distress after having been frightened by the sight of a spider. His phobia had escalated to the point where he was now convinced that the mere touch of any of the thousands of species of air-breathing arthropods would cause him to fall dead.

His secret was carefully guarded. Stuart Brown believed that only two people in his world knew of his phobia: his housekeeper and his secretary. Each was extraordinarily well compensated to ensure that his environment was spider free at all times. Brown spent huge sums on preventative pest control in both his office and home. At night, he slept in a specially designed cocoon made of super fine mesh mosquito netting. Under his business suits, he wore a skin tight body stocking at all times as well as gloves whenever he was not in the public eye. He took every precaution to ensure that his secret was safely hidden. Even Dr. Keitel was unaware of his patient's phobia — or that his overly liberal dispensation of controlled drugs helped keep it in check.

But Stuart Brown was wrong.

Arriving at his home near daybreak after participating in Phillip Granville's extraordinary meeting the night before, Brown was exhausted. The meeting had ended near midnight, but Granville had asked him to remain and compile information on "certain" of GIC's business transactions for review with him the next day. It had taken him nearly five hours and even Brown was amazed at the magnitude of what he had found. But now he needed just a few hours of sleep before sharing the information with Granville.

He waved to his driver after opening the great oak plank door to the house. Stepping inside, he went immediately to the security panel that controlled the sophisticated alarm system that was always armed and remotely monitored in his absence. A high-pitched sounder, emanating a steady beeping noise was already activated. The system allowed him 60 seconds to turn off the alarm and then rearm it to account for his presence inside. He entered the code without incident then walked through a grand foyer to the staircase leading to his private study and master bedroom. He walked slowly, extremely fatigued. The effects of the powerful amphetamines he had taken throughout the long day were wearing off and he was crashing fast. Typically, within minutes of taking several sleeping pills he would practically fall into his bed and lapse into a dreamless, near comatose state for several hours. He was so tired that he began shedding his clothes as he climbed the stairs to his bedroom, anticipating the luxury of passing out in the fresh sheets his housekeeper had put out just that day.

"Damn it," he cursed, realizing mid way up the staircase that he had forgotten to turn on the upstairs lights when he came in. The only illumination came from the moon, its glow through the oversized windows on the second floor casting an eerie shadow over him in the hallway before his room.

Without warning a second shadow appeared over his shoulder. For a moment, he was puzzled then realized he was not alone. Brown spun in his tracks to confront the intruder.

"Who is it?" he demanded.

There was no answer.

He began walking backwards towards his bedroom, where he knew he could lock himself inside and call for help. A voice rang out.

"Stop where you are, Mr. Brown," a voice commanded him. It was vaguely familiar.

"What? Who are you? What do you want?" he demanded. "I have very little money in the house. Take whatever else you want and just get out."

"It's not money I came for, Mr. Brown," the voice said again. The tone was low, husky, a voice that was no stranger to cigarettes or alcohol. Brown thought he recognized the voice, but could not place it.

"Then what do you want?"

There was silence as Brown began walking again.

"Go into your study, Mr. Brown or I will shoot you dead where you stand."

"What? How dare you… oh, my god," Brown said, suddenly aware of the danger he was in.

He turned to his left and entered his study, a library where he worked while at home.

"Turn on the lights and take a seat behind your desk. Now," the voice said. Brown did as he was told.

The intruder remained in the hallway for a moment then stepped into the lighted room. He was tall, dressed all in black and wearing a knitted facemask. Only his eyes were visible.

"There, that wasn't hard, was it?" the stranger asked. "You're not used to taking orders, Mr. Brown, are you?"

The executive leaned forward in his desk chair, peering at the figure dressed all in black. "No, I'm not.

What do you want? I'm a very powerful man, you know. Do you really want to do this?"

"Oh, I know exactly how powerful you are, Mr. Brown," the figure said. And that's exactly why I have come. I want you to tell me all about your power. All of it."

Brown squirmed in his chair, confused. The stranger removed a black backpack that he was carrying over his shoulders.

"Please don't hurt me, I'll give you whatever you want," Brown pleaded.

The stranger laughed.

"This is really funny," he said.

"What's so funny?" Brown asked, his voice trembling.

"You're just a bully, Stuart," the stranger replied. "And like all bullies, you're really a coward. Full of bravado one minute when you think your power will save you. Begging for your life when you know it won't."

"How do you know my name?"

"It's hard to forget bullies, Stuart."

"Who are you? I recognize your voice."

The stranger walked towards Brown who put his hands up to protect himself.

"Relax, coward, I'm not going to hurt you. You're much too valuable to me. Do you really want to know who I am?"

Brown swallowed hard. "Yes."

The intruder sat down in one of the two chairs in front of the ornate, hand carved desk that Brown treasured. He ran one of his hands over the surface.

"Nice. Bet it cost a pretty penny. Also bet General Industries paid for it. All in the name of shareholder value. What a joke." He laughed again.

"You know, you are a poor excuse of a man, Stuart. Absolutely pathetic. But I'm going to give you the opportunity to be worth something. To make up for all the wrongs you've done to your shareholders... and to me." As he finished speaking, the intruder pulled off the knitted mask, revealing his face.

Brown gasped.

"I know you...! Yes, I know you." He studied the strangers face a moment more. "But...you're dead!"

"Well, obviously not, Stuart. Can't remember my name, can you? But you remember my face."

"Yes."

"Do you remember what you did to me? What you and Granville and those pigs Stanton and Laabi did to me? What they took from me?"

"No, I don't," Brown said fearfully. "What ever it is, I didn't do it, it wasn't my fault... whoever you are. But I can make up for it. I can get back what they took from you. Really I can. What ever it was. Just give me a chance!"

"What you took from me I can never have back, Stuart."

"Don't be stupid..."

"It's gone forever!" the intruder screamed and slammed his fist down on the desk, causing Brown to push back from the desk in fear.

"But now, you are going to make up for it, you sniveling coward. You're going to give me what I need."

"What? Anything... just tell me."

"Open your computer, Brown, now."

The executive typed a password on his keyboard and his desktop monitor came to life.

"Turn the screen toward me."

Brown followed his order, turning the monitor towards the intruder.

"Now find every file that has anything to do with General sales to embargoed nations. And any violations of the Foreign Corrupt Practices Act. Bribes or facilitating payments, Brown. Any illegal transactions forbidden by the State Department or the Justice Department."

Brown looked at the man incredulously.

"You're crazy! There's no such thing... we don't play those kind of games with the government..."

"You're lying to me, Brown. And that's too bad. I know what I need is in that computer and I'm just going to have to find it myself."

"You're crazy!" Brown repeated.

"Insane, perhaps, Mr. Brown," the intruder grinned. Abruptly his face turned black. "You would be too, if you had lost what I have. But I'm not crazy. And you're in my way."

The intruder picked up the knapsack lying at his feet and placed it on top of the desk. He slowly unzipped the bag and reached inside. He pulled out a tall thermos with a screw on cap.

"Do you know what I have here, Stuart?"

"A bomb?" Brown said, almost relieved that it wasn't a gun. This crazy bastard would never set off a bomb and kill himself too, he thought.

"Oh, no. How parochial that would be. No, something far more terrifying for a coward like you."

Brown squinted, completely confused.

"What I have here is your worst nightmare, my phobic friend," he said sarcastically. "You see, you gave yourself away to me a long time ago."

"What do you mean? When? Where? What did I give you?"

"Your secret, Stuart," the intruder said with an evil grin breaking on his face.

"What secret?" Brown asked desperately.

"It was all so innocent," he responded. "We were at a meeting… I don't recall where. It was in a garden. But I was standing next to you when you saw…"

He paused, letting Brown swing in the wind. He so enjoyed toying with this little bastard.

"Saw what? What did I see?" He was completely panicked. The intruder was disgusted by the man.

"You sicken me, Brown. What you saw… was a cobweb."

Brown sucked in a huge breath, gasping at the vision the intruder was beginning to paint for him.

"It was a spider's web, in a flowerbed, something normal men would never have noticed. But you did. I thought you were going to wet your pants…"

"Oh my god… no…"

"It really was beautiful. Glistening in an evening dew, after a rainfall earlier in the day. How horrible it must have been for you, Stuart." He laughed out loud again.

"Why it positively gives me goose bumps when I think there you were, surrounded by people fawning all over you, thinking you were so important, so powerful, just dying for your undivided attention. But you couldn't pay any attention to them because you were shaking in your shoes, like a little boy, petrified of a tiny little spider."

The intruder reached out with the thermos and touched Brown's arm with it. The executive jumped at the sensation. A pitiful, guttural sound, much like what a wounded animal might make when cornered, rose from his throat.

"Yes, Stuart. I know your secret. I know how much you enjoy our eight-legged friend, the spider."

Stuart Brown began to hyperventilate. His chest began heaving as his breathing became more and more ragged. The intruder reached for the top of the thermos and began to unscrew it.

"No!" the executive screamed. "I have it! I have all of it! Everything you want. Granville had me pull it all together last night!"

"Where is it?" the man dressed in black asked, slowly continuing to unscrew the top of the thermos.

"Here, please, wait..." Brown begged him, turning to his computer, "I can access the file from here." Frantically, his fingers flew across the keyboard as he retrieved the file that he had prepared to discuss with Phillip Granville later in the day.

The document flashed onto the screen. The intruder studied it for a minute. "Scroll down," he ordered, his eyes widening as he read.

"Even more revolting than I thought. You're not only a coward, you're a traitor, Mr. Brown."

"No, I just followed my orders…"

"And you know the punishment for treason, don't you…"

"No! It wasn't me!" Brown begged. "Please, its all Phillip Granville's doing! I did what you asked… please," he whimpered, completely broken.

"Print it. And download the file to a disk."

Brown hesitated, his mind unraveling at the thought of what was in the thermos.

"Do it!"

In minutes, the intruder had a hard copy of the file and a disk loaded with all the information.

"Now, e-mail the file to this address: M.DeStephano@FarmingtonPD.com. Don't fuck it up. I'm watching." He turned the lid of the thermos another thread as he watched Brown frantically follow his instructions.

"Done!"

The intruder smiled. It was an evil grin, full of hatred for this man who'd had a hand in all that he'd lost.

"You took my life away from me."

"I did what you asked," Brown pleaded, tears now streaming down his cheeks.

The intruder stood up and slowly walked around the desk until he was standing over his terrified victim. A paralysis gripped his body; he was nearly unable to move.

"Not a day goes by that I don't live the terror of losing everything that was precious to me.

"And I can never get it back."

He hesitated for a moment. "I've dreamed of beating you to death with my bear hands, of cutting your throat... oh, there are so many ways to kill a man and enjoy watching him die.

"But this is so much better. I get to see the terror in your eyes as your mind disintegrates and your heart stops.

"Good bye, Mr. Brown. Have a nice trip... to hell."

The intruder picked up the copy of the document and the disk and put them in his knapsack. Then he slowly turned the thermos lid one more turn and removed it, placing it on the desk top for his victim to see.

Stuart Brown's eyes followed the path of the thermos as the invader raised it above him, then rolled completely back into his head as the stranger poured the contents of the thermos over the paralyzed man. Several dozen tiny brown spiders, hardly a threat to a normal man, fell out of the thermos and on to his head, his face, neck and shoulders.

Stabbing pain caused Brown's hands to involuntarily jerk up and clutch his chest over his heart. Spittle began to form at the corners of his mouth as his mind snapped from the sheer dread. In the next instant, his heart seized and stopped pumping, preventing circulation of blood to his body and the delivery of oxygen and glucose to his brain. Within two minutes he was unconscious. In three he had stopped breathing. The intruder watched as his body twitched, intrigued by the process of a man dying from fear. At five minutes, Stuart Brown was a lifeless corpse.

The stranger screwed the top back on to the thermos, replaced it in his backpack and looked around for any telltale signs that he had been there. On Brown's desk he saw the man's GIC corporate identity badge that allowed him access through all security doors. He picked it up and put it in his pocket. One never knew when something like that would come in handy. Then he walked out of the room.

He exited out the front door, the very same way he had entered the house the day before when the housekeeper had come and left it unlocked as she always did as she went about her business. It had been a long day, hiding motionless underneath Stuart Brown's bed as she worked, but well worth the wait.

Outside, the sun had not yet broken through the night. The intruder had at least a half hour yet to hide in the darkness. He ran through the back yard and waded across a stream that cut through the property, scaled a brick wall and casually walked across Homestead Avenue. A half block away he turned on to Albany Avenue, where he had parked his pickup truck the day before. Within minutes he was entering I-91 that would take him to Route 9 and back to the cabin in Old Saybrook. The sun was just coming up as he made the highway.

As he drove, he thought about the e-mail he had forced Brown to send. He imagined the look on Michael DeStephano's face when he got it and realized what had just fallen into his lap. But he knew that he had also just signed his own death warrant. It wouldn't take the detective long to begin to put the pieces together. No matter. What he had done this night would insure that he achieved his goal.

Get Phillip Granville.

Before Phillip Granville got him.

He downshifted the old truck to make the grade of a steep hill just outside Haddam. Then he pushed down on the heavy clutch again and yanked the long gearshift lever into fourth, steering the pickup into the far right lane at the speed limit. No sense in drawing any unnecessary attention. Unconsciously he began to hum.

"The itsy bitsy spider climbed up the waterspout… down came the rain and washed the spider out…"

Twenty-Nine

"Coincidence?" Farmington detective Dennis Leery asked his partner at the brownstone mansion in Hartford where the body of General Industries executive Stuart Brown had been found earlier that morning.

"Shit..." muttered his partner, Detective Sergeant Michael DeStephano. "If you can call the death of a fifth GIC executive in less than two months a coincidence, especially considering four of them were murdered, than yah, I'd say its just been a bad month for the company and we can close the file," he replied sarcastically.

The detectives had been invited to inspect the crime scene by the Hartford Police Department who thus far had not been involved in the GIC murders. DeStephano had gotten a call from the investigating detective that morning informing him that Brown had been found dead, victim of an apparent heart attack. The body had not yet been moved, awaiting inspection by the city coroners.

"Jesus, please don't move him, I'll be right there," DeStephano had pleaded. He knew instinctively there was no way Brown had died of natural causes.

A half-hour later, he and Leery entered Brown's study to find the body of the executive in the same place and position as it had been found earlier in the day by his driver. He was sprawled in his desk chair, his eyes rolled back into his head, vomit dried on his face and clothing. There was no sign of violence. The only thing unusual that either of the detectives noticed was Brown's computer screen turned away from him, as if he had turned it to share whatever was on the screen with a visitor. There were no signs of a break in and the security company that monitored the house reported nothing unusual.

"It doesn't add up," DeStephano said after looking over the scene. "We're going to have to wait until the toxicology and autopsy reports come in for sure, but I can't believe this guy died of poisoning or natural causes. Not now, not after the bodies of four of his best friends have just been dumped in Phillip Granville's lap."

The coroner saw nothing unusual although he said there were no indications from Brown's personal physician, Dr. Sidney Keitel, a GIC employee, that Brown had suffered from anything other than insomnia.

"God damn," Leery suddenly yelled, slamming the palm of his hand down hard on the surface of Brown's desk. You'd think a guy this well off would at least have a housekeeper. What the fuck is with all the spiders? They're everywhere?"

"Spiders?" the coroner said, immediately interested. His eyes scanned the room. "You're right, they're all over the place. Don't kill another one. Bag 'em. I'll check the body for bites. If that doesn't pan out, I have another idea."

Leery, ever the wiseass thought he was making a joke.

"Hell, maybe the victim was a wuss about spiders, " he laughed. "Might have scared him to death. My wife hates the damn things. Screams when she sees them."

"It's called 'Arachnophobia' — an irrational fear of spiders, detective," the coroner said to Leery, whose grin faded from his face.

"It's not uncommon, but only in severe cases could it frighten a man to death." He looked around the room. Dozens of the brown spiders could be seen crawling around if you looked close enough.

"But you know, judging by the number of spiders I can see scampering around aimlessly, these little bastards are new to this room. They don't have nests to go to. It's like someone brought them here and just let them loose. Unleashed them."

Leery was horrified at the scenario. Detective Sergeant DeStephano was intrigued.

"I wonder if Mr. Brown had a secret... that someone guessed..." he mused.

"This is one clever bastard we're looking for," he said to his partner. "C'mon, I gotta get back into the office and check my e-mail."

Thirty

Home.

The man now known as Tom Pulling found something oddly comforting about his tiny refuge in the North Cove of Old Saybrook. It was a long way from the mountains where he had hidden for so long, but the quiet and solitude were similarly calming.

He sat on the beach in front of the rented cottage, chain smoking and occasionally sipping from a quart of vodka.

The sound of waves lapping at the shore were all that filled the night this far from the road and the air was freezing cold, numbing him. He buttoned the worn, blanket lined denim chore coat he was wearing and pulled up its corduroy collar to ward off the chill. It was early morning, hours before sunup, but he knew he wouldn't be able to sleep. His head would be swimming with nightmares even before he hit the pillow. At least sitting out here he could relive the same dreams, but make them good memories instead.

After a while, a few more sips of vodka and the splashing of the waves drew him back to memories of the sound of his children laughing and playing, building sand castles at the edge of the water at Hammonasset Beach, just a few miles from where he sat. It was one of their favorite weekend family destinations. His beautiful wife, lying next to him on the blanket they had laid out on the hot sand, asked him to spread sun tan lotion on her smooth, white skin. He luxuriated in the feel of her, so soft and creamy and almost forgot about the children. He had to force himself to check on them every now and then while he fantasized over the woman at his fingertips. With one eye on his three children and the other on his wife's toned body, his whole world was within his vision. He could barely hold back the grin that came to his face.

For a few minutes at least, life was that good again.

A large wave suddenly broke over the dock where his boat was tied up. The fiberglass hull banged against the wooden planks, snapping him out of the dream. In an instant, he was alone again.

How ironic, he thought. That was exactly how his world had changed. In an instant.

The man put the bottle down in the sand and rubbed his eyes. He thought he smelled blood and raised his hands up to look. There was nothing. But the smell of blood, that rusty, metallic odor was on his hands, on his clothes…all over him. He knew a shower and a change wouldn't drive off the smell.

He'd killed five men in just a few weeks, with little effort and no hesitation. The stranger sighed, unsure if it was out of satisfaction or fatigue. Something was bothering him. He couldn't quite put his finger on it.

The vodka felt good, warming him as he dwelled on his feelings. More would die before he was done. He felt no remorse, had no thoughts of contrition. The act of murder was not difficult. It was reliving it — seeing the look of horror and recognition on a victim's face and watching him die with that look of shock in his eyes — that made him tired. Then it came to him in shocking clarity.

Despite his murderous spree, despite the brutal vengeance he had exacted on five men, he was not satisfied. He felt no elation at the success of his plan or thrill at watching the people who had destroyed his life die ugly deaths. And there was no sense of relief from the pain of his loss.

That was it. Nothing would ever make up for what they had taken from him. He would never stop grieving. Tears of frustration came to his eyes and rolled down his cheeks as he realized he would never escape the horror of his living nightmare.

He wept like a baby, finally after all these years of burying the agony of being gutted by monsters driven by greed and power. He screamed into the silence of the night, punching the sand beneath him with blow after blow until he was exhausted and could cry no more.

He looked down at the small craters his punches had created. It struck him that no matter how hard he smashed his fists into the beach, the grains would simply absorb his blows, only moving aside. No matter how violently he struck the sand, he could not destroy it. It was then that he finally accepted that no matter how much death and destruction he inflicted on Phillip Granville and General Industries, he would never kill it. GIC was like the mythical Greek Hydra of Lerna he had studied in school — the multi-headed serpent that guarded the Underworld. It could not be destroyed, for each time a warrior cut off one of its heads, two more would grow back to take its place. There was only one way to defeat it.

Cut off all the heads at once.

Pulling shook his head, knowing he would be caught before he could kill all those involved in the crime that had ultimately robbed him of his life. But the world would know what had happened and perhaps he could save his family, if not himself. Looking up into the heavens, he knew that his mission was as impossible as counting the stars. But still, he swore that "The General" would fall before they got him.

First, he needed to rest and to plan. The e-mail he had forced Brown to send would keep the police plenty busy, distracting them. It was an opportunity he had to take advantage of. But before he could consider that, abruptly a thought too dangerous to even contemplate entered his mind, having made the trip all the way from the tiny bit of soul that remained in him.

Could he possibly risk sneaking a look at his wife and children?

Risk? What was the risk, his alcohol addled brain challenged. He wasn't even sure if they still lived in the same house, and if not, he couldn't chance driving around searching for them. But if they hadn't moved away, the police in the driveway would be long gone, as would family and friends. They would be alone.

And even if they saw him, the chances were remote that they would recognize him. His hair was shorn down to just a stubble and he maintained at least a three day growth of beard to darken his looks. He was at least 35 pounds lighter than the day he disappeared and the life of hard, physical labor in the mountains had rid him of every ounce of fat he'd once put on living the "good life" of a globe hopping executive.

A flash of pain squeezed his chest. He had forgotten something. With sorrow, the thought occurred to him that his children were very young when he disappeared and probably wouldn't remember him no matter what he looked like.

He reached for the bottle and took a long pull, cementing his decision to drive to Canton tomorrow afternoon. All he needed was a look, a quick one at that, of the people who had been taken from him so many years ago. That would be enough to get him through the next part of his plan…and the final act.

The combination of fatigue and alcohol finally hit him and he slumped over onto the sand, passed out. He was too tired and drunk to fight it off and the worry of hypothermia had no chance of penetrating the fog he was in.

As he slept on the beach, the small transistor radio he'd left playing in the kitchen was broadcasting a news story about the death of the fifth General Industries Corporation executive in just a few days. The report quoted a Hartford police spokesman who said they had not determined if the death of Stuart Brown was linked to the four murders of GIC executives, but said the circumstances of his death were "troubling."

In Farmington, Detective Sergeant Michael DeStephano and Detective Dennis Leery were too busy to listen to the news. They had spent the entire day poring over the strange e-mail that Brown had sent to DeStephano obviously only minutes or hours before his death. The two were wide-eyed with the story they were piecing together from the information in the e-mail. It would only be days, after consultations with the FBI and the State Department that Phillip Granville's empire would come crashing down.

As a bleary-eyed DeStephano read, a bolt of lightening flashed in his brain.

Embargoed. Embargoed nations. He had seen the words a hundred times in the e-mail, but the truth finally hit him.

"Dennis," he hollered to his partner who was sitting no more than four feet away.

"What?" he said, startled. He reached for a napkin to blot the coffee he spilled.

"Of all those guys we checked who left GIC, you said all died of natural causes or retired... except one."

"Yah," Leery said. "Guy died in an accident in Canton. Drove his car off a bridge. Fully investigated but cause was never nailed down. No body was ever found. Keller was the guy's name if I remember."

"Kevin Keller."

"Yah that's it."

DeStephano put his hands to his eyes and slumped at his desk.

"Holy shit," he said.

"What?" Leery asked. "There's nothing there, Mike, I'm telling you."

"You're wrong," DeStephano said pulling Keller's file out from under a pile of paper on his desk. He opened it and pulled out an eight by ten inch glossy photograph of the executive taken just before his disappearance. He suddenly remembered him from the day he had visited Phillip Granville with his sister-in-law.

"It's him. It's Kevin Keller."

"What do you mean, it's him? Jesus, the guy disappeared, left a wife and a bunch of kids," Leery challenged him.

DeStephano stabbed a finger at the face in the photograph.

"This is the man who has murdered five General big shots in the last week."

He shook his head up and down, more convinced than ever.

"But he ain't done. Nope."

Leery looked at his boss like he was crazy.

"Not by a long shot, Dennis."

He stared at the picture for long moments. Then he grabbed his coat and car keys.

"C'mon. We're going for a ride," he said to Leery.

"Where?"

"To talk to his wife."

Thirty-One

DeStephano glanced at his wristwatch before ringing the doorbell at the home of Kate Keller in nearby Canton. It was nearly midnight. He had called her in advance to ensure that the young widow still lived at the same address and to try not to startle her any more than necessary by just showing up at the door.

"This is gonna suck, Mike," Leery said, unconsciously straightening the knot of his tie as if looking sharp was going to make the conversation they'd come to have any easier.

"I know. But that's why they pay us the big bucks." The senior detective took a deep breath and punched the doorbell.

The front porch light snapped on almost immediately and the door opened a crack. Kate

Keller's face peered through the space and both men flashed their badges before even greeting her.

She opened the door.

"Come in, please," she said, almost whispering.

"Good evening, Mrs. Keller. We're very sorry to..." DeStephano began.

She interrupted him immediately.

"You found his body, didn't you."

A stab of remorse hit the detective for not considering that the mother of three might have automatically jumped to that conclusion.

He shook his head in regret.

"I'm sorry, Mrs. Keller for bothering you so late," he said, ducking her question. "May we come in and speak to you? It's very important."

"Of course," she said, resigned to whatever conversation was about to happen. Her hands trembled as she showed the detectives in.

"Would you like some coffee or a beer or something?" she offered nervously.

"No, no, thank you, we're inconveniencing you enough. We'll try to be brief."

"Please, have a seat," Kate said showing them into the living room. She sat in the easy chair that had been her husband's favorite, motioning to the detectives to take a seat on the couch.

"Please answer me, did you find his body?" she asked. Leery dropped his head. It was a heartbreaking question.

"No," DeStephano said, shaking his head. "I'm sorry that our unexpected call might have given you that impression."

She sighed.

"So strange, the way he just disappeared... you would have thought by now that his body would have surfaced somewhere. But it's probably just as well. I wouldn't know how to break it to the children."

"It must be terribly hard for you, Mrs. Keller, I'm sorry," Leery said with genuine sympathy.

"Thank you detective, but my children have helped me through the worst of the grieving for Kevin, and after all, I have them to care for. But they give me strength. We're all doing okay."

"Mrs. Keller, what I wanted to ask you about was your husband's behavior before his death. The file indicates he was acting quite strangely at the time..."

Kate sighed. She had gone over the last conversations she'd shared with her husband a thousand times looking for clues. Unfortunately, based on everything Phillip Granville and Kevin's colleagues had told her about his last days at work, she had finally admit that her husband had become emotionally imbalanced, and his wild accusations were nothing more than paranoia as his world came apart.

"Yes, when Kevin disappeared... I'm sorry, died," she said, pausing, "he was not himself, certainly not the man I knew and loved. He was deeply depressed, signs of which were very obvious and that I should have recognized. He felt like his job was always on the line and particularly that Phillip Granville and Badr Laabi were out to get him," she continued. Tears came to her eyes.

"He would go on and on about the two of them leading General Industries down a path of 'treason'... he was convinced they had violated State Department regulations and had broken Federal law."

DeStephano and Leery passed a look between them. Based on everything in the e-mail that had come from Stuart Brown's computer before he died, Keller had been right.

"Detectives, forgive me," Kate interrupted, having caught their glance. "What exactly is this all about?"

DeStephano would have given anything in the world to confirm for Kate Keller at that very moment that her husband hadn't been off his rocker and that everything he claimed was actually true and probably had something to do with his ultimate death. He couldn't, but she would have no trouble in reading between the lines.

"I regret that I can't answer that right now, Mrs. Keller, more than you know. It's terribly unfair of us to come into your life and open this tragedy up again. But it is critically important that we know everything you remember about Kevin's accusations. It is possible that they have something to do with the murders of five General Industries executives over the last couple of months."

A look of horror came over her face.

"Are you saying..."

The two detectives were silent. Kate dropped her face into her hands and sobbed. They waited patiently for her to regain her composure. Finally she spoke again.

"The only other thing I remember was his fixation with an event that occurred years before he died, when he was the executive assistant to the CEO who proceeded Phillip Granville. It haunted him and he spoke to me freely about it just before he died... it was one of the reasons this supposed violation of the embargoes bothered him so much."

She wiped tears off her cheeks, leaned back in her chair and took a deep breath before continuing.

"It was just a few days before Christmas in 1988. I remember it so well, will never forget it because he was so distraught when he came home that night."

DeStephano had leaned forward in his seat on the couch. The date had intrigued him. Leery saw the look on his partner's face and was puzzled by his intensity.

"You see, it was in the middle of the General corporate staff annual Christmas party..." she paused, shaking her head with the aside, "how he hated that thing...

"But the party was interrupted by the news that Pan Am had lost a 747 over Lockerbie, Scotland...I'm sure you remember..." she continued.

DeStephano turned grey.

"It was a terrible tragedy made even worse by the conclusion of the investigators later that night that the plane had been brought down by a bomb."

The senior detective's hands shook as she spoke.

"Mike, are you all right?" Leery asked.

"Yes, detective, you look ill. Can I get you a glass of water or something?" Kate offered.

""No, no," DeStephano begged off. "Please, I'm fine, just continue."

Kate composed herself again, but was even more troubled.

"He was working for the chairman then, so he was very involved in pulling together information of the disaster. In fact I remember him being up all night working, trying to get the facts and to determine if any GIC employee had been aboard the airplane. It ends up there was a young man who was employed by General on board that flight who was killed. He lived not far from here. Kevin went to the funeral. I remember him saying how awful it was. But there are a couple of things about that event that bothered him even more."

DeStephano could not take his eyes off Kate's mouth as she moved her lips. He heard every word she said as if she was screaming it at him to the point where it hurt his ears. He was aware of nothing else around him.

"He told me that the only real concern the General executive team had that night was the fact that the news media was going to immediately put the blame for the disaster on the airplane's engines, and some components GIC supplied for them... and that they were going to lose millions because the company stock price was going to plummet the next morning. It bothered Kevin terribly that it was the money that bothered them, not all the students from Syracuse University who died on their way home for Christmas break or even the General employee who died.

"Actually, I think that night and the callousness he witnessed was the beginning of his doubts about the company and his life in the corporate world. I suppose, looking back, that was when he realized that he didn't belong there."

She stopped. DeStephano pressed for more, his fists clenched so tightly his fingernails were cutting into the palms of his hands.

"You said 'a couple of things' bothered him."

"Well... it was years later... but when he began claiming all this embargo business, it drove him literally to drink to realize that GIC had been selling parts and products to Libya for years before and after Pan Am 103 and that it was Libya that was ultimately held responsible for the bombing of the airplane."

She shook her head.

"I think he felt that his own company had something to do with the disaster — not directly — but because it had been doing business illegally with a country that supported terrorism. He went on and on about that young man's funeral, the General employee who was killed. He just couldn't get it out of his head. It was driving him crazy — crazy enough to threaten to take on Phillip Granville and Laabi."

She shook her head. "It was really terrible to listen to him, he was so torn up about something that had happened a long time before and that he had nothing to do with. But he couldn't let it go.

"The night before his last scheduled meeting with Laabi, we talked for hours. He was sure he was going to get fired. But one of the things he mentioned several times, was something he had come across years before while reading the final investigation report of the Pan Am crash.

"It was the fact that the GIC employee — I'm sorry, I can't remember his name — was specifically referenced in the report."

DeStephano was in agony.

"In what way?" he asked her, barely whispering the words, already knowing the answer.

"It seems his body landed on the sidewalk in front of a house in the village of Lockerbie and was discovered by the woman who owned it. She told the investigators that she covered the poor man with a blanket and reported the location of his body but that no one came. He was dead in the street for three days before anyone came for him."

Kate stared out the front window of the house at a streetlight a block away, her mind lost in a swirl of memories of those last moments with her beloved husband.

"The fact that his body was unattended to for three days while he and the rest of the GIC executive team were concentrating on shoring up the stock price nearly drove Kevin mad." She hesitated and held up a hand. "Mad is not the right word.

"He was so sad."

A deathly silence ended the conversation. DeStephano abruptly stood up and Leery followed suit.

"We've taken enough of your time, Mrs. Keller. Thank you," he said, choking on the words. He shook her hand and walked to the front door and Leery followed. Suddenly, he stopped and turned to Kate.

"Mrs. Keller, I didn't know your husband, but I wish I had. I know he was a good man."

"But how..." Kate answered, puzzled.

"Because he cared about that young man, the employee... who was also a good man with a wife and three children he dearly loved."

Tears streamed down the usually surly tempered detective's face unabated.

"I know all that... because...

UNLEASHED

"Because he was my younger brother, Stephen DeStephano."

Thirty-Two

He dreamt of his children as he slept on the beach. The sweet fragrance of their young skin, the touch of their tiny fingers on his face, the softness of their lips on his cheek. Playing with them on the swing set he had put together in the backyard, running back and forth to keep all three of them simultaneously in motion until he collapsed from exhaustion and they roared with laughter. Of the Christmas mornings when they would race into the bedroom to awaken he and Kate before the crack of dawn so they could scamper downstairs to see what delightful mysteries Santa had left them. Of their birthdays, of making wishes and blowing out candles on homemade chocolate cakes. Of weekends trips to the beach where they would bury him in the sand.

He dreamt of Kate, of loving her. Of holding her hand on their long quiet walks, of exploring the streets of Paris, of crying together as each of their children was born. Of making soft, silent love with her in the darkness of their bedroom lit only by the moonlight, deep under the covers in case they were caught by little eyes. Of surprising her with a kiss for no reason other than that he couldn't resist the temptation. Of her feigned protests when he would mischievously wrestle her into his lap and grope her unashamedly despite her squeals and cries of "Cheap feel!"

And then the dream ended, replaced by the cold that now saturated his bones and awoke him from memories of past joyous moments. Only the vodka had kept him from freezing to death. He forced himself to sit upright and staggered to his feet and into the cottage. Dawn light was just beginning to fill the kitchen. He made coffee and turned on the radio, trying desperately to shake off the pain that now replaced the happiness in his dream.

The coffee was black and strong. He guzzled it down and poured a second cup. The radio was reporting something about Stuart Brown but he wasn't interested. He grabbed the truck keys and went outside. It was waiting, calling him. He hesitated only a moment, knowing that if he blinked now it would never happen. He had to see them, the risk be damned.

Without another thought, he drove the truck along the dirt path out onto Saltus Road and made his way to Route 9. With no traffic, he could make Canton in an hour, perhaps even in time to see his children catch the bus for school near their house.

The bus?

It hit him hard. Sam was now almost 18 years old. Probably in his senior year of high school. Ben would be 15, his baby girl, Julie, 13. If anything, Sam was probably driving them all to school. He pounded the steering wheel with his fist at the frustration of all that he had missed.

He turned on the truck radio to catch the news. It didn't take him long to find what he was looking for. A reporter for WTIC in Hartford came on the air to announce that police were still investigating the death of GIC executive Stuart Brown, the fifth member of the company's executive team to die in less than two months. Four of the deaths were confirmed murders, two of which had occurred in nearby Farmington. The reporter switched to a taped statement by Farmington Police Detective Sergeant Michael DeStephano, who reiterated that the Beckham murder case was still open and there was no new evidence pointing to a suspect. The driver turned off the radio.

"That was a lie, Mike, he said aloud, talking to himself. I just gave you General Industries Corporation on a silver platter with that e-mail. What more do you want?" The truth dawned on him nearly as soon as he thought of the question.

"Me. You want me. You want the guy who murdered five of those bastards. Right?" The silence confirmed his answer. "Well, be patient, big guy. I'm going to give you another present before I'm done."

He took the exit for Route 72 and cut across to pick up I-84 to Farmington and Route 4 onto Collinsville Road in Canton.

Suddenly, he was on the bridge where his life had ended, less than a mile from his house.

Unconsciously, he slowed the truck to a crawl, seeking the spot where his BMW had gone into the Farmington River. A part of him expected to see a marker or a memorial of some sort. There was nothing. Why would there be, he asked himself. They had probably all concluded that he was crazy, perhaps that he had even taken his own life.

He glanced at his watch. 7:15 a.m. What time did school start? He had forgotten such things although they once were so important.

Abruptly, he gripped the steering wheel, startled by an abrupt sense that this was a bad idea. He pulled into the parking lot of a convenience store that was almost adjacent to the entrance of River Road where his family lived. Pulling took deep breaths, taking time to think through a plan. He only wanted to see them. It was all he needed to give him the courage and strength to finish the job.

He looked around and up and down Collinsville Road. Traffic was picking up. It was now or never.

He opened the door of the truck, pulled the collar of his coat up and his John Deere hat down low over his eyes and walked back towards the bridge, being sure to keep his head turned away from the video cameras he knew were mounted in the parking lot. Then he ran across the road at the first break in traffic, walked a few dozen yards and turned down River Road. He walked slowly, as if he were out for an early morning stroll until he was less than 50 yards from the house. Quickly checking in all directions and finding no one around, he ducked into the same underbrush in which he had hidden nearly six years ago.

Memories of watching police, family, friends and GIC executives, including Phillip Granville, Badr Laabi and Paul Stanton come and go after offering their condolences, came rushing back to him as he hunkered down in the brush. It all looked the same. The house was tidy but not quite as neat as when he and Kate built their home and landscaped the property. The swing set was still where he had assembled it, cursing the imbecile who had written the instructions. But two of the swings hung by one chain and the slide was lying on the ground, obviously broken.

Not everything was right here, he thought.

But how could it be.

Almost on cue, he heard the rumbling of the garage door open and he scrambled through the underbrush to get closer to the house without being seen.

Just as he positioned himself perpendicular to the garage, a small Ford sedan backed out and stopped in the driveway. From his vantage point less than 30 yards away, Pulling could tell it was his son Sam behind the wheel, fiddling with the radio.

Tears instantly came to his eyes as he took in the boy, now nearly a man. He was handsome, even from a distance. He felt his heart flutter. The boy was clearly his son by his features. He could only hope he had his mother's brains and compassion.

Before he could dwell anymore on Sam, the front door of the house flew open and Ben and Julie followed, flying down the front landing and hurrying to join Sam in the car.

"Shotgun!" he heard Ben yell as he threw a backpack into the back seat, slam the door then jump into the front passenger seat.

"You had it yesterday," Julie whined, accepting the inequity with a shrug and getting in the back seat. Pulling had just enough time to catch a glimpse of each of their faces. They were the spitting image of Kate.

He grabbed his thighs with his fingers, digging into the flesh even through his denim pants. He hadn't expected this to be so painful. Before he could absorb anymore of them, Sam backed down the driveway and pulled on to River Road on the way to Canton High School. The thick underbrush protected him from being seen but also blocked a last look at them.

His heart was beating furiously now. He had to see Kate, somehow. But he had no idea if she worked or not, if she would be leaving the house or would be inside all day. He looked to see a second car in the garage, but almost in the same moment, the door closed. At least he knew she was in the house.

For the next hour, he knelt in the brush, racking his brain for a way to draw her outside. But every idea he imagined was fraught with the possibility of alarming her. He sat tight, hoping, watching the windows for signs of her moving around the house. He was frantic for just a glimpse of the woman he still loved with all his heart. He felt like a teenage boy bearing the heartbreak of a crush on the school's unapproachable prom queen.

But instead of sorrow, he began to fill with rage again. There had been a time when he knew that Kate had loved him deeply. Now, he was unsure of her feelings, could not know how she remembered him or if she even thought of him. It came to him that hiding in the brush, just yards away from the woman who had been his soul mate, whom he still desperately loved and needed, might just push him over the edge to insanity. He was still sane enough to know, given the atrocities he had committed without an ounce of remorse, that he only had a razor's edge grasp of stability left in him and he was now capable of almost anything. It came to him in a momentary surge of clarity that he had to leave quickly or risk everything. Kevin Keller was on the verge of reemerging and giving in to the powerful ache in his heart. He couldn't let that happen or he would put them all in harms way again.

Instantly he jumped up from his hiding place and began moving back through the underbrush to a place where he could safely get back on to River Road without being seen. But just as he made the road, far behind him he heard a garage door open and knew instinctively that it was Kate.

He broke into a run, trying to get back to his truck before she came upon him. He was out in the open now with nowhere to hide. Pulling glanced over his shoulder and saw a car bearing down on him from behind. It was her. She would be on him in seconds.

He was sprinting now, urgently trying to reach the obscurity of Collinsville Road when the car overtook him. He dared not look inside it as it passed by and he continued to run. The car continued on and he thought for just a second that he was safe, that she had not seen him. Then, without warning, he watched as her brake lights flashed on and the car skidded to a stop. He kept running toward her as she stared, transfixed, into the rear view mirror as he approached.

The driver's door flew open and Kate jumped out wide-eyed at the stranger about to run by her car. Pulling grabbed the brow of his hat and yanked it down lower over his eyes and looked away as he passed her standing in the road, her mouth agape.

"Sir," she said quietly as he passed, "stop, please... please, stop just for a moment..." He kept running. He was nearly to the corner when he heard her yell.

"Kevin? Is that you, Kevin?" Her voice was breaking. "Please, stop...!"

He didn't break stride and ran across Collinsville Road without looking, barely escaping being hit by cars speeding by in both directions. He reached the truck, fumbled with his keys then started it, jammed the old Ford into gear and peeled out of the parking lot heading north.

Kate Keller still stood by her car, tears streaming down her face, her hands clutching her throat. It couldn't be, she thought, he's dead... he's dead, she repeated over and over, her hands trembling. She finally slumped to the road to her knees, overcome by emotions. Her heart and soul filled with sorrow.

But fear crept into her mind.

Thirty-Three
~~~ ◊ ~~~

Canton police came to Kate's rescue within minutes of an eyewitness in the parking lot placing the call for help. They found her lying beside her car, her eyes open, staring silently at clusters of soft cumulus clouds passing overhead. Tears stained her cheeks, but she appeared unhurt.

"Ma'am, are you all right?" a blue uniformed police officer asked her while waiting for an ambulance to arrive. He could hear the sound of an electronic siren whooping towards them.

"What?" Kate said, nearly whispering the words. She was dazed.

"Are you hurt?" Sergeant Doug Moore pressed, but she seemed to come around more with each passing minute.

"No, I don't think so." She looked at the young man. "What happened?" she asked in confusion.

"Let's let these guys take a look at you before we talk anymore, ok?" the cop said as a couple of EMT's rolled up. "You just relax, seems like something has upset you."

Kate shook her head. "It was him…"

The officer stepped back without comment and let the EMT's check her out. He turned to his partner, patrolman Rick Raymond.

"Weird. Must have had some sort of seizure. I'm sure she'd pass a Breathalyzer or drug test," Moore said. "But she did mumble something about, "It was him."

"I pulled a driver's license out of her pocketbook on the front seat, Sarge," the junior officer said. "This appears to be Kate Keller, address 50 yards that-a-way," he pointed to the house at the corner of River Road.

"She must have just pulled out. Keller… Keller… Rick, isn't that the guy who went off…"

"Yah, the BMW that went off the bridge, three, four years ago? He was a big shot with, uh… Beckham, in Farmington."

"Yah, that's the guy. Wonder if this is his wife. They never found the guy's body, did they?"

"I don't think so," Moore said. "But I think they closed the jacket after he was declared legally dead." He watched as the EMT's treated the attractive woman, thinking.

"Listen, these guys are going to transport her to John Dempsey Hospital, I'm going to ride along and talk with her. Get someone to tow her car back to the house and then follow me in. But let the watch commander know who I've got here. If I'm not mistaken, the Farmington Police are still interested in anything and anyone associated with Beckham after that double homicide a couple months ago."

"Got it, Sarge. Meet you at Dempsey," the patrolman responded, referring to the hospital at the University of Connecticut Medical Center in Farmington.

The Canton police officer jumped into the back of the ambulance after Kate was loaded aboard on a stretcher, despite her protestations.

"This is ridiculous, I'm fine," she said. " I think I just imagined something and it was so upsetting I fainted. Just silly."

"Are you Mrs. Kate Keller?" Moore asked her as one of the EMT's placed an oxygen line into her nose and attached a blood pressure cuff.

"Yes, I just live around the corner…"

"I know. They're just going to take a quick look at you at John Dempsey to make sure you haven't suffered any sort of event," Mrs. Keller.

"Oh, dear. Such a lot of bother. I'm sure you have better things to do, " she said, apologizing.

"It's ok, I'd rather be talking with you than my partner," he said in jest. "We run out of small talk after awhile." He smiled, trying to put her at ease.

"It was so strange," Kate said.

"What was strange?"

"Well, I was just driving to the supermarket while the kids were at school and as I turned onto River Road, I saw a man jogging. He was quite a bit ahead of me, but I swear…" She paused and put a hand to her eyes.

"What," Moore probed. "Please go on, Mrs. Keller."

She wiped tears away from her eyes.

"I thought his gait, you know, the way he ran, reminded me of someone. Someone who's been dead now for such a long time."

"You mean, you're late husband, Mrs. Keller?" Moore asked.

She looked at him startled.

"Why yes, but how could you know?"

"Well, I recognized your name from the accident a few years back. I was just a patrolman at the time but did some of the investigation at the scene. Also volunteered quite a few weekends looking for him along the Farmington River," he said.

"Oh…" The word caught in her throat.

"I'm sorry, I didn't mean to make you cry," the Sergeant apologized.

"It's not you, " she said. "The tears are always at the ready." A slight smile came to her face. Moore thought she was particularly beautiful. "I don't think anyone ever gets over losing a loved one."

"I know what you mean. My wife died of breast cancer shortly before your husband was lost. We were only married about 10 years. Not a day goes by that I don't think about her."

"Oh, I'm so sorry…" she said, reaching for the officers hand.

"Don't be. She was suffering terribly. It was a blessing. And I feel fortunate compared to what you've gone through."

"What do you mean?" Kate asked, puzzled.

"I got to say goodbye to her."

She managed to nod her head in understanding and choked out a few words. "That's the hardest part of all. He just disappeared."

"And I take it you thought you saw him?" Moore asked, turning the conversation back.

Yes. I think it probably has to do with a visit I had just last night from two detectives from the Farmington Police Department who came by to ask me some questions about Kevin's behavior before he died. They're working on some sort of investigation having to do with those awful murders at Beckham headquarters some time ago. "

Bingo, Moore thought. He was glad they'd called this in. The Farmington guys would definitely be interested. Probably DeStephano, he thought. The guy had a vested interest.

"So, did you finally get a look at this man, the guy running?" he asked.

"Yes... and that's what was so troubling. He had a hat pulled down low and seemed to be trying to hide his face as I passed. But I caught a glimpse. I could have sworn it was Kevin. My husband."

He squeezed her hand. "I'm sure that was very painful."

"My *dead* husband," Kate continued. "I yelled to him to stop but he wouldn't and ran across the street, nearly got hit by a couple of cars. Then he jumped into an old pickup truck and raced out of the parking lot. It seemed like he was trying to escape..."

Moore was silent. This was getting weirder by the minute.

"An old truck? Could you make out the plates or the make?" he asked.

"No, I'm sorry. I wouldn't know a Chevy from a Toyota and I was too shocked to even think to look at the license plates.

"Well, maybe we can check that out, make sure we know why the guy was in the neighborhood," Moore said. "Let me just make a quick call." He used his cell phone and called Raymond following behind.

"Hey Rick, have somebody get back to that convenience store and see if anyone saw a late model pickup pull out of the parking lot at a high rate of speed within the last 30 minutes. Pull whatever security tapes they might have as well, ok? Looking for the plates and a peek at the driver."

"Roger that, Sarge," Raymond responded.

Moore put his phone away and turned back to Kate.

"Standard operating procedure," he lied. "Just checking," he smiled to reassure her. "What time do your children usually come home from school? I'll have someone there to meet them, make sure they know you're all right."

"Oh, my god, no... I don't think seeing a police car in the driveway is going to be ok for them, they have enough memories, officer..."

"Geez, how insensitive of me... I'll make sure it's an unmarked car. Sometimes I don't think, Mrs. Keller."

"Don't be silly," she said. "I'm just overly sensitive to how they remember their dad. Try to make any mention of him a positive one. They've had enough police cars in their lives."

"I understand..." Moore said, silently kicking himself. He shook his head. His one shot at love was gone. His late wife was the only one who would ever understand him for what he was. As she used to tell her friends: "Dougie is kind with a touch of tough guy."

It seemed to him that Kevin Keller had been as blessed as he was until his luck ran out.

"Poor bastard," he mumbled under his breath.

"What was that?" Kate asked, puzzled.

"Oh, excuse me, Mrs. Keller. Just cop talk. Rest now. Let's make sure you're ok."

And he meant it.

Thirty-Four

The two Farmington detectives met the ambulance at John Dempsey Hospital as it pulled up to the emergency room entrance.

Moore jumped out of the truck first and recognized DeStephano and Leery. They'd worked a few cases together. He beckoned them to follow him inside where they could talk privately.

"Hey Mike, Dennis, good to see you guys. Think you'll be interested in the package we brought in. Beautiful lady. You got my call?" Moore said.

Detective Sergeant Mike DeStephano grabbed Moore's proffered hand. "Great to see you, Doug and congrats on that new stripe. Well earned, I'm sure."

"Yah, Doug," Leery chimed in. "And thanks for the tip. We were out to see Mrs. Keller just last night. So what went down?"

"She said you'd been by. Suspected it was you two. This is bizzarro, guys..." Moore replied.

"How so?" DeStephano responded.

"She's certain she saw her late husband, you know, the guy who died..."

"Yah, very familiar with it, Doug," the senior detective interrupted impatiently.

"She thinks she saw him jogging by her house. And when she asked him to stop, the guy ran through traffic, almost killed himself trying to get away from her. I'm looking into the make and registration on the truck she saw him jump into now. Hopefully we'll have security video to look at by the time I get back to the office."

"Kevin Keller," Leery said.

Moore nodded. "Yah. Now she thinks it was probably just something she imagined, maybe prompted by your meet with her last night."

"Shit..." DeStephano said while Leery groaned. "Never intended that to happen. But we had to talk with her, there's some odd connection we're trying to figure out between Keller and that mess at Beckham a couple of months ago. A real mind bender to figure out but we're trying to put the pieces together."

"What kind of shape is she in now?" Leery asked.

"Shaky, but ok. Not sure you're going to get anything more out of her than I did, to be honest. Maybe you could leave her to me," Moore offered. "I'll push a little more, gently and keep an eye on her at the house."

"You're probably right, Doug. Get back to me ASAP if you catch anything on that video. I mean, if it was Keller..."

"Jesus. I can't figure that, Mike. I hiked miles of that Farmington River section for weeks after if happened. Don't know how he could have survived the crash to begin with. And all we found was a wallet and some photos."

"Somethin' is snake eyes here, Doug..."

"But even if it was him, even if he isn't dead, why now? Why surface again after all these years? What's the point?"

"Dunno," DeStephano replied, shrugging his shoulders. "Maybe he never wanted to play dead to begin with. Maybe he's come back to hurt some people, get a little payback, but couldn't resist a look at the wife and kids. I don't know. But it doesn't add up."

The two detectives turned their backs as Kate was wheeled into the hospital. Moore waved to her. "I'll see you inside, Mrs. Keller," he said.

The cop's cell phone rang.

"Yah. No shit... where? Good job. Let's get a team over there and dust it." He was silent as he listened to additional information.

"A false bed? How deep?" DeStephano's eyes narrowed as he saw a look of bewilderment appear on Moore's face.

"Ok. Get the forensics guys all over that thing. Let's see what he was so eager to hide. Get back to me."

He hung up the phone and turned to the Farmington detectives.

"One of our patrol cars found the truck abandoned in a field just out of town. Matches the truck on security video we got from a parking lot camera. Truck is registered to a Thomas Pulling of Hamilton, Montana."

"Don't know the name… you Dennis?"

"No. What about the truck bed?" Leery asked.

"Apparently my guys found that the pickup had a false floor bed, about six inches deep. The truck was obviously modified to carry something without being seen."

"Drugs?" Leery asked.

"Could be, but I doubt it. Just a hunch," DeStephano responded.

"Get a look at the driver on the tape?" he asked.

"Yah," Moore replied. "Nothing conclusive. White male, six foot, slight build, 160 pounds, John Deere cap and jeans. Wearing work boots. This was no jogger."

"Wonder how Thomas Pulling matches up against Kevin Keller's profile," Leery mumbled.

"Yah, I was thinking the same thing," DeStephano said. "Can you ship the video to my office, Doug? Want to do some analysis."

"Sure, right away. I'm going to head inside and hold Mrs. Keller's hand for a bit. I'll call you if I get any more from her. In the meantime, I'm also going to have a car watch the house, at least for the next couple of nights."

"Thanks, Doug, let's stay close."

"Roger that, Mike," Moore said and walked into the hospital.

*　*　*

"God dammit, how stupid could I be," Tom Pulling screamed aloud as he struggled through heavy brush some two miles from where he had dumped his old pickup. He needed to get back to the main road and find another car somewhere.

But it wasn't his predicament or his instincts that told him the police were looking for him that had him enraged. It was the look in Kate's eyes when she recognized him. In the split second they had made eye contact, the hurt, the pain he saw in her beautiful blue eyes told him what her life had become since his disappearance. And he damned himself for being so selfish as to risk re-opening the floodgates of sorrow and regret that might finally overwhelm her.

"What was I thinking," he berated himself over and over as he crashed through the brush. Finally, he came to the road. He thought he had crossed over the Canton town line into New Hartford but couldn't be sure. He knelt low, out of sight of traffic in either direction, and scanned the scene ahead. He had lucked out by emerging almost directly across the street from a busy shopping center with multiple stores. There were hundreds of cars in a huge parking lot.

Acting quickly, he rose from his hiding place and walked into the first parking lot, searching out an inconspicuous late model sedan in a remote area. There. He spied a late 90's Buick four-door, beige. Nothing could be more boring or non-descript. The perfect car to steal because it wasn't worth stealing.

The police would put very little effort into tracking it down. Pulling approached the car, making sure he wasn't being watched, then slammed his elbow into the drivers side window, smashing it. He reached in, unlocked the door and jumped in, then pulled a Swiss Army knife out of his pocket and opened the flat blade screwdriver. He plunged the tip into the cylinder lock and slammed it in with the palm of his hand, then twisted the ignition clockwise and broke it. The car turned over immediately. Less than 15 seconds after eyeballing the car, he was driving slowly out of the parking lot.

Working to calm himself, Pulling backtracked on Collinsville Road eventually driving past the entrance to River Road. Kate's car was gone and there did not appear to be any police presence. He dared not drive past her house instinctively knowing the possibility that it was being watched. He smashed his fist on the steering wheel, not out of the frustration of nearly being caught, but by the pain he knew he had caused Kate. Even giving her a fantasy that he was still alive was so cruel.

He had to stop berating himself. It was done. It was stupid, but it was done. He had seen them. They were all safe, so long as he didn't blow it now. Pulling forced himself to refocus on his plan as he drove back to the beach house. He was close to ending this, but there was much work left to be done.

An hour later, he pulled off Saltus Drive in Saybrook and rolled the Buick up in front of the cottage. He lit a cigarette and took his time eyeballing the place. Nothing seemed out of order. He walked around to the front, checking for footprints on the beach. Nothing. Letting himself inside, he turned on the radio for news while he drank from a bottle of vodka to calm himself. The news was quiet. The River Road scene was quite dramatic, but hardly newsworthy, he figured. But Pulling bet that Kate had alleged to have seen her late husband and that the story had gotten back to DeStephano.

He walked outside and sat on the beach, watching the tide creep in and listening to it splash on the sandy shore. The afternoon sun had warmed the air and it was a comfortable place to think.

Detective Sergeant Michael DeStephano. Was he a friend or foe, Pulling wondered. He could feel his stomach churn at the memory of his interaction with the detective and his sister-in-law and Phillip Granville after the death of Stephen DeStephano in Lockerbie. Granville had been brutally cruel, even by his standards, almost hateful in his derisive treatment of the family. He wondered if the cop still hated him for not standing up to Granville.

The opportunity to test that theory was fast approaching.

But what did he know? Had he put the pieces together from the report he had forced Stuart Brown to send before he died? Had he tied together all the murders?

Had the name "Kevin Keller" crossed his lips?

He had to know.

The only way he was going to be able to carry out the rest of his plan was to understand what DeStephano did or didn't know. They would somehow have to talk.

Pulling dug into his jacket pocket and pulled out the "burner" cell phone that he had purchased at a 7-11 convenience store. It was prepaid under an assumed named. It was intended to be used only a few times before being "burned" or disposed of before the number could be traced.

He stared at it for a minute, thinking of how technology and the underground world was making law enforcement almost impossible. The ease with which he was able to buy this phone and others, fake passports, credit cards, driver's licenses, even birth certificates was almost comical. But worse was the frightening arsenal of weapons and explosives that he had been able to acquire on the black market with the same ease. If you had a reason to hide or a reason to kill, all it took was finding the right people and a wad of cash.

He pulled the number of the Farmington Police Department off the Internet and dialed it. It was 3 p.m. Probably at shift change but he doubted that the clock meant anything to the detective. Not with five linked murders on his desk and a file that proved Phillip Granville was the corporate equivalent of Satan himself.

Detective Dennis Leery had just put down the phone after an update from Canton police Sergeant Doug Moore on Kate Keller when his phone rang. He wanted to ignore it and brief his partner but something told him to answer it.

"Yah, Detective Dennis Leery. Can I help you?" he said in a monotone. After nearly 30 hours on the job without a wink of sleep he hoped it wasn't an old lady reporting her cat up in a tree. For the old lady's sake.

" Uh... I'm looking for Detective DeStephano."

"Well, I'm his partner, can I help you?"

"No. Need to speak with DeStephano."

Leery took a deep breath and let it out slowly.

"Ok, what's your name?"

"Not important. Put him on."

The telephone suddenly felt warm in Leery's hand. It was a common occurrence for the detective when he had someone important on the phone. His blood pressure shot up immediately causing him to have the equivalent of a hot flash.

He played along.

"Stop wasting my time. Your name?"

"Give the fucking phone to DeStephano. Last chance," Pulling replied firmly.

"Sure... whatever you say, pal." He pushed down the sudden vision of shoving a hot poker... Leery pressed the hold button and turned to his partner.

"Guess who?" he said. His boss barely acknowledged him. The senior detective was pulling the pertinent information he needed from the Stuart Brown report to brief the Feds and the State Department so he could get search and seizure and arrest warrants and make a move on GIC. They had to work fast on this. If Granville realized the report had leaked, he'd have shredders at work in a hundred offices around the world in a matter of minutes and make shambles of the detective's case. Surprise was the optimum word here.

"You gotta take this, boss..." Leery said. "It's him."

"Who is 'him'?"

"I think it's Thomas Pulling. Just a hunch. Guy won't give me his name."

DeStephano's jaw dropped. Fish rarely jumped into a held net.

"Pulling... a.k.a Kevin Keller."

"Just a hunch, boss," he repeated.

"If I was a betting man, I'd say he's trying to figure out what we know. Let's see what he has to say."

DeStephano stabbed the button for the line with his finger.

"This is Detective Sergeant DeStephano. Can I help you?"

There was a pause on the line.

"Hello?"

"Michael DeStephano? Had a brother named Stephen?"

The hair on the back of the detectives stood up. There were very few people who knew that or cared. It was Keller. He played it cool.

"Right. Listen, I'm very busy. What is it that you want? Maybe we can start with your name."

"Not important," the caller said again. "What is important is that we meet."

"Meet? Why the fuck would I want to meet a guy who won't even tell me his name?" DeStephano said, pushing.

"Because I have information you need. About Badr, Stanton, Stuart Brown and the Europeans. That enough for you to invest your time in a meeting?"

"You have my attention. Where?"

Pulling was smart enough not to be set up.

"Drive to the 7th floor of the parking garage at Merchants Plaza. Be there in one hour. Stay in the car. If I see anyone with you or any sign of cops anywhere near us, the deal's off. I'll disappear."

"Again?" DeStephano said sarcastically. There was no response.

"You think you know something, Detective. You're wrong. Be there. One hour." The line went dead.

Leery's eyes were bulging.

"Well... was it Keller or Pulling or whoever the hell we're looking for?"

"Pretty sure. Wants to meet."

"Meet?" Leery said. "You're going to? Do I have to remind you that this is one pissed off guy, a serial killer with a motive?"

"No."

"So?"

"I'm going. Alone. Merchants Plaza parking lot. We take two cars. Want you to park on Main Street and wait for my call. No one else is involved, understood?" DeStephano said, in a tone of voice that said his instructions were absolutely non-negotiable.

"What do you expect to gain from this? Accept maybe a bullet in the back of the head," Leery said, skeptically.

"Not sure. But he mentioned my brother. I think he may actually be looking for an ally. Maybe he's under the impression that we share a common goal."

"Such as?"

"Bringing down Phillip Granville."

Leery eyed his boss for a moment.

"He wouldn't be far off base, would he, Mike." It was a statement, not a question.

DeStephano didn't respond.

"Look, chances are he'll at least tip me off to his next move, and just maybe I can confirm that Keller and Pulling are the same people... "

"Which would mean you're right. Keller is still alive."

"And Kate Keller isn't crazy."

"Right," the senior detective said. "In fact, better call Moore. Tell him that we need to keep a 24-hour watch on the Keller family — all of them — for the next few days. We'll help if he has manpower problems."

"Why? You think Keller would hurt his family? What's his motive?" Leery asked, puzzled.

"No, not intentionally. I just don't think this guy is sane enough to realize what he would put his wife and kids through if he was to just reappear with every cop in Connecticut chasing him. That scenario has a bad ending. They've been through enough."

Leery had never known Michael DeStephano to look at the outcome of a case with compassion for the perp or the victim. It was always just "nail the mother, whatever it takes." His sudden concern for the welfare of the Keller family caught him off guard. His boss had some emotions invested in this case, something Leery was only beginning to understand. But he worried that it might cause his partner to lose his edge.

Now it was Leery who had a bad feeling about what was coming.

Thirty-Five

Exactly on time, Detective Sergeant Michael DeStephano pulled his unmarked Ford sedan into the above ground parking garage at Merchants Plaza, directly adjacent to the office tower that served as General Industries corporate headquarters. He wheeled the car slowly up to the 7th floor as the man on the telephone had instructed, keeping an eye open for anything that resembled a trap. It was a Friday afternoon and he figured a good percentage of the Pinstripers who parked here had already left for the weekend. After all, the stock market was closed now, there was no one left on Wall Street to help them cheat and steal.

"Now, now, Michael, keep an open mind," his conscience told him as it always did when he ventured into this world. Usually he tried. He didn't feel like putting much effort into it today.

"Screw you, Phillip Granville. It won't be long before your ass is mine," he thought to himself.

He arrived on the 7th floor and slowed his car to a crawl. There wasn't another parked on the floor. He stopped then backed into a parking spot so he could see in all directions. Despite the late afternoon chill, he opened the driver's side window and waited.

A moment later, it was more than the cold that chilled him.

The red light bounced off the driver's side windshield pillar and then quickly found his chest. It was so sudden that it took the veteran detective several seconds to process what it was.

Destephano looked down. There was no mistaking the glowing light, slightly smaller than the diameter of a dime focused directly on his heart. It was a red dot sight, probably combined with a day/night infrared illuminator vision scope. Somewhere out there at the other end of the light painting his heart was a shooter with a powerful, ultra sophisticated rifle that would disintegrate the vital organ with a single shot. He was a sitting duck.

He forced himself to resist the urge to fall across the bench seat in the unmarked car, knowing that the shooter could take him out before his muscles would allow him to move a fraction of an inch.

Instead, he slowly raised his two hands above the steering wheel showing that he was unarmed.

"Ok, you made your point," the detective hollered out. He had no idea where the gunman was hidden. There were no other cars in the lot, no visible spot where he might be hiding.

There was no reply.

Then his cell phone rang.

DeStephano nodded with understanding and picked up the phone.

"Stay in the car," the voice on the other end said curtly.

"Don't worry pal, you seem to have the upper hand. I thought you wanted to meet."

"We're meeting," the invisible shooter replied. "I just didn't think it was appropriate that we got very close on our first date."

"Stop jerking me around, Keller," DeStephano yelled into the phone, angrily.

"Kevin Keller is dead, Detective! How could you forget?"

"Keller, Thomas Pulling, whatever name you want to use makes no difference to me," the detective shot back. "You've murdered five men. You can call yourself Clark Gable for all I care. You're going down."

There was an explosion and a shower of concrete as a single rifle shot blew into the wall across from his car. Immediately, the red dot returned to his chest.

"Whoa. Something I said, Clark?" the detective said into the phone, dangerously baiting the shooter.

"Shut the fuck up, Mike," he replied.

"Mike?" Now we're on a first name basis? What is it that you want, man? If I didn't know better, I'd say you were a bit anxious. But any man who can wait for years for vengeance is probably over-endowed with patience. What's your story? And what do you want from me?"

"Patience..." the shooter replied into the phone. The detective heard the resignation in his voice. "You have no idea."

"I guess I don't, pal. I'm trying to pull this together, but..."

"I handed him to you, Mike? What more do you need?"

"Who? Who did you hand to me?" the detective replied, puzzled. "I'm lost."

"Phillip Granville!" he screamed. "Haven't you read Stuart Brown's e-mail? You think that just happened? Have you taken the time to read it? Answer me or so help me I'll put one through that lazy skull of yours..."

DeStephano had come to two conclusions. The first was that the shooter was not in the parking garage, but probably on the rooftop of one of several adjacent buildings. The second was that he was dangerously unhinged. Anything could set him off. He backed off.

"Yah, I read it," he replied with a gentler tone. "With great interest. Phillip Granville is going to get his. In fact, I'm betting General Industries Corporation shareholders are going to wake up some morning not too long from now holding a lot of worthless shares. The whole thing is going to collapse. Because of Stuart Brown's e-mail.

"Which, I'm guessing, you made sure I received."

"Ha!" the gunman laughed into the phone. "That's the understatement of the year. Let's just say Stuart wouldn't have sent it without a little... call it 'coercion' on my part. Spiders. Can you believe that a scumbag who wouldn't think twice about sending arms to a dictator could be frightened to death by a tiny little spider?"

"How'd you figure that one out, Kevin? I mean, that spider thing wasn't just an accident…"

"I was there…" Keller began, then hesitated.

"Kevin Keller is dead, god damn it. You want another demonstration, Mike?"

"Whoa, don't mean to excite you, pal. Just tying to have a friendly conversation."

"I'm not interested in chit-chat, detective. Let's get down to business."

"Ok, I'm all ears."

There was a pause. He's probably taking a scan of the area, looking for my backup, DeStephano thought during the silence.

"You probably wonder why I sent you the Stuart Brown report…?" the stranger asked.

"Well, I didn't know it had come from you. Until now."

"Don't bullshit me, Mike."

"I figured it came from the same guy who took out Laabi, Stanton and the two Europeans. That much made sense," DeStephano said, playing dumb. He didn't want to give Keller any more than he had to.

"Well then, I'll tell you. A whole lot of people hate Phillip Granville, you know? But there aren't many who are ready to kill him, or would celebrate his murder."

"I guess that's true," the detective replied, wondering where this was going.

"Accept for you and me."

The detective involuntarily jerked in his seat, he was so taken aback by the comment.

"What? What could possibly bring you to that conclusion?" he replied.

"Do you know that your brother's body was left unattended for three days on a sidewalk in Lockerbie, Mike?"

"What the fuck does that have to do with anything, you frigging psychopath?"

"Careful, I may be insane, but I still have feelings," the shooter laughed.

"And then, like pissing on your brother's grave, Granville didn't have the decency to bend the rules just a tiny bit... for something that would have made such a difference in your sister-in-law's life and for those kids. And from what I understand, for you too. Uncle Mike has spent the last ten years playing husband and father for his late brother. You've given up your life for his family. I admire that."

DeStephano couldn't answer. Memories of the conversation with Granville flooded his brains. He gripped the steering wheel hard and regained his composure.

"You were at the meeting, if I recall, Kevin. I guess you remember it the same as I do. So Granville's a scumbag. So what."

"He took your life away, Mike," he replied, ignoring the Keller reference. "Stephen's wife and kids are completely dependent on you. Without your help, they would have lost the house... everything. You go to work everyday, for them."

"That's none of your fucking business," the detective shot back.

"But it is, Mike. You've wanted Phillip Granville dead longer than I have."

It was as if Detective Sergeant Michael DeStephano had stuck his finger in an electrical socket. The hair on the back of his neck stood up with the shock of hearing the unvarnished truth come out of Keller's mouth. Not a day had gone by since Granville had trashed his brother's memory that the detective hadn't dreamed of cutting the GIC chairman's tongue out of his head and stapling it to his fancy desk.

"What he took away from me was even worse, Mike. He took my whole life away. My wife, my children. Everything."

"How?" DeStephano pressed. The real motive was about to come spilling out of Keller's guts.

"He and Laabi promised to kill my family if I went anywhere with the information in the Stuart Brown e-mail. He had them being stalked, a van outside watching their every move.

"Phillip Granville was going to have them killed if he thought they knew anything."

DeStephano thought a moment before he replied.

"So you faked an accident and disappeared... to protect them..."

"It was no accident, detective! I was trying to save..." Keller caught himself.

"That's not important. What I need to know is when you're going to move on Granville. You certainly should have enough information to whet the appetite of the Justice Department and the U.S. government."

"I can't tell you that..."

"I want to talk to Granville first," the gunman replied.

"You mean you want me to give you the opportunity to murder him," DeStephano shot back. "No frigging way. I don't care what he did to you... or to me... you can't just murder people and expect to walk..."

"I don't expect to walk," Keller replied. "I'm done. My life is over. I only have one thing left to do to ensure they're protected."

"Protecting your family is my job, Keller. Back off. Give yourself up and I can help you..."

"Don't be stupid, Mike, you've got enough protecting of your own to do. I've killed five men. More will die before I'm done. My life is already over."

He hesitated for a second, almost as if he couldn't bear to hear the words.

"Daddy's never coming home."

There was a long silence as both men thought of their next move.

"Will you tell me?" the shooter asked again.

"I can't." He thought for a moment. Maybe there was a way to stop him. He dropped the bait.

"But it will be soon."

Silence.

"Is Kate alright?"

"You mean the woman you frightened half to death today?"

"Is she alright?" he demanded.

"Yes. And surrounded by cops. Stay away," DeStephano warned.

"Don't worry."

"Yah, sure," the detective replied.

"Thanks for the meeting."

"My pleasure."

A long silence.

"Wanted to tell you something for a long time."

"What's that?"

"Your brother was a good guy. He deserved better. Was lucky to have a brother like you."

The detective couldn't find words to respond.

"Come in. I'll help you," he said instead. "You had a reason for your actions."

"Don't waste your breath, Mike, just do me one favor, ok?"

"What?"

"When Granville hits the pavement, take your time cleaning up the mess."

He paused.

"Three days ought to do it."

The cell phone went dead. DeStephano looked down at his chest.

The red dot was gone.

Thirty-Six

Canton Police Sergeant Doug Moore helped Kate Keller into his black and white patrol car parked in front of John Dempsey Hospital where she had just been released from observation. The traumatic experience of believing she had seen her late husband earlier that day had left her shaken and jittery, but otherwise ok. She was anxious to get home to see her children who were presently being looked after by Moore's partner, Patrolman Rick Raymond.

Moore eased into the driver's seat and radioed Canton dispatch that he was driving to River Road. Kate smiled at him, wordlessly thanking the Sergeant for his many kindnesses that day.

"It wasn't him, was it?" she asked, almost whispering the words as they drove back to Canton.

"No, I'm afraid not, Mrs. Keller," Moore replied with genuine compassion. He knew only too well what it felt like to be lonely.

"It must have been a horrible experience. I'm sorry," he continued.

"Don't be. I'm at peace with Kevin's death for the most part. It's just that the shock of seeing him... or someone who looked like him... it's just so confusing. I'm so glad the kids weren't in the car with me. They would have freaked out.

"We found him, you know," Moore said, hoping to put the issue to rest for her.

"The man I saw?" she asked in surprise.

"Yes. His name is Thomas Pulling. He's from Montana. He's been driving cross-country to see America, as they say, and just got out to stretch his legs for a while. Decided he would take a little jog. Unfortunately, he picked the wrong street."

"Doesn't he look like Kevin?" she asked, a slight bit of hope still ringing in her voice.

"I did some comparisons ma'am. I can see how you might have made the mistake. But it wasn't Kevin."

"Oh."

"For what it's worth, he was very sorry for any pain he might have caused you. I believed him."

"Why did he run?"

Moore chuckled.

"Actually, he said you frightened him the way you slammed on the breaks and jumped out of the car. He just wanted to get away from you."

Moore hoped she would smile. She didn't.

Kate lapsed into a long silence as they drove home.

"I'm not crazy, you know. I just miss him so," the widow finally said.

"Oh Kate...I mean Mrs. Keller, no one thinks you're crazy. After all you went through? I'm sorry if I implied that. And believe me, I know what it feels like to miss someone you loved with all your heart. It's an ache that never goes away."

"Can I see him?"

"I'm afraid not. We asked him to be on his way, considering the circumstances," he lied. "He understood and left for someplace up north a few hours ago. Told me to tell you how sorry he was before he left."

"That was nice of him." She paused for a moment, deep in thought. "For a while, while I was in therapy, I hung on to an idea that each of us has an identical clone, somewhere in the world, and all we have to do is find him or her... you know, to find peace."

Moore did not respond.

"I got over it pretty quickly with the help of my psychiatrist," she laughed. "You can relax, Sergeant."

He smiled. "Call me Doug, please, Mrs. Keller."

"So long as you agree to call me Kate," she grinned.

"Deal," he said, his eyes softening.

They drove in silence again for a while.

"I really am sorry you had to go through that this morning, Kate," Moore said gently, reaching down and touching her hand resting on the front seat.

She looked over at him, her blue eyes sparkling in the late afternoon winter sun.

"Thank you Doug. But if it hadn't, I might not have had a chance to meet someone as kind as you. I'm grateful for that."

Before he could think of anything to say that wouldn't give away how flustered her comment had him, they were turning into her driveway on River Road and her children burst through the front door.

"Well, here's the tribe!" she said. "My whole world. I wonder, if you have a moment, would you like to meet them, Doug?"

The Sergeant beamed as he straightened his tie and put on his hat, looking into the rear view mirror to make sure it was cocked just right. He was also checking to see that the surveillance car he'd asked for was in sight. It was.

"There's nothing I'd like more, Kate."

He'd forgotten how long it had been since he'd opened the car door for a lady, but he decided a good first step here was a wise investment.

"You wait right there, Kate," he said, and got out of the car, walked around to the passenger side and opened her door. It did not go unnoticed by the three Keller children who waited patiently while their mother got out of the car. Then they mobbed her with hugs and kisses. Eventually, Kate freed herself from their grasp and managed to introduce Sergeant Doug Moore as her knight in shining armor. The Keller children each shook hands with him.

A block away, Patrolman Ray Reynolds smiled as he watched the homecoming. It was about time his partner got a break. Something told him a seed of something really good had been planted over the last few hours. He looked on as the Keller family and their uniformed guest moved inside.

Then he took a long sip of his cold coffee and went back to watching. At the top of his list of things to be looking for was a black van.

* * *

On Route 9, the stolen beige Buick sedan was nearing Exit 2 for Old Saybrook. The driver was just a few minutes from the safety of his leased hideaway in the North Cove with it's comforting view of the ocean on one side and somewhat uneasy presence of the adjacent Riverside Cemetery on the other. It was possible both would be in his future forever.

He wheeled the Buick expertly through the small Connecticut shoreline town to Saltus Road, where he found the barely visible opening to the dirt road to his cottage. He was in a hurry and spared the old car's suspension no mercy hurrying over the pothole strewn dirt road to its door.

The "meeting" with DeStephano had worked out better than he had expected. The detective thought he was being coy by not sharing with him his plans for taking down Phillip Granville, until that one little slip.

"I can't tell you that. But it will be soon," Michael DeStephano had said.

Soon.

Kevin Keller was now fully in charge of what was to come. The false identity that had protected and hidden him for so long was rapidly losing its grip on his consciousness. Thomas Pulling was fading fast, practically as fast as Keller's thin grasp on his sanity.

But in his twisted mind, Keller was sure that DeStephano had inadvertently shared his plan with him. The cop was going to take down Granville and his empire tomorrow, probably with the full force of the FBI and Hartford Police behind him. He was certain of it.

It was late now, nearly 7 p.m. Keller suspected that the Farmington Detectives would spend the night putting their case together and present it to a Federal Prosecutor in the morning. Then while the lawyers were getting a judge to sign off on arrest and search and seizure warrants, they would be putting together the tactical plan to raid General Industries Corporation. He expected that would be a complex plan involving the process of seizing tons of documents and hundreds of computers. By this time tonight, the headquarters of General Industries would be a yellow taped crime scene, dozens of GIC executives would be under arrest here and abroad, and hundreds of cops and forensic accountants would be tearing GIC apart, file by file.

It all said that he only had a few hours to prepare. He went inside and cracked open a new quart of vodka and headed for the beach. There he sat, silently drinking from the bottle, celebrating the success of his mission well before its completion. It was now or never. He might not get another chance.

He also drank to the memory of his wife and children and savored the satisfaction of knowing they would be safe forever by this time tomorrow. It was his only legacy to them.

Then, the bottle half empty, he screwed the top on and walked back to the kitchen, placing it where he would need it later tomorrow. For now he had work to do.

Ripping up several loosely nailed floorboards, he began retrieving the items he had safely transported in the hollowed out bed of his dearly departed pickup and lined them up on the kitchen floor in a specific order. Everything had to be perfect. His plan was precise.

When he was done, he retrieved a large, canvas work satchel, the kind made for carrying heavy tools and carefully placed the items inside in an order that made sense to him. Finally, he loaded the pockets of a pair of navy blue coveralls, the type that Beckham mechanics used when working in building machine rooms with several small automatic handguns. He filled several additional hidden pockets that he had sewn inside the garment with a dozen clips of ammunition. The bright blue and white "Beckham" patch on the coveralls would instantly identity him as a service mechanic entitled to be on the premises and especially in the mechanical rooms he intended to visit the following morning. Finally he attached the identity badge he had pilfered from Stuart Brown's desk to a front pocket.

He filled several bottles with water and threw them in the bag with a couple of Snickers candy bars. Hydration and sugar would get him through what he expected to be a long day.

It was midnight by the time he was finished. He had to get some rest. Tomorrow he would leave for Hartford by daybreak, stopping for coffee on the drive in. It would be a leisurely trip early in the day and he expected the downtown business district to be a ghost town.

But first, Keller walked out to the beach one last time and sat heavily on the sand. He watched the waves and stars for long moments, knowing it might be his last chance to take in the glory of life. He said a prayer for the well-being of his wife and children and begged to God for himself.

But not for forgiveness.

He prayed that those he loved would never discover what he had done.

* * *

At the Farmington Police Department, DeStephano, Leery, Hartford PD detectives, the FBI and representatives of the State Department worked late into the night and planned to work the entire weekend preparing a case that they would to bring to a Federal Prosecutor at 9 a.m. on Monday morning. There were many counts to consider, but the ultimate charge to be levied against the targeted individuals and the Corporation as a whole was "Treason." Just the sound of the word gave DeStephano and Leery the energy they needed. Both were nearly exhausted.

All involved agreed that the odds of getting a judge to consider their requests, even with the support of the prosecutor's office would be very difficult on a weekend. So the decision was made to hold off until Monday morning. GIC headquarters would be raided with everything the combined law enforcement effort could muster on Monday afternoon.

Kevin Keller had guessed wrong. But the error in assumption was in his favor.

There would be almost no one in the building he planned to visit on Saturday morning other than a few security guards — and Phillip Granville, a man who had no other world.

General Industries Corporation, and the monster that pulled its strings, were about to feel the wrath of one very angry, one very unleashed, ex employee.

Thirty-Seven

February 28, 1998

As dawn broke on Saturday morning, February 28, 1998, just slightly more than 10 years since the hideous carnage had rained down upon Lockerbie, Scotland, Kevin Keller was already in the Buick, moving at the speed limit in light traffic, sipping his coffee and listening to the radio. Ironically, the news was full of the World Court's decision the day before in The Hague, Netherlands that ruled it alone had jurisdiction in the Lockerbie case and the deadlock that had held up the trial of two men accused in the bombing for nearly a decade. In doing so, the World Court completely rebuffed the arguments of U.S. and U.K. lawyers who had sought jurisdiction in the trial.

In America and Great Britain, families of the victims were aghast at the decision, feeling further violated.

"Well Mr. Granville," Keller said to himself, "by the time this day is done, I promise that you will regret ever hearing the word Libya, the millions in sales dollars you earned there on the backs of murdered men, women and children... and the names Stephen DeStephano and Kevin Keller." A grin slowly came to his face.

"You would be proud of me now, Kate," he concluded, his tortured mind now fixated on bloody vengeance.

Less than an hour later he took the Capital Area exit off of I-91 North and drove to Trumbull Street, where he patiently waited at the stoplight across the street from the empty Hartford Civic Center. He used the time to assess the traffic on the street and available parking. He turned right on Gold Street as the light changed, then took a left on to a deserted Main Street and pulled the Buick to the curb. He jumped out, full of adrenalin and took his canvas bag from the trunk. Then he crossed the street and walked a half block to a pedestrian door into the garage that led to the lobby entrance of General Industries Corporation.

But first he went to the special area where Granville's prized Aston Martin should be parked. If it was there, the man was upstairs in his office. Staying in the shadows, Keller peered around a concrete column and saw the car. The snake was in his nest. He smiled. All the pieces were now in place.

Wearing his Beckham overalls, he appeared to be a service mechanic. Saturday morning maintenance work on the huge building's heating ventilating and air conditioning was not uncommon at the tower. He used Stuart Brown's identification pass and slid it through the card reader on the door to gain access. Voila, just like that he was in. He looked up at the security cameras and waived his badge. Guards at the lobby console noted his arrival but thought nothing of it.

Just before the main lobby, he turned and opened a door that led him to the service elevator that travelled to all 26 floors of the building. He pushed the hall call button on the marble clad wall and the door to the oversized elevator car opened instantly.

Keller stepped into the elevator and was greeted by a robotic voice from the computerized car operating panel.

"Gooood Mornnig," the poor excuse for automation mumbled.

"Kiss my ass," Keller replied, pressing the illuminated button for the 25th floor.

As the car moved swiftly up the long dark hoistway, the former executive experienced several flashbacks of being in this building. He had hated it almost from the start. By the time he was transferred out to Beckham, he detested it. The building reeked of fear and intimidation, the management style of its chairman and CEO, Phillip Granville.

The car came to a gradual halt and the doors opened. He took a screwdriver out of his pocket and removed the four screws holding an access panel beneath the car operating panel in place. After removing it, he reached inside, located the alarm wires and with a pair of cutters snipped the ground, killing power to the circuit. Then he replaced the panel and pushed the oversized, red Emergency Stop button. No alarm went off. Effectively he had locked the service elevator in place so it would be right where he needed it, when he needed it.

Next, Keller moved with confidence to the elevator machine room for the eight, gearless traction elevators that served the building. He walked right in to the unlocked facility, the door kept open to add ventilation to the extremely hot environment. He smiled as he looked over the field of mayhem he was about to design.

Keller couldn't help but stop and run his hand over the casting for the first motor he encountered in the machine room. It was one of the eight that were going to help him achieve his plan.

Some five-feet long by three-feet high, each elevator machine was capable of hoisting up to 4,000 pounds at a speed of eight meters per second. The machine for each elevator weighed 24 tons. Hanging from a drive sheave attached directly to each machine were steel cables, which in the 26-story building that housed Beckham Industries Corporation, weighed an addition five tons per elevator. Add the controller, generator, car, car frame and brakes, counterweight, compensating rope, communications cable and other ancillary structures and components, and each elevator weighed in at more than 35 tons. The eight elevators serving the floors beneath Phillip Granville's palace weighed in at nearly 300 tons.

Well more than half a million pounds, Keller thought. And therein lay the plan.

It was quiet in the machine room now, with only an occasional use of any of the passenger elevators. Probably only a security guard now and then, Keller thought. During the week, with each car in nearly constant motion, the noise was deafening.

In the unusually quiet environment, he went to work grateful for the lack of distractions. The job ahead required patience and focus and would take several hours. Keller glanced at his watch. It was now 8:30 a.m. His goal was to finish within three hours. There was other work to be done — and a long overdue conversation to be had.

He shook his head to stop that last thought from growing. It was critical that he remain absolutely clearheaded for the next few hours. A careless mistake now would ruin everything. He began to unload his canvas tool bag, moving deliberately but cautiously.

Brick by brick, he lifted 20, one-pound bundles of Semtex, a reddish-brown colored general purpose plastic explosive out of the bag, placing them carefully on the floor. Composed of Pentaerythritol tetranitrate and mixed with a plasticizer and the explosive nitroamine RDX, Semtex was one of the most powerful explosives known to man. Keller had learned that it was used primarily in construction demolition because of its high threshold for temperature variations, stability and ease of handling. Because it also gave off a low odor (it smelled slightly oily), Semtex was also a favorite of terrorists.

In fact, as Keller removed the bundles from the bag, it occurred to him that Semtex was the explosive used to bring down Pam Am flight 103 over Lockerbie. He had acquired it in his last visit to Libby, Montana from one of the many wilderness "Patriots" that had befriended him and shown him the path he was determined to take. The ease with which he had accumulated so much killing power still amazed him. It wasn't just about money. If his supplier didn't trust him, no amount of money in the world would have convinced the owner to part with his explosives. Trust and belief in the buyer's intentions were required.

By 11:20 a.m., Keller had completed his task. He loaded up his tools and placed all the plastic wrappings from the Semtex and wire snippets in his bag, making sure the room was as pristine as he had found it with the addition of his handiwork as the only exception. In the nearly three hours he had been working, security had not checked on his whereabouts, but he noticed that every ten minutes or so, one of the elevator machines would start up, bringing someone somewhere in the building. He stopped to drink some water and ate half a candy bar. The hot environment of the Machine Room had dehydrated him. He splashed cold water on his face from a utility sink and felt refreshed.

Keller caught sight of himself in a small mirror hanging over the sink. With his nearly shaved head and gaunt appearance he barely recognized himself. He was amazed that Kate had. The look on her face still haunted him and he deeply regretted the decision that led to their meeting.

"I'm dead, Kate. Bury me," he said out loud.

But he couldn't wait to see the look on Phillip Granville's face in just a few minutes.

"Phillip, oh Phillip? Can you come out and play?" he called whimsically, sounding every bit as terrifyingly insane as he was.

Thirty-Eight
~~~ ෧ ~~~

The break of dawn also found the law enforcement team at Farmington Police headquarters still working feverishly to build its case against General Industries Corporation, its subsidiaries and companies and dozens of individuals. With the decision made to raid GIC on Monday afternoon, they would need every hour before then to prepare.

At 10 a.m., Detective Sergeant Michael DeStephano put a call into his counterpart at the Hartford Police Department.

"I'm assuming you know what's going down out here, Hal," DeStephano said to Harold Markum, a 28-year veteran detective.

"Hell yah, Mike. For Christ's sake, you've got half my men..." he said, an irritated tone in his voice. Then he laughed. "I'm just busting your chops, pal, wish I could be spending the weekend working with you. I am no fan of that arrogant SOB running GIC. Laid off my brother-in-law last year with a weeks pay in his pocket after 26 years. But I guess somebody's gotta play sheriff in Hartford."

"Glad you understand, Hal. We're going to be depending on you and the rest of your guys come Monday afternoon."

"Be honored to handcuff the bastard myself," Markum replied.

"Listen Hal, need another favor. There's a character that's going to play big in this investigation eventually, and he's also a prime suspect in the string of murders Leery and I have been investigating the last couple of months. All are related to GIC and Beckham, etc. He's been spotted locally and my bet is he's gunning for Phillip Granville himself."

DeStephano wasn't interested in sharing all the details yet with Markum. He was unusually confused by the Keller/Pulling involvement and had decided, at least for the moment to focus on getting the case against Granville and GIC nailed down first. Then he would tackle the killer.

"I have no reason to believe he's going to move on Granville in the immediate future and don't see that he'd have much of an opportunity. You can bet Phillip Granville will be spending his weekend in that crypt at General's headquarters like he usually does when he's not travelling."

"So what do you need?"

"I need you to have a couple of uniforms stop by the security desk at GIC and drop a picture of this guy in their laps, just in case."

"What's his name?"

"Thomas Pulling, hails from Montana. I'll fax over the sheet. Have your guys tell the GIC security people to keep a sharp eye out for this guy and to call you immediately if they see him. You can consider him armed and dangerous."

"Aren't they all," Hal Markum laughed. "Sure, just send me the fax, I'll take care of it immediately."

An hour later, a Hartford police black and white pulled up in front of GIC headquarters at the Main Street entrance. Two patrolmen exited the car and walked to the revolving door entrance. Since it was Saturday, the doors were locked. A General security guard took his time getting up from the security console where he sat watching a college football game and sauntered over to the cops.

"Sorry to bother you there, lamb chop," the driver of the cruiser said.

"Yah, we didn't mean to drag you away from your surveillance duties, pal. What's the score?" said his partner.

"What do you guys want? There's no Dunkin' Donuts here," the security guard said with equal sarcasm.

The first cop slapped his partner on the shoulder, feigning laugher.

"Damn, that's funny. You make that up, I mean about the donuts and everything?" he said, abruptly losing the smile on his face and forcing his way past the guard as he opened the door.

"We oughta run your fat ass in just for thinking you're funny, you moron," the cop said in utter disgust.

"Here," the second cop said, throwing a photocopy at the guard. It was a picture of a suspect that they'd been told by Detective Markum to deliver to GIC.

"There's a homicidal maniac on the loose, probably looking to grease your ass. Look out for him and if you see anyone who looks like this, call us. Wouldn't want you to break a sweat or anything."

"What?" the guard said picking up the paper. "Who is this guy?"

"Probably your worst nightmare, butterball. Just do what I said. Consider him armed and dangerous with a hard on for General Industries Corporation. Got it?"

The guard studied the photograph for a few seconds, now taking the cops seriously.

"Yah, yah, got it. Haven't seen him."

"Better hope you don't, asshole. But call if you do. You have a nice day, now." The cop pointed to the television set. "Hope whoever you bet gets their ass kicked."

"Assholes," the guard mumbled as the two patrolmen left the building. He walked back to his console and casually checked the half dozen surveillance monitors at his station, flipping through cameras that covered each of the 26 floors and saw nothing unusual. The building was deserted except for the few security guards working. He also noted that the elevator position indicator panel was motionless. The only signs of activity he saw were in Phillip Granville's office, where the CEO was working at his desk. Granville typically left the camera on unless he had visitors or a meeting in progress. Lately, he'd left the camera on more than off.

The guard picked up the police photograph again and studied it. No one he recognized.

"Screw it, " he said. "That's for the night guys to deal with." He threw it in a pile of reports to be filed, also someone else's job, and went back to his game."

As he turned his back on the floor video monitors and the elevator position indicator panel, the security guard might have noticed the inexplicable movement of the private elevator on the 24th floor. It only served the two upper floors of the building, including the CEO's suite of offices on 26.

Where Phillip Granville worked alone ruling his empire.

Thirty-Nine

There it was again, Granville thought, listening for the source. A noise outside his office. Something in the HVAC system, a rattle in the ductwork. So irritating. He'd have maintenance inspect it on Monday morning. Aggravated, he scratched a note to his executive assistant and got up from his desk to walk over and drop it on his desk in the anteroom.

An ominous voice suddenly filled the silent space.

"Stop. Turn around and go back to your desk, Granville. Now. Without any theatrics or I'll put a bullet between your eyes before you can blink," a voice said calmly. Startled, Granville spun around, searching for the voice, a cold chill climbing its way up his spine.

The red light on the security camera at the back of the room glowed.

"I said no theatrics!" the voice bellowed out in warning. "Go back to your desk and switch off the camera. Do it now... my finger is itching to put one into that nest of snakes you call a brain," the voice said in the same calm but demanding tone. Granville did as he was told, his eyes now focused on his desk. There was a silent alarm switch there, too.

"I know that the camera switch is on the right. Put your hands on the desk. If I see you move either of them below the desk you'll be dead where you sit. Understand?"

"Who are you? Where are you?" a trembling Granville choked out as he took the last few steps to his desk and slowly slumped down in his chair, careful to keep his hands in plain sight.

The voice ignored his questions.

"Now turn off the camera with your right hand."

Granville slowly dropped his right hand beneath the desk and flicked the toggle switch. The red light dimmed and went out. At the security console in the lobby, the television monitor for Granville's office went black. But that was hardly unusual

"It's off," Granville said. "Now what do you want?"

From the hallway, a figure dressed in blue Beckham overalls stepped through the doorway and into Granville's office. A German made 9 millimeter Sig Sauer P226 semi-automatic pistol was in his right hand aimed directly at Granville's chest.

The CEO slowly stood up from his chair, careful not to make any sudden moves.

"Who are you?" he demanded, but his tone was far less confident than when he was bullying his staff.

The stranger did not move, nor did he speak.

"What do you want?" Granville barked, already sounding somewhat wounded.

"Fear does that to cowards, doesn't it, Phillip?" the stranger finally said.

"Does what?" Granville said, his voice quivering.

"Makes a grown man sound like a sniveling child."

Right in front of his eyes, the all-powerful tyrant was coming unglued, Keller thought. He had never enjoyed watching anything more.

"I don't know you," Granville began to beg, "what do you want? I haven't done anything to you…"

"Shut up. Say another word and I will kill you on the spot just for the sheer pleasure of watching you bleed out. Do you understand?"

Granville nodded his head.

"Sit down and don't move. Hands above the desk and spread your fingers."

Again, Granville complied without a murmur of protest.

"Now listen very carefully, because I'm only going to tell you this story once."

Granville shook his head like a little boy afraid of being punished.

"Do you remember the name Stephen DeStephano?"

"No," Granville replied quickly. Almost a bit too quickly. He was lying.

"Think a little more. A man like you has a good memory. Even for the evil things he's done in his life."

"I don't know the name, I tell you. Now what is this all about? Please…"

"Lockerbie, an employee, dead in the street for days, his family came to you begging for your help… his health benefits, pension…"

A look of pained anxiety came to Granville's face. Recall was also hard to hide.

"Alright… yes, I remember. He died in the Lockerbie bombing, Pan Am 103… but my hands were tied. There was nothing I could do to help his family…"

The stranger sighed in disgust.

"That's not true, Phillip, is it? You could have helped them. All you had to do was authorize it and it would have been done. Just once in your life tell the fucking truth!" Keller screamed the last words as he rushed towards Granville's desk.

He stopped at the last second, grabbing the two chairs in front of the desk and tossing them aside in a rage. He leaned down until he was only inches from Granville's face and stared directly into his eyes. He intentionally acted insane.

"Tell me the truth…" he said again, his voice rising with each word.

Granville was completely terrified.

"Yes… you're right… I could have."

"Why didn't you? Why did you make them suffer?" Keller probed.

But then Granville's face suddenly changed, an evil darkness coming to his skin. He was like a snake that had been backed into a corner and was agitated enough to strike.

"Because I could!" he said, the words coming out of his mouth with a vileness that shocked even his persecutor.

"Because you could," Keller repeated, mocking him.

"Yes!" the CEO hollered, slamming both hands on the desk for emphasis.

Keller was unimpressed.

"And you could just as easily reverse that decision right now, couldn't you?"

"Yes! If I was so motivated..."

Keller laughed in his face.

"What exactly do I have to do to motivate you, Phillip Granville?"

The CEO stared back, still not recognizing the man who was tormenting him.

"Do it. Now," Keller directed.

"Why should I?"

"Because if you don't, I will cut each of your fingers off and shove them down your throat one at a time... before I kill you," he answered with a tone that said "Try me."

"How?" a shaken Granville immediately responded.

"Send an e-mail to your head of human resources directing him to restore all the benefits the family of Stephen DeStephano were entitled to after his death while travelling on company business."

Granville hesitated a moment. Keller raised his pistol, aiming the barrel directly at the CEO's left eye.

Immediately, the executive turned to his computer and typed the note.

"Send a copy to this address." Keller slid a piece of paper across the desk with an e-mail address: M.DeStephano@FarmingtonPD.com.

Granville typed in the copy address, knowing full well whom the recipient was.

"Turn your screen toward me before you send it." Keller read the words and nodded.

"Send it."

With an arrogant flourish, Granville stabbed the enter key with his finger, then turned to Keller.

"Ok? You made your point. Now will you please get out of my office and let me get back to my business?" he said arrogantly, hoping the intruder would be bluffed by his nonchalance.

"If only it were that easy, Phillip."

"What do you mean?"

"What I mean is we could spend the entire afternoon… hell no, the entire next year at this, atoning for all the evil shit you've done to innocent people."

Granville's cocky smirk faded from his face.

"But we hardly have that kind of time, do we, big shot."

The CEO was silent, not sure of what was about to happen.

"So, what I want you to do is atone for just one more sin."

A look of hope appeared in Granville's eyes.

"Name it."

"Not so fast. It's a big one," Keller said, grinning.

Granville swallowed hard.

Kevin Keller stepped away from the desk and spread his arms.

"Take a look at me, Granville. Take a long hard look. Don't you remember me?"

"No," he replied.

"Are you sure? Take a really hard look. Maybe it's the hair, or the weight loss, or the premature aging from being on the run, from hiding from you all these years. Maybe it's the pain you caused me. They say the pain of loss can really change the way a man looks... and thinks."

Keller saw it in his eyes when Granville suddenly remembered.

"Keller. Kevin Keller," he sputtered, nearly choking on the words.

"But you're dead. The accident... they couldn't find your body... how...?"

"You don't want to know, asshole. You simply don't. And I don't have time to tell you about my adventure anyway. All you have to know is this.

"You took my life away from me. You stole my wife, my children, years... all gone. You made me run so that they would be safe."

Granville began to perspire and his hands shook.

"I really never meant to... it was all a misunderstanding..."

"Don't! You coward! Don't lie to me or so help me I will... " He stopped himself, fighting to keep control. It wasn't going to happen here, not this way.

"Get up," Keller motioned to Granville, pointing the gun towards a door to the left and behind his desk. It was the CEO's private stairway to the helicopter pad on the roof above them.

"We're going to take a little walk, get some air."

"No, please. Let me explain." Granville began to beg.

"Stop!" Keller screamed at him. "No one can hear you except me. And I'm not listening."

He put the barrel of the gun in Granville's back and pushed him toward the door to the helipad.

"Open it."

It was four flights of stairs to the top, 48 steps.

"March, Phillip, and if you try anything I will shoot you in the kneecaps and drag you up."

Granville did as he was told and stepped slowly into the soft light of the stairwell. One step at a time they advanced to the top landing.

"Step outside," Keller ordered him. "Then wait."

The two men stepped out onto the rooftop helipad and stopped. The wind at this height made it that much colder and Granville shivered, wearing only a thin, white dress shirt.

From where they stood, Keller could see the two security cameras that covered the rooftop, each pointed across the pad in the direction in which the GIC corporate helicopters approached when landing. He raised his gun and quickly fired two shots, one aimed at the lense of each camera. Both were direct hits. At the lobby security console, the two monitors for the helipad suddenly went black but unnoticed by the guard who was still immersed in watching a football game.

Granville shuddered as he saw Keller's expert marksmanship at work and at the knowledge that unless a guard saw the cameras go out, no one would know he was up here.

It was time to plead, to promise anything in exchange for mercy. But Phillip Granville had very little practice at something so demeaning.

"Kevin, please…"

"Save it, Phillip. Think about all those people you've hurt. Think about all the good you could have done with all your money and power. Think about how many conversations you started with the question: What were your SAT scores? Think about what an asshole you are."

Granville began to cry.

"I want you to think about what was going through Stephen DeStephano's mind as he was falling to his death from 30,000 feet. Think about the terror he felt. And think about how I felt when my car went over the bridge in Farmington, knowing that my life was over — knowing that I couldn't save my wife and children.

"From you."

At that, one of the most powerful men in America, perhaps the world, fell to his knees, a groveling wreck begging for his life. It was a sight Kevin Keller had envisioned for six years.

"Stand up like a man!" he demanded, but Granville was incapable. Like a true bully, when outgunned, he reverted to form. He instantly became a sniveling coward.

The sight only enraged Keller more. From somewhere deep inside, he summoned strength he didn't know he had and reached down and grabbed Granville by the shirt collar. Then he dragged his prone body more than 50 feet across the rooftop flight deck. Keller stopped only a yard from the edge of the platform and looked down at Main Street, nearly 400 feet below.

"Funny thing about being blown out of an airplane or dropped off a bridge, Phillip. You simply lose all control. You're no longer in command of your own destiny. Wherever you land, you land. I guess how much it hurts depends on from how high you've fallen."

He looked down at the nearly invisible people and toy-like cars below. A black-hearted smirk came to his face as Kevin Keller uttered the last words the CEO of General Industries Corporation would ever hear.

"Trust me, Phillip Granville, this is going to hurt."

With long burning rage pumping adrenalin through his veins, Keller grabbed the collar of Granville's shirt again and hoisted the limp body of the CEO to the very edge of the roof. He raised his head to the heavens and roared in victory like a wild beast that had conquered his prey. Then with complete disdain and without so much as a thought of remorse, he tossed the tyrant off the helipad like so much trash. Keller watched as Granville fell, pirouetting through the air, his futile efforts to stop his free fall mindful of vaudevillian slapstick.

Just for an instant, he caught sight of Phillip Granville's face, his mouth agape in a silent scream for mercy as he fell helplessly through space. The terror in his eyes and the look of abject hopelessness almost quenched the never-ending pain in Kevin Keller's heart.

But just for a moment. For when Granville's body inevitably splashed on the pavement far below, all Keller felt was a wave of despair.

For the despicable creature he had just murdered was right about one thing.

Kevin Keller was dead.

But he would have to die all over again.

Forty
~~~ ෨ ~~~

It was a woman's scream outside the front entrance that finally got the security guard's attention. He ran across the lobby and immediately saw the cause of the commotion. A man's body lay on the sidewalk, hideously twisted, his skull smashed. A pool of blood was rapidly spreading beneath him. The guard went outside for a closer look and gasped when he recognized the distorted shape of Phillip Granville. He raced back to his console and dialed 911 and radioed the other two guards in the building who hurried to the 26th floor using the passenger elevators.

On the 24th floor, Kevin Keller had just reached the service elevator, still parked where he had left it hours earlier. He disengaged the emergency stop button that held the elevator in its location and pressed the button for the Lobby. The car doors slid shut instantly. Without interruption, the elevator reached the bottom floor within a couple of minutes and Keller stepped out of the car, allowing the doors to close behind him. He walked out into the main passenger elevator lobby without hesitation and used the ID card he had pilfered from Stuart Brown to let himself out into the parking garage. Then he retraced his steps from hours earlier, walking quickly out of the garage and to his car waiting just where he'd left it across the street.

As he pulled away from the curb, he could hear the sound of approaching sirens. He drove three blocks ahead and pulled back to the curb, watching as several police cars and an ambulance arrived from the opposite direction.

In the building, one of the two guards who had just arrived on the 26th floor frantically radioed the guard at the console.

"Christ, there's a sign on Granville's office door that says we have exactly five minutes to evacuate the building," he said. "There's no one up here, but I think there's a bomb somewhere. I'm out of here. Whatever you do don't pull the fire alarm. It'll shut down the elevators!"

The security guard at the console ran outside again and told the police who radioed the fire department and then began moving the growing crowd of spectators away from the General Industries Corporation headquarters.

"Hey Bob, call this in to Detective Markum, will ya?" one of the Hartford patrolmen yelled to his partner. "I don't know what he was working on but it had something to do with this building." Minutes later, the phone rang at Detective Sergeant Michael

UNLEASHED

DeStephano's office in Farmington. He picked it up with irritation, aggravated by the interruption. The caller was brief. The Detective heard only the first words. He looked at his partner.

"Keller. " He shook his head in disbelief.

"He did it."

On Main Street, the killer watched in his rear view mirror as three security guards burst from the lobby and ran across the street. The only person he could see within a block of the building was the body of Phillip Granville lying on the sidewalk.

"Time's up, fellas," he said, and pressed the button of a small transmitter he held in his hand. He couldn't resist getting out of the car and turning to look at his handiwork. Seconds later, the show began.

It started with a low rumble and a burst of smoke that seeped out a ventilation shaft on the 24th floor. There were more screams from spectators still shocked by the sight of the body that had plummeted from the rooftop. But a second later, a massive, fiery explosion blew out every window on the floor followed by a hailstorm of shattered glass and debris. Thick black smoke and leaping orange flames poured from the entire perimeter of the building just two floors below the late Phillip Granville's palatial private offices. A ring of fire encircled the entire building. The crowd instinctively moved back and arriving fire trucks halted their advance a half block from the building.

Inside, the shaped Semtex explosive charge that Keller had set along the base of the entire elevator machine room had detonated, shearing it from the core of the building and shattering the integrity of the 24th

floor's six inch thick concrete and metal plate slab all the way to the outside walls.

Suddenly, the thousands of tons of weight of the floor slab, the upper two stories of the building and all the elevator equipment, a force unleashing massive kinetic energy were released. In the next second, it collapsed onto to the 23rd floor, the free falling weight severing that slab as well. Like dominoes, each floor below the ever-increasing weight and speed of the falling mass failed with a growing roar that reached an absolute crescendo twenty feet from the street. In less than 60 seconds, General Industries corporate headquarters pancaked into a pile of burning rubble, smoke, concrete dust and debris that rose up into the sky like the fallout from a small nuclear weapon. The entire Hartford business district rocked with the implosion and collapse as tons of shattered concrete and twisted steel wreckage spilled out into the surrounding streets.

And there it buried the corpse of Phillip Granville. Fittingly, as if preordained by the ghost of Stephen DeStephano, the CEO's decomposing body would not be recovered for three days.

Three blocks away, a beige Buick pulled away from the curb and slowly drove towards the entrance to I-84, it's driver insanely reciting a childhood Mother Goose nursery rhyme.

"Humpty Dumpty sat on a wall, Humpty Dumpty had a great fall; All the king's horses and all the king's men couldn't put Humpty together again."

Kevin Keller chuckled, lit a cigarette and never looked back at the carnage mounting behind him. Instead, visions of the Bitterroot Mountains and dark memories of the time he had spent searching for his soul, desperate to find some reason to exist raced through his mind.

It occurred to him that it had only been a few months since he had left the safety of those Montana hills guided by Sam Dawkins' "three P's" philosophy.

He ticked them off in his head for the thousandth time.

Priorities.

Patience.

Penance.

Wrapped in the embrace of Sam's mantra, he had finally become resigned to his fate. The ensuing internal peace he found had enabled him to calmly mete out the brutal justice that was required to save his family. Without the discipline Sam had taught him, he would have rushed into battle against Phillip Granville and the others and lost the war. Instead, he was the anonymous, invisible victor.

He understood that most sane people would consider his actions barbaric. It mattered little to him. What was important was that his family was safe and would never know of his hand in their salvation, only the pain of his loss. That was enough for Kevin Keller.

Keeping to the speed limit and patiently avoiding any action that would draw attention to him, he drove home. It was time to get back to his secret hideaway by the shore, where he would deal with the last piece of his carefully woven plan.

The final victim.

Forty-One

He parked the stolen Buick at the back of the cottage and took his practiced stroll around to the beach front, checking the sand for footprints or any sign of visitors. As usual, there were nothing but his own boot prints.

Kevin Keller had come to like the tiny, ramshackle cottage only yards from the water. He found the combination of the solitude and the hypnotizing sound of lapping waves at the waters edge so comforting. He was exhausted and had a strong urge to lie back on the sand and take a nap. But the sun was going down and it was turning colder. And there was so much to be done. The boat, still tied up at the dock. A thorough search of the house and the grounds. He had to check everything and everywhere and eliminate or destroy anything that said he had once been there. It was vital.

He forced himself to begin the process of purging and walked to the dock. Keller jumped aboard the Bayliner cuddy cabin that had been sitting unused since the night he took out Laabi and Stanton. It had to go, quietly.

He found the keys he had hidden in the head below decks and crossed his fingers that the motor would turn over. The ignition turned, sluggishly at first, then caught and the engine roared to life. He let the boat warm up for a few minutes then went below and pulled the transom drain plug. Immediately, frigid water began to enter the hull. It wouldn't take long, he figured watching the rate of flow. He thought again about setting sail with her, leaving everything behind, but he knew it didn't fit the plan.

He went back to the wheelhouse and tied it off so that once he hit the throttle, the vessel would head straight out to deeper water. Keller looked around, making sure there was no sign he had been aboard the boat. Clean as a whistle.

With that, he tied another piece of rope to the throttle, then jumped back up onto the pier. He scanned the horizon to make sure there were no boats in the way or headed in, then yanked the rope to pull the throttles back to full power. Immediately, the small Bayliner leapt forward into the calm, cold waters and sped away from the dock. But already it was noticeably lower in the water. He watched as the boat continued to move out smartly for several hundred yards then visibly slowed by the weight of the water she had taken on. Ten minutes later and nearly a mile off shore, he watched as the craft nosed into the ocean. In seconds, she was completely gone from sight.

Keller walked back to the beach, policing it one last time, then went to the kitchen. He finished off the bottle of vodka he had left from the previous evening, then cracked open his last one, occasionally taking long pulls as he stripped off the Beckham coveralls, then went through each room and gathered his few clothes and other belongings. Maps, his collection of passports and other false identities, a couple of do-it-yourself instruction books, newspapers, fast food wrappers and empty bottles were next. He threw everything into a metal barrel on the side of the cottage, doused it all with a small container of lighter fluid he had bought just for this job, and set it afire. He drank heavily from the bottle as he watched the flames grow.

Finally, he pulled the stolen Buick around the cottage and down to the waters edge, opened all the windows, then fetched a cinder block from the fire pit someone had built on the beach and placed it inside the car. He pulled the column shift into neutral, then jammed the cinder block against the gas pedal. The engine screamed in protest at the sudden surge in RPM's. He closed the door, reached in and yanked the transmission stalk down into drive. The car lurched forward, momentarily spinning its rear wheels in the sand. Abruptly it found traction and drove into the water. The car made forward progress until its rear wheels lost contact with the sandy bottom because of its fleeting buoyancy. But the forward momentum was enough to keep it heading away from shore until it passed the underwater shelf where the depth dropped off to 15 feet or so. He watched as the vehicle filled with water then slowly sank, disappearing from sight in a matter of minutes.

Keller pulled the bottle from the pocket of his blanket lined denim chore coat and stared at it, realizing that other than the clothes on his back, it was his last possession. He drained it as he walked back to the barrel, still burning, and dropped the empty bottle in. The coat followed. He felt the sharp cold despite the alcohol coursing through his veins.

"What the hell, let's go all the way," he laughed, bending down to take off his shoes, socks and underwear and adding them to the flames.

In his growing fog of drunkenness, it dawned on him that being cold wasn't so bad. At least he could feel something. It had been a long time since he had felt anything other than sadness and rage.

Naked, he walked down to the water and waded in up to his ankles. The icy water stung his skin and his bare feet instantly went numb. He didn't care. The vodka lining his stomach began to warm him as he watched the sun just begin to settle on the horizon. It was the end of the day.

And the end of his long journey.

It was time. A price had to be paid in return for his family's safety. It was the penance he had to pay for satisfying his priorities.

Keller walked back up the beach several yards, sat down heavily on the sand and began to fulfill the promise he had made to himself when this moment came: He would think of nothing else other than his Kate and his wonderful children. He would take the time to say a proper goodbye, even if they couldn't hear him.

"I love you Kate," he whispered, not needing a photograph to remember how beautiful she was, the depth of her blue eyes, the softness of her kiss.

"I will love you forever. Know that when you were in my world, it was a wonderful place. I'm sorry that I didn't always know that. Please be sure that our children always remember me, and how much I loved them." He paused and buried his face in his hands, urgently wishing that he could turn back the clock, fix everything so he could be anywhere but here.

"Sammy, you're so grown up now," he continued. I wish we could talk. Take care of your Mom for me, never let her go. And remember me when I was your dad. The good one, and not that other guy I became. Ok?"

He thought for a moment about what he would say to Ben and Julia if he could be with them now. He hadn't read them a good night story in so long. He'd missed almost all of Julia's young life. She probably wouldn't even know him now.

He stood up. It came to him.

"I think I would sing you a song, kids," he said out loud. "That's what I would do. I wish you were here to sing with me."

Then, as Kevin Keller slowly walked back towards the water, he began to quietly sing a song that he and Kate had loved as they grew their family. In his eyes he saw them all together, laughing, happy.

Safe.

As the words came off his lips, he tried to envision them.

"I see trees of green, red roses too, I see them bloom for me and you. And I think to myself, what a wonderful world."

Tears streamed from his eyes as he took several more steps forward, his feet touching the icy water again but didn't stop as it reached his ankles and then his knees. He sang again.

"I see skies of blue and clouds of white, the bright blessed day, the dark sacred night. And I think to myself, what a wonderful world."

The water was up to his chest. Still he moved forward. He sang louder now, the vodka giving him courage.

"The colors of the rainbow so pretty in the sky, are also on the faces of people going by. I see friends shaking hands saying how do you do, but they're really saying, I love you..."

The water closed over his head as he felt the first pull of the North Cove's strong rip tide. With all his remaining willpower, he forced his body to relax and let the current pull him down to the depths.

As he took in a deep breath of the ocean and began to die, the eyes of the last victim were full of those he loved.

His final thought was a bittersweet recognition of what might have been.

"Yes, I think to myself, what a wonderful world."

Epilogue

March 1998

The Hartford Chief of Police, the FBI's top special agent for Connecticut and a spokesperson for the State Department had all made statements to the crush of press outside the State Capitol Building when finally Detective Sergeant Michael DeStephano of the Farmington Police took the microphone.

The speakers preceding him had laid out the facts related to the destruction of the General Industries Corporation headquarters and the extensive and ongoing investigation by the State and Justice Departments of GIC's criminal activity as it related to violations of federal regulations regarding the sale of goods to embargoed nations and the Foreign Corrupt Practices Act.

The FBI had concluded that the destruction of the GIC building had indeed been carried out by one individual whose motive had not yet been determined, but confirmed that it was not an act of terrorism by a foreign entity.

"Clearly this was an act of domestic terrorism not unlike the tragedy of Oklahoma City in 1995, perpetrated by a sole individual intent on vengeance, with one notable exception," said FBI Special Agent Thomas Steele. "This individual went to great lengths to insure that the building was evacuated before setting off the explosive charges that he had planted. However, his motivation has not yet become clear to us.

"We believe the man responsible for this crime was one Thomas F. Pulling, 43 of Hamilton, Montana. Despite intensive efforts, we have been unable to penetrate his previous history, whereabouts or relation to General Industries.

DeStephano listened intently, giving no indication that he knew any different than what Steele was reporting.

"Further, we believe that Pulling is responsible for the murder of GIC Chairman and CEO Phillip Granville, whose body was recovered from the rubble some three days after the explosion. Unfortunately, although we are continuing to sift through the wreckage, we do not expect to recover Mr. Pulling's remains. All available surveillance tape shows no evidence that Pulling escaped before the blast, and we believe that he intentionally sacrificed his own life. The magnitude of the blast and its close proximity to Mr.

Pulling's last known whereabouts in the building rules out the probability of any forensic recovery.

"Now, let me turn the proceedings over to Detective Sergeant Michael DeStephano of the Farmington Police Department, who will address the final piece of this extremely complex investigation."

DeStephano approached the microphone slowly, not one to enjoy the frenzy of news cameras and reporters all looking for their own angle on the facts. In fact, like most cops he found the media a hindrance to police work but a necessary evil that must be dealt with in a professional manner. He looked out over the audience and spied his sister-in-law watching. She smiled at him. His partner, Dennis Leery was standing next to her, grinning at his boss' obvious discomfort.

"I'll be brief," he began. "The Farmington Police Department has been investigating the deaths of GIC executives Badr Laabi and Paul Stanton in December 1997, and because of their relationship with the Corporation, the subsequent murders of Sebastian Oliviero and Jean-Pierre Chandon in Seville, Spain in January of this year. We believe that the death of GIC executive Stuart Brown in early February will ultimately also prove to be linked to this case.

"With the close coordination of the FBI and INTERPOL, we had identified Thomas Pulling as a suspect in those murders, and in fact were aggressively seeking his detention on February 28, when Phillip Granville was killed. We were unsuccessful in locating and detaining Mr. Pulling and believe that Mr. Granville was his sixth victim. As Special Agent Steele indicated, we have not yet arrived at any conclusions as to the motivation for Mr. Pulling's murderous actions."

Immediately, a flurry of hands rose in the audience of reporters and questions began firing at the Detective.

"I'm sorry, but because this is an active investigation, I'll have no more to say for the time being. Thank you."

He shook the hands of his colleagues and quickly went in search of his sister-in-law. She waved, drawing his attention.

"Hey, Lucy," he smiled at her and was rewarded with a kiss on the cheek. "Kids in school?"

"Yup. But so proud of their Uncle Mike. I showed them each the letter from the human resources man. You really pulled off a miracle here, Michael. Stephen would be proud of you, too. And so grateful." Leery winked at him.

"Well, let's get over to the Fidelity office tomorrow and talk to those people about what you've got coming to you Lucy. And don't forget, it's not like Steve didn't earn this for his family.

"Yah, I guess," Lucy said. "But if you hadn't kept pushing those SOB's, especially that guy Granville, it never would have happened."

DeStephano looked at his shoes. Leery did the same.

"Yah, I guess… " he reluctantly took credit just so he wouldn't arouse her suspicions.

"But I still find it amazing that Granville had a change of heart… I mean, like right before he died. It's sort of incredible, don't you think? I mean, you don't think this guy Pulling knew Stephen, do you? Like forced him into sending that e-mail?"

"Nah."

"No way," Leery said simultaneously.

DeStephano changed the subject. "The good news is that even though GIC is under investigation for breaking just about every international law in the books and probably won't survive as a corporation, the pension plan is in safe hands because the PBGC took it over.

She looked at him, puzzled.

"The Pension Benefit Guaranty Corporation. It's a quasi government agency that protects the average Joe from losing everything if his company goes belly up. It's complicated. But it works. That's all you need to worry about. Same with his life insurance. It's guaranteed."

"This means you're a free man, Uncle Mike," she teased him. "You might even have time for a girlfriend now..."

"Whoa!" the detective said as Leery laughed out loud. "From the frying pan into the fire, for cripes sake," he protested.

She gave him a hug.

"Love you forever, Mike. We wouldn't have made it without you." He kissed her on the cheek and couldn't speak. A portrait of his younger brother passed before his eyes. He was smiling.

"Get out of here. See you tonight." She turned and walked away, waving as she went, happiness and relief visible in her step.

"Lady looks years younger, Boss," Leery said.

"Yah."

"What's wrong?"

"Hell, it wasn't me, Dennis, you know that. Let's walk a bit, huh?"

"Sure. Yah, so may be it wasn't you, but you kept Granville's attention for a long time. Maybe he did have a change of heart."

"Something tells me he was looking down the barrel of a big piece of iron when he did."

"Well... maybe. But no one knows that and no one ever will. Let's not go tilting at windmills. This fight is over."

They walked a half a block in silence, each man lost in his conflicted thoughts.

"Keller cleaned up a lot of unfinished business on his way out. One smart guy with a big set of cujones. He took on the whole world and there's not a sign of him anywhere," DeStephano said.

"Poor bastard, he paid the price, set things right, but no one will ever know," Leery replied. "Think they'll find anything in that pile of concrete on Main Street? I worry about DNA ..."

They stopped and sat on a bus stop bench.

"Something tells me the answer to that question is no," the senior detective said. "Keller was way ahead of us in so many ways. We weren't even close to nailing him. I'm sure he thought through that problem. Hell, I wouldn't be the least bit surprised to find out someday he got out of there alive."

"Ya think?" Leery asked. "Na...."

"I don't know. You take everything away from a good man, push him to insanity? Most men would break. Not this one."

"So what's the final word?" Leery asked.

DeStephano paused, still contemplating the man he'd never met. A good man who had been horribly wronged, hurt till he bled and crushed with loss. And yet he had prevailed, even, it appeared, in death. He turned and looked up at the skyline, at the empty space where Phillip Granville once ruled an empire.

"I guess I see it a couple of ways, Dennis," he finally said. "There's a lesson to be learned from Kevin Keller."

"Leery turned to him, waiting.

"Never bet against a man who fears for his family…" he began, staring up at the hole in the skyline again.

He turned to his partner.

"Or an angry man unleashed."

Acknowledgements
~~~ ༖ ~~~

    From start to finish, *UNLEASHED* owes many thanks to many people.

    To my wife, Bobbie, who has owned my heart for 50 years, I know that I am blessed to have you as my partner, friend, counsel and the inspiration of my life and work. Your undying faith helps me to persevere when the words will only come one at a time. You are the only person who knows the story I am trying to pry from my heart and there are times that without your help, the words might remain locked up forever. Thank you for giving me the gift of encouragement, for without it, I might never have found what American mythologist Joseph Campbell wrote: "The privilege of a lifetime is being who you are." For that alone I will love you forever.

    To my sons Jack and Jay of whom I am infinitely proud, thank you for your unconditional love, for sharing with me your courage and strength and for being my best friends. And to my daughter-in-law, Andréa, one of the most wonderful surprises of my life, thank you for your love and for always seeing in me so much more than I deserve.

To my beloved Grandson, Charlie, the most profound blessing I will ever experience, know that your birthday will always be my favorite day of the year. Someday, I hope you will find the books written by "Papa" in the library and learn of the many adventures I have lived in my head. Remember that there is a thought of you on every page of every book I write. I love you, little man.

To my Grandfather, William J. McGrath, a man who epitomized love and humility, instilled in me a passion for history and filled my imagination, thank you for being there for me. I hope to see you someday to swap a few more stories. I'll bring the Ritz crackers.

Special thanks also to my friend Lisa Orchen, whose remarkable insights and sensitivities make her the consummate editor and author's friend; to Joyce Rossignol, my very first editor who taught me to love the art of writing; to my very special friend, Cathy King whose encouragement and support is boundless, and to her father and my eternal friend, Bob King, a role model who is, and always will be a gentleman and my hero. And to my age old friends Genevieve Allen Hall, Steve Bazzano, Diane Dustin Lord, Eileen McCarthy, Steve Zerio, Carol Russo, Gail Donahue, Carla Unwin, Michael Jordan-Reilly, Bill and Debbie Bartlett, Peter Larkin, Cheryl Zajack Barlow, Sharon Tomany Marone, Lisa Rivero Jankowski and Earl Flowers, my everlasting thanks for pushing me uphill.

And finally, my thanks to a few new friends who have accompanied me in my writing career and whose friendship and support I sincerely value: Captain (Ret.) Timothy J. Kelliher and Firefighter Frank Droney of the Hartford Fire Department; Hartford

Hospital Fire Marshall and Chief of the Rocky Hill CT Volunteer Fire Department Michael Garrahy; Jeff Mainville of the Hartford Public Library; and Michelle Royer of the Lucy Robbins Welles Library.

F. Mark Granato, November 2015

About The Author

F. Mark Granato's long career as a writer, journalist, novelist and communication executive in a US based, multi-national Fortune 50 corporation has provided him with extensive international experience on nearly every continent. Today he is finally fulfilling a lifetime desire to write and especially to explore the "What if?" questions of history. In addition to UNLEASHED, he has published *Out Of Reach: The Day Hartford Hospital Burned*, an historical fiction account of the tragic 1961 fire, the acclaimed novel, *Finding David*, a love story chronicling the anguish of Vietnam era PTSD victims and their families that was nominated for a 2013 Pulitzer Prize, *The Barn Find*, chronicling the saga of a Connecticut family brought to its knees by tragedy that fights to find redemption, *Of Winds and Rage*, a suspense novel based on the 1938 Great New England Hurricane, *Beneath His Wings: The Plot to Murder Lindbergh*, and *Titanic: The Final Voyage*. He writes from Wethersfield, Connecticut under the watchful eye of his faithful German Shepherd, "Groban." Readers are encouraged to visit with Mark on his Facebook page at "Author F. Mark Granato" or at fmgranato@aol.com.

Made in the USA
Middletown, DE
12 October 2020